Other Books by the Author

The History of the Child Actor (1990)
Natural Law (2018)
NSA Unzipped and Exposed (2019)

WREN'S
STORY

WREN RICHARDS

iUniverse

WREN'S STORY

iUniverse books may be ordered through booksellers or by contacting:

iUniverse
1663 Liberty Drive
Bloomington, IN 47403
www.iuniverse.com
844-349-9409

Because of the dynamic nature of the Internet, any web addresses or links contained in this book may have changed since publication and may no longer be valid. The views expressed in this work are solely those of the author and do not necessarily reflect the views of the publisher, and the publisher hereby disclaims any responsibility for them.

ISBN: 978-1-6632-0304-5 (sc)
ISBN: 978-1-6632-0305-2 (hc)
ISBN: 978-1-6632-0306-9 (e)

Library of Congress Control Number: 2020913815

Print information available on the last page.

iUniverse rev. date: 07/28/2020

Wren's Story is dedicated to the author's grandsons:
Justin
Vance
Alex

CONTENTS

PROLOGUE

The prairie grass danced with the wind in perfect rhythmic harmony as sprigs of sage applauded the performance. Few humans entered the thousand miles of empty acreage to upstage the principle dancers, and if mortals drew attention away from the main performers, the rocks, clouds, and creek objected loudly. They tattled to time and weather, who erased the humans' footsteps as if they had never existed.

Chapter 1

INDIAN MISSION

The moist, pine-scented path to Silas Lake absorbed the plod of four brown well-worn leather field boots. The right boot of both pairs imprinted scuff marks onto the forest mulch. Pigeon-toed prints smashed the fallen pine needles and released a strong pine-tar scent. The turned-in boot prints were indicative of the Shoshoni Native Americans who made them. The four walking boots emanated muffled scrunching as their wearers trudged the path without speaking. Silence was the communication between Native Americans, especially between these two, who had known each other for decades. A strong brown hand pointed to a rusted hubcap wedged in the low underbrush of the pine-and-spruce-rubbed earth.

"Wren's nest," the man said as he pointed for the other to see. Heads nodded as fishing poles and boots continued to move up the aromatic path toward Silas Lake's secluded pool of abundant water food waiting to be lunch. The smaller, trailing boots hesitated, and the wearer looked back over his shoulder at the wren's nest and saw it jiggling as he heard unusual muffled sounds.

"Mighty big wren," he said as he laid his handmade snare-fishing pole on the mulch-cushioned soil and retraced his steps. The bigger boots followed. Four boots squatted and supported strong, muscled thighs as hands grasped the sides of the hubcap and pulled it from the supporting branches of the spruce tree. Stuffed inside the hubcap was a soft, thick, aqua-blue sweater wrapped around a squirming newborn baby. Four dark brown eyes met as four hands grasped the hubcap and placed it back into the limbs of the spruce tree. The two men rose from their squatted position in search of the mother. Neither spoke. They both knew why they searched. Their eyes scanned the trail ahead, the surrounding forest, thicket, and around the lake itself. The two men saw no one. They were alone. They walked rapidly in each direction and searched for a new mother—or anyone. Two pair of brown, hooded eyes locked together in silent communication. Their tracking skills were the best in Fremont County, and they could have easily read the signs to follow the female prey, but homemade fishing poles remained unused as they returned to the wren's nest.

"Only takes a woman to ruin a good fishing trip."

"Yup, true words spoken."

Baby cries caused the boots to pick up their pace. No words were needed to express the priority and urgency of giving the newborn baby care. They mutually accepted that the baby was at greater risk than the mother who was able to walk away. Four big hands pulled the tin free from the low brush and gently unwrapped the small noisemaker, revealing black-feathered hair that surrounded plump brown cheeks below unopened eyes. Their own wide-opened eyes scanned the perfect form of kicking legs, toes, and tiny hands.

"What to do?"

"I don't want to be a mother."

"Me neither!"

"The Indian Mission will be her mother."

"Yup."

Big, rough hands rewrapped the tiny kicking legs and tucked them back into the hubcap. Within minutes the wren's nest rocked softly on the old truck seat between the two fishermen. Rounded, dented, and battered fenders rattled along the wide, long-hooded frame with a short-bed body of a faded green Ford pickup that banged its way to the Indian Mission.

The two old fishermen bounced along the graveled road and scanned the landscape through the cracked and pitted windshield, tinted greened with age. Four wrinkled, deeply set Hershey-brown hooded eyes swept across the Northern Arapaho and Eastern Shoshoni Wind River Indian Reservation that was nestled on the flat land between the Wind River Mountains and the Owl Creek Range in southwestern Wyoming. The size of the Wind River Reservation equaled the states of Rhode Island and Delaware combined. This peaceful land lay near the confluences of the Little and Big Wind Rivers about ten miles from the town of Riverton, population seven thousand, and fifteen miles from the smaller town of Lander. It was 1953, and Dwight D. Eisenhower was president, but no one around there much cared, especially not these sixty-year-old friends who knew reservation life. The pair of weathered men lived in isolation from the rest of the country and from the world, just as people in the area had been isolated due to its remoteness for centuries. It was sheltered from other humans before Shoshoni territory met explorers Lewis and Clark in 1803.

Isolation and remoteness had screened this land for over three hundred years and kept other cultures from tinting or erasing it before modern times. These two organically grown men—sprouted from nature without synthetic additives—were manifestations from the land. The two snare fishermen knew every crevice of the reservation boundaries that encompassed nearly 3,500 square miles of prickly, textured gradations of brown prairie until the land rose in elevation to the forested foothills of the Wind River Mountain range. In all this expansive land, only seven thousand Native Americans populated its surface, with the Arapaho tribe outnumbering the Shoshoni by almost three to one. This was part of the motivation for transporting the baby-filled hubcap rocking on the seat between them: the infant would add one more enrollment to their unequal tribal numbers.

The unfrequented land echoed the character of the people who occupied it, including these two Shoshoni men who rode in the 1943 Ford truck. Isolated inhabitants relied upon their own resources of creative ingenuity, personal skills, self-motivation, and the will to thrive. In some instances, self-determination alone was the reason for human survival. These two leather-tanned, tough people used their determination to live through the harsh thirty-degree-below-zero winters and the 115-degree, sun-scorched, dry summers to absorb the rare, pleasurable, short spurts of comfort during spring and fall.

The land's seclusion and insular space granted this traveling pair solitude for reflection and development of unique thoughts that built their physical and inner power. These two sturdy people did not ask for help. They believed that if someone asked for help they gave power away to another: the helper became stronger and gained prowess while the recipient grew weaker. Self-sufficiency was their solution for problem-solving. The emptiness of the land prohibited the search for help, as miles of obscurity separated friends. Persistence and self-reliance were the answers for survival when living on the Wyoming Wind River Indian Reservation.

The beauty of the land was reflected in the physical beauty and strength of their Native American tribe. The design of the tall lodge-pole pine tree was repeated in the stature of the larger person, the one who wore the bigger boots—he was, in fact, known as Big Boots. He had long, strong, sinewy arms and legs. The raw, hard horizon of the landscape was replicated in the chiseled bone structure of his facial features. The angular landscape was like his indigenous face, both naturally unadorned and copper-colored. The owner of the smaller pair of boots replicated the sturdy, closer-to-the-ground, tenacious sagebrush that grew across the prairie. He was known as Waffle Stomper.

The fishermen on their baby-delivery mission were descendants of the ancient eastern Shoshoni Plains Indians who migrated from the Rocky Mountains of Wyoming to southwestern Montana in the 1800s. The Shoshoni settled in the Wind River Valley, then named Warm Valley, during the harsh, coldest months. In the summer the ancient tribe migrated to the Fort Bridger area of Wyoming, where the higher elevation offered relief from the 115-degree sunny days.

Chief Washakie and the Shoshoni tribes were given choice lands because they were not involved with killing white settlers on the Oregon or Overland Trails. The Wind River Reservation began at the mouth of the Owl Creek and ran due south to the divide between Sweet Water and Popo Agie (pronounced po-po-ja) Rivers. The occupants of the truck knew the reservation boundary. As young braves they had walked along the crest and the summit of the Wind River Mountain Range to the North Fork and the Wind River that made a straight line to the headwaters of Owl Creek, forming its entirety. Through the years, Big Boots and Waffle Stomper had walked much of it many times.

The land belonged to the Shoshoni tribe, but in 1876, the

government allowed the Northern Arapaho tribe to settle temporarily in Shoshoni territory while they recovered from sickness. The Arapaho tribe and their Chief Black Cole wanted their own reservation in the Powder River country, but they remained as guests on Shoshoni land for eight years while the government had no intention of forming a separate reservation for them. The Shoshoni tribe was eventually paid $450,000 for the reservation land given to the Northern Arapaho. This government deal promoted everlasting resentment between the two tribes, and this ancient transaction instilled determination for the two Shoshoni friends to claim this baby as one of their own.

The ancient hatred between the two tribes was imbedded in the oral story tradition within both tribes, and the wearers of the four boots that traveled to the Indian Mission today knew the old stories by heart. The ancient enemy tribes had performed atrocities against each other. The old memories of hatred were scratched deeply into their minds and had been kept alive for centuries.

During the mid-1800s Jesuits established the Indian Mission to teach Christianity to both tribes. Big Boots and Waffle Stomper owed early childhood survival and education to the Indian Mission. Today Indian tribal councils governed the school and their communities while the Bureau of Indian Affairs funded the mission and supported Indian education.

The Indian Mission sat prominently on the land's flatness. The barren grounds supported a few large cottonwood trees that surrounded Incaranata Hall, which housed the sisters' convent. On this sunny morning of September 5, 1953, the old truck rumbled to a stop. The two fishermen carried the hubcap, climbed the few steep steps to the thick-walled, sand-colored building, and pulled the thick ropes to ring the brass mission bell. A small nun popped out.

"Good morning, Big Boots and Waffle Stomper! God has given us a beautiful September morning. How can I be of service to you?" Sister Margaret asked as she grasped the heavy door while her small, fragile body propped it open to the sunlight.

"We have something for Mother Superior."

"How thoughtful! I will go get her. Do step in."

"No—boots have mud."

Sister Margaret was the oldest of the Franciscan sisters, and she accepted the role of convent hospitality rector and served as an assistant to Mother Superior. Sister Margaret was a tiny, kind, and gentle soul who honored her vows to be of service. Her face looked like a small brown raisin stuck in the middle of the cream inside an Oreo cookie. The white wimple framed her face like the white cream center of the black cookie mantle that covered her head and joined the robe that dwarfed her four-foot frame. Even though she was in her late seventies, she moved spryly.

Sister Margaret darted back inside Incaranata Hall, and the door closed as the muddy-booted men waited on the steps. She returned and opened the door, and Mother Superior nodded her head in greeting to the two waiting fishermen. Strong arms sprang forward and presented her with the hubcap. Mother Superior looked puzzled as she accepted the gift. She pulled back the expensive aqua-blue sweater and gasped.

"My goodness, a little ragamuffin!"

"She's Shoshoni. We found her—so she is one of ours. She has turned-in toes."

"She is Shoshoni for sure," repeated Waffle Stomper.

Big Boots told the sisters the story of their find and emphatically stated, "Her name should be Wren, unless you want to call her Hubcap."

Mother Superior smiled. "Wren will do nicely," she said as she closed the door.

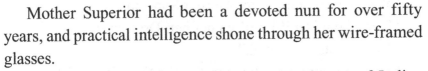

Mother Superior had been a devoted nun for over fifty years, and practical intelligence shone through her wire-framed glasses.

"Sister Margaret, please telephone the Bureau of Indian Affairs, Dr. Lawrence, and Katy Bear, who is a lactating mother. Have them all come immediately. This child still has the umbilical cord attached and needs care and nourishment."

Incaranata Hall became a lively hub of activity in contrast to the norm of soft steps and quiet prayers. Now the sound was joyous, excited chatter, baby cries, and the rushing rustle of black and white habits supplying clean, warmed blankets and fresh white diapers as Dr. Lawrence and Katy Bear gave childcare.

Katy Bear, a portly woman in her midthirties, had seven children of her own. Her rounded face held the characteristically Arapaho wide, flat bone structure with small eyes like Boston baked beans candy. Her face, with dimpled cheeks surrounding a warm smile, reflected her good nature and happy attitude. She had the demeanor of a mother hen when it came to children. Katy was an Arapaho but saw this child from God who needed attention as a by-product from the isolated forest. She saw a creature from nature, and it was of no consequence if this child was a proclaimed Shoshoni. The foundling nuzzled and latched onto the offered milk from the soft warmth of a generous human mother who was willing to share. Katy also shared her intellect with the people of her tribe as the first woman to serve on the Arapaho tribal council. Mrs. Katy Bear eventually raised a total of twelve biological children. All were well-behaved, gracious, athletic, and academically honored students. It was believed the ingredients for feminine strength, intelligence, and speed were given to the foundling through the lactating of Katy's human kindness. Katy held the kicking, strong-legged, four-pound, thirteen-ounce newborn while Dr. Lawrence completed the examination. He determined the birth had been at 7:30 a.m., September 5, 1953, and certified documents were given to the BIA, officially enrolling Wren as a new member of the Shoshoni tribe. When Katy finished nursing Wren and the waif was sleeping, Mother Superior placed the child into the newly prepared bassinet given by charity. The sisters' convent housed in Incaranata Hall had been transformed, and Mother Superior made long-range plans for Wren's care and religious education.

"Katy, would you be able to continue with the supply of nourishment for this child?"

"Yes, Mother Superior. My last child, Judy, is almost old enough for solid food."

"We know you have your own children to tend, but any extra milk would be helpful." Mother Superior then turned and addressed her assistant. "Sister Margaret, I think this child's daily care should be given to unruly Sister Samantha."

"I think that's a wonderful idea. Sister Samantha needs responsibility and to learn the frailness of life."

———◄—

Sister Samantha was never to be called Sister Sam in Incaranata Hall and within the Franciscan order of nuns. Mother Superior knew that Sister Samantha would learn more refined behavior if she were not called the tomboy name. The name change was only one of many ways Mother Superior and the twenty-three nuns living in Incaranata Hall tried to modify Sister Samantha's rowdy behavior.

Last month Sister Samantha had been disciplined for laughing loudly while she sat in the chapel's pew for third year novices during morning prayers. The front row was designated seating for the postulants, the first year trainees of the order, while the second- and third-year novices sat behind them to monitor the postulants' reverence. Sister Samantha was the youngest novice. She had entered the nunnery and accepted her vows to become a nun when she was only sixteen. The residents of Incaranata Hall granted tolerance to Sister Samantha for her youth, and they hoped she would soon outgrow her immaturity, but her behavior taxed everyone's patience. The three years of novice training were to teach the disciplines and benefits of poverty, chastity, and obedience—and Sister Samantha definitely had difficulty with obedience. Sister Samantha was now a knockout beauty. Her curly blonde hair was hidden under her habit mantle but remained part of the hidden picture for her flawless porcelain face that housed large, most vividly blue eyes. Her long blonde eyelashes and thick brows accentuated her cute snub nose. Her perfectly formed lips reflected her pure heart and good intentions. Sister Samantha's beauty and runway-model body were incongruent with the nun's habit.

Mother Superior's voice had been kind and soft when she summoned Sister Samantha to her office.

"Sister Samantha, what was the reason for the disturbing peal of laughter? It came from your third row of novices of all places! Not even from a postulant but from you, during the most reverent contemplation time of morning prayers."

"Mother Superior, forgive me, but Father Patty's vestments are hand-me-downs from tall Father Gregory. Short, fat Father Patty looks like Dopey from the seven dwarfs, and I couldn't control my laughter."

"I see your point, Sister Samantha." Mother Superior smiled.

"But if your heart and mind were engaged with the scripture to be contemplated, you wouldn't have been distracted by the visual image of Father Patty."

"Thank you again, Mother Superior, but I was contemplating the scriptures that Father Patty gave—Corinthians 1:27, 'But God has chosen the foolish things of the world to shame the wise, and God has chosen the weak things of the world to shame the things which are strong.' The sight of Father Patty with his oversized vestments looked foolish, shaming the wise, and he certainly looked weak. The scriptures and Father Patty's visual image made me laugh."

"We must remedy this." Mother Superior chuckled. "Sister Samantha, this week you will apply your seamstress skills and become Father Patty's personal tailor. You will hem all his garments, shorten the sleeves, and properly size the shoulders for all his robes. You will design Father Patty's image into one of distinction. You will do this task anonymously. You will remove and return his vestments from the chapel closet without revealing yourself. You will contemplate 'being of service' during your task."

The following week, Father Patty looked regal while he served the morning Eucharist. Extra fabric from the length of the robe had been added to the body to hide his portly size. His vestments fit and portrayed wisdom. He carried himself in a taller stance and moved without tripping on his garments. Mother Superior called Sister Samantha into her office to give praise for the transformation of Father Patty from Dopey to priest.

Sister Samantha stepped into Mother Superior's office covered with white, hand-printed note cards sewn all over her habit.

"Sister Samantha, what are you doing? Let me read those

note cards!" Mother Superior raised each card as she read them one by one: Nun Today, Nun Tomorrow, Nun Forever, Nun Whatsoever, Absolutely Nun, Nun Expected, Nun Wanted, We Have Nun, Nun of the Above. On the backside of Sister Samantha's habit the note cards read: Bad Habit, Good Habit, Addictive Habit, Habit Forming, Habit-Free, Habits? We Have Nun, Force of Habit, Nuns Are Habit Forming, Habits Become Addictive, Creatures of Habit.

"Please explain this, Sister Samantha."

"I'm doing penance to remember my calling and suppress my doubts," Samantha humbly answered.

"You transformed Father Patty's image in a positive way. He was exceptionally delighted with his altered robes. I am pleased you were of service to him and that you claimed no reward by revealing your identity. You may be excused." Mother Superior made no comment about the visual reminders that covered the Sister Samantha's garment.

Three years of unruly behavior clouded Sister Samantha's reverence, but her devout heart characterized her goodness. In addition to her seamstress skills, she had studied early childhood development and was an effective, fun-loving teacher for the Indian Mission day-care and prekindergarten children, who loved her.

Mother Superior's mind was firm as she and Sister Margaret discussed the new foundling's future on that September morning in 1953 when baby Wren would become Sister Samantha's charge.

Mother Superior rolled her eyes toward Sister Margaret, who closed hers in prayer at the sight of Sister Samantha, who had cut off the habit above the knees and shortened it in fifties' poodle-skirt fashion. The expensive habit made from the finest woven wool fabric was now only half its former length. Mother

Superior held her breath while aging Sister Margaret maintained silence when they presented Wren to the hep fashion queen.

"Sister Samantha, you have been given the most important task of a lifetime. You will be   in charge of this child's total welfare. You will see that baby Wren is nourished in both body and spirit. You will coordinate her feeding schedule with Katy Bear. Wren will depend on you for clean diapers, bedding, and clothing. Her total comfort is in your hands. You have been given a precious gift and the challenges of motherhood."

Sister Samantha cradled the tiny bundle in her arms as tears flowed from her cornflower-blue eyes. "I will love this child," she said as she left the room.

Chapter 2

TRANSFORMATION

S ister Samantha's steps echoed on the barren beige tile floor as she left Mother Superior's office with new purpose in her stride. The baby was warm and securely nestled in the new pink fleece blankets removed from the Charity Thrift Shop. Sister Samantha returned the used bassinet to the thrift shop and prepared the convent's wicker laundry basket as Wren's signature, designer-line custom sleeping quarters. The nuns within Incaranata Hall uttered not a grumble as they witnessed one of their laundry conveniences disappear and be transformed into a white-and-pink frilly but practical baby bed.

Sister Samantha's impetuous behavior was likewise transformed through the many hours of reading parenting books; visits with Katy Bear; and filling, refilling, and transporting bottles of breast milk to and from baby Wren's basket. Her shortened habit was replaced with the traditional long robe as she engaged in routine examinations and consultations with Doctor Lawrence about baby Wren's development.

The two fishermen delivered a Shoshoni cradleboard to Wren. The board was made from river willows. The curved woven canopy bonnet at the top of the board covered the baby's head and was trimmed with dangling beads for Wren to watch and grasp with her tiny hands. The head bonnet and the body of the cradle were both covered with soft white hand-tanned deer hide. Traditional Shoshoni American red rose beadwork was artfully placed against the white deerskin background. It was a work of art, with every individual bead properly placed, indicative of Shoshoni beading style. Other tribes beaded in the "lazy man style" by loosely attaching five or six beads together per strand. This cradleboard was beautiful, and Sister Samantha carried Wren everywhere in style, telegraphing her membership into the Shoshoni tribe.

Wren's christening was one of the most popular events at Indian Mission that fall, celebrated by both Shoshoni and Arapahos. She was presented to Father Patty in her revered cradleboard while the two Shoshoni fishermen stood in attendance and vowed to be her godfathers and protectors during her lifetime. Sister Samantha and Sister Margaret were her appointed godmothers and made the same vows to give Wren lifelong well-being. The chapel's simple wooden pews were full with members of the tribal community while the aisles and alcoves were full of children from the pre-K day-care classes and from the mission school, all there to witness the blessed event. Katy Bear and her growing family were among the many Arapahos who attended. As the nuns from Incaranata Hall served a pink-and-white cake, the new godfathers slipped away from the crowd to consecrate the newly accepted responsibilities in their own culture.

Big Boots and Waffle Stomper, the new godfathers, made dust as their old Ford truck left the convent driveway and headed toward the setting sun. Big Boots scoped the left side of the road looking for signs of an active sweat lodge while Waffle Stomper searched the right. The weather was in the low thirties, and the plume of smoke would be easily spotted. They had traveled close to twelve miles when Waffle Stomper called out.

"There!" The truck slowed as Big Boots looked off in the distance to see the smoke coming from a lodge.

"Yup, that sure is a sweat lodge or smoke from Martha's bad cooking."

The lodge was a small, handcrafted structure made from red willows lashed together to form a rounded roof ten feet in diameter. It was covered by an army-surplus tarp and a colorful Arapaho handmade quilt. The lodge was nestled twenty feet away from a rusted-out faded brown Chickasaw mobile home, stacks of old tires, a washing machine, and a shiny new 1953 sky-blue Pontiac. The godfathers' truck rolled in and parked beside six other vehicles with Gene Lee Motors stickers on their bumpers. Big Boots and Waffle Stomper watched as the door flap of the lodge rose and six glossy-bodied, low-crouched men came out, breathed deeply, and stretched their limbs. The godfathers grabbed their towels and boldly clomped to the sweat lodge. They nodded a greeting to the sweat lodge participants, but no conversation ensued. Outside the sweat lodge, the godfathers stripped out of their boots, pants, and shirts, down to their boxer undershorts.

Everyone was welcome to participate in a sweat lodge ceremony no matter what their tribal affiliation as long as the participant was not on drugs or drunk. The sweats included people from all cultures, from any race or age. It was uncommon, but not unheard of, that children as young as nine or ten participated. Modest dress was expected from everyone, and women usually wore shorts and T-shirts. This disparity of dress between men and women represented the double standard. It pointed to the superiority of male rule. It was thought that the female nude body was a distraction from the purpose of the sweat—or that men sweated more than women and would saturate clothing. However, women were welcome, but they could not participate if they were having their monthly cycle. It was unknown why the women's monthly rule was observed, especially since feminine hygiene products were available, but the old tradition was respected. Perhaps it was because the Shoshoni tribe had roamed and lived in the vast bear territory since primitive days. It was cautioned, even in 1953, that women during the monthly period were vulnerable to attacking bears when hiking or tent camping. Bears had poor eyesight, but they had an acute sense of smell. Perhaps this old tradition for survival was carried over into modern times, but tonight's sweat lodge ceremony was composed of all men.

The ceremony guide asked, "Does anyone need herbs or remedies for ailments or for pain?" Two people needed herbs, and the host distributed them during the sweat. The two participants rubbed the herb over their bodies. There were no herbs ingested, and the most common herb distributed was sage.

Big Boots crouched his six-foot-two-inch tall John Wayne body low. He was in his late sixties, and his facial features were replica of the Shoshoni high cheekbones with recessed eyes. His Shoshoni features looked to be more from ancient Asian descent. Big Boots was the first to enter the lodge and he sat the farthest from the door flap around the fire pit. The leader of the sweat entered last and sat nearest the east-facing door flap. He poured water over the rocks as he lowered the flap after Waffle Stomper trailed the other men and sat nearest the exit on the opposite side from the leader. All the men sat cross-legged around the fire pit in silence. Then the ceremony guide said a prayer, and each person in their silence had their own intentions. This was a sacred space, and there was no need for shared vocal expression. Every person's awareness was inward, and no one watched or judged others in the seated circle. When the flap came down, they were enclosed in total blackness. Big Boots closed his eyes and supposed that the others had done the same.

The ceremony host of the sweat lodge had given great care to build the lodge with the door facing east. The east-facing door collected positive energies from the morning sun. An east-facing door provided good health, prosperity, and eternal happiness for inhabitants. The sweat lodge host had carefully selected the red willows for their flexibility and strength to correctly build the lodge to purify the air and retain moisture. The two-foot-diameter fire pit was dug three feet deep inside the center of the lodge's earth floor to provide the carefully chosen sandstone rocks with long-lasting heat. It was known that sandstone rock held heat much longer than other types of rocks. Smooth granite river rock was not used. River rock when exposed to extreme heat and when water was poured over them sometimes exploded and dangerously threw hot shards of stone onto seated devotees.

The leader determined the lodge's temperature, which ranged between 160 and 180 degrees. To make it hotter he poured water onto the white-hot rocks in the fire pit. If the participants couldn't withstand the heat, they could cover their heads, shoulders, or body parts with their towels, but they couldn't leave until the end of the round as determined by the guide. If a devotee wanted the temperature to be hotter, he used an eagle's wing to fan the air onto his body.

There were four rounds to the sweat lodge ceremony, and each round honored one of the four directions. Big Boots and Waffle Stomper had missed the first round of the ceremony honoring the east, but they joined in time for the second round honoring the south.

Each sweat lodge experience was unique and depended upon the honorable qualities of the lodge host. The sweat experience depended upon his honor and his good intentions to provide a place where participants could seek connection with the source of creation, receive guidance or forgiveness, and gain physical strength or mental clarity. It was a refuge to gain a sense of well-being and productiveness. It was a place to purge wrongful actions, disease, personal weaknesses, impure thoughts, lust, or greed. The participants all had their own private intentions. Big Boots was there to give Wren protection and safety during her lifetime. Waffle Stomper devoted himself to assuring Wren had life-enhancing staples and was exposed to the arts, and he wanted to be a positive role model of fatherly love.

Each time the leader poured water over the rocks, the heat rose and the smell of the steam on the rocks mixed with the fragrance of the red willow. The scent was like a forest before a rainstorm. The sage smell helped to deepen the sweat experience by clearing the mind of random thoughts, sinking awareness into the blackness of the lodge, and magnifying the purpose of intentions. The experience was not unlike the sinking Wind River as it disappeared into the blackness of the Sinks Canyon. When the mind became self-absorbed, the body felt the burn of the intense humidity and heat. Self-absorbed, distracted thoughts caused discomfort to the participant, who suffered.

The perspiring participants felt the moist earth that they sat upon as the low roof of red willows brushed the tops of their heads and backs. They were aware of the movements of fellow devotees, but the blackness of the lodge kept their focus upon their purposeful intention. During the round honoring the south, the leader passed a ladle of water around the circle to the sweat lodge partners. When someone received water, he would pour half onto the ground to nurture Mother Earth before taking water for himself.

Waffle Stomper was startled when the lodge door flap was raised and the rush of thirty-four-degree night air hit his heated body, signaling the end of the second round. In a crouched position, he followed the ceremony guide outside, where his body was soothed by the September air. Big Boots was the last to emerge from the lodge, and he stood beside Waffle Stomper in silence for a few minutes before he grabbed the spare scoop shovel to help the host tote newly heated rocks back into the sweat lodge fire pit. The separate outside wood-fed fire had been heated for hours and was tended by the host's wife, who used it to prepare soup. The sweating members did not socialize or share their experiences, and after five minutes they crouched low again to follow the host with his shovelful of rocks and his bucketful of water back into the lodge. In this third round honoring the west, Waffle Stomper was first to follow the leader into the lodge and sat in the hottest part of the lodge farthest from the door flap.

Waffle Stomper was an enrolled Shoshoni, but he had been described in his younger years as a ten-years-younger look-alike of football hero Joe Namath. His body also did not reflect the slender lodge-pole pine. Instead, his five-foot-eight-inch frame was shaped more like the low, wide sagebrush. He had an exceptionally long torso, short arms, and short bowed legs.

Big Boots brought in the last shovelful of rocks and sat down last in the coolest position near the exit.

When the last round, which honored the north, ended, eight men stooped low and crawled from the sacred rustic dome to refresh their lungs and bodies under the starlit sky. The darkness engulfed the flat plains, and only the wood-fed fire pit competed with the many stars sprinkled in the black velvet sky. The fatigued attendees stood outside the sweat lodge and stretched and flexed their limbs and lungs. Their deep breathing sounded like a flock of geese flapping wings before taking flight. Hot, moist bodies began to cool, and the eight men began to rapidly sort through the piles of abandoned clothing like gophers searching for a mate. Lighthearted prattle spewed from the group as the near-freezing weather hastened their actions, but no one spoke of the sweat lodge experience. They kept the experience to themselves and bonded through silent respect for one another. They communicated best through silence. The host and his wife-helper served a warm soup in paper cups to prevent dehydration. Friendly male chatter and words of gratitude were given to the host. Then Big Boots and Waffle Stomper wearily ambled to their parked truck.

"You look like a newborn mouse." Waffle Stomper slyly smirked as he glanced toward his friend.

The newborn foundling as small as a newborn mouse brought days of joy for the convent. Mother Superior and the nuns couldn't have been happier. For the past three years they had patiently endured Sister Samantha's annoying practical jokes because the large grant donated to the Indian Mission by her parents, Bogetta and Lars Favre, gave the sisterhood subsistence. Much to the relief of the twenty-three nuns, Sister Samantha's convent pranks disappeared and were replaced with softly sung psalms to soothe the baby's cries. Wren in her cradleboard accompanied Sister Samantha to matins, mass, confessions, vespers, and evening compline. Baby Wren's cradleboard attached to the sister, who performed daily tasks for the pre-K day care. Wren was propped up in the cradleboard against a chair and watched the class at play. Sister Samantha and Wren both grew during the thirty-below-zero winter and into the sweet alfalfa smell of spring.

Wren at eight months was a beautiful child with abundant dark curly hair and large, round, vivid 7UP bottle–green eyes. Her facial features were like a painted china doll. Her delicate body had extralong legs, arms, fingers, and unusually long toes. Wren though small—a mere twelve pounds—was strong and agile.

"Holding Wren feels like I am holding a squirming noodle compared to my kids, who feel like bowling balls," commented Katy Bear. Eight-month-old Wren rapidly crawled down the slick convent hallways, grasped windowsills, pulled herself to a stable standing position, and watched the children playing on the school playground. She was in perpetual fast-forward motion.

She crawled and then stood and ran as fast as the seasons changed. Samantha applied her fashion designing skills to create Wren's hooded fuzzy pink snowsuit under the fur trimmed deerskin coat. The two fishermen brought the tanned hides, and Samantha created Wren's protective shield against Wyoming's painful winters.

Mother Superior and Sister Margaret smiled as they passed the open door and overheard Samantha lecturing three-year-old Wren about the dangers of smoking.

"You saw the eighth-grade boys out by the schoolhouse wall smoking! They think it makes them grown up, but you must never smoke. It is unhealthy for your lungs. Promise me, Wren, you will never smoke."

"Wren is only three," Sister Margaret whispered to Mother Superior.

"Sister Samantha is starting her preteen lectures early. It can't do any harm," Mother Superior said, snickering as they continued down the hall into the chapel.

"Okay, Wren, as soon as you put on your winter clothes and boots you can go outside," Sister Samantha said as she bundled the child into her Samantha-designed hooded snowsuit.

"I love you, Wren," she said as she nudged the small pink package out the iced-stuck front door. The thirty-below sunny midmorning weather in Wyoming was an experience unto itself. Even though the sun was bright, the frigid air smacked human skin with the sting of a fly swatter. The hard-packed snow had piled into six-foot-tall mounds each time the road was plowed since snowfall began in late September. The cold never relented to encourage melting, and the snow crunched under Wren's small feet. The white landscape looked like two-foot-deep sparkling sandpaper sheets stretched over the open pastures instead of the romanticized fluffy white stuff southerners imagined. The sun's rays glazed the surface of the snow and caused ice. Wren plummeted to waist deep through the crusted surface with each exhausted breath that she took. The sound of the snow crunching under her twenty pounds broke the crisp silence of the winter day.

Wren's shrill screams shattered the pristine air like glass breaking on a marble floor. As she shrieked, the door of the convent flew open and Samantha darted out in Wren's defense.

"Wren, what's wrong? Are you hurt?"

"No, I do bad. I do bad," Wren said between sobs. "I are smoking!"

Samantha laughed, gathered Wren into a snuggly hug, and carried her to the front steps. The sister demonstrated the lesson of breath condensation in the freezing air.

"See, Wren, I am smoking too, but it's condensation and not smoke. We are not smoking."

Wren's big round green eyes opened wide while her perfectly shaped fine eyebrows lifted. Her relieved face unfurled a smile as she learned that she had not performed a bad deed.

Wren learned many lessons about right and wrong in her developmental years at the convent, and she developed her own sense of self-governance. What was it that gave Wren her innate determination to perform right actions and to feel such remorse when she thought she had done something wrong? The local Christian folks said it was from being raised in the convent. Arapahos knew it was from the strong nutrition from Katy Bear's breast milk, and the Shoshoni elders of the tribe said it was because Wren was a product from nature's forest, and that she was given the ability to grow from the earth's strength. The tribal village also taught Wren things of a different nature.

At times Samantha left Wren with Katy Bear's family as she attended to charitable eldercare. It was during these times that Katy's three oldest sons, Darrell, Shram, and Speedbump, dragged Wren to the casino and sat her on top of the colorful nickelodeon while they played pool. Wren loved the music, felt the musical vibes on her bottom and through her entire body. The warm lights from the music box pulsated energy into her system, and she moved to its rhythm. Wren's thick, curly hair bounced to the beat of Tennessee Ernie Ford's song "Sixteen Tons." Her diminutive body became the music itself. Wren danced. She danced while the casino people smiled and applauded. Three-year-old Wren found her passion and talent. She discovered the love of performance at the Big Chief Casino, and it served as Wren's dance academy and studio.

Sometimes Darrell, Shram, and Speedbump took their little sister Judy to the casino too. Judy had been Katy's eight-month-old baby who was nudged from breastfeeding when Wren arrived. The two girls of nearly the same age were born to be friends, and they danced and sang songs together with the energy of pure joy. The Big Chief Casino served as the little girls' stage and music hall, where they learned song lyrics, limericks, and poems. The casino's influence was shown when Father Patty asked his young congregation if they would like to sing a song during mass.

"We are coming into the spring and Lent season. Would any of you like to sing a song for us today?"

Wren grabbed Judy's hand and bounced forward to the chapel altar. Katy Bear and Sister Samantha were dismayed. Wren had clear diction and a strong voice.

"Let's sing the song about the little dog," Wren suggested to Judy.

"Okay." The two friends' voices were crystal clear, and everyone in the small chapel could hear perfectly.

When Fido was a little dog and just began to crawl.

He hoisted up his right hind leg and peed against the wall

The firemen saw the smoke arise and thought it was a fire,

So he hoisted up the other leg and peed a little higher.

Muffled gasps, snickers, chuckles, and suppressed laughs crept from the gathered congregation, and the little girls smiled proudly.

"Oh my, this will never do—coming from a child raised at the convent. Wren and Judy know Psalm John 3:16 perfectly. I thought they were going to do that one!" gasped Mother Superior. And with that, Wren's Big Chief Casino education was abruptly altered.

Wren and Judy were in Samantha's pre-K class even though they both were too young, like underaged Big Chief Casino refugees. Sister Samantha traded childcare favors with Katy

Bear, and the two girls were together almost every day. Wren and Judy were sisters from opposite tribes, but no matter what the bloodlines held the power of their friendship was in their shared love, laughter, imaginary friends, dress-up, and mud pies. One day during class the older children were learning the days of the week.

"Who can name all the days of the week?" Samantha asked the round, upturned faces of the children who were sitting at her feet.

"I can!" shouted Wren.

"Great, Wren, please stand and say them for us."

Wren's diminutive stature was half-sized compared to the other children, but she had a strong voice. Her courage projected self-confidence unusual among the shy, reserved Indian Mission preschoolers.

Wren began. "Monday, Tuesday, Wednesday ..."

Silence ensued, more silence continued, more silence and fidgeting followed, and then from the back of the group came Judy's voice.

"Payday!"

Samantha laughed and knew the importance of payday to every resident living in Fremont and Hot Springs Counties.

"And is that the most important day of the week?" Samantha asked, hoping the response would be *No, Sunday is most important*, but the group shouted, "Yes, yes, payday is the most important!"

The children spoke their truth, and Samantha knew that she had hard lessons yet to teach. Sister Samantha was challenged. How she could possibly teach preschoolers that they lived according to the mandate of government decisions made 126 years ago?

Sister Samantha knew her school history well. She knew

that Andrew Jackson was president (and inadvertently created payday) when the Removal Act of 1830 mandated the Indian people live on reservations. The Removal Act contained a clause that stated Indian annuities would be paid directly to each enrolled tribal member rather than to the reservation's hosting state or the tribe itself to alleviate the temptation for corruption. Every enrolled Native American received a per capita check from the government. The money was earned from the mineral rights on the reservation land. Each tribal member, including Wren, received a share of the monthly royalties divided among tribal members. The Arapahos outnumbered the Shoshoni three to one, so their checks were smaller because they had a larger enrolled population. The per capita checks for Wren's future were important. Samantha received Wren's checks since she served as her guardian until she reached twenty-one years old. Samantha saved the payments for her future education, except for the dimes removed for payday treats, movie money, and for fabric to make Wren's Samantha-designed stylish wardrobe.

Judy Bear's family received a larger check per month. Katy Bear's children were well fed and well clothed. Other reservation children didn't fare as well as the Bear children. Many per capita checks were selfishly used by the parents until the child reached adulthood. Many Native American parents during the 1950s were alcoholics and abused the per capita money privilege given to the tribes. Many reservation babies were born as alcoholics, and children were malnourished, undersized, and neglected while child alcoholism and liver disease grew to epidemic proportions. It was a common practice and a quick convenience for alcoholic, uneducated, or young parents to pour wine or beer into their babies' bottles to calm or to feed them.

The once-a-month payday check was a big deal for the entire county. The nearby city's economy was also fed by the per capita checks. During the month, merchants gave credit at grocery stores, gas stations, dry goods stores, restaurants, car dealers, and bars to reservation residents. If establishments didn't receive payment to clear the account, hardships befell the families, credit was withheld, and anger raged. "See you payday!" was a common greeting. When Native Americans had payday money, they had friends.

Wren continued to learn what was appropriate and the difference between right and wrong—convent style. She also spent many hours at the Bear family home learning social skills.

"Judy calls you Mother. Shouldn't she call you Mother Superior?" Wren asked Katy Bear one day when Wren and Judy were playing.

"Oh, I would like for Judy to call me Mother Superior." Katy chuckled.

"Should I call you Mother Superior too?"

"No, Wren, you call me Katy Bear." And so it was forever more—katybear.

During her kindergarten year and for many years after, Wren attended the community center dance hall with katybear's family, which had grown to become twelve children. Wren as a five-year-old danced with the proficiency of an adult. She would hold her space and dance as the crowd changed partners. Rotating partners gave Wren a different dance partner every half song. Wren followed any adult's lead, kept perfect time with any music, but the new 1950s' jitterbug was her favorite, and the Bears' seventh-grade son Speedbump was her favorite partner. As his name suggested, he was doughboy portly, but he could lift, twirl, drag, and flip Wren with the grace and energy of a smooth ballroom dancer. Wren danced at powwows, community hall dances, sports intermissions, and Sister Samantha's transistor radio added to her dance opportunities and performance skills.

When Wren went to katybear's house, she and Judy danced to her brother Shram's record albums for hours.

At age seven, Wren ran or danced everywhere. She was perpetual motion except when she would lie flat on her tummy as still as the fence posts that surrounded the pastures of prairie grass. She watched the herds of pronghorn antelope as they came out to graze in the late afternoon sun. Wren knew there were more antelope than there were people where she lived. These animals were tan-colored with white rumps, underbellies, and rings around their necks. They also had a white streak along the jawline, under the nose, and above the mouth that accentuated their narrow faces. Wren thought about the song "Home on the Range."   "Home, home on the range, where the deer and the antelope play," she sang. "Home, this is 'my' home." Wren thought that her home looked like a flat piece of squared brown cardboard with hard gray mountains that jutted straight into the sky and bordered the edges like they were holding everything together. Her treeless, wide-open flat spaces were covered in dry, straw-colored grass that camouflaged the antelope as they bedded down. She was awed that the antelope knew they were unseen. Wren equated herself with the fawns who had no sisters or brother because antelope had only one baby at a time and lived in the wild to be eight to ten years of age. These antelope were her age, but they could run much faster. *Maybe I am part antelope, and maybe I can run as fast.* Wren watched them for long hours until she saw their silhouettes grow dark against the soft pink, orange, and lavender setting sun. She studied the way the animals ran, how they stretched two of their long legs into fast strides, and how they pulled the other two legs back under themselves in midair before they touched the ground for another power forwarded stride. *I will try that with my own two legs.* Antelope were the fastest animals on the plains compared to the white tailed deer, elk, mountain sheep, moose, and wild mustangs. Wren had seen the antelope run at their top fifty-mile-an-hour speed. She watched, jumped up, and chased after them, imitating their stretched legs during their stride, and the quick pull tuck-up underneath themselves before they took another surging step. The antelope ran and leaped over the fences for self-defense as Wren chased after them. She imitated the running antelope, practiced their technique, and forgot about the light of day.

"Wren, where have you been? You have been gone for hours. It's after sunset, and I was getting worried about you! We are going to be late for compline evening mass. Tell me on the way where you were!" Sister Samantha queried as they hurried to the chapel.

"I was chasing the antelope."

"Well, I hope you didn't catch any."

Wren laughed. "Nope—they are faster than me, but maybe next time!"

Chapter 3

THE PLAYGROUND

Wyoming was special. The Wind River Indian Reservation was unique, and the Shoshoni and Arapaho people made it the most exclusive of all places in the United States, or at least it was for Wren, who knew nothing about other places.

The convent's ten-party phone line was known as the reservation drumbeat. All people who had a phone listened to anyone's conversation, a practice known as "rubbering." Rubbering was a form of news and entertainment.

The "drumbeat" rang at the convent, and Sister Samantha picked up the receiver.

"Hi, Sister. This is katybear. Wren just arrived."

"What? How could that be? She left here just thirty-five minutes ago."

"Well, she's here now, huffing and puffing. She said she ran all the way."

"Katy, that means she ran three miles in thirty-five minutes. She knows never to accept a ride, even from people she knows. With drinking being a problem out here, I told her never to ride with anyone except you. Do you think she caught a ride?"

"No, I don't think so. She is just a fast runner for an eight-year-old. I will call you when she leaves."

"I saw her run past the intersection of Deaf Smith Road about fifteen-minutes ago."

"Hilda, is that you?" Sister Samantha asked.

"Yeah, I'm rubbering! Wren was running wide open when I saw her."

"Well, at least we know she is safe and can outrun most anything bad." Katy hung up.

Wren ran the distance to spend the day with her friend Judy Bear. Wren was always exhilarated by Judy's noisy, chaotic household. The dark-green house was a small three bedroom with a remodeled basement where Judy's parents slept. The three upstairs bedrooms each held two sets of bunk beds to accommodate the twelve children. Judy's house was strewn with yellow-and-orange push toys for children under seven. The olive-green countertops and wooden desks held various piles of books for school assignments. Judy's twin brothers, Ronny and Donny, who had been withheld a year, were in her same third-grade class. Wren recognized the math book that she too had not finished and had brought to the convent for Samantha's help. Wren was aware of the mounds of clutter and the piles of shoes at the front door. Native Americans routinely removed their shoes before they entered anyone's home. They believed the energy of the host was absorbed through the soles of the feet, and the simple act of removing shoes spoke of friendship, trust, and acceptance. The custom could have been a tradition from past days of the tipi, where removed shoes kept the limited space of the interior clean. The old custom still held practical application for 1960.

Judy's home was a striking contrast from the minimal living provided to Wren in the convent. The house didn't provide much play space, so the Bear children—like most rez children—used the outdoors as their play area. When Wren arrived, katybear was combing Judy's hair. Wren watched the tenderness and attachment shown to each of the long, black, shiny strands of Judy's hair that katybear combined into one-inch-thick pigtails. Wren watched the peaceful, contented expression on katybear's round brown face as she finished Judy's braids. Wren knew that Samantha touched her hair with the same affection she saw in katybear's eyes. *Judy and I share the same expressions of endearment given to us by women who care.*

"Okay, Long Legs! Let's go help Speedbump and the twins sell lemonade," Judy sang out as she jumped down from the stool.

"I never noticed before, but, Wren, you do have long legs. Maybe you are related to the antelope," katybear said, laughing.

"Yes, I am! Sister Samantha thinks I may have some white blood. My skin is lighter, and my hair is curly, but I know that I have antelope blood, because we are almost the same color."

"Don't slam the screen door, but close it so the flies don't come in," katybear reminded the girls as they left the kitchen.

The Saturday outdoors was as inviting to children as any candy store. The fragrance of blooming sage sedated living creatures into a state of relaxation. Wren and Judy flopped on the unfolded blue plaid blanket. The two eight-year-old friends held hands as they looked up into the brilliant blueness of sky obscured by fast-moving white, fluffy clouds that was their own private slide show.

"What do you think that cloud looks like, Judy?"

"It looks exactly like a dead owl. See that one? It looks exactly like a whole flock of dead birds."

"Yeah, it does, and look at that one! It looks like a butterfly, or it could be an open Bible. Do you think the Bible tells us what will happen to us?"

"Nope, the clouds tell us what happens."

"Come on! I'm tired of this cloud game. Let's go get lemonade from the twins." Wren jumped up and pulled Judy up with her, and they raced to the lemonade stand where they met resistance.

"Hey, Mom, the twins won't give us any lemonade unless we pay them five-cents a glass," Judy shrieked as she slammed the kitchen screen door.

"Don't slam the screen door, Judy—you will wake up the baby. My purse is in the drawer. You can have a dime for you and Wren."

"Do you want a lemonade too, Mom?"

"No thanks. I am drinking the new stuff Slim Fast for fat girls."

"You are only fat when you are going to have a baby." Judy laughed, slamming the screen door as she and Wren ran out to get their lemonade.

The Bear boys had made a lemonade stand out of an overturned wagon and covered it like an umbrella-stand by using an old army-surplus blue parachute. The stand was decorated with old tires with hand-painted signs that filled the round empty centers. The signs read, "Lemonade made by real American Indians," "Last chance for lemonade," "Next lemonade stand 25 miles," and "Do you need government aid? Try our lemon-aid."

"Ronny and Donny, we have our dime for lemonade," Judy called.

"Show me the dime," Ronny demanded.

"Show me the lemonade," Judy retorted.

"It is right there sitting on the counter," Donny scoffed.

"Here, Wren, this lemonade isn't even cold. It feels warm!" Judy complained.

"Well, it was sitting in the sun while you looked for a dime, what do you expect?"

The girls took their glasses over to a nearby rusted wrecked pickup and sat down on the open tailgate to drink.

"This tastes terrible! This is the worst lemonade I have ever had," Judy shouted as she poured the remainder on the ground. Wren, being convent trained, knew never to complain about food or drink. She ingested anything that was placed before her so she wouldn't appear to be rude or ungrateful. Wren drank until the cup was empty.

"Ronny, the lemonade is spoiled. You can't sell it. What did you put in it?" Judy screeched.

The boys broke out into peals of laughter. "We peed in it!"

Wren jumped from the pickup tailgate, grabbed Judy's skirt, and dragged her to a private corner behind the house.

"I feel sick. I am going to throw-up," Wren announced.

"I am sick too," Judy agreed.

"Judy, I think we have morning sickness," Wren proclaimed.

"My mom always gets morning sickness before another baby comes."

"I am so ashamed! Sister Samantha told me that this is the worst thing that can happen to a girl, and it is happening to us," Wren lamented.

"What should we do, Wren?"

"We won't tell anyone, and we will plan what we should do."

"Mom said that she would take us into town and we could go to the movies this afternoon. Do you want to go?"

"Yes, I want to go, but I am such a disgrace, and I'm scared. Sister Samantha said that a girl in trouble without a husband is a drain on the tribe. I don't want to be a drain on the tribe. I don't want to be a charity seeker as a grown-up. I want to run away, but I don't know where to go!" Wren sobbed, and tears spilled into the dirt.

"Please don't be sad, Wren. I will be a drain to my tribe too, but we will always be friends. We get payday money today, and Mom is letting us go to the movies. I want to show her we are happy about that. Can you be happy about going?"

"Yes, I don't want anyone to know what a rotten girl I am."

"Can you forget about our morning sickness and have fun at the show?" Judy pleaded.

"Yes."

Katybear's van pulled up to the Acme Theater and unloaded thirteen eager children with money in their pockets.

"It is a double feature today, so I will pick you up after the show about four forty. Look for the van parked out front by the Teton Hotel. Judy and Wren, look after the younger kids and sit near your older brothers," katybear instructed.

"I will not sit next to Ronny and Donny," Wren announced to the surprised group as she climbed down from the van.

"We don't have cooties," Donny said defensively.

"Even cooties wouldn't want to stay on you."

Wren and Judy were in Riverton, the biggest city in Fremont County, to spend a portion of their per capita money on a movie ticket, buttered popcorn, a Carmelo candy bar, and a Coke. All these were Wren's favorites. Judy chose her favorite Necco Wafers, a box of Baked Beans, a Fire Stick, and a Sugar Daddy. Saturday "payday" movie matinee was an event for the children of both tribes and local town kids too. The Acme Theater was full of children from six years to teenagers. The younger kids were to sit downstairs while the teenagers were allowed to sit in the balcony. Kids had to prove that they were thirteen by giving a note from their parents. This rule resulted in many child-written, rejected notes presented to the box office. The Acme Movie Theater had a big marquee with chasing lightbulbs advertising today's double feature of Zorro and Tarzan. Both of these were Wren and Judy's favorites. The theater interior made troubles vanish. The opulence of the gilded crown molding, red velvet curtains, and plush fold-up seats pushed any sadness or troubles aside. Wren was not heavy enough to keep her seat from folding up with her inside. Judy had to keep putting her weight on the seat so Wren could watch the movie without her legs sticking straight up into the air. The theater's opulence transported everyone into a displaced suspension, even Wren.

During the movie, Wren ate all her treats and even some of Judy's Necco Wafers. The movies ended, and the audience of children clapped and screamed. Wren wiggled through the seats to reach Judy's brother Shram.

"Judy and I are going to the bathroom. Please don't leave without us." The two girls walked the incline of red and gold patterned carpet to the ladies' room. When they got inside the closed door, Wren pulled up her shirt and examined her protruding belly. Her eyebrows were raised as high as they could arch, and her green eyes glistened with tears.

"Judy, look at my big belly. It looks just like katybear's before a baby comes. Let me see yours." Judy pulled up her shirt, and they both stared at their round stomachs.

"Yes, I see yours too! Oh, Judy, what are we going to do? We should think of someplace to run away."

"Come on, Wren. We will have to think about running away later. Shram is waiting for us."

Wren's heavy heart showed in her slumped shoulders, her slow, pigeon-toed gait, and her little grim face.

"Mom's van isn't here yet. Do you guys have any money

left?" Shram asked his group of siblings, who indicated with a nod that they did.

"Far out! Let's cross the street to Pop Logan's Popcorn Wagon and get some caramel corn."

Seventy-nine-year-old Pop Logan sold tasty real buttered popcorn with peanuts and genuine maple-caramel syrup popcorn from his antique carnival wagon parked on Gene Lee's Used Car Lot. The wagon was huge and at one time was horse drawn. The wheels were as tall as the top of Wren's head. She loved to run her hands over the red and gold gilded, hand-carved scrolled relief as she waited for the Bear kids to buy take-home treats. Wren had spent all her money, but she was full of treats and had morning sickness. The ornate wagon made her feel less deserving and more ashamed of herself. *I don't deserve to see the beautiful wagon.* Wren tried again to seek comfort from Judy and to explain her guilt and depression, but Judy was in a state of Pop Logan's popcorn euphoria and couldn't appropriately respond. *I don't deserve movies, movie treats, or even to touch Pop Logan's wagon.* Many people came to admire Pop Logan's wagon but ended up buying the salty products. The delicious aroma fragranced the entire west end of Main Street.

"Here comes Mom's van!" Shram yelled and then herded his siblings back to the Acme Theatre curb. Wren followed Judy to the van and sat on the floorboards so she didn't have to sit beside any boy with or without cooties.

"Wren, what's wrong? Didn't you like the movie?" katybear asked.

"I loved the movie. Thanks for bringing me," Wren responded. She was quiet all the way to the convent. "Thanks for inviting me. I had a good time. Goodbye, Judy. See you at school," she politely said as she climbed out of the van. Wren then ran up the convent steps and into her cell, flopped down on her cot, and cried. The loud sobs were heard everywhere.

Sister Samantha went to Wren's bed. "Whatever is the matter, Wren?"

"Nothing!"

"Why is nothing making so many tears?"

Silence.

"Wren, it's okay if you don't want to tell me. It's time for compline evening mass. Will you come with me?"

Wren grabbed Samantha's hand, pulled herself up from the cot, and gave her a tearful hug. Together Wren and Sister Samantha walked to the chapel.

"Wren, you can always talk to Father Patty if you don't want to talk to me. I love you, and my heart breaks when I see you in such unhappiness."

"I am afraid you won't love me anymore if I tell you."

"Nothing could ever make me stop loving you, Wren."

"You will know that I am a rotten girl and that I am a drain on my tribe."

"I would never think such a thing! I would never think that about you! Never! We all make mistakes, Wren, and a mistake doesn't mean that you are rotten."

"I didn't make a mistake."

"Wren, you and Judy have received strong praise from Mother Superior and Father Patty. They both complimented how well you know your lessons for first communion. Next week is your confirmation! You must be so excited! Aren't you twitterpated by the thought of this?"

"No."

The conversation dissolved into the chapel's candlelight. Sister Samantha was aware of the intensity of Wren's prayers as she watched the tears slide down Wren's strained little face.

On the way back to the nunnery, Sister Samantha tried again to reassure Wren of her steadfast love.

Throughout the week, Wren remained aloof in her classes. Before evening prayers, she didn't run with the antelope. After evening prayers, she cried herself to sleep. Sister Samantha watched Wren on the playground during the lunch hour from Mother Superior's office window after consulting her about Wren's troubling behavior. The playground lay wide open, as spacious land was abundant without fences to corral. The open pastures didn't limit a child's imagination, games, or territory. The spring sun, even during high noon, was soft butter yellow wrapping everything it touched into a mood of security. A group of fifteen mostly sixth-grade boys were lined up at the sidewalk edge for a footrace. Wren pushed through the group to Bradly, the organizer and the biggest boy.

"I want to race, too," Wren asserted.

"Nope, sorry, this is just for sixth graders," he responded.

"Ronny and Donny aren't sixth graders."

"Yeah, but they are big boys and fast runners for third graders," he boasted.

"Why are you racing?" Wren asked.

"To see who is fastest and strongest, which you are not."

"Why would it matter if I joined the race?"

"Because you are a girl and the littlest third grader that I have ever seen. These boys will just run over you."

"Not if I am in front of them," Wren protested with her large green eyes and perfectly arched raised eyebrows.

"Everybody starts on the same line, and no-one gets a head start."

"I don't want a head start. I can follow the rules," Wren said as she lined up between Ronny and Donny.

"Come on, let's get this race cookin'," demanded Donny.

"We run to the road, touch the marker, run back, and the first one to touch the line wins!" Bradly announced.

Other kids on the playground began to gather to watch the race. Bradly lined up with the rest of the runners, took a whistle from his pocket, and blew the shrill sound. The whistle blower gave himself a slight edge of preparedness, but the pack was off with Wren at the front. Wren's sinewy legs pumped up and down on the gravel road like blades of a rotating motored fan. Her thin brown legs were a blur of motion as her arms and hands reached in front of her tiny body as if she was pulling herself forward by an imaginary rope. The air filled her lungs to capacity as she inhaled through her nose and released the used air out her mouth. Wren ran to the road marker, touched it, sped around, and was standing on the finish line when most of the boys reached the road turn-around marker. The boys couldn't deny that they saw Wren in front of them the entire race. Boys panted to the sidewalk finish line where Wren calmly stood waiting for them. The race had gained the attention of some of the teachers and Father Patty, but none of the boys said a word to Wren. Judy pushed through the onlookers to reach her.

"That was so neat, Wren! You won by ten horse lengths," she said as she handed Wren a blossomed willow twig. Wren raised her eyebrows, and her green eyes flashed.

"I wanted to prove to Ronny and Donny they shouldn't take advantage of us girls."

"Wren, you showed them just fine."

The last boy touched the finish line, but none of the runners looked at Wren. Bradly stepped forward.

"We didn't have a chance to warm up."

"I think they are warmed up now." Wren's eyebrows arched in a comical way as she tilted her head to gaze up at Bradly. "But the race was way too short. Let's race around Littelshield's pasture and back to this sidewalk as the finish line," Wren suggested.

"That sounds like a good race," interjected Father Patty. "I will be the starting and finishing official. Can we use your whistle again, Bradly?" Father asked as he stuck out his hand.

The whistle blew and fewer runners left the starting line this time. The runners pack was reduced to Wren, Bradley, the twins, and John Eagle, but the spectators swelled to include most of the noontime students K–12 and six of the teaching nuns. Wren's feet left the starting line like an antelope jumping a fence. Her small thin legs pumped up and down imitating the pronghorn's legs stretching and tucking-up that she'd learned by chasing them in the pastures. Wren ran as if she was full of fever and was running from a disease. Her legs raced, but her mind raced even faster.

I must show these boys that they should never take advantage of anyone because they are bigger, stronger, or feel superior. I have been humiliated by what they have done. Their actions have been recklessly poured over me, and they don't even think about what consequences it had. My shame has cut me from my tribe and left me with no place to run—but I run, I run to prove that I am worthy.

◄———————◄═

Sister Samantha wanted advice from Mother Superior. "I know something deeply troubles Wren, but she refuses to confide in me. Her grades have plummeted, she is sullen, cries at night or when she is alone, and she fervently prays during mass."

Mother Superior listened to Samantha, but was distracted by the cheering crowd outside. She moved to her office window to watch.

"Who is that little boy?" She asked as Sister Margret and Sister Samantha moved beside her to gaze at the crowd on the playground.

"That's not a little boy! That's Wren! She is running like a wild animal, or running like the stories of Job in the old testament from Father Patty's lessons" Sister Samantha sobbed.

Wren was now on the near side of the pasture while the other runners remained on the far side. She had distanced her lead by one-half of a pasture. The crowd was now clapping and cheering, "Run Wren run!"

Sister Samantha loves me. She said that no matter what mistakes I make, she will still love me. I know she stands by her word and always tells me the truth. She has my love too, and I want to be a nun like she is, but now I can't be a nun anymore. I know what I have to do. Wren relinquished her thoughts and focused on her racing legs!

"Do you see what I mean?" Sister Samantha lamented.

"Yes, we see, Sister Samantha, she is running to prove something."

The school bell rang signaling the beginning of the afternoon classes. Wren touched the finish line as the crowd congratulated her. Judy hugged her and handed her one of her baby sister's diapers to dry her wet face and arms.

"That was sooo neato! You showed them! The bell just rang so we had better hurry up!" Judy burst out.

"I'm afraid those boys will get detention for being tardy." Mother Superior chuckled as she watched the boy's on the far side of the pasture.

When class was released at 3:00 p.m., Wren bolted from her wooden desk with the flip-up top, ran to Judy, and helped to gather up her books.

"Come on, Judy, we have something that we must do!" The

two friends marched into Sister Samantha's cell where she was ironing her wimple.

"Sister Samantha, Judy and I are pregnant." Startled Sister Samantha nearly burned a hole in the wimple at Wren's proclamation.

"My goodness, what makes you think that?"

"Ronny and Donny peed in our lemonade. We drank it and got morning sickness."

Sister Samantha burst out with laughter that brought tears rolling onto the scorched wimple. Samantha's laugher was the sound of church bells from the chapel tower with a symphony of angels' voices to Wren's ears. The celestial sound made Judy and Wren's eyes lock together as their faces changed from fear into amazement and wonder.

"Girls, I see it is time for a lesson on how babies are made. There is *nothing* that you could ever do to make me or katybear stop loving you. You are our girls."

Wren was relieved to learn that she was not pregnant and vowed she would never be humiliated again.

Chapter 4

FRIENDSHIPS

Wren's esteem among the Indian Mission student body from kindergarten to seniors gained acceptance and recognition. Her popularity was not the big boastful type, but it was a bonding affection earned through her good character. Her approval was not built on 'race glory,' but it was her quietness, kindness and unspoken leadership that branded her. Wren reigned silently producing strong bonds of friendships given to her from upperclassmen, who patted her on the head as they opened the heavy school doors for her. Kindergarten children took her hand and looked eye level with her small face and felt a kindred bonding since they were the small people of the school. Both kindergartener and third grader knew it wasn't size that was important, but it was inner stature that counted.

Wren's quite nature served her well as she lay on the new sprouts of spring prairie grass that emerged in the pasture. She could feel the moisture on the backside of her Levies as she listened to the clear shrill song of the meadowlark. She loved that sound and listened for more as she waited for the antelope to arrive for evening grazing. It wasn't the meadowlark that she heard now. It was human voices wafting across from the convent side of the open field. She sat up and could see two figures silhouetted against the setting sun walk toward her. She moved unto her knees for a better look. Wren sprang to her feet and ran to greet Sara and Owl, two teens from the Indian Mission junior class.

"Hey Wren, we are looking for you!" shouted Sara as she gave a broad arm wave from across the pasture.

"Why are you looking for me?" Wren shouted back as the three figures closed space.

Owl picked Wren up and tossed her over his shoulder as he spun circles prompting her laughter.

Owl was striking with his handsome looks. He was the image of the brown, chiseled Indian featured on western calendars. His shiny black hair resembled the pop star Fabian and casually fell onto his forehead. His black eyes were hunter alert and surveyed a wide span of awareness. His six foot two inch body was strong and lean with wide shoulders framing his long arms and legs to grant the grace and strength of his agility. He was the center starter for the Indian Mission basketball team, the Eagles. The team was known for running ability and won many games, placing them into the top position of their division. Owl and his team weren't the most skilled of players, but endurance and their ability to run up and down the court wore down opponents while the scoreboard recorded victories for the Eagles. Owl's Shoshoni good looks granted his choice of attractive girls, but he had been friends with Sara since the fourth grade, and they were 'an item.' Sara was a good student and helped with Sister Samantha's day care where Wren had been her favorite kid since she had been three years old.

Sara was pretty, exhibited humility, and her fair complexioned Shoshoni Indian ancient Asian features granted her attractiveness. Her small boned facial features portrayed delicacy. She wore her dark brown hair in waist long thick braids that reached the small of her back. Her narrow framed five-foot, five inch stature was shapely slender. Her strong, perfectly postured body was filled with happy energy, and she enjoyed being of service to the Indian Mission nuns and to Sister Samantha's day care.

"We are looking for you! We want to invite you to go with us tomorrow," Sara explained.

"Where?"

"For a ride to a special place. Do you want to go?" Owl asked as he stood Wren on her feet.

"Yes, Yes! And more yes," Wren shouted as she did birdie hops around her two friends and Owl laughed at her antics.

"We thought you would," Sara said smugly.

"We will pick you up early in the morning," Owl instructed as they walked toward the convent.

Wren lagged behind her friends, dragged her feet with slumped shoulders, stopped and dejectedly looked at the ground. She opened her big round bottle green eyes, titled her head toward Owl, and raised her eyebrows like a comic.

"I am not allowed to ride in cars."

"We know! That is why we invited Sister Samantha to go with us too. See you at the crack of dawn."

Wren's mood brightened like the dawn, and the three friends sprinted back to the convent.

Dawn's butter cream light pushed into the corners of Wren and Sister Samantha's tiny cell as Wren's eyes opened to the soft morning light. Wren sat up, cleared the hazy film from her eyes, and saw Sister Samantha standing by her cot.

"What are you wearing?"

"This is my new hiking habit."

"Where did you get those pants?"

"From the Charity Thrift Shop. Quick, jump up and get dressed while I go to the galley and make some snacks for the day. Owl and Sara will be here soon."

Wren was dressed and saw Owl's chariot, the old faded gray Dodge, come down the convent driveway. Sara moved from the front seat, held open the back car door for Wren, and sat beside her.

"Where is Sister Samantha?"

"She is coming with the food basket."

Owl and Sara stared at stunningly beautiful Sister Samantha who lugged the heavy basket. She wore a red plaid long-sleeved flannel shirt with blue bell-bottom pants that actuated her well-shaped bottom, and her curly blonde hair was piled high in the ratted big-hair trendy fashion.

"You look great, Sister Samantha! You look like one of us."

"Thanks, Sara, we are all from the same source! Owl, let's peel out of here. I don't want Mother Superior to see me without my habit," she said, sliding into the front seat beside Owl. Sister Samantha remembered when she was thirteen, and the clothing she wore today was her Saturday attire when she joined friends to prowl the department stores of Chicago. Samantha was the only daughter of wealthy Swiss parents Bogetta and Lars Favre who were renowned clothing designers and owners of the most expensive and coveted Avonelle Boutiques in Chicago, on Michigan Avenue. Sister Samantha evaluated the changes in her life since she had taken her vows at sixteen, and how childish her past seemed now that she was twenty-three and Wren's guardian.

Owl's chariot rattled west in the same direction the godfathers drove to reach the sweat lodge, but Owl traveled thirty miles beyond. Owl followed the one car trail through open range with cows and horses grazing along both sides. He tooted the horn and watched the startled horses run with their tails up, their necks arched, and their long mains blowing in the wind. The cows merely looked up at Owl's passing car and continued grazing. Wren sat on her knees and stretched up to look out the side window at the band of galloping wild quarter horses on the run.

"We have gone so far. Are we almost to Chicago?" Wren asked.

"Chicago is east in the other direction. We have been traveling west and we are still on the rez. One-third of Fremont County and one-third of Hot Springs County are Indian lands. This land is so open and free with nothing to confine the huge spaces or to squish the sky with Chicago skyscrapers." Sister Samantha's voice resonated the love she felt for her remote convent life, and she knew that Wren had no idea what a skyscraper was.

"This is my first car ride, and I have seen prairie chickens, a fox, deer, antelope, lots of cows, an eagle, a coyote, turkey, and bands of wild mustangs."

"Now that you are seven years old, it is time for you to know where you live," Sara added.

On her knees, Wren continued to have a transfixed gaze out the side window watching the passing vast unobstructed landscape. Owl and his party of explorers drove west for over an hour and didn't seen another human. This remote land was tucked behind other towns and cultures that screened it from the probing fingers and eyes of outsiders. The side window of Wren's backseat car door framed the view of aesthetics like a local Wyoming artist Georgine Lee painting, critiqued by a European art critic as "colorless and void of primary shades." Today, on this adventurous sunshine day, the reservation was like the painting tinged in a monolithic beige gradation with latte, crème, ecru, brown, and pale sand colors. The graveled trail traveled upon by Owl's faded gray dodge was the color of popcorn as it receded in perspective over the khaki prairie and faded into the distant fawn, tan, and milk chocolate tones. The hills were the hue and texture of natural wool, Irish linen and buff leather. The entire scene was blended as if the huge mountains were draped with a fabric of unbleached raw silk. In reality, the extremely harsh, dry panorama gave a false appearance of softness like jackrabbit fur.

Owl pointed to the mountains and asked, "See the largest peak in the middle of the caulk, blanched area? Union Carbide is extracting number nine coal, and our per capita checks may increase."

His comment quickly set Wren to singing Tennessee Ernie Ford's song, "Sixteen Tons," about loading number nine coal. She knew all the words from her Big Chef Casino education. Everyone applauded and then joined her in singing other songs. It was a thrill for Wren to have Sister Samantha sing the McGuire Sisters' "Sincerely." Wren thought, *Of course Sister Samantha would know songs by the McGuire Sisters—they are sisters just like she is.*

Owl's car choir was amazed to learn that Owl could sing just like Elvis Presley when he belted out "Love Me Tender" and "Heartbreak Hotel." Sara led a nice rendition of the Chordetts' "Mr. Sandman" with a surprisingly strong voice. Songs of the 1950s served as entertainment until Owl's voice dropped from the ensemble in the middle of "The Purple People Eater." He slowed the car, songs ceased, and silence swept through the interior until Owl announced, "We are here!" He parked the car on land that looked like the acres and miles of environment they had passed all morning.

"How do you know we are here, when this place looks just like all the rest?" Wren asked.

"You will soon see the difference," Owl explained as he opened his car door and his passengers followed his example. Wren jumped out and turned a perfectly executed cartwheel and a walkover that she'd learned from the Indian Mission high school cheerleaders.

"Wren, Stay behind me," Owl directed.

Wren was compliant, fell into Owl's cadence, grabbed his shirttail, and sang "Three Blind Mice" as Sara and Sister Samantha trailed. The terrain remained the same bland wash of variegated beige. It was the same special butter cream color produced by Wyoming cattle when they grazed on yellow carotenoid pigment in natural pastures and produced cream of the same hue. This cream-colored prairie, mixed with the bone-white cliffs with their dark chocolate crevices, and cream vanilla colored pathway made up the landscape they walked. The area was like being inside a giant peanut butter milkshake. The four Indian Mission friends blended with the environmental color scheme as naturally as the rocks blended with the hillside. Their DNA was the same as the land they inhabited. They were by-products of the reservation and blended with nature as they walked single file behind Owl. Their pigmentation ranged from Owl's tanned leather color, Wren's tawny antelope hue, Sara's cattail-coffee tint, and Sister Samantha's Swiss crème shade. These humans blended into the total swirled beige marble, earthy effect.

The colorless, muted landscape scheme gave the illusion of softness, but in reality it was extremely arid. When human skin was exposed to the harsh dryness of the Wyoming air, it quickly drew up tightly, attempted to retain every droplet of liquid like a starved bear grasped for a berry. The dry sage aromatic path was inclined, and the sun approached midmorning, but the air was juiceless. Any perspiration was undetected and the moisture quickly evaporated. The thirsty breeze scraped the skin like sandpaper rubbed on pine bark. The parched ground lay open, and Owl led his scouting party for over an hour by using a barely visible ascending cow trail as his map.

There was something kindred to the feeling of being in mass that caused Wren to fall into silence as she hiked. She felt hushed and so did the others. The quietness of the trail was accentuated by the snapped spring sage. It released a strong scent as the eight shoes stepped on the young sage twigs and filled the air with the aroma that sedated the hikers. Wren had absorbed the Indian culture. She had an honest love for her country and possessed the earth's tranquil qualities. She knew that she was part of this land, and that the land possessed part of her. She was as much a part of this landscape as were the rocks in front of her. There was no separateness from soil and herself. She was the rock and the rock was her.

The followed cow trail ended, and Owl motioned to his band of Shoshoni to wait for him on the fallen boulders that had cracked loose from the barren cliff that they hiked toward. The waterless countryside had changed from prairie grass and sage to baked openness with large boulders strewn about like some giant had flung popcorn for the birds.

Owl sprinted across the barren, empty space and crouched beside three look-alike boulders. He squatted beside each one, lifted and shifted it to one side, looked underneath, and moved on to the next.

"Sara, what on earth is he doing?"

"I have no idea. This is the first time that I have been here."

After peeking under the fifth boulder, Owl straightened and motioned for his small assembly to join him. The three women listlessly ambled the two city blocks across the drab, hard, dry ground to where Owl stood.

"I am really thirsty," Wren, cranked as she tugged on Owl's shirttail.

"We can fix that soon. You have been a great hiker," he said, patting her on the head.

"Come on now," he said after he'd laboriously moved the boulder to one side and exposed a dark hole. "Wren, watch what I do, and you do the same." He dropped to his knees and slid onto his belly head first into the hole. Wren sent a worried look toward Sister Samantha, who shrugged her shoulders in puzzlement. Wren heard Owl's faraway voice say, "It is your turn, Wren—go into the hole."

She dropped to her knees, flattened onto her belly, and disappeared into the hole. Sister Samantha stood and hesitated beside the opening as she heard Wren's faint voice exclaim, "N-e-a-t-o!"

"Do you want me to go first?"

"Oh no, I am fine, Sara. I was just thinking what a funny sight I would have made if I had worn my habit." Sister Samantha gave a little chuckle as she dropped to her knees and slid head first into the dark portal. Sara was last to enter. She felt both Owl's and Sister Samantha's grasp on her arms and waist as she slithered into darkness.

"Far out!" Sara gasped when she became upright.

"This is so neato kabeto!" Wren cheered as she looked around the underground cavern, waiting for the others eyes to adjust to the darkness. The light from the entrance portal streamed in to reveal the three friends as they stood on a wide ten-foot ledge that descended to a fresh estuary where Wren lay on her belly and lapped up the clear stream water like a cub wolf.

"Wren, come and see the pictographs," Sister Samantha

whispered. There was no need to shout because the water and the shape of the grotto magnified every word and footstep. Wren ran back up the incline and gathered joined the others on the ledge. Owl pointed to the cave drawings for Sister Samantha and Sara to see. The light from the portal illuminated the cave enough to clearly see the drawings. Sara and Owl made their way to the clear-pure stream below, drank, and absorbed the surroundings. They sat on the ledge with their legs dangling, and Owl put his arm around Sara.

Sister Samantha called to Wren. "Wren, do you see these drawings?"

"Uh—yeah." She peered at the marks on the walls. "Why did kids draw on the walls?"

"Why do you think they were kids?"

"Because the pictures look like Mickey Bear's pre-K pictures on katybear's refrigerator."

"Yes, they do, don't they? I think they were painted by someone who was waiting for a hunting party to return, and they stood in this very place like we are doing. Do you see this one? What do you think it is?"

"It is sisters cooking over the fire, and this one is a kid."

"I think you are right, Wren, look at these—"

"They hunted antelope instead of deer. You can see the pronghorn."

"You are so right, Wren, I didn't notice that. You are very observant. You might make a good archaeologist someday. Wren, when you go into Littelshield's pasture with the antelope, what are you doing there?"

"I am learning."

"What do you learn?"

"I am learning stillness."

Sister Samantha wasn't sure she totally understood. "Wren,

can't you learn stillness at matins, lauds, vespers, or compline mass?"

"No, I learn stillness and feel God in myself when I am outside."

"Don't you feel that inside the chapel?"

"No, when I am in the chapel or mass I practice stillness and God, but when I am outside I learn it from the pronghorn antelope and the meadowlarks."

Sister Samantha grew silent.

"I can feel stillness from these old pictures. Do you feel it too, Sister Samantha?"

"Yes, Wren, I do."

Wren and Sister Samantha discussed the drawings at length. Sister Samantha gave a detailed lesson about the three-thousand-year-old drawings and the story they told. Sister Samantha held Wren's attention, allowing Sara and Owl alone time as they conversed and sat on the lower ledge next to the crystal-clear stream.

"Sara, I brought you and Wren here to give you this as a gift from my legacy."

"And what a beautiful legacy you have given. This place is so hep. I like this place a lot."

"I wanted you to know about this place after I am gone."

"Where are you going? Can I hang out with you?" Her voice filled with surprise.

"No, Sara, I must go alone. You and Wren have a future. You respect nature, know about sacred places, and care about our tribe. You have very strong and powerful ancestors that you can call on to give you guidance and strength. You came from the most powerful Shoshoni woman in our history—Sacajawea—and she will show you how you can be of service to our tribe. Wren is just a very smart and strong little kid with a lot of years yet to live. She knows what is right and wrong and has proven she will stand up for her values. She has Sister Samantha as her guardian and the entire Shoshoni tribe looking after her. I wanted to gift this place to you and Wren to protect it and to keep it sacred."

"Is this place your deeded property to give to Wren and me?"

"No, Sara, It is Shoshoni tribal land."

"Why are you leaving? I don't get it! When will you come back?"

"I'm not sure, but I think I will leave after the powwow."

"Owl, you have been my best friend since I was in the fourth grade and I don't understand why I can't come too."

"I am required to go alone."

"Oh—like you will be on a spiritual journey?"

"Exactly! I think you do understand, Sara. That is why we have been friends for so long."

Wren quickly spun around from Sister Samantha's lecture, sat down on her Levis-clad bottom, drew her feet and legs up to her chest, wrapped her arms around her legs, balanced on her rear end, gave a push with her arms, and allowed gravity to coast her down the decline like a slide on the playground. She crashed into the backs of Owl and Sara, who released startled yelps.

"This place is *neato kabeto*!" Wren laughed. "Can we bring the food basket? I am getting hungry."

Owl reached behind him, grabbed Wren and began tickling her as he said, "We left the food basket in the chariot, and it is about four or five miles away. Let's all go, and we can have a picnic on the way back to the mission."

When they returned to the convent, Wren let out a screech of delight when she saw the godfathers' old faded green truck parked in the driveway. When Owl stopped his car, Wren leaped out and ran to the waiting truck with napping godfathers.

"Godfathers!" she shouted.

"Hi, Wren." Big Boots yawned. "We have a present for you," he said as he handed her a pillowcase that was stuffed with something.

Sister Samantha used this distraction to make her exit. She grabbed the empty food basket and darted for the convent door before anyone saw her without her habit.

Wren peeked inside the pillowcase and pulled out its contents. "Neat! It's a powwow dress!"

She held up the white deerskin dress and rubbed its softness against her cheeks. She traced the Shoshoni beaded rose on the yoke of the back of the dress and on the front of the skirt with her small, willow-twig fingertips. Wren danced with the dress so that the long fringes on the hemline, sleeves, and belt bounced up and down. She absorbed the godfathers' love and knew that this dress was made especially for her. Standing in the driveway, she pulled the dress on over her head and jingled the handmade bells that were strewn over the dress to make the tinkle sound as she danced.

"Godfathers! Godfathers! Thank you! Thank you," Wren chanted to the rhythm of the bouncing fringe and tinkling bells on her dress.

"How beautiful!" Sister Samantha exclaimed as she rushed from the convent, now more appropriately clad in her habit, and saw Wren dancing around.

"It was a wonderful day, Owl and Sara." Sister Samantha thanked them as she waved.

"Owl and Sara, I had a blast," Wren shouted.

"Godfathers, thank you for Wren's powwow dress. Would you like to join Wren and me for vespers and evening mass? I am sorry to rush off, but we are late." Sister Samantha took Wren's hand as she jingled into the chapel. After they had disappeared behind the thick wooden door, Owl drove his gray chariot beside the godfathers' truck and rolled down his window so they could talk.

"You guys brought Wren a good gift."

"Owl, for powwow come join our drum circle," Big boots invited.

"Thanks, but I am going to dance this year. I need to have hides to make my dance outfits. You guys are keen hunters. Can I go with you when you go hunting?"

"Yup." Waffle Stomper nodded his approval.

Chapter 5

PREPARATIONS

Owl and the godfathers were three tribesmen out of the two thousand Shoshoni and five thousand Arapahos that prepared for the first annual Wyoming powwow in 1959. This was a really big deal for the Native Americans on the Wind River Reservation. The powwow gave normally idle tribal members purpose. Dance participants prepared their dance dresses and crafted feathered shields. They hunted and gathered eagle feathers, designed and beaded dresses, belts, shawls, moccasins, leggings, headdresses, and arm bands. They made ankle bell bands and men's aprons. Even children like Wren were busy with powwow preparations.

Wren ran the three miles to katybear's house to practice her dance with her friend Judy and all the Bear siblings. Being at katybear's house was like having her own private powwow rehearsal that was conducted every day that school was out for the summer. Some days the rehearsals consisted of over thirty youth participants who competed for katybear's homemade fry bread. Katybear was on the women's committee to gather and store ingredients for the coveted delicious Indian fry bread that would be for sale during the powwow.

Contacts for sponsors were made. Donations funneled into the tribal council and were saved for food, building materials, prizes and awards. Suitable expansive land was sought to host both the Arapaho and Shoshoni tribes as well as visiting tribes from other states. The powwow grounds location remained secret and was only known to tribal members. The location was obscure from main roads or populated areas. It was located on flat roadless prairie land hidden to any nontribal member.

In the late 1950s and the early 1960s, the powwow was not meant to be entertainment for non-Indians. There were a few white visitors who understood the Indian culture, but they were sparse and were always accompanied by a Native American friend. The powwow ambiance was a manifestation of art and skill and fostered respect for Indian culture.

In 1959, the godfathers and Owl hunters returned from a successful hunt with deer hides that needed to be tanned. Their mission was to deliver the hides to Suzy Pavora's camp. Big Boots drove to the remote location tucked beside the Little Wind River. Suzy's camp was an army surplus tent secured onto a two foot elevated wooded platforms. Suzy Pavora was thought to be in her late nineties, and was known to be the best tanner in the county. She had made the white soft deerskins for Wren's dress. Suzy's workshop consisted of a large black iron kettle that looked like the witches caldron from one of Shakespeare's plays. She could have passed for one of the witches until you looked into her black, kind, intelligent eyes. Suzy was no taller than four foot seven. Her abundant hair had turned white and she wore it loose giving the impression of the big hairstyles of the '60s. Her brown skin draped her bones like her dark blue Charity Thrift Shop dress draped her body. The loose-fitting dress was beltless and hung in folds where former roundness and curves once had been. Her physical strength shown in her snappy alert eyes and her smile was as wide as the Wind River Canyon as she greeted her three visitors with a toothless comical grin.

Suzy was the most educated member of the Arapaho tribe. She held a PhD in education. Andrew Jackson was president of the United States when he passed the Indian Removal Act of 1830 mandating that all Indians were to live on reservations. White migration affected Wyoming later than other tribes living in the east like the Cherokee who were removed to reservations after 1830. When the Wind River Indian Mission was first established, the government's strategy was to send the Indian children to eastern schools to hasten cultural assimilation and Suzy was one of the many children designated to attend. Suzy was jerked from her Arapaho parents when she was five. She lived a lifetime with white families learning refinements and academics. She was educated in Massachusetts and earned her doctorate in education from Harvard. Her degree was monumental in the early 1900s when few women of any race were educated. While she lived in the east, she raised her own family, but Suzy's heart longed to be with her related Arapaho people in Wyoming. She returned to Ethete (pronounced Eee-the-tee) after her own children were grown. Suzy continued to utilize her education. She spread her Harvard degree into the Indian High school where she taught children for fifteen years, and remodeled a small shack into a library. The government assimilated Suzy, but what she felt in her soul would not be erased. Suzy watched Big Boots, Waffle Stomper, and Owl unload the fresh hides. She loved her Indian life, and knew that she had purpose for as long as she lived.

Suzy's kitchen was the vast outdoors and the workshop's roof was the blue sky thatched by the overhanging branches from the two large cottonwood trees. The caldron sat over a pit like the sweat lodge fire dugout. The boiling mixture would oscillate for many hours to separate the fur from the skins. Big Boots gave Suzy the meat from the freshly killed deer in neatly labeled, cut and wrapped packages as payment for her tanning services. The three men waved goodbye and would return in three days to collect the soft tanned hides. Suzy's work had just begun.

The skins had appropriately boiled to accommodate the separation of hair from the hides, and now it was easier for Suzy's flat scarping stone to scrape off the remaining hair. When the skins were completely hairless, she unwrapped the deer by-product packages of lard, brains, and intestines and boiled them together for many hours until a milky soup mixture occurred. Then the deer hides were lifted into the large black caldron to boil with the mixture for more days until they were as soft as rayon velvet fabric and equally as supple. It is unknown how Suzy's tanned hides were rendered into such softness.

The godfathers and Owl collected the hides from Suzy and artistically embellished them with the help of fellow tribesmen known for their proficient dressmaking and beadwork skills. Owl drew his own beadwork designs, but trusted the finished product to faster and more skillful artisans than himself.

Chapter 6

POWWOW

Today would be the most important day for the rest of Owl's life, and it would be one of the most memorable days for Wren too. The clandestine powwow area came to life midafternoon. Hundreds of late model abused cars and pickups, branded with Gene Lee Motors stickers attached to the bumpers, and signified their mortgage formed a circle around the powwow performance area, not unlike the old prairie schooners from days long past that circled in protection from attacking Indians. Today they circled for protection from the white people. Now the cars parked side-by-side instead of from end-to-end like the frontier wagons. The cars were parked close to each other and spaced tightly for passengers to squeeze on and off through the partially opened doors. The Indian people didn't get in and out of cars, instead they got on and off, this was one regionalism of their language. The car headlights would produce the necessary light for the after sundown dance events. The performance area ground was well worn and void of sagebrush and prairie grass by late afternoon. Noticeable puffs of dust raised with the step of each moccasin or boot print that transported drums, tables, chairs, benches, and judges platforms. Women sat up makeshift food booths behind the performance area and in front of the parked cars. The freshly made fry bread's sweet aroma wafted in the dry air and mixed with the smell of uprooted sagebrush, hamburgers, hot dogs and beer. Spectators and participants roamed the area munched on something from the food booths while dignitaries and sponsors paraded to applause when introductions were made from an announcer's microphone that was activated by a generator placed on the brownish-tan ground.

The colorful feathered and beaded dance regalia festival converted the normally drab scenery into an artist's paint palette rarely seen by native eyes. The display of color telegraphed the excitement of the day's events. It was if color energized these usually laid-back indigenous people into a busy anthill. They rushed everywhere in exuberant industry of construction and creation. This kindred group heard spoken words and greetings from normally wordless friends who lived in seclusion and silence with minimal opportunity for conversation. The sound was an astonishingly pleasant social chatter that colored primitive ears. The resonance was as delicious to the ear as sweet honeyed fry bread was to the ethnic tongue. Today's totemic unit was accustomed to the native drum sounds that splattered into the air. The sound of the drumbeat was considered to be sacred, and Big Boots and Waffle Stomper believed it to be the heartbeat of their tribe.

The drum circles consisted of three to five drummers seated around the large tribal drum on the perimeter of the performance area. Each tribe had their own drum and drummers, and today there were five drum groups representing the Arapaho, Blackfoot, Cheyenne, Sioux, and Shoshoni tribes. The Shoshoni and Arapaho drums were made from the large cottonwood trees found near water sources. The drums were made from trees that were four feet to six feet in circumference and cut into three-foot-long hollowed out logs. Each log retained three inches of thickness with the bark shaved away. Elk or moose hides were dried and stretched over one hollowed end of the log, and a new drum was born. The drumsticks had sheep wool wrapped around one end to mellow the sound of the strike.

Wren learned to recognize the different tribal songs by their pitch. The Cheyenne's songs sounded to her like high pitched, sharp rapid desperate yelps while the Arapaho and Shoshoni songs seemed to be of lower register, intensity, and rate. Wren could hardly wait until it was her turn to dance. She came to the powwow with katybear's family in their van. Judy and she had signed up for the same dance events. They were elegantly outfitted in their native dress and impatiently waited for their turn.

The first event was the Northern Buckskin Warbonnet dance, which didn't much interest Wren. The dance consisted of older grandpa-type men in their later years. They mostly danced in beautiful feathered bonnets that reached from their heads to their ankles and some actually drug on the ground identifying their participation in many wars of World War I, and II, or Korea. Most of these dancers wore buckskin pants and shirts, but others wore a chest shield made from horizontally placed small hollowed bones or porcupine quills. Some men were shirtless with red, white and black designs painted on their bodies. The Warbonnet dance focused on the artistry of their costumes and reflected respect and stoic grandeur toward the men who wore them. Many of these men earned the right to wear the Warbonnets because they had earned each of the feathers that signified a battle that they had survived. After the Warbonnet dance had finished the Tiny Tots ages one to six were pushed and placed into the center by their parents. Little boys and girls danced together in this event. Some of the two-year-olds knew the steps and could keep time, but they didn't compete for the prize money. Wren's age group was the first to compete for prize money where $1,000 was given for first prize, $800 for second prize, $600 for third prize and fourth place received $400. Wren didn't care about the cash prizes. She just wanted to dance and now it was her turn.

Wren moved with perfect posture to the center of the circle and had her foot poised for the first drum strike. She was the smallest contestant competing in the eight to thirteen Girls Traditional Dance age group. She was no bigger than the six-year-olds that were in the Tiny Tot division. The judge held up his hand to signal the drum circle of a delay and walked over to her. "Are you sure you are in the right age group? How old are you?"

"I am eight years old."

Judy waited next to Wren, and stepped forward assuredly.

"Yes, this is my friend, Wren and she is in my class at school."

"Okay, let's get started." The drum pounded its steady pulse and Wren's blue beaded moccasin-shod foot touched the ground precisely with every beat. The attached bearskin strips on the sides of her blue beaded headband and the fringe on the hemline and sleeves of her dress gyrated with perfect synchronistic, forceful, sure-footed step. Her white deerskin dress with the red beaded Shoshoni rose on the yolk and skirt reflected the afternoon setting-sun as she restrained her energy to conform to the regal, sedate, requirements for Traditional Dance. *What I really want to do is to cut loose*, she thought, but she maintained controlled compliance to the rules of the dance. The primordial drumbeat entered her nervous system and transported her to another state of consciousness where she was aware of nothing but the joy of the deep vibrating sounds that surged into her movement. Wren's small stature drew the focus of spectators and judges alike who noticed the perfection of her strong toe-heel footsteps in sync with every drum thump.

Wren's Shoshoni godfathers provided the drum music from the tribal drum for the days dance events. They were pleased when they saw their small charge walk in her Shoshoni dance dress to the judges stand to receive the second place envelope, but they showed no expression of pride or joy to Wren or to anyone. Bolstering and feeding the ego was not a part of the Wyoming Indian culture during the 1950s, and extra parental caution was taken not to inflate or cause conceit in offspring. Praise was rarely given, if ever. Children were taught to use their full potential without fanfare. Children did not strive to receive praise or recognition as the end goal. They learned the lesson of self-development as their reward for learned skills. Contests were the way to determine and evaluate their abilities, and the Indian culture loved competitive games. The foot races, beanbag toss, hand-jive, jacks, hopscotch, basketball games, and powwows, were the thermometers used for self-evaluation.

In remote, barren Wyoming, the beloved powwows gave families, friends and children the rare experience of being together and for learning social skills. This event inadvertently prompted the inbred DNA alcohol-drinking problem. Sister Samantha was very aware of the existing alcohol problem and knew that it would be magnified during the powwow. She cautioned Wren about the dangers before Wren left Incaranata Hall in her exuberance to dance. As Wren stood waiting for the judges' result, she remembered Sister Samantha's words of caution. "Wren, stay in areas where Big Boots, Waffle Stomper, or any member of katybear's family can see you or where you can see them. Stay away from people who are drinking. If a drunk person approaches you, run away." Wren was pulled back into the powwow ambience and saw the judges as they approached.

The judges explained to Wren, "You could have won first place, but your movement was too animated for Traditional Dance." Wren knew that the judges' words were true, but the Fancy dance was her favorite event, and that was what she really wanted to dance. She wanted to watch Owl's Prairie Chicken Dance, which was a later event, so she sat down at the foot of her godfathers' drum circle as they pounded out the rhythms.

The afternoon sun slipped into twilight as the other events for adult men eighteen and older, women eighteen and older, teen girls thirteen through seventeen, teen boys thirteen through seventeen, Traditional Dance, and Women's and Men's Southern Traditional rolled on. Twilight had disappeared into darkness by the time that Owl's event of teen boys thirteen through seventeen Prairie Chicken Dance emerged. The circled car lights had all been turned on, and it was an optimism that the cars batteries were strong enough to last when most were not. Some cars had only one headlight, some were turned on bright, and others were yellowed by age or dirtied lens. The dead-battery cars were pushed back away from the circle by four strong men and cars with stronger lights replaced the dark ones. The quality and intensity of light was constantly variable. Portable stronger carpenter bench lights were hooked up to the generator and lighted the ground to expose the dancers' feet. The car lights emanated a strange unintended light effect that cast elongated moving shadows of feathered or grassed regaled Indians and made weird human shapes. The organic, esoteric effect rivaled a theatrical stage production of the late 1950s. The lights and moving silhouetted figures looked otherworldly and eerie to superstitious spectators, but Wren was fearless and understood her culture.

Seated at the godfathers' feet beside the throbbing drum, Wren waited to watch Owl's Prairie Chicken dance. Wyoming Indians developed their culture around the environment they viewed daily. Prairie chickens were once abundant in Wyoming but now had become rare because of the loss of their habitat due to coal, uranium mining, and oil exploration.

Judy Bear knelt down beside her friend and handed her a Coke with hot Indian fry bread that dripped honey.

"Owl will be next," Wren said enthusiastically with outstretched hands accepting the treats.

"Oh, wow! And there he is!" Judy slid down next to Wren to watch.

Owl's dance outfit was stunning. He had chosen a most untraditional black and white color theme trimmed with red. He sported an all-white roach, black-and-white tail and arm feathered medallions that mimicked the birds full breeding plumage and Owl's headband, moccasins, wristbands, and apron were white with black nontraditional Indian designs. When Owl stepped into the center of the performance circle the crowd gave a collective "Aaah." Owl's roach, the three inch strip of headgear that stood four inches high and went from the middle of his forehead to the nap of his neck. It looked like a mohawk haircut that kids wore in later decades. The roach was made from the fur of an albino bear. The roach was a rare item. The contrast with Owl's black hair parted into two long braids and tied with red ribbons was eye-catching. The feathered medallion with a bright red teardrop shaped center was worn on his behind. The medallion measured three feet in diameter, and the circle of black feathered plumage was atypically fluffy ostrich feathers with white tips. The smaller one-foot-diameter arm medallions were made from the prized traditional black-and-white, spiked eagle feathers. These matching arm ornaments also had the red teardrop shape in the center of the black and white color theme. The arm medallions were traditionally worn on the arm above each elbow. Owl's headband, moccasins, wristbands and apron were beaded with solid white background, and had the special black design that he had crafted. His ankle bands were beaded black background with large white bells.

Owl's seventeen-year-old body was bare except for the white apron that covered the loin area. His physique was beautiful with well-defined pectoral, abdomen, thigh, and calve muscles, all of which complemented his broad back and shoulders. His long torso created his six-foot-two-inch stature with sinewy, lanky arms, and legs. He captured everyone's attention even though he was but one of the nineteen colorful contestants ready to dance.

Owl took his beginning position in a low, crouched stance kindred to a sage chicken hidden in the prairie grass. He waited for the palpitation of the drum, and his feet stamped the fast foot rhythm of the mating male grouse as he remained crouched. This initial dance maneuver exhibited impressive creativity. The torturous position required extreme thigh strength, and he held his rapid foot motion longer than other dancers. He stretched up tall into a shaking head and arm movement stance that quivered his roach, arms, and tail feathered medallions. His chest heaved out in replication of the strutting bird, and his head jerked and peered for female companionship. His shoulders shook and shimmied while his arms flapped the feathers and quivered the tail plumage. He strutted his prowess like the mating bird around the perimeter of the lighted area and abruptly stopped in proud posturing. Owl leaped and spun in midair, crouched and sprung up again into high vaults all the while keeping the perfect beat of the drum rhythm.

Wren and Judy were spellbound by Owl's dance. Sitting on the ground, they could see the height of his leaps and the low squats of his crouches. Owl suddenly sprang up higher than their heads.

"Judy, look! Owl's moccasins are beaded on the bottom of the soles." Judy became quiet. She reached over and held her friend's hand, while her eyes flooded with tears. "Remember, Wren, the cloud game that we played in the springtime, and you said that the cloud looked like a dead owl?"

"Yes, I do remember that day, but what did that mean?" Both of the eight-year-old girls who'd been friends from birth fell silent. They both knew what that meant. They watched Owl undulate, quiver, writhe, and leap to end his dance with perfection to the last spanked drum whack. He finished his dance and the crowd was wild with strong applause and cheers.

Owl stepped down from the judges' stand with his first place envelope in his hand and gave Wren a folded paper.

"Wren, this is the map of our special secret place. Don't lose it—give it to Sister Samantha for safekeeping. You can go there whenever you want."

"I want to dance like you."

"Okay—then do it!" He smiled at her and disappeared from the headlights into the darkness that swallowed his being.

The darkness provided Wren and Judy a screen from which they could wash the sticky honey and fry bread residue from their faces and hands in preparation for their favorite Fancy dance girls ages eight through eighteen event. The two friends had stashed their dance gear in pillowcases inside katybear's parked van. They dressed in the van. Then they took their places with the other twenty-two girls. Judy and Wren spaced themselves around the dance area close to the godfathers' drum. Judy, now twice Wren's size, was dressed in her traditional Arapaho designs. Her dress had been a hand-me-down from her three older sisters, who had all outgrown it. The dress was no longer the bright white like Wren's, but it had turned a cream-beige color with age and wear. The multicolored greens, blues and purple geometrical bead insignia of the Arapaho tribe embellished the dress and preserved its beauty no matter how many children had previously worn it. Judy had her hair braided into naturally long pigtails trailing down her back, but Wren had to wear the strips of dark brown bear fur attached to her headband beside the temples of her head. The bear strips gave the illusion of long braids that conveyed the traditional look to her curly, short-cropped hair. Both girls stood poised in readiness like katybear had coached them as the godfathers' drum thundered out the first sounds. Both girls toe-heel step hit the ground with every drum down beat. The roaring sound vibrated into Wrens body and blood. She felt a swelling of energy in her core that could not be harnessed. She opened her white long fringed shawl that made her appear like a flying white owl with spread wings. Her feet pounded the ground like the drumsticks pommeled the elk hide, and all the fringe, bells, and feathers on the deerskin dress were a jumping jive of gesticulation. Wren danced hard with the force of stampeded wild mustangs that surged through her. Owl's dance had been her inspiration and now she could cut lose with every drum slap. She flapped her wings until her body lifted into flight and she spun in midair. *I want to dance like you*, her mind echoed. *Okay, then do it!* She remembered what he had said. Wren became a miniature white Owl. The beaded red rose on her opened shawl was a replica of Owl's red teardrop on his medallion tail feathers. She swooped, ducked, and soared hunting for prey.

She spotted the victim, pounced on it, and soared again. Wren gave a high kick in victory of the captured prey. The skirt of the buckskin dress was too straight to accommodate the high kick and knocked her standing leg out from underneath her. She landed splat on her bottom. Wren danced beside Judy who witnessed the crash and laughed so hard tears ran down her face. The crowd laughed at the humorous sight as if they had just watched a slapstick comedy show. Wren didn't lose the rhythm or her composure. She jumped up and continued the toe-heel rhythm without losing a step. She twisted, turned and circled the performance area undaunted. The spectators applauded her skills and tenacity. Wren learned on the spot that the beautiful dress had its limits.

Big Boots watched Wren's disaster out of the corner of his eye and saw her strength of resilience. He continued with the plangent but his eyes were on her. He noticed a stranger had his focus on her too. Wren had held the crowds attention, but this man's stare was about Wren and her dancing skills. The stalker seemed to be hidden between two parked cars and was alone. Wren ended the dance at the far side of the circle away from the godfathers' drum. Big Boots noticed Wren standing by herself and he saw the isolated man move toward her from the shadows. Big Boots tossed his drumstick to another drummer and sprinted across the circle to where she stood. The man that approached Wren saw Big Boots, retreated like a weasel between the parked cars, and disappeared into the darkness.

Big Boots remained beside Wren while the drums were silent and everyone waited for the judges' decision. The master of ceremonies announced the winning contestants. The fourth place $400 cash award was given to Judy's thirteen-year-old sister Susan Bear, and the third place $600 cash award was given to thirteen-year-old Betty Oldman. The three judged huddled together in discussion for over ten minutes that seemed ten hours to Wren.

"We have decided to give two awards for second place. The winners will both receive the prize cash award. There will be no first-place award given at this powwow for the eight-to-thirteen age division. Judy Bear and Wren will you please step forward?" Judy started laughing again when Wren stepped up to the judges, and she remembered the funny sight of Wren's wild kick into the air that brought her suddenly to the ground. Both girls giggled uncontrollably when they saw each other. The audience chuckled too at the little girls' infectious laughter as they recalled Wren's humors spill.

"Girls, here's what we decided. The judge stoically announced. Wren, you were given first place, but your fall caused you to receive second place instead. Judy, you were awarded first place when Wren landed on the ground, but for the rest of the dance, you were laughing so hard that your composure was gone—so you earned second place too. Maybe next year we will award a first place." The audience applauded in agreement as both girls received their envelopes.

Big Boots and Waffle Stomper stayed beside the little eight-year-old girls until katybear was there and gave the girls a hug and hamburgers. Big Boots wondered about the man in the shadows. Did the man think that Wren would get first prize and that he would steal the $1,000 he thought that she would win? Was he a member of another tribe? Was he young or old? Was he drunk and without malicious intent? Who was he, and why was he there?

Big Boots and Waffle Stomper returned to their drum circle to finish the remainder of the events that lasted until 1:00 a.m. Judy and Wren were hungry, ate their hamburgers, and fell asleep in katybear's van with the three younger Bear children who had already zonked out. Eventually eight Bear children slept in the van as katybear, her husband, and four of the older children helped the drummers to pack up their drums, folded up tables and chairs, disassembled the judges' stand, bundled up the unsold food, removed food booths, carried the generator to a parked truck, and were the last to drive away.

Katybear carried Wren into the dimly lit silent convent and tucked her into bed. She handed Sister Samantha the two envelopes for second place that were stuffed with the cash award of $1,600 that Wren had earned. She gave Sister Samantha the folded paper that Owl had given to Wren. Katybear slipped out quietly to take her own twelve children to their beds that were three miles away.

The vast, empty prairie returned to aloneness, and eventually replenished its own prairie grass and sagebrush. The wind erased the human telltale signs of a powwow that upstaged its own natural splendor. The moon sighed in the breath of night-darkness and felt relief that every human had gone.

Chapter 7

WHY?

Sister Samantha jolted up in her bed as red flashing lights beamed into the tiny cell windows, bounced off the walls, and glared into her eyes. She eased up on her knees in bed to peer out the window and saw the arrival of two more tribal police cars as they entered the grounds of the Indian Mission. She watched several other cars drive all around the grounds, and she spotted the ambulance as it parked near the gymnasium. A soft rap sounded on her door, and she saw that it was Mother Superior, who opened the door softly and whispered.

"Sister Samantha, I think you should come with me." Sister Samantha grabbed her wimple, robe and mantle.

"What's wrong?"

"We need to go to the gymnasium." Sister Samantha pulled the door closed silently as not to disturb sleeping Wren. She left the snug tiny room, and accompanied Mother Superior. The two nuns walked through the convent halls that now were awake with many nuns that asked questions in soft voices, opened doors, and had curious, concerned eyes peering from the windows into the red-lighted school ground. The sisters watched all the urgent care men with the ambulance gurney, tribal police, and the coroner. Some of the nuns recognized school administrators and the superintendent who all rushed inside.

The night was warm and the stars were abundant in the black-velvet night sky as the two nuns crossed the distance through the schoolyard to reach the gymnasium.

Mother Superior and Sister Samantha opened the heavy double door into the Eagles' basketball court.

"Oh, God in heaven, *no, no, no!*" Sister Samantha gasped as she grabbed the ends of her mantle and pulled it to over her eyes as she turned to face the wall with her back to the sight of Owl's body hanging by his neck from the basketball hoop. He was still dressed in his beautiful powwow black-and-white Prairie Chicken plumage. Several men lowered his body onto the gurney, covered and zipped it with the thick black leather bag, and slowly wheeled it to the waiting ambulance.

"*Why? Why? Why?*" The sports court echoed Sister Samantha's words. The two nuns huddled together on the vast, emptied, brightly polished gym floor, comforting each other as best they could.

"The janitorial staff found him," Mother Superior said. "We don't know why. There are no answers. We should go to the chapel." She tugged Sister Samantha to her feet. "The other sisters will want to offer prayers, and I am responsible to tell Father Patty."

"I need to check on Wren to make sure she is still asleep."

"Yes, Sister. I will meet you in the chapel." Mother Superior rushed from the death scene to fulfill her nunnery duties. Sister Samantha ambled back into Incaranata Hall but was numbed and had lost the sense of herself. Her thoughts, breath, sight, and body had vanished. She moved empty of her emotions and felt as hollow as a machine. She moved like a programmed robot back into the familiar nunnery. The dimly lighted hallways illuminated the twenty-three informed nuns who silently prepared to attend a last-rights mass in the chapel. Sister Samantha crept back into the tiny cell she had always shared with Wren who was thankfully still asleep.   Within the darkness of the room, Sister Samantha's hands searched for the folded paper that Owl had given to katybear only hours ago. She slipped back out into the dim hall light and slowly unfolded the paper expecting to find some explanation. The opened paper showed a clear drawing of the underground caverns location with the pictographs and Owl's hand written directions to find the area. Sister Samantha studied the drawing and looked for notes, or clues, or tell-tale-signs of what could have prompted Owl's desperate action. She turned the paper over and over, examining it carefully, but found no answers. Sister Samantha eased silently back into the dark room and placed the map into a shoebox for her keepsakes. She opened the door softly, stepped back into the now empty hall of Incaranata Hall, and walked toward the collective sound of the murmured prayers from the chapel that floated into the star-studded black night sky and the warm night air.

Wren had managed to sleep soundly through all the night's chaos, but Sister Samantha was still unable to sleep at six in the morning, when she knew that it was time for her to call katybear. Sister Samantha slipped out into the hall where the telephone was on a small wooden table with a stool. She sat down, dialed the numbers on the black rotary phone, and waited.

"Hello."

"Hi, am I talking to Susan Bear?"

"No, I am Judy Bear."

"Hi, Judy. Is your mama busy?"

"Are you calling to tell her about Owl?"

"Uh ... yes, I am. How did you know?"

"Wren and I knew a long time ago. Wait—I will go get Mama."

Sister Samantha was confused by what Judy had just said, and she also heard the sound of ten telephone clicks of rubbering listeners seeking information. With the ten additional listeners, the sound of the original caller became weakened, and it was difficult to hear katybear's voice.

"Hi, Sister Samantha. Did you get any sleep?"

"No. Do you know about Owl?"

"Yes, Joe Oldman with the Arapaho tribal police told Shram about it last night. Have you told Wren?"

"No, I don't know how I should tell her. She slept through the whole ordeal and is still asleep. I wish that I could sleep like that."

"Why did he do it?" a woman's voice broke in.

"Is this Hilda?"

"Yeah, I am rubbering, but why did he hang himself. Didn't he just win the first prize at the powwow?"

"He was also selected as most valuable player for the Eagles basketball team," Dotty added.

"No one seems to know, Hilda. He left no note or anything." The reservation moccasin telegraph was smoldering with everyone asking questions and putting in their opinions.

"Katy, it's impossible to talk to you now. I need to tell Wren about this after she wakes up." Sister Samantha hung up and turned to find Wren standing behind her.

"Tell me what?"

"Let's jump back into bed and we can talk where it's cozy." Sister Samantha pulled the covers up around both of them, and they snuggled down together.

"Wren, our friend Owl died." Wren was quiet and made no

response. Sister Samantha worried that the information was too harshly given, so she tried a softer approach.

"Wren, Owl will no longer be with us. We will remember his goodness and the fun adventure that we had with him and Sara." Sister Samantha didn't know what to make of Wren's silence, but she continued to hug her close.

"Judy and I have known for a long time that Owl would die."

Wren's words were like ice on Sister Samantha's skin.

"How did you know that?"

"We saw a dead owl in the clouds."

"When was that?"

"When we played the cloud game."

"Did you play the cloud game yesterday?"

"No, that was a long time ago, but we saw the beaded soles of his moccasins yesterday."

"You did? Tell me about that."

"Owl did a big leap when he was dancing, and Judy and I saw the bottom of his moccasins because we were sitting on the ground."

Sister Samantha realized that Owl had danced in his burial moccasins. Sister Samantha sighed. "Wren, what did Owl say to you when he gave you the map?"

"He said that I could go there any time that I wanted."

Now it was Sister Samantha's turn to be silent. She realized that Owl's suicide was contemplated for a very long time. Wren and Sister Samantha both knew that the answer to Sister Samantha's unspoken question was inherent in the Native American culture itself.

"I want to be with Sara. I think she wants to be with us too."

"Oh, Wren, yes, you are so right! We will go now."

The nun and the small child walked five miles of dusty

country road in the morning sunlight to give comfort to their bereaved friend.

Sara was sitting alone on the steps of her house in the warmth of the morning sun. Her family left Sara by herself while they spent summers on the Blackfoot Reservation in Idaho. Sara's thick, long, cattail-coffee colored hair cascaded onto to the porch steps as she slumped over her drawn up legs and stared vacantly out into the distant prairie landscape. She aimlessly poked a stick into the cracks of the porch steps. Her head perked up when she spotted Sister Samantha and Wren walk in the distance, and she sprinted to greet them. Wren did a jackrabbit start and ran to meet Sara when she saw her run toward them. At the connection point, they both threw their arms around each other and waited for Sister Samantha to catch up.

"You came to visit me?" Sara asked.

"Yes, we came to be with you."

"I am alone every summer, but my parents will be back before school starts. I was just waiting for Owl."

"Let's go sit on the porch. I am sweaty from the walk and from the weight of this habit."

"Owl isn't going to come anymore." Wren blurted. Sara looked into Wren's bright green eyes.

"Oh, I guess he left on his trip already." Before Wren could say more, Sister Samantha quickly asked, "Sara, when was the last time that you saw Owl?"

"Last night at the powwow. He gave me the envelope with his first-place money and the map. He said that he was going to go alone on his journey after the powwow, but I thought he might change his mind, and come back to take me too."

"Owl beaded the soles of his moccasins." Wren stated as Sara stared at her.

"Sara the reason that Wren and I have come to visit is to

tell you something. Owl took his own life." Sister Samantha sat close to Sara and told her about the night's stressful ending in the gymnasium. "Sara, it was beautiful how the Incaranata nuns carried a lighted candle into the chapel and compline prayers from the Psalms were chanted. The full choir with the best voices, like Waffle Stomper, sang the Gregorian chants and Father Patty blessed the newly released soul to find peace on his journey." Sara didn't make a sound, but tears poured out of her brown eyes like a waterfall down the mountainside. She stood up suddenly and disappeared into the house allowing the door to slam. Wren and Sister Samantha sat in silence for a few minutes while Sara returned with scissors. "Cut it all off." Sister Samantha slowly accepted the scissors from Sara's hands.

The Shoshoni and Arapaho tribes expressed grief by cutting off their hair, and they grieved until the weather changed. They grieved during windstorms, until the calm come, or when sunshine turned into rain. The change in nature eased grief. When the spring turned to summer, summer to fall, or fall changed into snow, that was the length of endured sadness. Grief still remained, but the mourning period ended to allow life to continue for the living. Family and friends grieved until the old tracks of life on earth were erased. They grieved until nature or a new season created new tracks. Sister Samantha knew that Sara erased Owl's tracks by the cut of the lengths of her hair.

"Sara, we will need a rubber band, or string, and something to wrap it in."

"Yes, I will get it," she darted back into the house and returned with rubber bands and a white, freshly ironed pillowcase. Sara sat on the middle step while Sister Samantha stood over her and cut off her beautiful hair. The nun cropped the tresses to the nap of her neck, carefully wrapped the thirty-six inch lengths with the bands, and placed them into the pillowcase. Sara remained on the step bent over to her knees and sobbed. Sister Samantha and Wren sat down one on each side of her. No one spoke.

Wren wondered how Sara had so much water in her eyes. She suddenly jumped up, sped into the kitchen, returned, and handed Sara a glass of water.

Sara looked up in surprise. "Thank you, Wren. I know that I need to be the one to prepare the giveaway. Luise has nothing to give. His grandmother has his six brothers and sisters to look after, and his beautiful mother Patty, who is a real cow Patty, ran off with some man nowhere to be found, he never had a dad, and I am the one who loved him."

"May I help Sara?" Sister Samantha knew that the Shoshoni people never asked for help.

"Yes"

"Can I help too?"

"Of course you can Wren! Please come with me to visit Owl's grandmother, Luise"

"Does she know about Owl?"

"Shhhh, Don't ever say the name of a dead person aloud. It causes them great unrest."

Wren's question was answered when the three visitors opened the flap to Luise's army surplus tent built on the wooden platform and saw her jagged cropped hair and red-rimmed eyes.

"Luise, he gave me this envelope at the powwow, and told me to give it to you."

Luise stood transfixed. She knew what the contents of the envelope held. Luise had seen her grandson's performance, but she had taken her other grandchildren home before the powwow ended. As the four bereft women of different generations stood in Luise's tent, Sara leaned forward, took Luise's hand, and stuffed the envelope into her hanging clenched fist.

"He was a good boy and my daughter Patty is a beautiful

woman," she said, as tears flowed down her old weathered face like water ran down a dry eroded riverbed.

"Luise, I need to go howl into the prairie. Do you and your grandchildren want to come?"

"Yes."

"We will go at sunset. You and the children can meet me at Nutty Nan's Road."

"Sara, I expected you to come today. I have hot dogs, Cokes, and fry bread." Wren suspected that katybear had something to do with this available food.

"I am really hungry!"

Wren had already squirted on the catchup after she dove into the hot dog kettle like a starving gopher. The women and children sat at the picnic table outside on the small, extended platform around the tent base, and ate with their hands clutching hotdogs wrapped in napkins. Owl's brothers and sisters of various sizes, shapes and races stared at Wren in silence as they sat at the table and on the floor. These children, born to Owl's mother all had different fathers. Two had dark hair, one had red hair and blue eyes, another looked more like Owl and there was another that had yellow hair and one that had mouse colored hair. This assortment of kids looked like kids from a school or something. The three women and Wren sat at the table without talking while the children stared and ate in silence. Wren wished these kids wouldn't look at her. She could withstand it no longer! She jumped to her feet and said, "I am Wren, and he was my friend."

The small yellow-haired boy said, "I am Corn Tassel, and he was my brother." The other children barely audible offered the words "brother too."

Sara stood up and picked up the trash. "We can all meet at sundown."

Luise opened the flap for her guests and stated, "Attractive women in heat have a great variety of puppies."

Sister Samantha nodded, understanding the plight of Luise's life.

When Sister Samantha and Wren returned to Sara's house, they knew they would stay with her until sundown.

"Come with me to howl in the prairie," Sara invited.

The nun was astonished to see how many women had gathered at Nutty Nan's Road and carried blankets and containers of water. The group was quiet and walked together to a secluded area of unfenced prairie where it was miles to anywhere and no one would hear their voices. The group dispersed and each person found their own space of seclusion. There were at least fifty women and children, some sat on the ground while others stood. Sister Samantha pulled her habit around her legs and sat down on the ground. Wren walked a few yards away from her nun, and got comfortable by sitting cross-legged on the ground too. Sister Samantha could see Luise and many of the grandchildren scattered in the distance. She spotted katybear, Judy, Susan, and the other Bear girls who had found their space of isolation.

The big ball of orange sun threw sheets of pink, lavender, green and magenta across the wide sky over their heads like a native quilted blanket that gave comfort and warmth. When the sun disappeared into the earth and the Mardi Gras–colored skylight changed into twilight, Sara stood up, threw her arms open to the world and howled at the sky like a wounded, deserted coyote who was in great pain. Wren's wail answered her friend in grief and was joined by Luise's angry growl and loud barks. Wren was filled with a consuming energy that blasted the night air in an enormous sound of lament. She watched the twilight fade to darkness in the west and saw the white shiny moonrise in the east. This natural act of nature prompted her to howl like the animals she had heard so often from her bed at night. She knew and understood how they felt as she too bayed at the moon. The flat sage covered prairie was alive with the sound of a pack of wild wolves, barking dogs, and angry coyotes from the bereaved women. The sound was a therapeutic serenade of shared grief, and tonight it was a replica of the ancient Shoshoni Death Wail.

Sister Samantha opened her mouth wide and released the stored up grief into a loud screech and a howl that expressed the injustice done by humanity. She continued the forlorn sounds that melded into the tribe that cried together. Sister Samantha surprised herself at the freedom she felt, and how the black, torturous image of Owl hanging in the gym was seeping from her mouth into the open black night. Sister Samantha, Wren, Sara, and all the women howled until their anger at the injustice of it all had left them drained and empty, but peace flowed into their vacated inner cavity. Sister Samantha was aware that she felt better, lighter, and happier about reservation life. In the cavern that Owl had taken her to, she remembered that Wren told her that she learned from being outside and practiced what she learned inside the chapel. Tonight Sister Samantha learned what Wren had experienced and understood how nature was God's teacher, and that nature was a powerful cathartic healer. This was how Native Americans survive. This rural setting was therapist, counselor, nurturer, friend to the abandoned, and companion to the lonely. Nature and the chapel were both teachers about God. Calm and peace replaced the disquiet from the women's howls and silence overtook the field once again. The prairie became as it formerly was, filled with its own natural night sounds. Samantha felt Wren's warm little body snuggle up next to her and together they absorbed the night's quiet blanket that cuddled them. Wren and Sister Samantha listened to the movement of the jackrabbits and nocturnal creatures beneath the millions of stars. Relaxed into the blackness of the night the Sister was startled by a tap on her shoulder.

"Would you and Wren like to ride home with us?" katybear whispered.

"Yes, we would! We have walked over twelve miles today. Can we also take Sara with us? I don't think she should be alone tonight, and she can stay in our cell at the convent."

"I know right where she is sitting. I will bring her here, and you can ask her."

Katy Bear's van was full of riders that she dropped off on the way to Incaranata Hall. Sara, Sister Samantha, and sleepy Wren walked softly into the convent. Sister Samantha slipped into the galley and picked up three bananas and a pitcher of milk. The nun smiled to herself at the joy of having an overnight visitor and memories of her advantaged Chicago childhood slumber parties. Sister Samantha gave her bed to Sara, and she made a pallet on the floor for herself. Everyone was hungry and ate in their beds in the tiny room before Sister Samantha said bedtime prayers and hugged each girl goodnight. She turned off the light, and in the dark she whispered to Sara, "Sara, we are glad you came home with us. Tomorrow we will plan for the giveaway."

Tomorrow bounced into the diminutive cell wrapped in glorious cellophane sunlight and accompanied by the smell of pancakes, hot honey, eggs and fry bread. The sun and scent prodded the residents from their convent beds and directed them into the galley with a satisfying reward of breakfast. The black and white clad group of nuns vacated Incaranata Hall as fast as they had filled the breakfast galley. They flocked into the chapel for their matins. Sara had never been to morning prayers before and she was contented to be in the chapel.

Mother Superior moved near the altar and made an announcement. "We welcome Sara and thank our Lord for her presence. Today is cell change day. Please refer to the schedule posted in the office of Incaranata Hall."

After the matins psalms for morning prayers, and Father Patty's Eucharist concluded, the nuns poured out to do their daily duties. Some worked in the hospitals, health centers, or charity stores. Others gave home help to the housebound or served as social workers, teachers at the Indian Mission, or for Wind River High School. Wren and Sara walked back to the convent while Sister Samantha explained about cell change day.

"Nuns have adopted a life of poverty and to be of service to others. Our minuscule bedrooms are called cells. Cell change day requires us to change rooms every two weeks to encourage us to disavow attachments. We don't want to become attached to our rooms or to our possessions, and so we rotate on a regular basis. This move keeps us from accumulating." Sara stopped abruptly in her walk and no longer listened to the nun's words. She saw Owl's gray dodge chariot parked by the gymnasium.

"Sara, this cell change will only take Wren and me about twenty minutes to complete. Why don't you stay outside and enjoy the sunshine?" Sister Samantha and Wren went on ahead to the cell.

Sara moved hesitantly in the direction of Owl's parked car. Her eyes dripped a cup full of clear, salty moisture that evaporated into the dry air. She walked to the back of the car and ran her hands over the gritty trunk tracing it around to the driver's side door. She opened the driver's door and was startled by Owl's scent. She sank into the driver's seat and her hands bumped an envelope attached to the steering wheel. The envelope had her name on it. Sara carefully and slowly opened the brown packet. It contained the car keys! Sara sobbed in grief, but more in appreciation and admiration for Owl's thoughtfulness and the clear sign of his love for her. Sara had searched for a message from Owl, and she found more than a message, she found a loud and clear announcement! Sara sobbed.

Wren was kept busy with the room change and she was joyous about the location of their new cell. It was between the galley and the outside door to the chapel. "Perfect!" She knew that Sister Samantha and she would have easy access for snacks, and it might keep them from being late for lauds, the prayers before lunch.

"I'm going to go find Sara."

"No, Wren, give Sara some time to be by herself. Wait for her to come to you on the front steps so she can easily find you when she is ready." Wren nodded with understanding and waited patiently for her friend. Sister Samantha joined Wren in the warmth of the morning sunshine.

Sara with her shirt wet from tears, slipped in between the nun and the small bird as they sat together on the front steps of Incaranata Hall.

"Look what *Owl* left for me!" Sara held out her hand with the envelope and the keys. Sister Samantha's eyes flooded with tears, and she hugged both of her girls.

"Oh, Sara, this will make it so much easier for you. You can get groceries, come to school every day, continue to work at the school, and haul things. Perfect!"

"This is neato kabeto!"

"Can you drive?"

Sara's big brown eyes opened wide, and Sister Samantha saw the truth.

"Good enough," was her answer.

Chapter 8

THE GIVEAWAY

Owl's gray chariot lurched, jerked, jumped, and died. The engine turned over again as Sara experimented with the standard shift mechanism and the driving process. The car and she lurched and stalled, started again and bumped the bumper into the gym wall until she found reverse and managed to get the car headed in the right direction leading away from the mission. During the first mile, the car wandered from the right edge of the road to the left edge, but Sara kept it on the road. By the third mile, she discovered that if she sighted the car's hood ornament directly in the middle of the road the car behaved and navigated straighter and easier. The applied pressure on the gas pedal was another matter. The car raced to fast sometimes and slowed too much in others. She learned to read the speedometer and keep the pressure even to make a consistent thirty miles per hour. "Rats"! It was the intersections that were the killers! The car died every time she hit the brakes. Sara sat in the middle of the road with the car stalled. She had pumped the gas pedal too often.

Big Boots and Waffle Stomper drove up behind the car.

They both got out of their old green Ford truck and walked up to the driver's side and recognized Sara who was driving Owl's car.

"Are you having car trouble?"

"Yeah, I guess I am. I can't figure out how to make it go again."

"Oh, easy fix!" Big Boots showed her how to shift the gears to keep from stalling. He showed her how to shift according to the rate of speed and how to avoid the biggest danger, which was to keep it from flooding.

"Don't pump the gas pedal. It will flood the car and keep it from starting. How about if I ride with you, and Waffle Stomper can follow us in my truck until you get the hang of it? Where are you going?"

"I'm going to my house. I'm going to get ready for the giveaway. Where were you guys going?"

"We were going fishing," replied Big Boots.

"Only takes a woman to ruin a good fishing trip." Waffle Stomper winked.

"Yup, true words spoken."

Sara couldn't keep her smile hidden at their humor as she realized that they were going to help her.

She practiced driving with Big Boots beside her, and Waffle Stomper followed. She worked the clutch, shifted gears, kept the car in the middle of the road, and managed to drive the twelve miles without a lurch. She even managed to successfully stop at two intersections even through there were no such thing as a stop sign on the reservation. It was only out of cautious driving on her part that she stopped at intersections.

She pulled up to her bright purple HUD, wooden framed house and stopped the car without a lurch. Native Americans hated HUD homes. They were too clustered together, caused claustrophobia as the Shoshoni were used to having miles of space, and the colors were selected for inner-city black culture, they did not face east —so exterior doors were cut into them to accommodate an east entrance, and occupants cut each room in the house to have an outside entrance. This many exit doors helped the residents to feel less trapped. These HUD homes fostered crime and anger on the rez and were known as a dangerous zone.

"What do you need to do to get ready for the giveaway?"

"I need to shut off the gas. I am going to give away the stove and the refrigerator. Sister Samantha allowed us to have the giveaway in the Eagles Gymnasium to erase death with new beginnings."

Big Boots and Waffle Stomper said nothing, but got out, shut off the gas, disconnected the stove and the refrigerator, and loaded them into the back of their truck. Sara stripped the two beds of blankets and washed them in the washer. She hung the bedding on the line to dry. "Take the washer too." The two fishermen understood the Native American life and silently loaded the washer into the overloaded truck.

"That's all she will hold!" Waffle Stomper yelled as he rolled up the window, and they drove away.

Sara boxed up dishes, pots and pans, and bedding and placed them into the trunk of Owl's car. There was nothing left to give. There was a small pile of her clothes that she stuffed into a pillowcase and placed it into the back seat of the car. Sara got into the chariot and drove the distance to Luise's. Owl had never lived in a home, but he had spent his life in this tented place that was filled with Luise's love where he had known happiness.

Luise and some of the children saw the cloud of dust from the car coming up the road, and a pang of emotion hit her heart when she saw it was Owl's car on the move. The chariot only lurched a couple of times before it came to rest in front of the canvas structure.

"Hi, Luise," Sara called as she shifted the car into park as Big Boots had taught her to do.

"I have two boxes ready for the giveaway," Luise called to Sara.

Luise pushed the boxes forward. Sara nodded, but knew that she was not emotionally strong enough to look at the contents inside. Corn Tassel continued to hold Owl's basketball, but Luise gently removed it from his hands and put it on top of one of the open boxes.

"Wait! I have something else to give."

Luise's determined stride revealed her resolve to give away the only possession of artistic beauty that existed in her practical world of items for survival. She returned with a beautiful, black, white, and red handmade quilt. The two women's eyes met and held their gaze, but no words were exchanged. Sara took the quilt, opened the car door and carefully laid it in the backseat. Sara got into the gray dodge and drove away without a lurch, without a backward glance, or without a wave goodbye.

"Gone is Gone, is Gone is Gone" Sara repeated to herself as she drove back to her deserted, empty, wooden, purple hovel and parked the car a half mile away from the front door. Sara walked to the back of the house and picked up several pieces of dried kindling and carried them around to the front. She dug into her pockets and retrieved a packet of souvenir matches from the Big Chief Casino, stuffed the entire packet into the crevices of the wood pieces, ignited them, and tossed them inside the front door. She slowly walked back to the car, sat inside, and listened to the radio. Elvis Presley's voice flowed out: "Love me tender, love me true and never let me go." Sara recounted the many times that she had heard Owl sing that song. She examined her life and the path it took.

Sara watched the gray smoke billow and puff up in the sky like the steam raised from a sweat lodge. She saw the house burst into flames that resembled a Fourth-of-July sparkler she had held as a child. The flames were angry, hot, immense, and imitated her grief. Within the hour, the house was gone and left the smell of burned charcoal in the mound of its own ashes. Sara put the car into gear and drove surprising well to Incaranata Hall.

Sara got out of the car, walked the few steps, and rang the mission bell. In a few minutes, Sister Margaret opened the convent door.

"Oh, my darling child Sara! Do come in. I am so glad to see you."

"Thank you. I would like to talk to Mother Superior."

"She is in her office. Come right this way, dear."

Sara knew the way, but Sister Margaret enjoyed being hostess, and she opened the door into the office. Mother Superior was sitting at her desk and looked up,

"Sara, how nice to see you. I enjoy seeing our students during the summer months. Please have a chair."

Sara sat down and held out her hand with the car keys.

"I want to give his car to the nuns of Incaranata Hall to be used in their service to help others."

"That would certainly be helpful." Mother Superior had experienced many years of the giveaway culture, and accepted the car keys without hesitation or praise.

"Mother Superior, I want to become a nun."

"You have helped at the mission since you were in junior high, but being a nun is a full-time job, not just during the week."

"I want to always make right choices at every intersection and to choose the crossroad that will help my Shoshoni people. I am a descendant of Sacajawea, and I want to be of service as she was, and to honor her for what she had given to her Shoshoni tribe. I want to work for a better goodness."

Mother Superior sighed, pushed her glasses down her nose, and peered over the rim at Sara. "I have always said that you would make a splendid nun, but you must finish your school first."

"Can I begin my postulant training and finish my senior year at the same time?"

"Yes, that would be possible, but what about your parents?"

"My folks are in Idaho, and that's where they want to be."

"You may begin in September when school starts if you would like."

"Can I start now?"

Mother Superior looked surprised, and pushed her glasses back into position. She knew that Sara's short-cropped hair was a signal of urgency.

"Do you mean today?"

"Yes, I brought my clothes with me."

"Well ... hmmm ... let me think. Two of our nuns have transferred to work in Philadelphia ... uh, I guess you could start today, but, Sara, if you started now you would need to lead the life of a nun today."

"Yes, that is exactly what I want. I need to finish the giveaway, but since it will be in the gym, I could be right here. I would like to start today."

"I will ask Sister Margaret to begin your orientation this afternoon, and we could have the ceremony this evening." Mother Superior consulted the new cell change chart. "Sara, you may have the cell named Hope. It is available now. That seems appropriate for your first day as a new postulant. The cells are labeled with the name on the doors. Welcome!"

"I will get my bag of clothes from the car."

"Sister Margaret will bring your appropriate postulant clothing to the cell."

"Then, I guess that I can take everything out of the car and put it into the giveaway! Do you want me to park the car somewhere?"

"I think that you will make a fine nun, Sara. Park the car in the space for the maintenance workers. There is plenty of space there." Mother Superior returned the keys.

Sara left Mother Superior's office and opened the door of Hope.

The following day in the late afternoon, the gymnasium was blanketed with a flock of black-and-white magpies that helped organize the inventory for the giveaway in honor of the new resident postulant. This group was a replica of the birds that enveloped the schoolyard and prairie every spring and summer in Fremont County. As the black-and-whites flitted about, Sara, wearing her new postulant white blouse with the small black ribbon tied in a bow at the neck and her midcalf-length, black, full skirt, greeted the guests with Sister Samantha and Luise. The three of them directed people to sit in the stadium seating surrounding the basketball court floor. Long buffet tables laden with potluck community contributed dishes were placed along the east wall, and katybear and her family managed the food detail for the soon to be served feast. Waffle Stomper had been invited to be the master of ceremonies, and he requested Father Patty to bless the gifts and the food. After the blessing, Waffle Stomper sang the Lord's Prayer in his beautiful tenor voice.

He also had an announcers speaking voice, and served as presenter for many bingo fundraisers, basketball awards celebrations, tribal rodeo's, school graduation, or school activities. His talent was ironic because he never said more than two words if asked a question, and he never took part in dialogue or conversations. He believed that talking was a waste of time, but to officiate an event, or to be in front of a crowd as a performer he had showmanship. He had no family, but he and Big Boots had been friends since the second grade. The two of them were known as a pair like the Long Ranger and Tonto, and he was Tonto. He had earned sixty annual hunting trophies. Waffle Stomper had an atypical Shoshoni stocky body build, bowed legs, and turned-in-toes. His face was a benevolent oval shape, with black, deep-set eyes, and a thick crop of speckled dark gray hair.

Waffle Stomper invited the two hundred people who had assembled into the bleachers to join the banquet line. There was a smattering of card tables set up around the perimeter where Sara, Luise, and the six children sat, but most people filled their plates and returned to the stadium seating.

After the food was gone and the nuns and Sister Samantha had cleared away the trash, Waffle Stomper announced, "Native Americans understand the rituals, customs, and the Shoshoni way of thinking. They know that possessions mean nothing. They understand a life without ambition to gain materialism, and that we do not work and strive to accumulate stuff! Our people have not lived in a culture that promoted greed, gathered money, developed arrogance, or bullied to prove strength to demise another. Our way of life is not a culture to bolster or to feed our ego at others expense. Please remember these words. We will help to erase our friend's footprints. Deceased's close friends, please come forward and select a gift at this time."

Twelve Eagles basketball team members all wearing their black, white, and red team jackets, descended the stairs onto the floor. Sara, Luise, and the children remained at their table as they watched the parade of students wander the area and select items to be taken away. Sara and Luise's eyes met as they watched the captain of the team pick up the black, white and red handmade quilt that Luise had made for Owl's upcoming senior graduation present. Sara grasped her hand and nodded approval to Luise. Corn Tassel watched as one of the Eagles' guards for the team picked up Owl's basketball, tucked it under his arm and left the gym.

"Ethete community members, please come forward and make your selection," Waffle Stomper announced. Big Boots noticed that Suzy, who had tanned Owl's hides for his dance outfit, chose the cooking stove, and he knew that she would need his help to transport it home. He would also need to help her to get electricity for her place to make it work. Sara watched as she saw other families remove the other appliances, boxes of dishes, bedding, pots, and pans. Soon all the giveaway possessions were gone, and Owl's Funeral would begin.

<hr />

Four days had passed since the powwow. Owl's funeral was held in the Indian Mission chapel where Father Patty said the funeral mass. Every pew of the chapel was full of people who had known Owl, and he crowd overflowed into the schoolyard. Luise and Sara sat together with the six children in the front row of the chapel that had been reserved for family. The Indian Mission High School shop class had made Owl's casket from cottonwood and pine. Luise was overcome with emotion when she saw that it had been lined with the quilt she had made for his graduation. The pallbearers wore their Eagles team jackets and carried Owl to the Shoshoni Indian Cemetery. The nuns and Father Patty did not attend graveside internment. The Catholic Church respected the difference between the cultures and looked the other way during their ancient rituals and pagan customs. The internment ceremony was conducted by the Shoshoni elders, Big Boots, and Waffle Stomper. They had their own songs, chants, prayers, and eagle feather ritual. Family and friends placed items they believed Owl would need for his journey to the beyond into the casket. Sara placed the long tresses of her hair into his hand as a memento of their friendship. Another male friend placed a Mars candy bar, and a comb, someone placed Owl's gym towel, a math teacher placed a junior class ring, and Waffle Stomper laid an eagle feather fan onto his chest.

Owl was dressed in his exquisite prairie chicken dance outfit, and Sara and Luise noticed that Owl's moccasins were beaded on the bottom as Wren had reported, but some of the beads had been worn away by his last dance, which validated what she had seen. The students, Luise and Sara were demonstrative with the body. They kissed Owl's face and held and touched his hands, but after the travel items were placed into the casket, the elders closed the lid and lowered it into the ground with chants and the blessings of eagle feathers. Seven men with shovels covered the casket with dirt, filled in the hole until it made a mound, and the mourners walked away to become mourners again on another day.

Sara was one of those mourners. She sat on the front steps of Incaranata Hall waiting for the seasons to change. She watched the little girls, Judy and Wren who chased the antelope in the Little Shield pasture near the convent. She more correctly watched Wren do the chasing and Judy was more of a spectator, like herself. Sister Samantha slipped down beside Sara and watched the chase.

"Where does that small child get her energy and inspiration to run like that? Sara, I am happy that you have come to live with us. It seems such a natural choice. You have been helping us since you were in the seventh grade."

"It seems right to me too. Now, you are really my sister. I was an only child, and I have always wanted a sister."

Sister Samantha gave her a hug. "Now you have twenty-two sisters! Not a bad step to take as an only child."

The two little friends loped across the field and plopped down beside the nun and the postulant.

"Well, I see that the antelope managed to win the race!" Sister Samantha teased.

"They won today, but maybe they won't win tomorrow!" Wren retorted.

"Girls, I was wondering about something." Sara hesitated. "When did you know about his death?"

"We knew about it in the spring. We saw the dead owl in the clouds." Judy assertively explained.

"What else did you see?" The little girls looked at each other, waiting to see who would answer first. Neither child understood the significance of their cloud game. Sara quietly waited for an answer when Wren blurted, "We saw a whole flock of dead birds in the clouds. Come on, Judy, let's go play hopscotch."

The two little friends ran to the sidewalk with chalk in their hands, leaving Sister Samantha and Sara to reflect, and they grimaced upon their answer.

"I believe that these innocent children are prophets!" Sara marveled.

"Are they both soothsayers for the future, or is only one of them a gifted seer?"

Chapter 9

PROPHECIES

The future and the march of reservation time would answer the nuns' questions. The dry air of August cracked the faces and hands of the organic residents of Ft. Washakie and Ethete, and turned them into brown leather. Even children's skin looked older than their tender years in the dehydrated air. The white-hot sky did not lend itself to the children's cloud game, but instead dried the clothes on the line in less than ten minutes, and sucked up any drop of moisture that it could drink.

It had been two weeks since Owl passed, and on this cloudless, parched day sirens from four speeding tribal police cars pierced the thirsty air as they sped down the road in a cloud of dust while spinning red lights flashed. The drumbeat rang, and twelve rubbering voices told the alarming news: a nineteen-year-old youth who had been arrested for disorderly conduct had hanged himself with his socks in the Arapaho jail. This was only the beginning; Owl was the first of the suicide epidemic. Four days after the jail hanging, Donovan Blackburn, sixteen and a sophomore, hanged himself from a tree with his sweatpants.

Father Patty, Postulant Sara, Sister Samantha, and the other twenty-two nuns at the Indian Mission worked tirelessly to prepare the chapel and provide funeral masses for the teenagers who were victims of suicide, and yet the deaths didn't stop. On another arid day a few days after the Blackburn boy's suicide, the fingers of death found a fourteen-year-old eighth grader Darren Shakespeare, and assisted him as he hung himself from a cottonwood tree using hay-bailing twine. After the fifth reservation suicide, the wide-open spaces of the prairie were marred with reporters, cameras, reservation police cars, Bureau of Indian Affairs, Federal Bureau of Investigation agents, Wyoming State congressmen, the county coroner, and many religious affiliations. The fervor and the attention from government agencies only seemed to acerbate the problem, and seven more suicides occurred. A flock of dead birds echoed from Judy and Wren's words into the busy Incaranata Hall.

Wren and Judy occupied their time and waited for the antelope at grazing time. They continued to chase them, danced to records, looked at magazines, and played games while their adult guardians helped others, but even children were affected by this tragic epidemic. They sensed the grief that cascaded over everyone, and they knew how this black cloud affected happiness and caused fatigue on these cloudless days of August and September. The nuns, Father Patty, and the adult Indian community helped to organize giveaways, feasts, funeral masses, and home help care. They held prayer vigils and ministered the bereaved as best they could for families of a total of fourteen suicide victims.

The nuns from Incaranata Hall were exhausted and worked in shifts to allow for sleep and prayer time, but through their fatigue, they had thwarted forty other attempted suicides by teenagers. There was twenty-four more attempted suicides among young adults ages twenty to twenty-nine.

Many government services, programs, and events were created to stop the epidemic that slapped the reservation community and knocked it to its knees. Alcoholism programs, suicide prevention, recreation centers, Behavioral Health, Social Services, Community Health Nursing, Dental, Diabetes Programs, Medical Services, Optometry, and Office of Environment Health were all created. Clergy and community members assisted or volunteered to provide manpower to staff them. There were eighty-eight total attempted adult suicides that involved alcoholism with the statistics between men and women being nearly equal with forty-six male attempts and fort-two female.

Indian Mission and other schools extended their gymnasiums to be opened for recreational basketball, teen dances, and adult social and business meetings. Even with the provided services, the tribes continued to suffer from alcohol abuse and other diseases, especially diabetes and cancer. Some members were still carriers of tuberculosis even though they were mostly symptom free. The tragedy left unhealed wounds on the hearts of the reservation people, and emotional scars were lodged in their minds.

The suicides ended as quickly as they had begun. Priests and nuns of the Catholic faith spoke about the importance of life and the difficulty of the souls for those who committed suicide. Congregations believed that faith was the remedy that stopped the tragedy. Some people pointed to the many newly provided community services that were long overdue as the reason for the halt to the deaths. Others explained that it was simply the imbalance of nature, and that nature had corrected itself. Others believed that the suicides ended because the four tribal elders known as the Tribal Old Man Brothers performed a ceremony where they painted spiritual red designs on their faces and covered the palms of their hands in red paint. Whatever the reason for the halt to death, it didn't matter—the important fact was that it ended.

Wren understood without asking any questions about the loss of her friend Owl. Perhaps her young years protected her from the full impact, or perhaps she understood something deeper than what others knew. Wren accepted death so matter-of-factly.

"Wren, come sit on the steps with me for a few minutes before we go to vespers. We have time. It's only three-thirty p.m. I have been so busy, and I have missed being with you. Come and tell me about the clouds that looked like a flock of dead birds. Did you know any of those dead birds?"

"The clouds looked like a flock of dead birds. That is all. I want to tell you about Owl."

"Okay, what do you want to tell me? I would love to know about him."

"He was a good friend, and he was honorable like Jesus and Tarzan. He died and made good things happen. When he went away, he helped Sara to become a nun, and before he left he showed me how to dance."

"Do you think that Jesus, Tarzan, and Owl were all alike?"

"Yes, they are exactly alike."

"How do you believe they were alike?" Sister Samantha stretched her Catholicism and tried to understand Wren thoughts.

"Jesus and Owl died to make things better, and Jesus, Owl, and Tarzan were strong, brave, and always did the right thing, and Tarzan and Owl liked to be outside. I don't know if Jesus liked to be outside or liked animals. Did he?"

"Yes, Wren, he did. Don't you remember that he was a shepherd? He also loved little children like you."

"Oh yeah, I forgot that part, but I'm not a little kid anymore. I am almost nine years old."

The hot dry summer had changed into the yellow-golds of September and erased the tracks on the earth that left ruts on Sara's heart. The change of season renewed her energy, and she knew that it was time to celebrate life again. Wren's birthday gave her zeal to plan for something special.

September 5, 1962, was Wren's ninth birthday. Postulant Sara and katybear decided to take Judy, Ronny, Donny, and part of the Bear clan that were close to Wren's age range to the casino for her birthday celebration. Katybear thought that it was time for Sara and Wren to experience their own Shoshoni Tumbleweed Casino, located just outside Lander, instead of the Big Chief Casino, which was Arapaho. Neither of them had been to the Shoshoni Tumbleweed Casino. Katybear pulled up in front, and they all tumbled out of the van. They walked in as a group, and Wren noticed something strange. She didn't know what it was, but she felt unwelcome. The people didn't smile at her, and they seemed offended.

A small, thin, wrinkled man who appeared to have had too much to drink approached katybear. "This casino is only for Shoshoni people."

"Wren and I are Shoshoni, and these people are our friends," Sara responded.

The man said nothing and walked away. Wren's birthday party was ushered to a large table in the back of the room. Everyone ordered what they wanted from the menu, and the Bear family had begun to relax when the birthday cake with lighted candles came from the kitchen and everyone sang the birthday song to Wren. Wren was standing in the middle of the room and blowing out all the candles when a big white man wearing a black cowboy hat and smelling of beer approached her.

"Hey, little girl! Pick out the jackpot!" he said as he held out a colorful punchboard that was divided into squares with pictures. There was a square of a bear, deer, snake, butterfly, rabbit, fox, and a turtle.

Judy stepped up beside Wren and shouted, "The jackpot is in the butterfly!"

"I was asking the birthday girl. What does she say?"

"Wren, do you remember seeing the butterfly in the clouds when we played the cloud game?" Judy prodded.

"Yes, I do, and this picture looks exactly like that butterfly," Wren said as she pointed to the butterfly. "I say choose the butterfly! Punch out all the holes in that butterfly!"

"Well, okay, I'll choose the butterfly! Have a happy birthday, little girl!" The big man patted her on the head and swaggered off to the bar area.

Katybear cut everyone a piece of cake while Sara served ice cream to all the kids. A huge roar of voices and applause came from the bar area. Loud laughter and shouts filled the casino, bells chimed, sirens blew, and lights flashed. Suddenly a crowd surrounded Wren's table. Two big men picked Wren and Judy up and paraded them through the casino on their shoulders. The girls had surprised looks on their faces. Sara and katybear raced after the men who carried the children.

"Where are you going with my kids?" screamed Katy.

"Put her down," Sara shouted.

The parade of people had formed a conga line and were shouting, laughing, and singing. The black-hatted white man grabbed a hold of katybear and twirled around with her. "We won! We won the hundred-thousand-dollar jackpot! The butterfly won the jackpot—we punched out *all* the holes in the butterfly and won!"

Wren and Judy were carried around on the shoulders of big men and tossed up in the air. They had no idea what had happened. They didn't know if it was fun and they could laugh, or if they should be frightened. Wren reached for katybear and missed her hand, but she read katybear's lips that said, "It is okay!"

The crowd danced, sang, and toasted the girls. Eventually the black-hatted man and the crowd returned the girls to their table and stood them on their feet.

"Hey, little girl! What's your name?"

"My name is Wren, and this is my friend Judy."

"Is today your birthday?"

"Yes, I am nine years old."

The man reached into a bank bag. "You get one hundred dollars for every year."

The crowd counted out loud together. *"One"*—the man handed her a hundred-dollar bill—*"two"*—he handed her another—"three—"

"No, no, please wait," Wren shouted. The crowd grew quiet to hear her voice. "It was my friend Judy that remembered the butterfly in the clouds. This money should be hers."

The crowd was amazed at her honesty, her boldness, and her modesty. They remained silenced.

"Then she shall have hers too." The man with the black hat counted out three hundred dollars for Judy too. He turned back to Wren and said, *"Seven,"* and handed her another hundred dollars. He turned back to Judy and said, *"Eight,"* as he handed her another bill. He turned back to Wren and said, *"Nine. Happy birthday Wren!"* The man and the crowd dispersed, and left the birthday party in a calm like it had been hit by a tornado. "Thank you!" Wren waved.

"I haven't had any cake or ice cream. And neither has Judy," Wren whined.

"We can fix that right away." Sara said as she hugged both of the girls and handed them their cake with melted ice cream. "When you finish let's go home."

The van pulled up in front of the convent, Wren jumped out, and handed Sister Samantha $500. Sister Samantha's face looked stricken, and she gasped.

"You let her gamble?"

Katybear burst out laughing. "Wren has quite a story to tell you, Sister Samantha."

"You are invited to stay for Wren's convent birthday party following vespers," Sister Samantha shouted to katybear.

"We need to get home to the other kids," katybear called out from the car window as they drove away.

Wren had been a part of the nuns schedule since she was born, and she accepted the daily ritual of prayers as a normal way of life. Matins were morning prayers before breakfast, lauds were the prayers before lunch, vespers were usually at 4:00 p.m., and compline were the prayers before bedtime. The Indian Mission nuns were only steps away from the chapel and, all these prayer sessions were done together with Father Patty. He always added a short mass with at least one daily Eucharist. Wren had had a raucous casino party, but she was excited to learn about the party after vespers. It felt like she was safely at home.

Everyone remained in the chapel following vespers to celebrate Wren's birth. Father Patty removed his vestments and sat in the first row pew with the postulants, which now included Sara. Mother Superior stepped up to the reader's pulpit. "Wren, the entire Incaranata Hall wishes you a happy birthday. Our gift to you is this:" She held up a key with the word *determine*. "This is your key to your *own* cell." The audience of nuns cheered and applauded. Sister Samantha looked surprised. "Your cell is named "Determine" because at nine years old it is time to determine what the world means to you. You shall determine who you are. You shall determine what school subjects are of interest. You shall determine your true friends, who you love, and who loves you. You shall determine what ideas are important and which ones are unimportant. You will determine the boundaries to be explored. Are your boundaries the reservation, Fremont County, Wyoming, The United States, a foreign country, or the entire world? Wren, because you have so much to determine you will not do room change with the nuns, but you will keep your room until your next birthday, and throughout this year you will determine answers." Everyone gave applause as Wren confidently approached Mother Superior and accepted the key.

"Now that you are almost a grown lady, you also will have convent responsibilities. You will consult the Chore Chart every two weeks to have a change of chores like the nuns."

"Yes, I will. Thank you, Mother Superior."

Sister Samantha stepped to the reader's pulpit carrying a gift-wrapped box and handed it to Wren. Wren opened the pink wrapped box and looked into Sister Samantha's blue eyes. The Sister Samantha, designer-line, handmade dress was adorable. Wren's green eyes revealed her surprise and her joy. The dress was a navy blue print with tiny bright yellow roses. The dress was designed with three lengths of poplins that added volume to Wren's body so she wouldn't look so small. The first poplin started at her waist and ended in the middle of her rear end. The second poplin was midthigh in length, and the third was dress length just below the knee. Every poplin hem was trimmed with yellow satin ribbon, and the sleeves were long-sleeved Victorian and trimmed with yellow ribbon at the wrist and elbow. The belt was made of yellow satin that tied in a big bow in the back.

"This dress is so neato kabeto! Thank you!" Wren threw her arms around Sister Samantha. The nuns served pink cake with rocky road ice cream. Wren ran to her new Determine room and put on her new dress. She returned to eat cake, ice cream, and wore her special dress. She wore it for every special occasion for over two years. On the walk home to Incaranata Hall after compline prayers were said, Wren took Sister Samantha's hand.

"Will you still tuck me in at night, even though I have my own room, and even though I am nine years old?"

"Yes, I will do that for as long as you want me too. I will come to your room before lights out." Sister Samantha knew that this was a big milestone for her too, and she knew that she would struggle with the adjustment. Both the nun and the child got ready for bed, and when Sister Samantha opened the door softly to the cell Determine, she saw that Wren was sitting up in bed waiting for her. She sat down on the edge.

"You know that you can come into my room anytime that you want too."

"Okay, and you can come into Determine anytime that you want to too."

"That's good! Our rooms are very close to one another."

"I know that you have been my mother, katybear and Judy have been my best friends, Sara is my big sister, I have Big Boots and Waffle Stomper who are my two godfathers, Mother Superior, and Sister Margaret are my godmothers, Father Patty is my father, but why do I only have one name? Everyone else has two names. Sister Samantha, katybear, Big Boots, Waffle Stomper—everybody has two names but me. I only have Wren."

"Oh my goodness! You have only been in this room named Determine and already it has begun to make you think. Wren, I have told you many times the story of how the godfathers found you."

"Yes, but I only have one name."

"Well, for that to change you must wait until you grow *into* having another name. It will come, but you must be patient. I love you the same with one name or with two. Everyone loves you the same with one name or two. It is the same amount of love. You have had quite a big birthday today, little girl. Good night! Sweet Wren," Sister Samantha blew her a kiss and closed the door.

Sister Samantha stopped by the office and checked the Chore Sheet to find Wren's chores. The list made her smile.

1. Empty the wastebaskets for the first floor.
2. Water the plants in the office.
3. Check to see that napkins are stacked in the middle of the table in the galley.
4. Chase the antelope.

Chore lists were definitely used at the Bear's house. Katybear was CEO and Mother Superior of her household, and she made lists of chores for each of her twelve children. She had to be organized because she volunteered and loved to be active in the community. She often joked that she had only been pregnant ten times, but she got the Big Bingo Bonus Babies. She ended up with twelve children. She had had two sets of twins, Ronny and Donny, who were in Wren and Judy's class, and a set of twin girls, Malissa and Monica, who were in the first grade, but now she knew that she had an especially gifted child to monitor: Judy! Wren's casino birthday party exposed Judy as a gifted prophet with divination. This scared katybear big-time. What was she to do for a child like that?

Katybear wanted to be a parent who gave her children as many opportunities as possible. She made sure the children had access to sports. This prolific parent had four children who competed on the swim team RATS (Riverton Aquatic Team). All her boys were signed up for basketball, baseball, weight lifting, and martial arts. Katybear's children had access to library books, math games, and four kids participated in the spelling bee tournaments, but what to do to encourage Judy? Katybear had so many questions about what she had witnessed. It seemed that Judy had foreseen Owl's death, the suicide epidemic, and the Butterfly jackpot, but could this have been coincidental? Katybear knew that a meddling parent could ruin a child like Judy. She reasoned that it was probably best to let nature do its work and allow Judy to grow in the direction like flowers grow to face the sunshine. Her parental instincts would pay closer attention to Wren and Judy's cloud game. That was for sure.

"Hey Wren, today is a good day to play the cloud game. Want to?"

"I don't know. I feel weird about playing that game. I don't want bad things to happen."

"Good things can happen too! Remember the butterfly? Don't you want to know what will happen? Come on let's go outside." Wren went outside reluctantly, and katybear stood by the screen door. The girls sat down on the steps and looked up at the beautiful, billowing, fluffy overhead stuff.

"Look, Judy. What do you see in that cloud?"

"It looks like a car is stuck in a rut. Do you see it too, Wren?"

"Yes, I do, and it looks like the car is full of people."

"Yeah, the car is full of mean boys. Look at that big bright fluffy cloud that is so white and trimmed by the gold sunshine."

"It is beautiful, and I am happy just looking at it. What do you see in it, Judy?"

"I see an Indian chief holding his hand out to a little girl."

"Maybe it is God, like the Bible says in Mark 10:14–15, saying 'let all of the little children come to me.'"

"No, Wren, it is an Indian chief, and he is pointing to you. Don't you see?"

"Yes, Judy, I see his finger pointing and motioning toward the child to come. Oooh, here comes a big dark cloud!"

"It looks like a speeding car passing by, and the cloud is getting dark as it passes over us, do you see it, Wren?" Judy buried her face in her hands. "It will bring hurt and sadness, Wren."

"Will it make you sad too, Judy?"

"No, it will only make you sad. I won't be sad."

"Then let's run away from that dark, fast-moving cloud so we won't be hurt or sad!"

"Wren, you can't run from a hurtful cloud. It is only telling you what will happen."

"Judy, look, it isn't a dark cloud anymore. It is only bright, happy clouds now."

"Yup, you will only be sad for a little while. Look at that cloud." Judy pointed to another on the horizon. "It looks like a giant schoolhouse."

"Yes, it does. Look at that one, Judy."

"It looks like a fancy dress in the magazines. It is a fancy dress that you will own, Wren!"

"I don't want a fancy dress and I don't want to play this cloud game anymore."

Katybear was stunned as she absorbed the words from the

children's cloud game. What was the car stuck in the rut? What was the dark cloud that caused hurt and sadness, and was the big schoolhouse college? Katy was convinced that Judy possessed divination, but she didn't feel satisfied, and she needed more information about the predictions that she had overheard. She wanted to be a good parent for Judy as she was for her other elven children. Katybear wrote down the cloud game divinations that she had overheard. She made a copy to give to Sister Samantha so both women could document the power of Judy's shamanism. Katy had concerns for Judy's development.

"Judy, can we look at the new magazines that Waffle Stomper gave to you? Is it okay if we bring them outside?" The girls carried armloads of magazines out onto the front steps, and began turning pages.

"Oh look Judy at this beautiful toe-dancer standing on her toes. That is what I want to do. I want to dance like that. It says here that ballerinas practice eight to ten hours every day. I guess that is what they must do to make their toes strong enough to stand on the very tip like that." Wren jumped up and began her new goal of standing on her toes. She practiced standing, later she would practice walking, and eventually she would learn to dance on the ends of her toes. She practiced this new art for hours, months and years. When Wren wasn't chasing the antelope, she practiced dancing on her toes. *I want to dance like that more than anything else. I will practice every day to balance on my tippy-toes and to be a toe-dancer.* Wren was charged with an excitement that swelled in her chest whenever she thought about those ballerina pictures.

There were no ballet schools, teachers or knowledgeable adults that could nudge Wren into the right direction, so she became autodidact, and developed an unusual talent to dance on her toes without toe shoes. Judy showed no interest in Wren's newly devoted aspirations of this new self-disciplined art. Judy's skill were for something else, and she was content to sit on the sidelines, which made her an excellent spectator and audience for Wren.

Chapter 10

SEGREGATION

Wren's life was surreptitious. Her reservation home was a brown square piece of cardboard that floated in space with no sound or light to penetrate its surface. Wren and Judy had no television in the 1950s and 1960s to explain the civil rights movement or the Martin Luther King marches. Their life was an insulated dark pocket where they created their own entertainment.

The mountain range obscured airwaves, and Wyoming was too sparsely populated for television companies to invest. Radio too was limited to the local Riverton and Lander stations, and it was forbidden in the convent where silence was the accepted norm. Judy on rare occasions used her older brother's ghetto blaster, even though they had no idea what a ghetto was. The young friends knew no diversity of people. Judy and Wren had never seen a black person, but the disparity of equality that the black race struggled to gain was the same oppression that every reservation inhabitant endured.

The difference between the black race oppression and the Wyoming Native American was a complete opposite. The tribes had no voice, no platform, no speech, and no words, or means to express themselves. Judy and Wren had their songs, dances, and rituals, but no one outside of the reservation heard them. The young girls were born into a race of silence and their feelings ran deep, but remained unarticulated. They knew unhappiness, but it remained concealed and unexpressed. Shoshoni and Arapaho adults were their role models, and they learned that their tribes were nations of deep stillness, gentleness, modesty, and kindness, yet they possessed a boiling undercurrent of violence, and the young girls witnessed this reservation unrest.

The resentment Wren experienced at the Shoshoni Red Flower Casino when the skinny man mistook her for an unwanted Arapaho, was similar to what the Natives encountered when they traveled into the towns of Riverton or Lander. The animosity was faint compared to what the blacks experienced in the large inner cities. The blacks knew fear and hate, but those elements were missing from the tribal experience.

Wren played in the Riverton City Park with Judy and the other Bear children when she saw a sign posted in handwritten words on the bathroom door that read, "No Indians allowed." This was a startling revelation and her first step to determine who she was. She was an Indian.

"I don't think this sign means us Judy, because we are Indian Kids. The park is full of adult Indians who are drunk, and I don't think they are wanted in the bathrooms because they make a mess. It is okay for us to use them because we won't leave a mess!" They used the restroom many times without repercussions. There was no one to enforce the posted sign.

Katybear took Wren shopping in downtown Riverton where they openly used the public bathrooms that were inclusive for all public use. The resentment against Native Americans was not wide spread, and the malice against the many drunk reservation persons was justified. The rural towns of Lander, Riverton, Thermopiles and Dubois were small, and merchants needed business. Water fountains were not segregated either. The city's economy was not so flush as to afford separate facilities. It was the same for restaurants and stores where non-Indians and Indians ate and shopped together. Everyone's business was needed and racial differences were overlooked.

On another occasion, Wren went into the sparsely populated town of Lander with Sister Samantha and Sarah. They walked by a restaurant with a sign in the window that read, "No dogs or Indians allowed." The sign made Wren think about herself. She thought, *I was once humiliated by the lemon-aid pregnancy, and I vowed that I would never be degraded like that again! I know who I am, and a sign will not take away my dignity. Mother Superior told me to determine who I am, and that sign will not determine who I am. I will determine who I am.*

"Come on, girls, there is delicious little restaurant around the corner that sells great hamburgers!" Sister Samantha marched on, and hoped that Sara and Wren had not seen the offending sign. Sister Samantha however could not shelter the girls from the larger problem of alcoholism that loomed over their young lives.

It was illegal to serve Indians alcohol, but bar owner's found ways around that law, and the liquor law was impossible to enforce. The towns had few law officers, and it remained undetermined how to enforce the law if a person was a full Indian, half breed, or some part Indian blood. If the natives' tribes were of age, they were served. White, unlicensed folks also supplied them with the addictive drink for a fee, and liquor stores supplied them on the QT. Most of the alcoholics were winos and their favorite drink was Muscatel Wine, or Mad Dog 20, which was only $1.25 per bottle. If they couldn't afford wine they drank Vitale's hair oil, which made them smell good and relieved their addiction but hastened an early death, with the average life span being only forty-nine years. Judy and Wren were surrounded by children who were abused by alcoholic parents, and the rez addiction colored their world. Judy had nonalcoholic, caring parents, and Wren knew only the guidance from the convent. That delineation bonded the girls' friendship and separated them from other rez classmates.

On the rez there was a much stronger stigma of resentment between the Shoshoni and the Arapaho tribes than there was between the Native American and the Caucasian culture. Historically, the Arapaho had always been enemies of the Shoshoni. These historic enemies encountered each other in thousands of raids and skirmishes, and they regarded the other as untrustworthy. Wren and Judy's friendship broke the ancient rules of rivalry and caused resentment among their respective tribes. The little girls were oblivious to the resentment that they encountered from the other schoolgirls who refused to play with them.

When Wren was ten years old in 1963 resentment and segregation ran strongly. Each tribe had their own schools, fire departments, tribal police, and separate governing councils. The two tribes youth did not date each other, socialize, or intermarry, and if they did punishments would occur to the offender, and retaliation followed from the opposition. Modern atrocities occurred between the tribes. The Shoshoni people were spurred on by hundreds of years of resentments toward the Arapahos who had encroached upon the host tribe when the US government put the two tribes on the same reservation. Both tribes were innocent victims that suffered from a forced mandate. Savagery of the most unthinkable type transpired from both tribes. An Arapaho clan would war against a Shoshoni family and vice versa. That was the world that Judy and Wren were shrouded under.

During the time of Wren's birth in the early 1950s Arapahos openly degraded Shoshoni by calling him a dog-eater. Waffle Stomper had a radio announcer's voice and served as the oral historian for the Shoshoni tribe. He would hold sessions of oral storytelling, and one time Waffle said, "During this era of turmoil, one Shoshoni was arrested for drunkenness and was sequestered in the Riverton City jail. An Arapaho clan bailed him out, took him to an obscure reservation area and applied torture. Hot nails were seared into his eyes, and he was dragged behind a vehicle until dead. The Shoshoni clan retaliated with the use of fire. They burned down three Arapaho homes that resulted in five human casualties."

During Wren's rez childhood the Riverton and Lander City Law Enforcement had no jurisdiction on Native American territory, and a Caucasian citizen had no protection on tribal lands. The reservation was known as no man's land as far as law enforcement was concerned. The land mass was 3,532.010 square miles and this wide open space was lawless. There were only a handful of tribal police to keep law and order which could not be done. Reservation inhabitants governed themselves by their own innate principals and Waffle Stomper and Big Boots were no different. They managed to remain highly principled, strong of character, and guided Wren to grow in their reflection. Their self-governing habits were helpfulness to whomever needed it, or whenever there was work to be done, and they gave their efforts toward community service. They were Wren's benefactors and protectors; they both were devoted to a life of self-improvement and self-development. They grew in their practice of spirituality through regular sweats, Catholic mass, and performing good deeds. They learned from their observations from nature, respected and cared for the environment, and participated in community cultural events. They were self-sufficient and autodidact. They learned to be innovative and provided for others. They built their own home, helped to build houses for others, fixed cars, created their own music, planted gardens, gathered herbs, hunted, and fished.

Big Boots and Waffle Stomper were best friends since the second grade at the Indian Mission. They both grew up in families where their parents drank themselves to death, and they learned to fend for themselves like Huckleberry Finn and Tom Sawyer. They loved their unstructured life, the rez culture, humanity of all races, and they loved each other as brothers.

The sharp September wind forced itself onto any creature that roamed and torturously stabbed Big Boots and Waffle Stomper who returned to Waffle's home after they had been to a Friday night sweat. It was dark, moonless, late, and their bodies were dehydrated, depleted of strength, dreamy, and mellow. They both experienced a state of bliss as Big Boots steered the old green dented Ford tuck down the familiar narrow irrigation canal. Waffle Stomper called attention to the older model black Ford blocking the cow trail that he used to reach his house. There was no way to pass around the stalled vehicle. So they parked behind it and got out into the knife-sharp, killer wind to offer their mechanical skills. This act of assistance was true to their nature. Big Boots's tired feet wedged between the deep ruts of the hardened mud car tracks as he made his way to the stalled vehicle, and nearly lost his balance from the force of the icy wind. He maneuvered the distance and shouted above the gale to the occupants of the stalled car.

"Are you high centered on the rut?" Big Boots questioned as he leaned on the fender of the driver's side of the car.

"No way, man!" said a young male's inebriated, arrogant voice.

"What are you boys doing out here on this dead end trail?" Big Boots asked as Waffle Stomper made his way around to the passenger's side of the car, and inspected the front and rear flat tires. He could tell that these kids had gunned the motor to force the vehicle through the hardened deep ruts, and the old thin tires couldn't withstand the pressure.

"Worn out blown tires," Waffle Stomper yelled to Big Boots over the howl of the wind. "Do you guys have a tire iron or a jack?" He asked as he peered into the back seat.

"Nope, we don't got a goddamn thing," one insolent kid from the backseat slurred.

"Well, how long you gonna sit here?" Big Boots challenged the driver. Waffle Stomper had already retrieved two spare tires, tire iron and jack from Big Boots's pickup.

"We was gonna walk to the queers house and borrow tools," the driver mush-mouthed.

Two pairs of boots recognized the 'trouble alarm' when it sounded from the rude voices of the teenagers. They knew that it was best to get these kids moved out of the way so they could pass around them and head to Waffle's house as fast as they could. Waffle Stomper had already removed the hubcaps, lug nuts, and was ready to jack it up.

"I need you boys to get off the car before I can jack it up." Waffle Stomper calmly directed.

"No way in hell I gitt'n off," sneered the driver.

"We are trying to help you. We need you to get off so we can jack it up," countered Big Boots.

"Hey! Ain't that the little shit queer that's change'n the tire?" The kid in the back seat said, as he leapt out, grabbed the tire iron away from Waffles hand, and brought the weight of it down across his back as he crouched by the rear tire. As fast as lightning, two of the punks riding on the driver's side of the car jumped out and pinned Big Boots to the fender. The flung open door whacked his head and back. The other two kids on the passenger's side of the stalled car kicked and beat Waffle Stomper repeatedly with the tire iron across his face, neck, and head. He dropped in unconsciousness, but they continued to kick and pommel him as he lay in the hard rutted mud. Another teen grabbed the tire iron from his friend, swung it to crush Waffle Stomper's head, but missed, and the iron gashed his neck.

Big Boots freed himself from his attackers. He kneed them in the groin and left them to writhe on the ground. He ran to the passenger's side of the car, grabbed the iron in midair as it was about to come down on Waffle again, but instead Big Boots took a couple of whacks at the two other teens, and sent them sprawling face first into the ruts. He gathered Waffle Stomper up in a fireman's rescue stance and dashed for his truck. He expertly backed out on the trail for over a mile before he was able to turn around. His heart raced in time with the engine of the old truck as it headed straight for the Riverton Memorial Hospital on Park Avenue. The twenty-six-mile drive felt like the distance to the moon and back, but he pulled up to the emergency room door where the ambulances dropped off patients, and blasted his horn. The well-trained staff were prepared for emergencies and quickly responded to the sonorous truck horn. The orderlies moved the unconscious Waffle Stomper from the blood soaked truck seat onto the gurney and wheeled him into the ER.

Prompt and efficient emergency care was administered, but Big Boots was not allowed into the emergency exam room with Waffle Stomper. Big Boots John Wayne swagger——was more like a dragging wagon. He collapsed into a green naugahyde waiting room chair and noticed his own clothes were smeared with Waffle's blood. He remembered that he had a change of sweat pants and jacket in the truck from the sweat ceremony. He looked up at the clock on the waiting room wall and it read 2:05 a.m. It seemed an eternity since he and Waffle Stomper had left the peacefulness of the sweat lodge before midnight. It had only taken an hour for this senseless debauchery to have occurred and changed the course of life.

Big Boots cleaned himself up and changed his clothes in the waiting room restroom. He unwound a pile of paper towels from the bathroom dispenser, walked out to his truck in the parking lot, and attempted to clean the blood from his truck. He ambled back into the waiting room lobby and sank down into the chair again to wait for news from the doctor. He was the only person in the room and the quietness prompted him to fall asleep. He was startled awake by screams from a mother who carried a lifeless battered three-year-old girl into the ER. A group of family members accompanied the women, and everyone shouted and cried. The receptionist and a nurse tried to bring order as the child was taken from the mother's arms and rushed into the ER exam room. The din shook him fully awake, and he noticed that the time was 5:12 a.m. on the wall-mounted clock. The nurse turned and spoke to Big Boots.

"Mr. Stomper is still unconscious. You will need to fill in admitting papers at the reception desk."

Big Boots nodded his acceptance.

"The doctor has had a very rough night, but he will talk to you if you want to wait."

Big Boots nodded again and rearranged his six foot two inch thick heavy body to fit more comfortably into the stiff slick naugahyde chair that did not lend itself to the contour of his build. The thirty extra pounds in his midsection made his body and that green chair unlikely companions. His sixty-eight-year-old shoulders and back overflowed the chair's chrome frame, and complained that they had had enough discomfort for this endless night. He folded his arms, rested his chin on his barrel chest, and his braided long pigtails that had unraveled several hours ago fell onto his biceps. His mind drifted to thoughts about his many years of friendship with Waffle Stomper.

Waffle Stomper was the only person that Big Boots considered to be his brother and family since his parents died when he was eleven. State Child Protection Services were out of their jurisdiction on the rez and the tribes had no services of their own. Children's welfare became a catch-us-catch-can community responsibility. Suzy Pavora, who tanned hides, took an interest in Big Boots out of her kindness toward children and also because of his hunting skills. She left food and books for him beside his tent where he lived alone, and in return Big Boots kept Suzy and himself supplied with wild game. Their mutual cooperation grew into a profitable business that was based on the law of supply and demand. When Suzy needed hides to tan, Big Boots hunted and supplied them for her, and Suzy shared her profits with him. Waffle Stomper when he came to school also helped to feed Big Boots. He brought Fritos, potato chips, Twinkies, and other packaged foods from of his own school lunch.

Waffle Stomper was two years older than Big Boots, but his formal education at the Indian Mission began when he was placed into Big Boots second grade class, and they became buddies. Both of the second graders wore field boots given to them from the Charity Thrift Shop. Even though Waffle Stomper was older he was smaller than Big Boots. The second grade class nicknamed the boys Big Boots and Waffle Stomper. The soles of the field boots left waffle-like prints when imprinted into the mud, and the boots left mud daubers on the school floor. Their nicknames stuck for life like mud daubers stuck to the school floor.

Waffle Stomper's widowed mother died of cirrhosis of the liver when he was thirteen. The boys continued to live in separate houses, but managed to get themselves to school in spite of the harsh winters. Winter weather attributed to many absent days, and the attended school days were motivated more by their friendship than by their respect for education.

A few months after Big Boots parents died frozen in a snow storm the two pair of field boot clad friends played horseshoes in the middle of an open country road with six other school kids. One of the boys threw a horseshoe at Big Boots. It smacked him on the temple and knocked him cold. He dropped to the ground, and the boys all scattered like prairie chickens. Waffle Stomper called to them, "I will stay here with Big Boots. Go get my dad or someone to help."

Waffle Stomper stayed with Big Boots all night, but no one came. Waffle Stomper never knew if the boys tried to get help, or if his dad was too drunk to care. He didn't know if the boys were afraid they would be in trouble, so they didn't tell anyone. He didn't know the truth, but Waffle Stomper stayed with Big Boots and tried to help him as best he could. He keep him warm by placing his own jacket over him.

Big Boots remembered seeing the most beautiful magenta and purple sunrise when his eyes opened the next morning. He saw his friend sitting beside him silhouetted against the backdrop of the dawn. This was the silhouette of an honorable and caring friend.

"Excuse me, Mr. Boots. I am Doctor Fernau." Big Boots pried himself loose from the butt-gripping chair.

"Please stay seated, and I will drag up a chair. I am so tired. I need to sit down. Your friend is in very bad shape."

"Will he live?"

"He seems to be a strong man, but he has lost a lot of blood. He was given a five-unit transfusion, and we had to do immediate surgery on his neck to stop the bleeding. His carotid artery was spared; the lacerations were deep but repairable. He suffered severe blows to the head, and has a brain hematoma; the brain is edema, very swollen. Until the swelling goes down, we don't know if there is brain damage. His body was also badly beaten. He has broken ribs and a ruptured spleen, which we had to remove. He has been moved into ICU and will be closely monitored. He can't have any visitors, and he won't likely regain consciousness for hours, or maybe days, or it could be weeks. The best advice for you is to go home and return midday tomorrow—I mean today late in the afternoon or this evening. We will know more if he makes it through these next few days. I am sorry that I can't give you more information. The severity of his injuries required me to contact the police. They are expecting you to file a report and to press charges." Dr. Fernau stood and shook Big Boots hand.

Big Boots ambled to his truck in the early morning haze of his mind. He felt more alone now than when he was orphaned as a child. He was dehydrated from the sweat, depleted from the lack of food, and had sleep deprivation. He felt cruddy, but he was compliant, and stopped at the Riverton Police Department, but he knew that they could not take any action. They would only forward the report onto the reservation police. The crime occurred on the rez, the victim was an enrolled tribal member, and the perpetrators were also Native American. He climbed on his old truck and drove the twenty-six miles back to his house. As he drove Big Boots chanted his Indian prayers, said, 'Hail

Marys' and many 'Our Fathers' in Waffle Stomper's name. He pledged that if the Great Spirit would heal Waffle Stomper, he would dance in the Sundance in gratitude for his friends spared life. Big Boots reached the comfort of his home, and dove into his bed like a gopher disappears into a burrow.

Big Boots woke from seven hours of sleep, and his first thoughts were about Waffle Stomper. He stuffed some clothes, toothbrush, comb into a pillowcase, and headed out to his truck. He drove to the canal trail that led to Waffle Stomper's house, but stopped when he spotted his discarded tire iron and car jack. The midday sun warmed last night's frigid, cruel temperature and arrested the angry wind. His long legs stretched out of his truck, and he inspected the ground and assumed that the teenagers had backed out of the trail the same way he had done. The tracks revealed that his spare tires were placed onto their stalled vehicle. It was evident that the boys must have sobered up enough to realize what they had done, and the abandoned tools indicated that the kids were not thieves. Big Boots picked up his tools, tossed them into the pickup bed, and drove on to Waffle's house. The teenagers also did not take revenge on Waffle Stomper's house by committing vandalism or arson. The interior was clean and orderly, but it had a minimal of possessions. Big Boots placed some of Waffle's clothing items into a pillowcase, grabbed up some of his unread books, and his guitar. He fed and watered Waffle's mixed-breed dogs named Fast Forward and Rewind. Big Boots drove to Ft. Washakie to give information that might be helpful to the tribal police to reign in those ill-tempered tanked teenagers.

Big Boots had deep sorrow for the peril of his friend's life, but he felt no anger toward the young insolent teens who used bravado to mask their immature insecurities. He had seen years of alcohol related destruction that ravaged the tribes lives worse than the savages of war. This disease was a playful trickster that snuck up, joked, laughed, provided frivolity, and gave good times with friends. Alcoholism was a seductive curvy, cuddle creature, and comforter for sorrow, loneliness, or depression. It was the malady that hid in the tribes DNA for hundreds of years and would spring forward without provocation. Alcoholism was the reservation plague that intruded every household, infested it with heartbreak, and child neglect. Many Native American babies were born as alcoholics and lived their lives staving off the craving.

The strongest individuals with the best of intentions and will power were the most vulnerable. They not only had the cravings for the languishing liquid, but their fun-loving friends who were on the sauce, pressured them into the bottle. Only a handful of Native Americans who lived on the rez were vaccinated to withstand the tempting allure. The injection consisted of education, employment, productivity, human services, and spirituality. Big Boots had his vaccination when he was seven. His drunken father passed out twenty feet from the door of his platformed tent in a snowstorm and froze to death. His friend Waffle Stomper realized the dangers of alcohol as a nine-year-old. He saw his parents dying each day until he was orphaned at thirteen.

Another stranglehold on individuals like Big Boots and Waffle Stomper, who resisted the reservation curse and worked toward self-improvement were labeled 'Apples,' red on the outside, but white on the inside. The white man's ways of employment, improved living standards, and education were renounced, objected, and scorned by the majority of tribal members. Assimilation had been forced onto the tribesmen, and they resented the slow death of their nomadic culture. It was accepted that the white culture bred greed, corruption, and selfishness. The majority of Native Americans resisted white culture, and disavowed employment they believed encouraged accumulation of materialism. They lived in poverty, shunned acquired personal possessions, and yearned for freedom, but they didn't know how to find it.

Big Boots arrived at the Riverton Memorial Hospital at 7:00 p.m. The hospital smell hit his senses and identified his location. A hospital always had the same hospital smell.

"I am here to see Waffle Stomper."

"Yes, Mr. Boots, I will tell the nurse that you are here. Please have a seat."

Oh no, not the pain of the green naugahyde steel-framed chair again! After he had the negative thought a second thought reminded him of the pain that his friend endured. He squeezed himself into the naughty green vice and waited. The nurse came more rapidly then he expected.

"Mr. Boots come with me into the conference room please." Big Boots followed the nurse into a small office with two chair.

"Please have a seat." The chair was a more comfortable fit and Big Boots stretched out his long lanky legs.

"Your friend is still in ICU. He has suffered a brain hematoma and ruptured spleen and throat lacerations. The internal organs are bruised, but there is no more bleeding. He is hooked up to IV fluids, but he is still unconscious. We want to keep him in ICU until he stabilizes. You may come again tomorrow and the best time would be around two p.m. Do you have any questions?"

"Will he wake up?"

"Sometimes a patient gives small signs that brain activity is resuming. We will give you a report when you come tomorrow."

Waffle Stomper remained in ICU for ten days, and every day the report was the same, but on the eleventh day the news was different.

"Good morning, Mr. Boots. We have good news! Your friend has been moved into room number 505, and you may visit him if you wish. He is still unconscious, but please talk to him. The sound of your voice may help him to recover."

Big Boots gingerly opened the door to room 505 and stepped inside. He was shocked to see his friend's bruised face. He still had a swollen rearranged nose and lumps on his forehead above the eyebrows. Big Boots stood there just staring for a long time before he spoke.

"Hi, Waffle Stomper, Good to see you. You look like a trout that was caught and tossed back. The nurse said to talk to you. Well, that can be hard for us 'cause we didn't much do that. No need to talk. You knew my thoughts, and I knew yours. I will tell you about things that happened. Those Arapaho boys got arrested——" Big boots was interrupted by a nurse coming in to check the fluids in the IV.

"Please keep talking to him as if I weren't here."

"You know. Four teenagers arrested and in Ft. Washakie jail. Police found them by tracking spare tires on their——"

"Look at *that*—his eyes fluttered. That is a sign that he can hear you. Keep going! Keep going." The excited nurse wrote on the chart on the foot of his bed. Big Boots began again to relate current events.

"Waffle Stomper, guess what! The prosecutor on the kids' case is Darrell Bear, Katy Bear's oldest son. He passed his bar exam and was lawyer last Christmas." With that bit of news, Waffle Stomper's eyes popped open.

"Wow! This is wonderful," screeched the nurse. "Keep talking to him."

Big Boots halted. He was stunned by Waffle Stomper's unfocused, glassy, dilated pupils. His eyes didn't seem to move or to show that he understood what he had heard.

"Mr. Boots, this is great progress, and if you would like we will move a cot and a chair into Mr. Stomper's room so you can be with him as much as you want. Your presence and talking to him is definitely promoting progress."

The nurse turned and hurried from the room. Big Boots was relieved to be alone with his childhood chum. Talking and making conversation was a rarity between them in normal times, and now he was under pressure to do so. He felt genuine fear that his words would cause Waffle Stomper anxiety or a relapse. He worried that he might say the wrong things.

It was his experience that unspoken thoughts were clear, precise, and honest, but when they became spoken, the sound distorted the crystalline cerebration. The sound of his words caused the clarity, purity, and exactness to vanish, and left only the shell of the word. His spoken words became discolored and slightly distorted the preciseness of his thoughts. Words, when spoken, were eschewed and left only a shadow of their intended meaning. Speaking for him was like trying to explain a dream, only to realize that the telling of the dream was not like the original dream at all.

"I want to be here but don't want to crowd you up. This is tiny room to be all bunched up in, when before we had pretty much entire Fremont County to ourselves." Waffle Stomper's eyes showed no comprehension.

"Ten days I carried things in the truck for you. Do you want them?" After Big Boots asked the question, he felt guilt and remorse. Waffle Stomper could not answer because of his damaged throat, and he was not fully emerged from unconsciousness. "It will be okay if I don't say much. Maybe you'll be ready for things in a few days," Big Boots stood beside his friend's bed and was silent for over ten minutes. He shifted his weight from one foot to the other in his discomfort. "Maybe it will be enough for you to feel my presence."

"Maybe this is good lesson for me to be better talker. I will come back tonight." He gave the John Wayne cowboy two-fingered salute. "Later," he said and left the room while his friend lay flat on the bed with his eyes in a wide-open, glazed stare.

The medical staff at the Riverton Memorial Hospital began a vigorous regiment of therapies to assist with Waffle Stomper's recovery. The staff was encouraged by the progress that was observed from Big Boots's visitation. He was given physical therapy twice a day, aroma therapy, light therapy to enhance eye movement, music stimulation, and touch therapy.

Big Boots had his own form of therapy. He checked on Waffle's house, fed and watered the dogs. He assisted anyone who needed chores done, he completed car or house repairs, and he performed requested errands in the small squalor of Ft. Washakie. In the early evening on Monday Big Boots returned to the Riverton Hospital to spend the night with his friend.

Big Boots opened the door of hospital room 505 and saw a cot and chair. Waffle Stomper had been raised into a sitting position.

"You look like a prairie dog just stretching up out of your burrow." Big Boots greeted his friend as he arranged his toothbrush and comb on the bathroom counter and sat down on the cot beside the hospital bed.

"You need to go home soon. Rewind won't eat unless *you* feed him. Fast Forward eats everything when I feed him, but not Rewind." Big Boots noticed that Waffle Stomper continued to stare straight ahead instead of turning his head to the side. Big Boots got up and moved to sit in the chair at the end of the bed more in line with Waffle's vision.

"Rewind misses you. He drinks the water, but as long as I stay there, he does not eat. The food is gone the next day when I return, but I don't know if a coyote eats it or if Fast Forward eats it. He wants you to feed him."

Big boots noticed that Waffle's eyes weren't as dilated as they had been yesterday. "I haven't pressed charges against the teenagers. I wanted to see how you were doing." With those words, Waffle's legs jerked like he wanted to walk. Big Boots pressed the nurse call button, and a nurse opened the door. Big Boots told her about Waffle's legs.

"This is good news! His nerves are starting to wake up his body." She began to exercise his legs in walk patterning for ten minutes and left the room.

"The four hoodlums have been incarcerated for six days waiting for charges to be filed. You are doing better." Big Boots stood and moved around the room within Waffle's perihelia vision and suspected that his eyes were trying to follow his movements. Days and nights passed and the two men followed the schedule that involved their own recovery therapy.

On Wednesday, Big Boots returned. He opened the door slowly and peaked inside. He saw that Waffle was no longer hooked up to IV fluids.

"Okay, he is awake. You can go in." Wren bounced through the open door, climbed onto the bed and gave Godfather Waffle Stomper a hug that didn't stop. She cuddled up beside him and looked into his eyes.

"Godfather, your eyes look different. They don't look like Boston Baked Beans anymore. They look more like Oreos." Wren touched his eyelids and eyebrows as she spoke.

"Godfather, look what I can do." She jumped off the bed and walked around the room on 'point'. She had developed the strength in her toes to balance and dance.

"Wait, Wren. We have some music." Big Boots punched the buttons of the ghetto blaster that the nurses had used for Waffle's music therapy. Wren went up on her toes and danced to Beethoven Moon Light Sonata piano #14. Three of the nurses heard the music and came into room 505. Wren had an audience and danced stronger than she did in her practice sessions in her room named determine at Incaranata Hall. One of the nurses moved to the end of Waffle's bed and wrote a note that recorded his eye movement.

"Godfather, when I dance for you next time, maybe I can stand on my toes with one foot and do this." Wren stood on one foot and grasped her other leg and stretched it higher than her head.

"I want to dance like the toe dancers do in the pictures on one tippy-toe and not two."

The hospital staff applauded her performance, and for an encore Wren did the splits.

Wednesday's hospital visit had been successful, so Big Boots invited more guests. More visitors took the pressure off Big Boots's responsibility to carry on a one-way conversation. On Thursday Big Boots opened the door slowly, and saw that Waffle Stomper was dressed in street clothes and sat in a chair. Wren bounced into the room and landed in his lap. Sister Samantha, Mother Superior, and katybear followed Big Boots, and stood against the wall. Mother Superior stepped forward and presented Waffle Stomper with a basket.

"Waffle Stomper, the nuns at Incaranata Hall have made you Indian fry bread with honey. They wish you a speedy recovery." Waffle reached for the basket, which surprised Big Boots, who stepped forward to help.

"Godfather, can we have some now?" Wren asked with her comically raised eyebrows.

Waffle Stomper nodded a slight positive head movement. Big Boots eyes brightened when he noted the progress. Sister Samantha carried a large laundry basket taken from the convent. She removed the cover and revealed the listless dog, Rewind. The dog sprang up at the smell and sight of Waffle Stomper. Mother Superior gave a surprised gasp and a scolding glance of disapproval toward Sister Samantha who gave back a humble smile and an innocent shrug. Sister Samantha possessed spontaneous right action and good intentions of the heart, but she still had trouble with obedience. That dog was clearly against hospital rules. Her actions made Mother Superior smile.

The dog became lively, jumped out of the basket, and dived into the freshly baked fry bread. "Wait! Save some for us." Wren squealed as she rescued some of the gift.

Waffle's eyes changed from Oreo flat-black into the shiny color of the Boston Baked Beans they had formerly been. Rewind, whined, wiggled, wagged and took Wren's place in Godfather's lap. Waffle Stomper awkwardly pet Rewind as the dog snuggled down into his lap. Katybear stood close to the wall in the cramped hospital room and realized that her daughter Judy had read this tragedy in the clouds.

Katybear said softy, "Waffle Stomper, I have some news for you too. You knew that my son Darrell will be the prosecutor, but what you don't know is that my second oldest son, Shram, passed his bar exam and got his law license on September 8. He will be the defense attorney for this case. How about that? Two brothers on opposite sides of the case." Katybear laughed uproariously. The people visiting Waffle Stomper cheered, clapped their hands, and the dog barked loudly. The room was full of happy chaos and din as the door of room 505 flew open.

A stern, dried prune, faced hospital administrator who wore a brown business suit and strappy high-heels burst into the room. Sister Samantha held up her hand to stop the woman from speaking.

"It's okay, we are leaving," Sister Samantha moved forward and removed the barking, whining dog from Waffle Stomper's lap, and struggled to stuff him back into the laundry basket. Big Boots quickly ushered everyone from the room.

Mother Superior in her white superior habit was the last to exit, but she turned, and authoritatively declared, "The dog's visitation will hasten this patient's recovery." Mrs. Brown Suit, not wanting to be outranked replied, "Mother Superior, you may be guaranteed that Mr. Stomper will have a hastened, premature release!"

And he did.

Chapter 11

TRIBAL COURT

The October morning was as golden and crisp as the prairie grass that forecast the beginning of the harsh winter to come. The windows of katybear's van had Jack Frost white paintings etched onto them as Judy, Wren, and Sister Samantha rode with her to the tribal court building of Ft. Washakie. Wren's window still exhibited the frost mural from the night's low temperature, and she traced its beautiful tree-forested pattern with her fingers and watched it disappear. The frost melted into rivers that slid down the glass. Wren felt that something important took place even before she saw the many parked cars that looked similar to the powwow grounds. Cars were parked everywhere, but katybear meandered through them. It looked as if she were driving in the middle of Gene Lee's salvage yard. She parked in front of the building reserved for council members.

Ft. Washakie in the early 1960s was a generic, nondescript cluster of small wooden framed homes, trailer houses, and several overpowering solid redbrick government buildings, one of which was the tribal court facility. The other brick structures were also government BIA, the Ft. Washakie Post

Office, Out-Patient Health Service, and Ft. Washakie Law Enforcement. This smattering of humanity comprised a population of no more than one thousand people who mostly worked as staff in the government buildings and lived nearby in the small houses and trailers. The settlement was void of any special identifiable landmarks other than the loud declaration of US government property. The buildings were randomly plunked down, seemingly without streets, and gave the appearance of unplanned disorder. The roads leading to the area were graveled dirt and appeared randomly wherever a car could maneuver or park. There were no trees or planted vegetation to soften the harshness of the sage covered prairie. Ft. Washakie did not reflect Native American pride. It was almost as if the residents yelled, "We don't like these government buildings!"

The tribal court facility was one of the largest structures, which included the medium-security prison and yard. The complex had double-strength fencing with three rows of razor wire on top that guarded the perimeter. The tribal court facility housed the justice system for both tribes. Each tribe had their own tribal council members who were elected. In 1962, Katy Bear was the first woman to have been elected and reelected to serve on the Arapaho Council. She was a political activist and served on different councils throughout her active career. Katy served on the Arapaho Education Council and was responsible for extending scholarships to any student that graduated. Students could use the scholarship to any university of their acceptance. She later served on the Business Council, Records and Census Committee, and Arapaho Council for Mental Health. The brick buildings were Katy's workplace, and she worked there for over twenty years. Five miles east of Katy's office was Big Boots's house, and eighteen miles west of Ft. Washakie was the trail where Waffle Stomper encountered the four Arapaho youth that placed his life in jeopardy.

Katybear believed the Waffle Stomper trial would be a good lesson for Judy and Wren to attend on inner-council tribal affairs. Judy should witness her two older brothers' attorney careers, and become inspired toward law, or perhaps it would give her some direction for her divination shaman skills. Sister Samantha knew that Wren should experience the justice system and understand how it related to the welfare of her godfathers.

Katybear saw groups of people huddled together but individually wrapped in colorful Indian designed wool Pendleton blankets. The people were standing in groups holding cardboard signs that read, "Place your bets for the prosecution" while others grouped around signs that favored the defense. These Arapaho and Shoshoni people had the same look of blanketed wrapped natives that weathered the frosted mornings in the 1800s. Back then they were wrapped in the Hudson Bay Co. blankets they had traded with the fur traders, but today they traded their money for a chance to win the home-style lottery.

October 16, 1962, was the World Series between the New York Yankees and the San Francisco Giants, but the reservation trial of a severely beaten Shoshoni versus four Arapaho youth was far more alluring than the World Series. Arapaho brothers, Darrell Bear served as the prosecution attorney and Shram Bear represented the defense. These brother-related councilmen added competitive drama while multitudes of Native Americans laid wagers. Hundreds of cars surrounded the destained redbrick tribal court building on this frigid morning. Inside the bland courtroom, every chair was taken, and the small interior didn't allow for standing room. People filled the isles and spilled over into the hallways, but katybear had reserved seats for herself and her three guests. The beige tile floor was tracked up with the melted snow clumps from spectators' boots. Close bodies, packed chairs, and the low ceiling gave the room a cramped atmosphere that smelled of tobacco, leather, and wet dogs.

The trial held promise for fairness. The judge was Clarence Eagle Feather, whose heritage was a ShoRap. Clarence Eagle Feather was sixty-three-year-old son of a Shoshoni mother and an Arapaho father. His heritage had made him an outcast all his life, but this trial presented the opportunity to put tribal animosities aside. It allowed the attorney brothers to exhibit pure logic, sound reason, skillful strategies, and oratorical arts.

It seemed incongruent that this isolated Native American court procedure would follow the old British style of formality, but it did. The bailiff announced, "Hear ye, hear ye, all rise for the presiding Judge Eagle Feather."

Judge Eagle Feather entered the courtroom wearing the traditional black robe and took his place at the judge's bench. The theatrics were the strangest blend of British / Native American cultures that collided and splattered into the makings of this trial. Wren felt that this grown man Judge Eagle Feather played "dress-up."

When he sat down, the bailiff announced, "You may be seated."

The two attorneys were seated at separate, side by side, rectangular tables with their clients facing the judge's bench. Darrell Bear wore a long-sleeved turquoise and red plaid shirt with Levis and brown loafers. His shirt looked snappy against his dark skin and complimented his youthful twenty-six years. Darrell was a sturdy build: five feet, ten inches tall and 160 pounds with a stylish haircut with trimmed bangs swooped to the left side of his forehead. He was movie star good looking, unmarried, and attracted the attention of the shy, soft giggling teenaged girls that were in the courtroom.

The courtroom was void of anyone who wore suits. The Native Americans hated the suit attire. Government men always wore suits when they were on the reservation, and those suits were as offensive as the redbrick buildings they strutted into.

Waffle Stomper sat in his rented wheelchair beside Darrell at the left table facing the judge. He was still not able to speak or walk, but he could write, and his eyes were able to focus. He was wrapped with a red robe over his shoulders and legs for warmth on this nippy morning. Waffle was able to turn his head, and he glanced around the room and searched for Big Boots. Big Boots tapped him on his shoulders to reassure him that he sat directly behind.

The defense attorney, Shram Bear, and the four defendants sat together at the table on the right facing the judge's bench. Shram was a year younger than his brother Darrell, but he was bigger. He stood at six feet, two inches, and had the body built of the weight lifter that he was. He weighed in at 175 pounds and competed in that division around the state as an amateur. Shram was a handsome man too, but his looks were more the look of a military officer. His hair was not a crewcut, but it was cut short in the '60s trendy flattop. He projected the look of intelligence as he placed his black rimmed glasses on the table in front of him. He resembled a sturdy Buddy Holly, and he projected the same showmanship confidence. Today he was like a racehorse at the starting gate— ready and raring to begin the trial.

The Judge spoke to the jury. "Charges have been filed against the defendants. Please stand, defendants, as I call your names so the jury can know you." The four defendants all wore the BIA black jumpsuits as they sat erect. "Weasel White Horse, Gary Frazier, Fox Goodman, and Wyman Large." The four defendants each stood as their names were stated. "As you can see for yourselves these defendants are all juveniles. This is not a Juvenile Court, but because all the defendants are Native American and the charges against these youth are severe, so the Justice Court will hear the case. Weasel White Horse just turned thirteen on September 27, he was born in 1949." Weasel Whitehorse stood his five foot two inch height and made eye contact with the judge and several of the jury members. "Gary Frazier is fifteen years old, born March 11, 1947." Gary was five foot five inches in height and his demeanor reflected his shame to be in the courtroom. "Fox Goodman is fifteen years old, born April 18, 1947." Fox was a well-developed youth, and stood at five foot and ten inches tall, and he played basketball for the Eagles. He looked directly at the judge and smiled. "Wyman Large is fourteen years old, born September 2, 1948." Wyman was five foot four inches, and ran distance for the Eagles track team.

"Gentlemen of the jury, you have met the defendants, and now you will hear the charges against them. There are four counts of intoxication against all four of the defendants, four counts of underage alcohol possession against all four of the defendants, four counts of assault against all four defendants, two counts of assault with a deadly weapon against Weasel Whitehorse and Fox Goodman, two counts of intent to do bodily harm against Weasel Whitehorse and Fox Goodman, and one count of car theft against Wyman Large. You may be seated, gentlemen." The four BIA black-jumpsuited young men took their seats as Judge Eagle Feather had instructed.

Judge Eagle Feather scrutinized the all-male jury seated in the jury box in the front of the room on the left side from the judge's bench. He nodded his head in approval. The jury was a well-balanced selection. Five were enrolled Arapaho members, and five were Shoshoni. The other two men on the jury were white farmers with reservation-deeded land; one lived fourteen miles from Ft. Washakie and had been a farmer for twelve years and raised his family there, and the other had lived on deeded reservation land for more than forty years and was well known by both tribes. Judge Eagle Feather was well acquainted with all the selected jurors, and he knew them to be fair minded.

"Bailiff, please lead the defendants out of the courtroom until they are individually called to testify." The bailiff escorted the prisoners back into incarceration.

"Prosecutor Darrell Bear, are you ready with opening remarks?"

Darrell Bear stood and nodded his respect to Judge Eagle Feather. "Yes, Your Honor. My client, Mr. Waffle Stomper, is the injured victim in this case and wants justice be served in his regard. He is seeking full restitution for medical bills now totaling $4,389 to the Riverton Memorial Hospital. He had spent ten days in ICU and another week in physical therapy recovering from a brain hematoma, a spleen removal, lacerated throat surgery, broken ribs, and severe bruises over eighty percent of his body and internal organs. There will be significant additional expenses after he recovers from the concussion. The brain damage affected his motor skills. He does not have the use of his legs, and it is unknown whether he will speak or walk again. Big Boots is seeking that justice be served, and the return of his two undamaged spare tires."

Prosecutor Darrell Bear stood composed for a few minutes then crossed the room from the left rectangular table to stand directly in front of the jury box.

Chapter 12

TRADITION VERSUS YOUTH

"Gentlemen of the jury, picture this scene: It is Friday night, September 27, 1962. The weather is cold and windy, the night is dark and moonless, and the time is eleven forty-five p.m. Two men—Waffle Stomper and Big Boots—had been at Jake Oldman's sweat lodge since seven p.m. Big Boots was driving Waffle Stomper home in his truck. Waffle Stomper's house is not on a street. It is not even near a graveled road. It is located eighteen miles out on the prairie by way of a rutted cow trail. Big Boots's truck is the only vehicle that travels into that remote area. Waffle Stomper has no family, and friends do not travel eighteen miles into that isolated, sage-covered prairie for visits. These two friends"—Darrell walked back to Waffle Stomper and Big Boots and put his hands on their shoulders—"these two friends were returning from the sweat lodge and were startled. Two miles from Waffle's house on that evening a black four-door Ford was stalled on the trail so no vehicle could pass or go around. On the right side of the trail, there is a five-foot-wide irrigation ditch, and on the left side of the trail there is a rocky-cliff drop off. The only way in or out from Waffle's house is on the one-car-wide trail." Prosecutor Darrell Bear walked back to the jury box to drive his next point into the attentive jurors' eyes.

"The point is this: the carload of boys inside the black Ford were out there for a purpose. That purpose was to do bodily harm. There are no Texaco gas stations, no A&W drive-ins, no Marvin's liquor stores, no movie pickup places, no Burlesons Drug Stores, no soda shops, there is nothing at eleven forty-five p.m. in that empty space except Waffle Stomper's house. During the course of this trial, the prosecution will provide the jury with witnesses to show that two of the defendants wrongly misread and misunderstood Mr. Big Boots and Mr. Waffle Stomper. The defendants, Weasel White Horse and Fox Goodman, had malice and immature resentments against these two lifetime friends. The prosecution will provide witness to demonstrate the truth of that statement." Darrell Bear addressed the jury in a personal, friendly style as he established eye contact with each juror.

"These two gentleman, these two friends, are not queer, but others believe that they are. They live separately in their own self-constructed homes, but they are constant companions, never married, and neither of them ever traveled outside of Fremont County, except when Big Boots earned his degree in sociology from the University of Wyoming. There was never a public physical display of affection, and no one over the seventy-year span of their friendship has witnessed an alternative lifestyle, but they are labeled queer. The love they share for each other is the same universal love they have for all humanity. They have always cared for each other's well-being. Their kindness is misread and misjudged by people who are immature or less evolved. Rumors about them are widespread, but untrue. The prosecution concludes opening statements."

Darrell Bear took his seat with Waffle Stomper and Big Boots at the prosecutors table. The spectators were emotionally affected by Prosecutor Bear's oration, and a handful of men hurried to the outside to adjust the betting numbers under the "Prosecution to win" sign. Wren listened to Darrell's beautiful words and remembered how these two attorney brothers had taken her to the Big Chief pool hall and taught her poetry about "Fido the Little Dog" that she'd recited in mass. Wren vowed to herself, *I will learn to use words like Darrell.*

"Thank you, counselor. Will the defense present opening remarks?" Judge Eagle Feather inquired.

"No, Your Honor, the defense defers opening remarks."

"Okay, are you ready to call your first witness, Prosecutor Bear?"

"Yes, sir, the prosecution calls Mr. Big Boots." Big Boots walked with the stride of a lone male prairie chicken and took his place on the witness stand. The bailiff swore him in. Prosecutor Bear, being Arapaho himself, was aware that this older Shoshoni might follow the ancient Shoshoni tradition of never speaking his own name. He glanced in the judge's direction, made eye contact, and his eyes signaled his intent to deviate from the norm. The judge nodded.

"Is your name Mallard C'Hair, and do you go by the name of Big Boots?"

"Yes."

"Please tell the jury your age and what relationship you are to Waffle Stomper."

"I am seventy, and I consider Waffle Stomper to be my brother. We are the only family that we have."

"How long have you considered Waffle Stomper to be your brother?"

"From when I was seven years old. We have been friends for sixty years."

"Big Boots, please tell the jury why you were out on the cow trail at eleven forty-five p.m. on September 27, 1962."

"I was taking Waffle Stomper home after we had been to Jake Oldman's sweat lodge."

"Do you and Waffle Stomper always go to the sweats together?"

"Yes, most always, but sometime we go alone."

"Why do you go together?" Prosecutor Darrell Bear prodded.

"Because Waffle Stomper's car was repossessed."

"When was his car repossessed?"

"I think it was about twenty years ago."

"Have you been driving him around since then?"

"Yes, sir, I have."

"The prosecution has no further questions. The prosecution reserves the right to recall this witness. Your witness."

Shram Bear stood and moved like a military tank to be closer to the witness.

"Now, tell me, Mr. Big Boots, you live five miles east of Ft. Washakie, and Waffle Stomper lives eighteen miles west of Ft. Washakie. So altogether you drive twenty-three miles to be with your friend?"

"Yes, sir."

"Do you drive twenty-three miles every day, Mr. Big Boots?"

"Yes, most every day except for winter when snow blizzards keep the truck from reaching Waffle's house."

"That seems like a very impractical arrangement. Why over these fifty years don't you share a living space?"

"All men have the same needs—each has thirst, hunger,

and a desire for land. Man is but his land, and our land is our connection to our ancestors. Waffle Stomper and I have different ancestors."

"You have different ancestors, and you both want to stay at your own houses? Please explain what you mean, Big Boots."

"Our ancestors give us guidance, and it is much more than ancestor worship. We feel closer to receive their guidance, their blessings, and their protection when we are in our own houses, and on our own land."

"I have no more questions, Mr. Big Boots. You may be excused."

The gambling gang that collected bets out in the cold morning changed the "Prosecution to Win" sign, giving 2 to 1 odds that favored a win for the prosecution after Big Boots testified.

"The prosecution calls Jake Oldman to the stand." Jake, a solidly built man in his midfifties, walked with perfect body alignment and was sworn in by Bailiff Monroe.

"Mr. Oldman, did you hold a sweat on September 27, and were Mr. Big Boots and Mr. Waffle Stomper in attendance?"

"Yes, I did, and both men were there."

"The prosecution has no more questions. Your witness."

"The defense has no questions. You may be excused, Mr. Oldman."

"The prosecution calls Turtle Blackburn to the stand." Turtle Blackburn was a small boy who looked malnourished and unkempt. He slouched to the stand, visibly trembled, and was sworn in.

Prosecutor Darrell Bear smiled at him and tried to dissolve his fear. "Please state your name and tell the court how old you are."

"My name is Turtle Blackburn. I am twelve."

"How do you know the defendants?" Prosecutor Bear prodded.

"I only know Weasel White Horse."

"Tell the court how you know Weasel." Darrell Bear resumed questioning Turtle from his seat at the prosecutor's table to be less intimidating for this witness.

"Weasel and I share a locker for gym class."

"Tell me, Turtle, have you ever heard Weasel talk in the locker room about queers?"

"Oh yeah, we talk a lot about queers."

"Really? Did Weasel ever mention anyone that he thought was queer?"

"Oh yeah, he said that Waffle Stomper was queer and he and his friends were going to beat the shit out of him and make him be a real man."

Prosecutor Darrell Bear stood up, smiled at the witness, and said, "Thank you. Your witness."

Shram Bear stood, walked closer to the witness, leaned on the railing around the stand, and talked to the boy in a conversational tone. "Tell me, Turtle, what do you know about queers?"

Turtle shrugged his shoulders and replied, "I know that I don't want to be one."

"Why not?"

"Because it's not cool. If you are queer, you are girly pink."

"How do *you* keep from being girlish?"

"In the locker room, we are careful to walk tough, smell our armpits, adjust our nuts, check our fly, that kind of stuff, so we show that we are men and not fairies."

Counselor Bear smiled and nodded. "I got it. Do you know anyone who is a fairy?"

"Yeah, the dentist at the BIA Health Clinic. We call him the tooth fairy."

"Objection!" The prosecutor shouted over the roar of laughter from the jury and the packed seating area.

Judge Eagle Feather rapped his gavel. "What is the reason for this line of questioning, Counselor Bear?"

"To establish innocence about the topic."

"That's clearly been established. Let's move on," Judge Eagle Feather instructed over the continued chuckling of the crowd.

"The defense has no further questions." Shram Bear took his seat at the defense table.

"The prosecution calls Weasel White Horse."

Weasel Whitehorse, the youngest of the defendants, was a skinny, small-framed boy with hair in a crewcut. He was well groomed wearing the black BIA jumpsuit, but his body language revealed discomfort, and he walked like a beaten dog with his tail tucked between his legs. His name was well-suited as he weaseled toward the witness stand.

"Please state your name and age."

"My name is Weasel Whitehorse, and I turned thirteen on September 27." The witness's voice cracked like a squawking parrot, and the boy flushed and winced in obvious embarrassment.

"Mr. Whitehorse, what were you doing the night of September 27?"

"Sir, I was out celebrating my birthday with my friends."

"Please explain to the court what you mean by 'out celebrating.'"

"My friends each brought bottles of booze, and we drove around drinking."

"Drove around to where?"

"Nowhere in particular. We cruised to some of the cute girls' houses to talk to them, but only Connie Oldman came out to talk to us, and she wouldn't go drink with us, so we kept cruisin'."

"What time was that?"

"I don't remember."

"How much did you have to drink?"

"I brought three bottles of Muscatel," he boasted.

"Did you drink them all, or did you share?"

"There was no need to share, man. Everyone had their own."

"Where did you get the Muscatel?"

"From the bottom of my mom's closet. She has emergency cases stacked and wouldn't notice if three bottles were missing."

"Would she care if you took them?"

"Probably not, as long as she had some left for herself."

"Why did you go to Waffle Stomper's house?"

"It was just something to do."

"Were you the man that told your friends that Waffle Stomper was queer?"

"Yeah, Fox was hep about hearing that. He wanted to go beat the shit out of him to get him straight."

"What do you mean by 'getting him straight'?"

"That he would learn to be a man."

"Do you think that a seventy-year-old man getting a beating from a thirteen-year-old would teach that lesson?"

Weasel Whitehorse shrugged his shoulders.

"Answer the question, Mr. Whitehorse," the judge demanded.

"I don't like queers," he resentfully snarled.

The trial produced a casino atmosphere outside. The cluster of women and men that supported the prosecution placed their bets as the crowd swelled. The bet broker in his black-and-red plaid wool hunter's cap with a black bill and red earflaps was mobbed by outstretched fists holding cash. These gamblers scurried back inside the tribal court building to observe the proceedings after they raised their bets.

Darrell Bear walked back to the prosecutor's table, shaking his head, and sat down.

Judge Eagle Feather looked up from his notes. "Does the defense have questions for this witness?"

"Yes, Your Honor." Shram Bear pushed his chair back and slowly adjusted his black glasses as he moved closer to the witness.

"Weasel, where were your parents and sisters on the night of your birthday?"

"My sisters were out with their boyfriends, and Mom was at the casino."

"How did your family celebrate your birthday?"

"I just told you that they were gone."

"What about your dad?"

"My dad is in Rawlins since I was a year old."

"Do you mean that your father is in Rawlins Wyoming State Penitentiary?"

"Yes, I wrote to him once, and he told me not to bother because he doesn't think I am his son."

"Do you want to be his son?"

"Naw, I don't care. I never see him anyway. I just don't want to be a sissy or become sissified."

"Is that why you beat Waffle Stomper with the tire iron because you thought he was sissified?"

"Yep, and I proved to my friends that I am not sissified."

"No further questions." Shram Bear returned to his seat.

"The prosecution calls Fox Goodman to the stand."

Fox Goodman strutted past the jury box in bold, elongated steps, but he took care to establish eye contact with several of the jury members as he passed. He flashed a winning smile to them as he took his place on the witness stand. It was obvious that this witness had followed Counselor Shram Bear's directions to exhibit friendliness and straight-forwardness. Fox applied the instructions to his physical good-looking appearance and to his charming persona. Fox exhibited school popularity as he recognized several of his friends in the audience. He gave them the two-finger cowboy salute. The defense attorney grimaced as he saw that his witness's instructions were extended to include the court audience and that Fox's body language would be viewed as arrogant.

"It would please the court if you would state your age and name," the prosecutor requested.

"I am fifteen years old, and my name is Fox Goodman."

"And are you a good man?" The question threw Fox a curve ball and took him off his game.

The defense attorney thought, *Thank you, brother, for knocking this kid down a peg.*

Fox answered in a bewildered, small voice, "I … I … uh … I am the son of Irene and Robert Goodman."

"Yes, I know that, but my question was are you a good man? Are you an honorable man?"

The question clearly flustered Fox, and he ran his hands through his perfectly coiffed Fabian haircut, leaving it in an uncool bed-head look. "I am an honor student, I go to mass, and I am not in trouble at home or with teachers."

"I think that you were recently invited onto the Eagles basketball team. Is that correct?"

"Yes, I was on the second string, but all the suicides left available positions on the team, and I was moved up to play with the main Eagles team."

"On September 27 were you in the car celebrating Weasel's birthday?"

"Yes, sir, I was."

"Where were you positioned in the car?"

"I rode in the front in the passenger's seat."

"Please explain to the jury where the others rode in the car."

"Wyman Large was driving. I rode shotgun, Weasel Whitehorse rode in the back seat behind me, and Gary Frasier rode in the back seat behind the driver."

"How much did you have to drink by the time you were at Waffle Stomper's cow trail?"

"I don't know about the others, but Weasel and I were at the bottom of our bottles."

"Did you and Weasel share his three bottles of Muscatel?"

"Naw, I had my own bottle of Jim Beam."

"Wow, that's impressive. Jim Beam is expensive whisky. Where did you get that?"

"From Marvin's liquor store in Riverton."

"Where did you get the money to buy that?"

"I didn't buy it, man! I liberated it from its confinement on the shelf. I set it free." The court audience and the jury snickered.

"Are you telling the jury that by the time you were sitting on the cow trail with two flat tires you had finished the entire bottle of Jim Beam?"

"No, at that time I had about one finger left in my bottle, and I know that Weasel was down to his last bottle. He only had about one finger left of the wine, too, because we measured."

"Did you do the first strike on Waffle Stomper?"

"No, Weasel discovered that the queer we went out to get was right there changing our tires, and he jumped out of the car and hit him with the tire iron."

"So you are telling the jury that you were on the cow path because you were going to beat up Waffle Stomper?"

"I grabbed the tire iron from Weasel and whaled on Waffle Stomper because I didn't want any queer near me. I was protecting myself and my friends from queers."

"No further questions. Your witness."

Counselor Shram Bear slowly and deliberately walked to the witness box. "Fox Goodman, are you an only child?"

"I am an only child in my grandma Goodman's eyes, but I have three sisters and a baby brother who stay with my aunt Kathleen Tall Tree."

"You told the prosecutor that you were an honor student. How many hours a day do you study?"

"Me? I never study!"

"On the night of September 27, where were your parents?"

"They were home and told me to be home by eleven p.m."

"You were not home by eleven p.m. What time did you get home?"

"I looked at the clock on the kitchen stove, and it said three-thirty a.m."

"Were your parents waiting up for you?"

"Naw, they were asleep. They had gotten home from a Casper square-dance jubilee—I was careful not to wake them."

"No further questions. The defense reserves the right to recall this witness."

Outside the courtyard, casino was in play, but the betting fervor was less active. Only a few straggler bettors approached the "Place your bets for the defense" sign, and inside witnesses continued their testimony.

"The prosecution calls Sister Margaret Thompson."

The oldest nun at the Indian Mission, Sister Margaret knew everyone in both Indian nations. Counselor Shram jumped from his seat to help her up the stairs, but she shooed him away as if swatting a fly. She demurely sat down.

"Sister Margaret, please tell the jury how you know Big Boots and Waffle Stomper."

"Oh my goodness, I have known them most of their lives. Big Boots was five when he was enrolled at the mission, and Waffle Stomper was seven."

"As a character witness, how would you describe these two men?"

"Waffle Stomper and Big Boots are men that God has made in his own image. They have spent their lives helping each other and helping everyone else besides. They have no desire for material wealth but work diligently to protect their Shoshoni culture. They have built over twenty-three homes for members of both tribes. They deliver groceries to people who can't drive, and they do errands for anyone who needs help. They rescued a newborn abandoned baby in the wilderness and serve as the child's godfathers."

Drowsy Wren became alert when she heard those words.

"Waffle Stomper gave his beautiful voice to cantor for mass," Sister Margaret continued. "He served as emcee for forty years for rez events. He sang for weddings, funerals, giveaways, fundraisers, and powwows. These two are stewards of God's planet, his helpers to humankind and especially to the Native Americans."

"Thank you, Sister Margaret. No further questions." The seated people who observed the trial stirred, and several men rushed outside to the gambling area where a sign read, "Place your bets for the prosecution." After Sister Margaret's testimony, the sign changed to "Prosecution gives 2 to 1 odds. Place your bets now." The men standing at the opposite end of the courthouse building huddled together and wore dour looks on their faces. One man lowered his sign that read "Vote for the defense here." The wagers hustled back inside to the in-session trial.

Judge Eagle Feather asked the defense, "Do you wish to cross-examine?"

"The defense has no questions."

"Thank you, Sister Margaret, you may be excused. Do you need any help with the steps?" asked Judge Eagle Feather.

"Don't be silly—of course I don't!"

"Okay then! Call your next witness, Prosecutor Bear."

"The prosecution calls Gary Frazier."

Gary Frazier walked confidently and made friendly eye contact with specific people in the jury box. He smiled and nodded in the judge's direction as the defense attorney had coached. This fifteen-year-old's demeanor reflected humility and compliance, but his thoughts were projected as discomfort at being in this disgraceful situation.

The prosecutor stood, and the sound of the scraping chair was like the abrasiveness of the trial that scraped on Gary's nerves.

"Mr. Frazier, please explain to the court how you know the other defendants."

"I have known them all my life. Fox is in my same class at school, Weasel and Wyman were in my confirmation classes, and I have known them all since I was in preschool at the Indian Mission."

"Do you consider them to be your friends?"

"Yes, they are the *only* friends that I have."

"Were you riding in the back seat on the driver's side of the car on the night of September 27?"

"Yes."

"How much had you had to drink?"

"I brought a bottle of Mad Dog 20 wine, and I finished about a third of it."

"Were you drunk?"

"I do not think so. I had a little buzz on, but I don't think that I was drunk."

"Why were you at Waffle Stomper's house?"

"I don't know. We were just cruisin' around, and that was where Wyman ended up."

"Why did you attack Big Boots?"

"I did not attack him. I held him. I thought that I had to help my friends. When Weasel and Fox jumped out to clobber Waffle Stomper, Big Boots was on my side of the car, and I knew he would go around to the passenger's side of the car and jump the guys, so I helped Wyman hold Big Boots."

"Did you know about the plan to beat Waffle Stomper because he was queer, and was that the reason that your friends were out there?"

"No, Fox had just said come go cruisin' with us on Friday to celebrate Weasel's birthday."

"No further questions. Your witness, Counselor Shram Bear."

The defense attorney moved to the witness box with the prowl of a grizzly bear protecting its cub.

"Mr. Frazier, do you make it a habit to drink to celebrate someone's birthday?"

"No, sir, I don't get invited to drinking celebrations or to anything."

"Why don't you get invited?"

"I am busy with church work."

"So where did you get the Mad Dog 20 wine?"

"I found it in the rectory at the Indian Mission Chapel. I think it's the wine they use for the Eucharist, and I had been invited to bring a bottle to drink to go cruisin', so that is what I brought."

"Are you saying that you swiped the bottle of wine from the church?"

"No, sir, I am not. I left an IOU note it its place and signed my name explaining that I would replace the bottle on payday."

"Gary, what is your intent when you graduate?"

"I have been working with Father Patty to enter the seminary."

The betting hawkers' voices from outdoors wafted into the courtroom as three older women wrapped in gray Pendleton wool blankets placed their bets with the defense broker that held the pink poster board pegged to a stick. These ladies completed their wager and entered the courtroom. The seated spectators scooted over to make room for them to sit, and then their attention was given to the speaking defense.

"No further questions." Gary Frazier left with the bailiff, and Shram Bear resumed his seat at the defense table.

Darrell Bear stood beside his table and announced, "The prosecution calls Wyman Large to the witness stand."

The bailiff approached the defense table, bent over, and whispered into Counselor Shram Bear's ear. Shram looked up at the judge with *emergency* blazing from his eyes.

"Your Honor, the defense requests a ten-minute recess."

The judge tapped his gavel and then said, "Granted. I think we all can use a lunch break. It's almost two p.m. We will recess until three-thirty p.m."

Chapter 13

TRADITION VERSUS YOUTH REACTIVATED

"**M**an, I'm tired of sitting here," ten-year-old Judy Bear said as she rubbed her plump backside. "Come on, Wren. Let's go to Mom's van and see what Sister Samantha packed for us to eat in the laundry basket."

"I am so hungry, I hope it's a great big peanut-butter-and-jelly sandwich. Sister Samantha, can I bring sandwiches to the godfathers?"

"Wren, they don't allow food or drink inside the courtroom, but why don't you invite them to join us at katybear's van?"

Wren bounced her way through the crowd like a little Ping-Pong ball to reach her godfathers. She threw her arms around Waffle Stomper and announced her lunch invitation to the men.

"Wren, we are going to meet with Darrell Bear now."

"I bet that his mom would give him a peanut butter and jelly too."

Godfather Big Boots smiled. "Thanks, Wren. I bet she

would, but we are going to the casino for lunch. You go and enjoy your peanut butter and jelly."

Wren scampered away like a squirrel on a phone wire.

The bailiff and Shram Bear looked like speed-walkers as they took long strides to Judge Eagle Feather's chamber door. The bailiff tapped lightly, but Shram Bear didn't wait for the judge to respond and assertively entered his chambers.

"Judge Eagle Feather, I am sorry to disturb your lunch, but defendant Wyman Large—the fourteen-year-old—attempted suicide in his cell."

"Oh my God, we don't want another suicide epidemic. What is his condition?"

The bailiff stepped into the office and closed the door. "Wyman hanged himself with his jumpsuit. He was groomed and waiting to be called by the prosecution when I checked on him. I told him he would testify about three p.m. When we took the prisoners their lunch, we found him. He had taken off the jumpsuit and was wearing only his undershorts. He was hanging above his cot, which he had jumped from. We must have found him within minutes—he was still breathing when we took him down. His neck was not broken, but he was gasping for air. A deputy gave CPR, and I ran to the outpatient clinic next door. A doctor and two nurses took him into the clinic on a gurney and stabilized him. He is there now."

Judge Eagle Feather abruptly left his chambers and marched back into the courtroom. He rapped his gavel at 2:15 p.m. and announced to the reassembled courtroom, "The trial of Tradition versus Youth will be postponed until further notice. I would like to have the prosecution and the defense meet in my chambers immediately. Jury, please remain in the jury box for a few minutes. Bailiff Monroe, please clear the courtroom. Court adjourned." The judge tapped his gavel.

Prosecutor Darrell Bear looked surprised while he remained seated with his clients. "Big Boots and Waffle Stomper, you may wait here until I return. Excuse me."

After the judge explained the situation to the prosecution, he gave decisive and clear instructions. "Prosecution Darrell Bear and Defense Shram Bear, it is important for the jury not to know what has happened. It may evoke unfair sympathy toward the defendants. The other defendants are in separate cells, and this tragedy can remain unknown to them. I will go to the clinic and impress upon the medical staff the importance of their silence so we won't need to declare a mistrial, and I will get a report on Wyman's condition. You attorneys will need to speak to the jury. We will need to resume the trial as soon as Wyman Large is able. Big Boots and Waffle Stomper should not be told what has happened either. Let's all follow tight procedures for the sake of justice for everyone." The two trial lawyers closed the chamber doors and plotted their course of action as they walked back to the courtroom.

"Let's help Big Boots get Waffle Stomper into his truck, and then we can talk to the jury," Darrell Bear told his brother.

"The hard part will be to keep this information from Mom." Shram grinned at his brother.

"Yup, that will be the hardest task of all." The brother counselors sent the two old friends to lunch by themselves at the casino and then briskly returned to the courtroom to address the jury.

"Ladies and gentlemen of the jury, we know that you must have a thousand question to ask, but please don't. We will not accept *any* questions," Shram instructed once the murmuring twelve had quieted.

"Do not talk to each other about this trial or try to speculate about the delay. Give your location to Bailiff Monroe as to where we might find you. It may be tomorrow or it might be next week, but you must stay available. Do not leave the reservation, and try to avoid each other socially," Darrel Bear directed. The jury filed out in silence with wide eyes, seeking the bailiff.

"We need to caution the security staff about not talking about this."

"Ha! How long do you think this can be kept quiet?" Shram smirked.

"Maybe five minutes! You know the drumbeat has already begun to sing with plenty of rubbering going on. The trial delay *and* the reason for it will spread like butter on hot fry bread."

Darrell and Shram saw their mother as she approached the courthouse doors.

"Quick, quick, lock the front door and don't let anyone inside," he urgently prompted the security guard, who followed his instructions.

"But ... uh ... it is your mother," he stammered.

"We know!" replied Darrell and Shram in simultaneous attorney voices.

"Sister Samantha, while you and the girls finish the hot fry bread and butter, I am going to ask my sons what is going on." Katybear buttoned up her coat, opened the door, and slipped out of the van. She stood outside the closed doors, and the security guards turned their back as she peered into the fogged-over windows. She was aware of her breath vapor in the cold afternoon air when the guards refused to acknowledge her, so she returned to the van and drove Sister Samantha and Wren to Incaranata Hall.

Judge Eagle Feather visited the fourteen-year-old defendant

Wyman Large every day to monitor his recovery. He was also in contact with the BIA Indian Health Services and discussed with the psychologist whether Wyman was mentally strong enough to stand trial. After three days of bed rest and therapy, the doctors and the judge declared that the trial could resume. Ft. Washakie and the justice building returned to its former state with randomly parked cars and blanketed, huddled Natives waiting for the trial to resume. Katybear drove her van to the reserved parking space and noticed there was a third gambling sign on the court grounds. The new sign read, "Make your guess! Why the trial delay?" Surprisingly, there was a crowd beside the new sign. There was a thick crowd around the prosecution and a sparse cluster near the defense pole. Katybear chuckled at the sight. She knew that her son Shram had not begun to make his defense case, but that too would change like the seasons.

The Wind River Mountain Range was beginning to winterize itself. By mid-October the distant gray granite had turned snow-covered white, and the flurries had come down to the valley floor. By the end of the month, this whiteness would remain until spring. The twenty-degree morning was wrapped in yellow-gold cellophane and trimmed with diamond-sparkling brightness as the sun reflected on ice. The weather was never a deterrent for the leather-skinned humans drawn together by an event, and today the trial was that event.

The attorney brothers had vetted, probed, dismissed, and replaced two members of the jury who had heard about Wyman Large's attempted suicide, but on the whole, the jury remained intact and was ready to serve. Judge Eagle Feather presided.

"Is the prosecution ready to call your first witness?"

"Yes, Your Honor. The prosecution calls Wyman Large."

Wyman Large had a sturdy, strong gait as he took his place in the witness box. No one would have guessed that he had attempted suicide. He appeared to be in good health, as one would expect of a distance runner. His five-foot-four-inch body was sinewy and strong, but he kept his gaze on his moccasins, not looking at anyone.

"Wyman, were you the driver of the black four-door Ford on the night of September 27?"

"Yes, you know that I was."

"Are you old enough to drive?"

"I don't have a driver's license, if that's what you mean, but I've been driving since I was eleven."

"Whose car were you driving on the night of September 27?"

"It belonged to my aunt. She got home from her job, and I took her car."

"Did she give you permission to use her car?"

"No. She took a nap, and I took the car."

"Are you saying that you stole her car?"

Wyman sat in silence.

Judge Eagle Feather's strong voice boomed. "Answer the question, Mr. Large."

"Yes! I stole my aunt's car."

"Tell me, Mr. Large, were you soused when you were stalled in the rut?"

"Yeah, I drank four cans of Budweiser."

"Where did you get the beer?"

"From my aunt's refrigerator."

"The prosecution has no more questions. Your witness, defense."

Wyman seemed to relax as he saw defense attorney Shram Bear ambling toward the jury box.

"Wyman Large, what was your reason for taking your aunt's car?"

"Fox Goodman asked me to go crusin' with him and some friends, and he asked me if I could get a car."

"You stole a car because Fox asked you to?"

"Well, not exactly like that. I knew that I could take my aunt's car, and it was cool that Fox asked me to go crusin'."

"Mr. Large, tell the jury why you were at your aunt's house."

"Because that's where I stayed that night."

"Why didn't you stay at your own house?"

"Because Mom and Dad were on a bender. When they get drunk they don't know what they do."

"How long has it been since you were at home?"

It took Wyman several minutes to count on his fingers before he replied. "It has been about four months," he answered hesitantly.

"Why did you leave?"

"Because my dad shot my mother in the stomach."

"When she got out of the hospital, did she go back home?"

"Yep. They both drink until they conk out, or sometimes if my dad doesn't conk out, he shoots up the house with his rifle. He doesn't like me, and I try to keep out of his way."

"That is all the questions that I have. You can be excused, Wyman." Bailiff Monroe escorted Wyman out of the courtroom.

"Prosecutor, you may call your next witness."

The prosecution called Dr. John Fernau to the witness stand. Dr. John Fernau held his head erect, and his posture portrayed fifty-four years of professionalism. He gave a slight nod of recognition to Waffle Stomper and Big Boots as he lowered his medium-sized frame into the curve of the wooden witness chair.

"Dr. Fernau, were you the attending physician on the night of September 27, when Waffle Stomper was admitted to Riverton Memorial Hospital?"

"Yes, I was."

"Please tell the court what Waffle Stomper's condition was when he was admitted to the ER."

"Mr. Stomper was covered in his own blood, and he was barely alive. He was unconscious and unresponsive. The staff worked on him for over five hours before he was moved into ICU."

"When you say that he was barely alive, can you please describe his condition in more detail?"

"The patient had bruises on 80 percent of his body and required five units of blood transfusion immediately. He had throat lacerations that required one hundred and thirty-three sutures to stop the bleeding. He had bruised organs and a ruptured spleen that required removal through emergency surgery. He had five broken ribs, but luckily none had impaled his lungs. The most life endangering injury was to his head. Mr. Stomper suffered from a brain hematoma that left him unconscious for ten days in ICU. It remains unknown how much damage there might be to the brain. Today the damage affects his speech and motor skills. The prognoses are that the brain may heal, and these brain functions may return, but at this time it remains unknown."

"Thank you, Dr. Fernau. That is all the questions from the prosecution."

"Does the defense wish to cross-examine this witness?" asked Judge Eagle Feather.

"Yes, thank you." Shram Bear adjusted his black-rimmed glasses and strolled nearer to the witness box.

"Dr. Fernau, you gave a vivid picture of your patient, Mr. Stomper, upon admission, but could you give us the result of the lab report drawn on your patient?"

"Yes, but I will need to find it. I brought the patient's file with me, and I have it in my briefcase. It will take me a minute to find it."

It was obvious that this question was not anticipated by either the witness or the prosecution. Darrell gave his brother an annoyed glance as the doctor fumbled through his files.

"Here it is! Riverton Memorial Hospital, Laboratory Report, September 30, 1962. Doctor John Fernau: A microalbumin creatinine test was ordered along with a lipid panel. Other tests included alt, urine, and blood tests. Everything was within the normal range, but an unknown virus was detected. This virus was sent to a larger laboratory in Salt Lake City, but the sample was returned as unknown. The lab reported that the virus could be a form of meningitis or perhaps associated with mononucleosis, but the findings were inconclusive."

"Dr. Fernau, what does that report tell us in layman's terms?"

"It explains that there was a virus present, but neither the Salt Lake lab nor our local lab could identify what the virus was."

"Is the unknown virus contagious?" Shram asked in a bewildered tone.

"I have been practicing medicine for over thirty years, and I have not seen anything like it. Mononucleosis is known as the kissing disease, so it is possible that it may be contagious on contact, but any guess is a bad guess without knowledge, and I just don't have the answers."

"One last question, Doctor. Could this virus be the result from the beating, or was it a preexisting virus?"

"It could be that the virus is called a latent-period virus, which means that the virus may not cause recognizable symptoms for a long period after the initial exposure, but many knowledgeable researchers don't have the answer, and neither do I."

"Thank you, Dr. Fernau. The defense has no more questions."

"Call your next witness, prosecutor," Judge Eagle Feather urged.

"The prosecution has no more witnesses, Your Honor."

"Very well. Is the defense ready to present witnesses?"

"Yes, sir. The defense calls Mother Superior."

"Good morning, Mother Superior. Are you well acquainted with the four young defendants?" attorney Shram Bear said.

"I am well acquainted with everyone involved with this trial."

"We know that's correct! Tell the jury what you know about Weasel Whitehorse."

"Weasel Whitehorse is a good boy. He is compliant and does what he is asked to do, but he is immature for a seventh grader. He is in the stages of discovery about himself. He lives in a household of women, and he is insecure about his manhood."

"What do you mean, Mother Superior, when you say that Weasel is in the stages of discovery?"

"Weasel is searching for his identity. He is bouncing about trying to discover what a man should do, what he should think, speak, and act like. He needs to bond with a male role model, and he is searching for a male friend that he can imitate. He doesn't accept himself as he is. He is small compared to the other seventh graders, and he is fearful that he doesn't look like a man. Most of all, Weasel needs male acceptance."

"Thank you, Mother Superior. Please tell us about Fox Goodman."

"Fox Goodman is a charmer. He is popular at school, and he has friends because he is a good-looking fifteen-year-old and well developed for his age. He has learned how to use his physical appearance to his advantage. The disappointing thing about Fox is he doesn't really grasp who he is either or what important qualities he possesses. He is a very gifted student, and he has an exceptionally high aptitude for mathematics. Fox also has a beautiful singing voice, and he sounds similar to his father, Robert Goodman. Fox also has a sense of humor that makes his friends laugh, but Fox has learned that his physical appearance can get him everything that he wants. He doesn't need to exert himself, and it has taught him how to manipulate others to do his bidding. Fox Goodman needs direction, and he needs to be challenged."

"What is the role of Fox's parents?"

"I don't know his parents very well because they travel a lot. His dad is a nationally known square dance caller, and his parents leave Fox to stay with his disabled grandmother, who lives with them. Fox is the apple of her eye, and to her he can do no wrong."

Counselor Shram Bear moseyed to the small table beside the bailiff that held a pitcher of water and poured a glass. He returned to the witness box and presented Mother Superior with the liquid.

"Oh, thank you, Shram, for your thoughtfulness."

"Mother Superior, please tell the court about Gary Frasier."

"Gary Frasier is the apple of *my* eye. Gary was three years old when he first came to the mission preschool, and all the nuns from Incaranata Hall proclaimed that this was a child made in God's image. At an early age, he exemplified signs that he was interested in learning more of Christ's teaching. Once, after he had heard a Bible story he asked, 'What makes Jesus so good?' On another occasion, one of his classmates brought an orphaned kitten to school, and the class discussed what name to give it. Gary spoke up in a determined voice and said, 'He should be named *God* because that is the nicest name that I know.' That is how our fifteen-year-old cat God got his name." Mother Superior smiled and lowered her steel-blue eyes. "All through school Gary has been interested in philosophy, theology, and the lives of the saints. Gary loves to help out in the rectory, chapel, and Incaranata Hall. When there aren't errands or chores that he can do, he spends hours in the music hall practicing to be a cantor. He also volunteers at the health clinic. Gary has a great attitude, and he is a happy kid."

The defense attorney asked in earnest, "How is it possible that he is on trial for such a violent crime?"

Mother Superior's body slumped in the chair, and she answered with sadness, "Gary has been without close friends throughout school. He is fifteen years old now, and when the most popular kid in his class invited him to a birthday party he probably was flattered and thought that it was his chance to be included."

"Mother Superior, how well do you know Wyman Large?"

"I feel that I know all my students as individuals. I have known them since they were in preschool, and I have seen them grow into who they have become at this stage of their development. In some cases I feel that I know them better than their parents do.

"Wyman is the most vulnerable of our St. Stephen's students. Wyman Large is an average student, but he does excel in track. He received a bronze metal as a distance runner at the state track tournament in Cheyenne last year. His ability to run is his only mark of visibility. Wyman is a boy that no adult really wants, and he knows it. He doesn't have security, a stable home, or guidance of any kind. At age fourteen he has become a drifter. He stays with friends, relatives, or wherever whenever he can. His aunts and uncles keep four of his younger siblings, and he mostly rotates among them. He has even spent a couple of cold nights sleeping in the chapel. Being fourteen comes with its own problems. He is surly, defensive, unfriendly, ungrateful, and dislikes adults in general. Father Patty has tried to motivate Wyman toward church activities, but he hasn't shown any interest. His goal is survival. He looks for a place to stay most nights, and Incaranata Hall gives him food when he comes around. The nuns give him shoes, coats, and clothes from the Charity Thrift Shop when it appears that he needs them, but he expresses no gratitude. Wyman can run, and he does plenty of that every day just to stay warm. He runs without a destination."

"Thank you, Mother Superior, for giving the jury a knowledgeable and heartfelt assessment of these defendants." Shram wondered whether Mother Superior knew about Wyman's suicide attempt or if she truly knew her students so well as to give such an accurate account of their characters. "Your witness, Brother Darrell Bear."

"Thank you, *Attorney* Shram Bear. Mother Superior, how can you look at these two men before you at the prosecution table and not see a badly battered man? He can no longer walk or speak, and yet you tell the jury that these four defendants are good boys."

Mother Superior's face clouded over, and her eyes filled with tears that ran down onto her white wimple. "Darrell Bear, my heart and love go out to the plaintiffs Waffle Stomper and Big Boots. I love these two men as if they were my own sons. This trial is the symbol of tragedy that plagues our reservation life. The plaintiffs, the defendants, and our entire Indian Nation are products of our environment. We are living the tragedy of our lives that are symbolically portrayed in this trial today. Both the victims and the perpetrators are blameless and faultless. Everyone involved collided at the wrong place and the wrong time, resulting in heartbreak and physical pain." Mother Superior voice's was strong with conviction as she wiped away her tears.

"Thank you, Mother Superior. The prosecution has no more

questions of this witness." Prosecutor Darrell Bear nonchalantly strode past the defense table and whispered to Shram, "Way to go, brother. Mother Superior outranked Sister Margaret! Nice work to have your witness make closing arguments for you." He winked.

There was a sound of shuffling and scurry in the courtroom as several men rushed outside to the betting areas. Men scrambled to change the betting signs, giving odds in favor of the defense after Mother Superior's testimony. The casino atmosphere outside replicated the inner courtroom drama.

"The defense has no questions for this witness."

"You may be excused, Mother Superior," Judge Eagle Feather said softly. "The defense may call its next witness."

"The defense calls Stephen Moss."

A portly Arapaho man in his forties trudged to the witness box and was sworn in by the bailiff.

"Good afternoon, Mr. Moss. Please tell the jury your occupation."

"I have been the guidance counselor at the Indian Mission for the past five years."

"Do you have knowledge of the defendants' parental involvement with their school activities?"

"Yes and no." He gestured with a wavering hand. "During the five years that I have been at the mission, I have met on two occasions with Fox Goodman's parents during his basketball games, and I know Gary Frazier's parents quite well. They are involved in his parent/teacher conferences, school events, and church activities. The other defendants' parents I have never met."

"Is there a correlation between a student's academic behavior and the participation of parents?"

"Most definitely! Students with caring parents perform

much better. I am amazed how our students function at all without parental assistance. It is a major effort for them to get to school in the winter or to even have food or a place to sleep, but yet they go to their classes."

"Thank you, Mr. Moss. The defense has no more questions, and the defense has no more witnesses."

"The prosecution has no questions for this witness."

"Very well, counselors. Tomorrow at ten a.m. we will hear closing remarks, and the jury will then deliberate. Court adjourned." The jury and the spectators dispersed, and the attorney brothers helped the plaintiffs into the old faded-green Ford truck.

"Darrell, I am going to invite Mom and Judy to go for ice cream and to play the cloud game. Do you want to come?"

"Brother Shram, the answer is a resounding yes, and I know your intentions. I can read your defense like a telegram!"

Shram chuckled as the attorneys left the courtroom.

Chapter 14

PREDICTIONS

"I find this to be a humorous situation! We both have worked hard to graduate from law school, we are well grounded in Plato, Aristotle, and Quintilian philosophy, reason, and logic, and yet we are racing off to seek council from our ten-year-old sister. Now how funny is that?"

"Yeah, that's pretty funny all right," Shram agreed as he put the car into park and darted into the casino to pick up four ice cream cones. The two attorneys parked in front of their Arapaho family home as ice cream dripped between Darrell's fingers.

"Hey, Judy, come outside. We have ice cream cones," coaxed Darrell.

Katy, wrapped in a blanket, opened the storm door and came out to sit on the steps. Katy gave her sons a knowing look out of the corner of her eye. "You are bringing gifts to your little sister, I see. You know that Judy knew about Owl's death, the suicide epidemic, and the godfathers' tragedy before any of those things happened? You will treat her with reverence and respect if it is your intention to play the cloud game."

"Come on, Mom, cut us some slack. Our intentions are honorable," Darrell demurred.

"Oh, neato kabeto! Rocky road ice cream is my favorite," Judy said as she slammed the storm door, pulled her coat closed, and plopped down to sit with her family on the steps. When they had finished their cones, Shram approached his intention with caution.

"Hey, Jude, do you want to play the cloud game? The clouds are beautiful this afternoon."

"I know, and Wren doesn't like to play the cloud game very much. I think it will be fun to play with you guys."

"Well, I really want to play. There are so many clouds." Shram became reflective and quiet, and he gazed upward.

"Judy, look there! That cloud looks like a puppy jumping up on someone."

"That is Waffle Stomper's dog, Rewind, and he is happy to be playing with him. Oh, look at that one—it looks like two men shaking hands because they both won something. Do you see that?" Judy clapped her hands in joy.

"Yes, I do see that." Darrell showed a knowing smile and agreed.

"What about that one? It looks like a pile of dolls," Shram stated.

"No, it's not dolls. It is dead men," Judy softly corrected.

"Is it from a war?" Shram probed.

"No, all those men died from germs."

Judy's answer alarmed Shram, and he related her answer to the trial when Dr. Fernau had explained about the lab report's mystery virus. Shram was fascinated and could not leave the topic without further inquiry. "Darrell and I are men. Will we die from germs?"

"No." Judy laughed. "The dead men will happen many, many, many years from now."

Shram looked at a grouping of cumulous clouds and remarked, "That cloud looks like a bunched of spilled marbles, but one of them is away by itself."

"They are not marbles. They are boys at the gymnasium, and that one by itself is Wren."

The Bear family remained silent without understanding, and Judy smiled and assured them. "That's a really good thing."

"Look at that dark rectangular cloud that looks like a box moving right over us." Darrell pointed to the cloud he was asking about. "Do you see the one?"

"Oh no, here it comes again!" Judy covered her eyes with her hands and rested her head on her knees. She spoke muffled words through her covered face. "That dark cloud is the reason that Wren won't play the cloud game with me."

"Why won't she play?" Katy was now drawn into the game.

"Because the dark cloud is a car that will make her sad."

"Will that cloud make us sad too?" Katy asked as she looked up at the dark shadow blocking the sun.

"Yes, you all will be very sad for a season, but look, the sun is shining through now."

"Can we chase off the dark car cloud?" Katy studied the disappearing cloud.

"No," was all that Judy said. The older brothers masked their concerns and bewilderment as they stood up to leave.

"Judy, thanks for letting us play. We have closing arguments to prepare for tomorrow's trial. Will we see you there?"

As Darrell and Shram made their way to their car, Katy answered their question. "No, Judy, I, and the other kids have school stuff to do, but I might place my bet tomorrow though!

Maybe I can get rich! Good luck to you both." She waved and
blew kisses to her sons.

————◆————◆

The sunlight bounced from the shining mountain and began
the second day of the trial. The courtroom was filled to capacity.

"All rise for the Honorable Judge Eagle Feather." The
bailiff's booming voice settled the din from the spectators on
this fifteen-degree, snow-covered morning of October 25, 1962.

"You may be seated." The bailiff addressed the storm-coat-
wearing, blanket-wrapped, and snow-booted-attired crowd.

The judge settled himself into the judge's bench and began
the proceedings. "We will start the morning with the trial
Tradition versus Youth by hearing the prosecution's closing
statements."

"Thank you, Your Honor." Prosecutor Darrell Bear walked
with determined clipped steps to present his oration directly
to the jury. He took a moment to establish eye contact as he
addressed each member with a greeting and thanked each by
name for serving.

"Ten days ago you agreed to listen to the evidence provided
by the prosecution to show the guilt of the defendants. One,
all four defendants have been charged with underage alcohol
possession and intoxication. The prosecution has unequivocally
proven that charge from the defendants own admissions. Two, all
four defendants have been charged with assault. The prosecution
has shown the jury proof that the four defendants assaulted Big
Boots and Waffle Stomper. The defendants have all admitted to
these charges in their testimonies. Three, there are two charges
of assault with a deadly weapon against Weasel Whitehorse
and Fox Goodman. The prosecution and the jury have heard
how both defendants admitted to Waffle Stomper's beating

with a tire iron, and they have unquestionably admitted their guilt to the crime. Four, there is a charge of car theft against Wyman Large who admitted his offense. Five, Fox Goodman and Weasel Whitehorse were indicted on the charge of intention to do bodily harm. Both defendants admitted their intentions were to, as Weasel said, 'make Waffle Stomper into a real man.' These were the words of a thirteen-year-old stating what he thought the image of a real man should be. The testimony from Turtle Blackburn described the physical habits of what a real man should do—adjust your nuts, smell your armpits, and walk tough. These were the requirements of manhood for which Waffle Stomper received the lesson that has possibly disabled him for life. The prosecution has proven without a doubt the guilt of these four youth in the trial of Tradition vs. Youth.

"The prosecution requests payment for Waffle Stomper's initial hospital bill of $4,389 plus any additional cost that he may incur for rehabilitation. The plaintiffs Big Boots and Waffle Stomper have requested first and foremost that you will grant them *justice*. Their plea is not for extravagant monetary gains. They both have stated ultraconservative repayment for actual financial outlays that they will incur. Big Boots asks only for the replacement of his two undamaged spare tires. Mr. Big Boots does not ask for the loss of the mobility of his friend of over sixty years. He does not ask for compensation to replace his full-time companion, his hunting buddy, his fishing partner, his house-builder-business co-owner, his duo in the joy of song and drumming, his philanthropic teammate, his cultural preservation protégé, his only family member, his brother. He does not seek restitution for any of these losses. Instead he asks for a meager pittance. He asks for the replacement of his spare tires. Why does Big Boots only ask for spare tires? Big Boots exhibits the Shoshoni way. He has no interest in accumulating material goods or money, he has no greed, and he does not lust for undeserved status. He knows that all the intangible damages incurred to him and to his friend can *never* be replaced with wealth that is deemed important to some other white man's culture."

Darrell Bear took a twenty-second pause to allow his words to make a deep impact on the ears and thoughts of the attentive jury. When the prosecutor began again, his tone had changed. His approach toward the jury was as soft, consoling, and comforting as a mother would comfort her child.

"Our beautiful, joyous entertainer, Waffle Stomper, now sits muted and is bound to a wheelchair. His loss is the community's loss. It is *your* loss. It is *my* loss. *We* may never be able to hear that tenor voice sing "Amazing Grace" or "Love Me Tender" again. We may never be able to enjoy his announcer sound belt out on our bingo nights, our funeral giveaways, our auctions, or our school awards night. Our loss is greater than his personal financial loss or Big Boots's loss of companionship. It is a community loss. He fed our human enrichment needs, and it is a great loss. It is a loss to every member of the jury who serves here today."

Prosecutor Darrell Bear stood before the jury in complete silence for a long time before stating his final position.

"Jury members, the prosecution speaks to you openly today. You know that a Shoshoni's tradition is never to do anything that is useless or that is without pleasure attached to it. Evaluate the useless act against these gentlemen and evaluate the future pleasure that their life holds. The prosecution begs for the jury's *guilty* verdict, and to present these plaintiffs with a gift of *justice*. The prosecution rests its case."

The courtroom was as silent as a prayer group during mass.

Darrell Bear softly and slowly sauntered to the prosecutor's table and sat down with the plaintiffs.

"Does the defense wish to present closing argument?" Judge Eagle Feather could see that Counselor Shram Bear was already taking his stance in front of the jury.

The judge smiled. "I guess he does!"

"Good morning, fellow Indian Nation members. My brother's words should ring in your ears as truths. None of us should deny the benefits our tribesmen have reaped from the plaintiffs' many years of service. These four young men on trial today could be the Big Boots and Waffle Stomper of our future. These youth are our next adult tribal kinsmen and perhaps our leaders.

"Our Indian Nation has a legacy of freedom to roam through our spacious vast lands. We do not thrive in confinement, small spaces, caged up, or impaired from movement. These four youth would not do well confined in Worland, Wyoming's Reform School for Juveniles.

"It is our youth that we need to think about now! Our youth are the future providers of benefits to our Indian Nation, and we should listen to the four distinctive voices pleading for our help and our guidance. All four of the defendants are shouting the same message: 'We need to belong somewhere. We want to be men, but we don't know how.'

"One, Weasel Whitehorse, barely a teenager, is neglected and desperately needs a male role model. Weasel is consumed with fear about his male body image, and he has insecurities about his development into manhood. His inner fear is about being a sissy. His incarcerated father has denied his birthright, and he is drawn into friendship with Fox Goodman because Fox represents an image of manhood.

"Two, Fox Goodman has mathematical aptitude that could be tossed into the rubble heap because he is a fifteen-year-old swaggering with good looks. Both of these adolescents are charged with intent to do bodily harm. Their bravado was enhanced by alcohol, and they became a product of their environment—alcohol. Neither of these youth has a past of violence in their personalities.

"Fox is a team player on the Eagles basketball team, and Weasel needs a team. They are not angry youth, and they did not attack Waffle Stomper out of hatred toward him, but they attacked because of their dislike for themselves and because of their own insecurities and fear that they might be sissies. These adolescents thought that Waffle Stomper symbolized what they hated about themselves. The charges of intent to do bodily harm are projections of how Weasel loathed himself. In fact, Weasel and Fox thought of themselves as heroic in protecting themselves and their friends from homosexuality.

"Three, Gary Frasier is innocent of all charges except possession. He was not intoxicated. His assault on Big Boots was only with the intent of holding him pinned to the car to protect his friends. He did no damage to either man, and he did not steal the liquor. He left an IOU for repayment. His error in breaking the law was that he was underage and in possession of alcohol, and even that was in innocence. His intent was not inebriation, but he wanted friendship and to be with his classmates.

"Four, Wyman Large, a fourteen-year-old, is charged with underage possession, intoxication, assault, and car theft. The car was returned without damage, plus it was returned improved with new tires. Even though he admitted to car theft, he is not a thief. His transgression was in holding Big Boots, but he caused no physical harm to either Big Boots or to Waffle Stomper.

"Wyman is an example of our reservation's pathetic neglect for our youth. His crime is our crime. His abilities to run and earn a bronze metal happened for the most grievous reasons. He had to run to find food and to find a place to sleep every night. He had to run to keep warm and to find clothes in the winter. He had to run to survive, and for that he earned a bronze metal. Is our Indian Nation not ashamed for the neglect of Wyman and maybe others? Aren't we sorry about what we have done to all four of these lonely braves who have experienced the age of indiscretion?"

Counselor Shram Bear glided to the water table and poured himself a glass of water while he allowed his words to wash down the throats of the silent, attentive twelve all-male jury members.

He strolled back, and swept his eyes over the seated group. He acknowledged each jury member with either a nod of his head, a sincere smile, or a wink of his friendly eyes. He charmed and nearly flirted with the jury.

"The defense has one last point for you astute gentlemen of the jury to consider. Doctor Fernau reported a mystery virus that the lab found in Waffle Stomper's blood work. All of us in this courtroom can see the physical results of the beating he received. We can observe a man who cannot walk or speak. The doctor implied these two impairments were the result of a brain concussion, but I ask you, could it be that the mystery virus affected his brain and produced the affliction attributed to his physical damage? Can you be one hundred percent sure as you pass judgment on our four adolescents that they are entirely guilty of his existing condition? Are we scapegoating our youth for our own reservation shortcomings, our offenses or sins, and for a mystery virus that holds no answers? The defense asks you to carefully consider the lifelong judgments that you will place upon our youth. Perhaps you will determine their only crime is the crime of being youth, and that should be read as *not guilty.*"

A teenage girl in the courtroom wiped her eyes and blew her nose while the three older women shared a tissue. Several spectators rushed out to the courthouse yard and placed their bets on the defense. The raised voices from the gathered spectators outside sounded like hawkers from a boisterous carnival at fair time. Judge Eagle Feather rapped his gavel to no avail because the noise was not within the courtroom.

"Gentlemen of the jury, you are excused to the jury room to find the verdict." The bailiff escorted them from the courtroom, and the judge announced, "While the jury deliberates, I would like to see three tribal council members from the Arapaho tribe. One of those members should be Katy Bear. I would also like to see three tribal council members from the Shoshoni tribe, the defense attorney, the prosecution attorney, Steve Roberts from the Indian Mission School Board of Trustees, and Father Patty in my chambers as soon as everyone can assemble."

Judge Eagle Feather held his meeting behind closed doors during the jury deliberation process, which lasted for over six hours. The bailiff escorted the jury and the defendants back into the courtroom. He sat the four youth at the defense table, and at 7:00 p.m. the judge rapped his gavel before asking, "Has the jury reached a verdict?"

"It has, Your Honor," responded the jury's spokesperson.

"Will the defendants please stand to receive the verdict?"

The defendants stood.

"How do you find the defendants?" The judge's voice was amplified within the startling silence of the courtroom.

The jury speaker reported, "The jury finds Weasel Whitehorse guilty on all charges. He was found guilty of underage possession, intoxication, assault with a deadly weapon, and intent to do bodily harm. The jury finds Fox Goodman guilt on all charges. He was found guilty of underage possession, intoxication, assault with a deadly weapon, and intent to do bodily harm. The jury finds Gary Frasier guilty of one charge of underage possession. The jury finds Wyman Large guilty on two charges: possession of alcohol and intoxication."

"The defendants may sit down until your name is called for sentencing," Judge Eagle Feather directed. "Sentencing will proceed immediately with the first sentence being given to Gary Frasier. Please stand, Mr. Frasier. Gary Frasier, you will be placed under the guardianship of Father Patty, and the sentence will be considered completed when you enter the seminary. You will give twenty-five hours of service to Big Boots. You will learn to be a cantor for mass and begin to serve in that capacity under Father Patty's tutelage. You will join Attorney Shram Bear's Big Brother program and his weight-lifting team until you graduate.

"Wyman Large, please stand for sentencing. You are placed under the guardianship of Attorney Shram Bear, who has agreed to provide food, clothing, and shelter until your graduation. In return for his hospitality, it is your duty to help Mr. Bear start a weight-lifting team and a Big Brother program for all age-appropriate boys on the reservation. You will give an appropriate number of hours working for the Arapaho tribal council in exchange for earning money to replace Big Boots's spare tires. You must attend AA meetings, provide twenty-five hours of service to Big Boots, and qualify to be on the St. Stephen's track team every year until you graduate.

"Fox Goodman, please stand for sentencing. You will begin studying college placement courses, advanced placement classes in mathematics, and science under the direction of Mr. Steven Roberts. You will attend Attorney Shram Bear's Big Brother program, and you will be on his weight-lifting team until you graduate. You will attend AA meetings and give two hundred hours of home-care service to Waffle Stomper and do errands for Big Boots as part of your sentence, which will conclude upon your graduation. You will learn to cantor for mass with Gary Frasier and Father Patty. You must qualify to be on the Eagles basketball team every year until you graduate. You will donate twenty-five hours to Marvin's Liquor Store in Riverton for the bottle of Jim Beam that you liberated. If you don't have a car for transportation, you will ride your bike or walk the seven miles into Riverton to complete this service.

"Weasel Whitehorse, please stand for sentencing. You will be Attorney Shram Bear's assistant with the Big Brother program, and you will be a member of his weight-lifting team until you graduate. You will attend AA meetings and donate two hundred hours of home-care service to Waffle Stomper or do errands for Big Boots. The defendants may now be seated.

"The Arapaho tribal council has agreed to pay Waffle Stomper's entire hospital expenses in order for justice to be served toward the plaintiffs. Big Boots's spare tires will be replaced through special services given by Wyman Large to the Arapaho tribal council, who in turn will oversee the fair exchange.

"The Shoshoni tribal council will sponsor the reservation Big Brothers and Big Sisters programs. They will fundraise and pay the travel expenses for all members who qualify to compete in weight-lifting tournaments." Judge Eagle Feather stood and moseyed to the side table, poured himself a glass of water, and returned to the judge's bench but remained standing. "Can we now have the two chiefs of the Arapaho and Shoshoni tribal councils come to the judge's bench?" The two portly chiefs ambled toward Judge Eagle Feather's bench.

"Gentlemen, if you agree to these terms, please shake hands." The chiefs shook hands and expressed good will.

"May we now have the prosecutor and the defense approach the bench?" One Bear brother sprinted and the other lumbered to the judge's bench. "Attorneys, if you are agreed that justice has been served for the trial of Tradition vs. Youth, please shake hands."

The two brothers grasped each other's palms in professional respect. "We look just like the cloud game predicted," Shram said with a smirk as he put his arm around his big brother.

Outside in the courtyard, arguments and discussions took place to determine the winning bets. "Do you think they will need a lawyer to settle the matter?" Darrell asked his brother.

"I'm not volunteering!"

"Me neither!"

Chapter 15

NEMESIS LOO

Life in Wyoming was closely intertwined with nature's changing seasons and conditions. The environment determined the stipulations placed upon its inhabitants, and the human character was shaped by the weather that Wren experienced daily. She sat in summer and gazed through the cottonwood branches overhead that made it cool as she looked at the huge blue sky, and wondered about the endlessness of the reservation land. She hiked to the hills in the spring and drank from the clear, fresh streams where she learned the strength of aloneness, but it was the weather that taught, disciplined, elated, tortured, soothed, gratified, and gave or claimed life.

In the year of Waffle's trial Wren endured the harshest of winters. The thermometer recorded forty degrees below zero in the months of November through April. She wanted to run with the antelope and was properly bundled in winter clothing, but the instant she stepped outside Incaranata Hall her nostrils closed tight with frost as if someone had placed a clothespin on her nose that forced her to open her mouth to breathe. Wren felt the frozen air on the roof of her mouth like ice cream when it's eaten too fast, and it caused sharp pains in her temples as she gasped for air. The iced inhalation punched her lungs; her chest ached after taking in less than one hundred breaths. Wren felt her nine-year-old heart begin to pound after twenty minutes of running with the antelope. Her face, hands, and feet were without feeling, and her knees and shoulders were turned to unmovable stone. No human could withstand more than an hour of the deep-freezer agony that forced Wren back inside to the warmth of Incaranata Hall. Her flesh tasted the warmth of her room, and she tried to unfasten her heavy snowsuit, but her hands, face, and feet burned and tingled as they thawed while feeling ebbed back into her iced limbs. Wren accepted and endured the weather's lesson that built her physical strength and shaped her tenacious character, but the shortness of the antelope chase disappointed her. She knew that winter's weather pushed her into another direction where she would spend the winter months practicing her toe-dancing. The weather determined who she was, and it selected her activities.

The seasons changed, and so did Wren. She grew through eleven winters and three room changes named Determine, Resourceful, and Generosity now to experience the pleasures and warmth of 1964's spring. The prairie unfurled itself from the grasp of winter's icy fist to delight her senses with fields of bright red Indian paintbrush, emerald-green cottonwood leaves, and yellow buttercups that comprised the foreground under the azure sky above the shining granite mountains. Spring air opened Wren's pinched, cold-winter nose and allowed her to sniff the air that smelled like fresh clean linens from the clothesline. The fragrance from budding lilacs mixed with the scent of prairie flowers made her think that she stood in the middle of a flower bouquet. The flower fragrance, running sap, and budding greenness seeped into her skin and enlivened her hormones to sprout from the dormant winter. Wren did a jackrabbit jump out the convent door and leaped into the fresh smell of Little Shield's alfalfa field where the antelope grazed. The startled antelope jackrabbit jumped in unison, and the beloved race was on! It was Wren versus the antelope. The race finished after an hour-long chase, but the antelope remained the victors.

Wren panted into the convent galley where Sister Samantha waited for her.

"Wren, do you know Mr. Gamble? He is the Indian Mission's athletic coach."

"Yes, I know who he is."

"Well, he is waiting in Mother Superior's office to talk to you."

Wren tilted her curly, dark head and raised her eyebrows in a humorous expression. "Why?"

"I don't know, but let's go find out."

Wren and Sister Samantha walked into the office. The nun and the foundling both shook hands with Mr. Gamble and sat down in the wooden visitors' chairs beside the desk. Mr. Gamble was a sturdy, muscular Shoshoni who wore the Indian Mission school team jacket with Levis. He stood until the ladies were seated, and then he sat in the chair facing them.

"Wren, I have asked you and Sister Samantha here to talk today because I want to ask you for a favor." Wren looked toward Sister Samantha, who shrugged and showed no indication that she had previous knowledge of this meeting.

"Wren, you know that the track team is short of members because of the suicide epidemic, and we don't have enough members to have a team. I have talked about this problem with the boys, and Wyman Large nominated you to be on the boys track team so we will have enough to compete against the other high schools."

"I'm a girl, and they won't want me because I am only in the sixth grade."

"They all voted that they wanted you. Ronny and Donny Bear are on the team too, and they are only in the sixth grade. The twins cheered your nomination and told the story of how you beat them all in the playground race when you were in the third grade. Bradly confirmed that the story was true."

"It was Bradly Deepwater that didn't want me in the race at all."

Sister Samantha and the godfathers had carefully trained Wren never to harbor resentful thoughts toward anyone. She was taught that hateful resentments were self-destructive, and Wren did not hold a grudge against Bradly or the other boys, but Wren lamented her thoughts aloud. "I want to be wanted."

"Well, Bradly is team captain now, and he wants you to be on the team. They won't have enough participants to have a team if you won't join. The board of trustees will not sanction a team unless we have thirty runners to compete against the other teams. No one will go to the track meets without you, because we won't have a team. Wyman Large, who is cocaptain, has worked hard in training and spoke highly of your abilities. I was just watching you run from this window, and I think you will do fine."

Wren tilted her fine-featured face that looked like a china doll and raised her perfectly painted eyebrows while her small mouth faintly smiled. "But the antelope won."

"Yep, but with my good coaching and training maybe they won't win next time." Coach Gamble chuckled, and Wren giggled.

"Mr. Gamble, I have great concerns." Sister Samantha's icy

words doused the sparks of electricity that emitted from the conversation.

"Please tell me, Sister Samantha, what are your doubts?"

"There is the problem with her being the only girl on the boys' bus and in the locker room."

"Of course that would not happen. My wife drives our car to all the meets, and Wren would travel and stay in the room with her. My wife would be there for her at all our meals. Wren would also have her own change room at my wife's motel, and she would not be in the boys' locker room. We would have all our pep talks at a restaurant away from any area that was meant for only boys. Wren would be respected for who she is. We have our training sessions right here at the school, and Wren can come to Incaranata Hall to her own room whenever she wants."

"Wren, do you have anything to say?"

"I want to be on the team! I would like real people to run with instead of antelope."

"Mr. Gamble, will the other schools allow for her to compete?" Sister Samantha asked.

"The mission's administration is supportive of this idea and will help persuade the other school districts. They will accept us as a laughable underdog with three sixth graders on a high school track team, one being a tiny girl. Father Patty has weighed in on this discussion, and he has given his approval. You must know that Wren will be confronted with hurtful heckling. She is a woman walking into a man's world, and it might not be pleasant for her. She is breaking a huge, solid cultural traditional barrier, but her own skills and her team will protect her. Sister, you would be welcome to attend anytime."

"I have my responsibilities to the young Indian Mission students and to the convent. I would attend when possible, but it would be a rare occasion."

"Wren, I believe that the boys on our team would look after you when we are competing at other schools, but there would be rules for you to obey for your own safety."

"I know how to do the right thing, I know right from wrong, and I know how to follow the rules."

"Do you two ladies want to discuss my proposal before you commit?" His question prompted Wren to her feet, and she almost jumped as high as the desk.

"No, no, and more no! I am ready to commit if Sister Samantha says I can join."

"Wren, you know that you being the only girl might not be easy," Sister Samantha cautioned.

"I know, but I have lived in the cell of Determine, Resourceful, and Generosity, and I can be strong! I want to generously accept this invitation."

"Mr. Gamble, I guess you have a new team member!" Sister Samantha stood and shook his hand, and then Wren gave him a hug.

"My wife and I will do our best to take care of her. Wren, come to the gymnasium tomorrow after your last class at three thirty to begin your training with the team. Come dressed in your gym clothes."

"Thank you, Coach Gamble. I will be there." Wren walked away like the young woman she had become, and Sister Samantha unobtrusively wiped the tears of joy from her eyes so Wren wouldn't notice.

Wren's excitement filled Incaranata Hall. The twenty-three nuns were ecstatic, and Sister Sara swept her up into her arms and whispered into her ear, "You have become a woman leader, just like my ancestor Sacajawea, and we are sisters in many ways."

Wren's excitement spilled out at school when she told Judy what was taking place at three-thirty in the gymnasium.

"I already knew, and I am glad we are friends. My brothers and my mom saw it in the clouds," Judy explained.

Judy and Wren had been friends since birth when they shared the same breast milk, and now that they were eleven, the silent bond grew stronger. Their unusual friendship transcended historical hatred between Shoshoni and Arapaho, and the girls knew nothing about that historical ill will. Judy was raised with eleven brothers and sisters by fair-minded parents who believed there was no love for abstract humanity, only love to be shown to each person as an individual. Katybear loved the squirming new human inside the hubcap, and she taught that love to her family. Wren, by contrast, was raised under the tutelage from twenty-three nuns spewing universal love, and so their friendship existed undisturbed.

The rez was steeped in the tribal prejudice of Arapaho versus Shoshoni, and only now did Wren wonder why she and Judy didn't have other close friends, but this cultural animosity was not her concern or of importance to her. Both girls were content to know their friendship was genuine, and it transcended time and culture.

Their nemesis was LOO. It was not tribal warfare nor petty cultural restraints. Their enemy was something silent, unkind, and never spoken aloud. The antagonist in Judy and Wren's world was seldom understood by judges, priests, lawyers, nuns, or teachers. Some parents and many rez alcoholics knew that there was a black vapor without a name that seeped into every reservation shanty, chapel, or army surplus tent. Accusing fingers pointed to drugs and alcohol as the cause for Native American demise, but those were only by-products used to mask the real foe. The true adversary for reservation children who grew to be reservation residents was much bigger and all consuming. This shapeless backbiter restrained creativity and innovation and sucked up innate motivation. This villain had no name, but its identity was known to be an assassin of goals and dreams. The saboteur had no single word to describe what it was, but it was *LOO*, Lack of Opportunity. The reservation was insulated in the interior of the state, and Wyoming remained isolated from the country by its enormous mountain ranges and inclement weather. Wyoming residents lived inside a dark, thickly lined pocket of insulation. They could not taste, see, hear, or smell much of anything from the outside world. The slowness of reservation progress was understood, endured, and accepted as normal life. Parents like Katy Bear and Sister Samantha practiced patience, persistence, and progressiveness with their children.

Judy was a maturing eleven-year-old who had changed from the plump child that she had been into a sturdily built beauty. Her thick, straight hair was shiny raven black and reached below her rounded behind. The preteen's oval face was flawless with good health, and her high cheekbones complemented her bright, almond-shaped black eyes. Her skin was the darker complexion typical of the Arapaho, but it was her lips and beautiful white teeth that made Judy so attractive. She was a tall five foot five, and the top of Wren's head barely reached as high as her shoulders. The girl's always downcast eyes gave the impression of shyness. Judy preferred to read, converse with Wren, or reflect by herself rather than hang out with the popular kids. Judy and Wren shared their lunchtime every day, attended payday movies, told their secrets about classmates, explored the details concerning Judy's gifted abilities, and discussed Wren's courage to be the only girl in a boy's sport.

Wren's mind was definitely not on the geography lesson that

she was assigned to read before her next class. Judy understood and shared Wren's wild anticipation for three-thirty.

Finally, it was three-thirty! Wren closed her flip-top desk, sprinted to her cell named Generosity, and changed into her u-g-l-y gym suit. It was a cobalt-blue, midthigh-length, bloomer-legged, one-piece jumpsuit that snapped up the front and had a belt with metal ring fasteners. Wearing dirty white sneakers Wren sprinted the thirty-foot distance from Incaranata Hall to the gymnasium, and opened the heavy doors that she remembered she couldn't open as a third grader. How embarrassed she felt then. She was grateful that she opened the doors to this opportunity by herself. The gym was empty except for Mr. Gamble, who sat in the first seat on the bleachers.

"Hi, Wren. The team is in the locker room and will be out in a jiffy. Have a seat."

Wren sat down beside the coach, and soon the jostling, boisterous team filed in and sat in the third row bleachers behind her. Coach Gamble stood and began looking over his clipboard notes while Wren sat uncomfortably isolated.

Mr. Gamble gave out directions for use of the sparse equipment and talked about proper footwear. He looked up. "Wren, why don't you sit with your team?"

"Why don't they sit with me?"

Coach Gamble masked a smile. "Wren, I guess you are right. After all, you were the first to arrive. Okay, guys, move it down to the front row."

The guys rolled their eyes at each other and moved at a sloth's pace down to sit in the first row. Ronny Bear was the brave one that elected to sit next to Wren. Coach Gamble stood in front of the first row in his well-worn gray sweat pants and T-shirt.

"Today I will evaluate what track events will be the best

for each of you. I will decide if you are a distance runner or a sprinter. Let's have Ronny and Donny Bear, Wyman Large, Weasel White Horse, Phil Oldman, Wren, and Clarence Moss line up against that far wall. You will all run to touch the home wall and race back to that red line as the finish. Bradly, go stand at the far wall to make sure that everyone touches it before he or she turns to run to the finish line where I will be monitoring. Okay, gang, let's line up!"

Wren marched to the center line, and her team filled in on both sides of her with Ronny Bear on her right and Donny Bear on her left. She felt comfortable and relaxed between the Bear twins.

"Starters, take your mark—get set—hold it! Hold it. Wren, when the official says 'take your mark,' show her what she should do, Bradly." After Bradly showed her the starting positions and commands, Coach Gamble whispered into Wren's ear, "I guess the antelope don't start on a starting line, do they!" Wren's big green eyes looked up at him, her eyebrows arched with an unspoken response, and she gave him a faint smile. The coach gave her a sly wink.

"Gentlemen, let's try this again. Starters, take your mark, set," and he blew his whistle. The race was off with Wren in the lead the entire distance. She tied with Wyman Large being first to reach the finish line, but Wren knew that she had not run her fastest.

Coach Gamble took notes. "Okay, we will race this distance three times to get an accurate assessment. Line up again, but this time let's have everyone line up. You too, Bradly. We will trust that everyone will be on their honor to touch the far wall." The team lined up for the second time. This time Wren pumped her legs as if she was chasing antelope and was the first to turn to run back to the red finish line, but again Wyman Large caught her, and they tied.

"Okay, team, this is the last time to show me your stuff for the dash. Starters, take your mark." Wren left the starting line like a startled jackrabbit, and she could feel the gymnasium air on her skin as she passed the other runners. She touched the wall with chunky Clarence Moss on her left. She saw from her peripheral vision that he had tripped on the ripped sole of his shoe, and he fell directly into her running path. She stretched her sinewy strong legs and jumped over him, but now Wyman Large was ahead of her. Wren dug deep into her inner power box, moved her legs like a motored machine, and she tied again with Wyman on the finish line.

"Good job, team! Let's all walk over to Deaf Smith Road and test for the distance runners." Coach Gamble reassembled his team. "This race is for three miles, so keep that in your minds. I don't want anyone to fall over from exhaustion. We don't have any water out here, so pace yourself. Many of you haven't been actively running all winter. No need for heroics! Just do what you can. Who thinks that they can run the three miles?" Several boys raised their hands.

"Okay! Fox Goodman, Bradly Jenkins, Wyman Large, John Eagle, and Bill Oldman. Does anyone else want to try out for this race?"

Wren noticed that these were the really big boys. She questioned if this would be fair, since Deaf Smith Road was the road that she ran every day to Judy's house. She knew this road like she knew John 3:16, but she reasoned that they were all much bigger than she was, so maybe it would be fair.

"I want to run this race too!"

"Okay, Wren, sure! Why not give it a go? All right! Starters, take your mark, get set ..." Coach Gamble blew his whistle, and the runners were off. Wren bolted from the start and passed the big boys like they were spectators. Her mind was free of competitive challenge, and she felt the pure joy of movement. She wanted to fly as only a Wren could do. Half way to the three-mile marker she peeked over her shoulder to see that Wyman Large, John Eagle, and Fox Goodman were three fence-post lengths behind her, and they were duking it out among themselves. Coach Gamble waited at the three-mile marker as she ran in.

"Nice run, Wren. I am astounded by your performance. I am glad that you decided to try for distance. I can't determine if you are a sprinter or a distance runner, and you might be a rare person who can do both."

"Thanks. Are we finished with practice for the day? I am really hungry."

"Yup. See you tomorrow!"

"Thanks! I had fun," Wren shouted as she sprinted toward Incaranata Hall.

Wren bounced into Sister Samantha's cell with leftover high spirits from her workout. "Sister Samantha, I love, love, love track practice!"

"And, so how did you do?"

"Fine," she said through mouthfuls of Coke and glazed donuts.

"I know that you are a special girl, and I am proud of how hard you work." Sister Samantha hugged Wren.

"Come on—it's time for chapel."

Chapter 16

THE TRACK TEAM

The school day dragged on, especially during math and science. All Wren could think about was track practice. Yesterday's evaluation races granted Wren her rightful place of respect and acceptance on the boys' track team. The three-thirty bell jolted Wren to her second day of track workout, and again she was the first to arrive.

Coach Gamble was seated in the first row waiting for the team to emerge from the locker room. "Hi, Wren. Have a seat!"

"Thanks, but I think I should sit in the third row where my team chose to sit yesterday. I need to practice generosity."

"Good thinking! I hope they will notice your kind gesture."

"It doesn't matter if they don't! After all"—she rolled her eyes—"they are boys."

The boys jostled, pushed, and shoved each other as they entered the gymnasium, and they saw that Wren waited in the third row. Fox Goodman elbowed Ronny Bear.

"Look who's sitting in our third row!"

"Nice choice of seats, Wren," Ronny said as he sat down

beside her. From that day on, the third row bleachers became the standard routine for the track workouts.

The month of April was peppered with daily practices, and at the end of the month on Friday afternoon, the Indian Mission had a match with the Pavilion High School track team.

"Now listen up, team." Coach Gamble began his instructions. "You will be excused early from your last classes. The bus will leave promptly at two p.m. We will take the bus and drive one hour to Pavilion High School. Come dressed in your workout clothes and shoes. You can use our gym locker room to change out of your school clothes before we leave. Wren will ride in the car with my wife, who will follow the bus. When we get there, now listen to this carefully, you boys will surround the passenger's side of my wife's car where Wren will be riding. The entire team will stand so that Wren will not be visible. She will walk in the middle of the team pack, unseen because she is so small. Your team will stay grouped until your individual events are called. No one will see Wren until she runs her events. We don't need to expose her to any unnecessary heckling. When the meet is over you will walk Wren in the center of the pack to the car just the same way that you arrived."

The coach's plan worked, and Wren's team was compliant to follow directions.

The Eagles team sat in silence as they watched the Pavilion team enter the outdoor track. The team sat huddled together in the bleachers as they waited for the first event. Their uncharacteristic silence was noticeable. The team was in awe and spellbound as they watched the parade of uniformed track shorts, tank tops, and track shoes mosey past the scruffy attire that the Eagles had donned. One of Wren's teammates had mismatched socks, one yellow and the other black, and a torn tee shirt, while several others had cutoff Levis or wore swimsuit trunks; Weasel had no shirt at all. The boys' hair ranged from mangy to savage and most were matted with Vitale or Brill Cream. The Eagles track team wore the style of traditional poverty. Coach Gamble sat in the first row like he did at home. In a speaking voice audible only to his team, he said, "It's not about how we look! It's about how we run. You all will run prettier than they look. The Indian Mission has a reputation for their ability to run, so go out there and do it!"

"We did it!" Wren screeched as she slid down the hall of Incaranata Hall to Sister Samantha's cell.

"We won the meet, and I won first place in the sprint, and Ronny Bear won second. I won first place in the distance run, and Wyman Large won second. All our team placed in their events! We did so good, and, Sister Samantha, let me tell you about how they hid me. It was so cool, and so much fun!"

Wren's fun lasted throughout the track season. The Indian Mission school gained a reputation for hiding their secret weapon. Her team qualified for the state track meet hosted in Laramie for the C-class schools on June 5, 1964, and Coach Gamble prepared his team.

"Listen up, team. We have a lot of work to do before we go to Laramie, but I have a surprise for you. Bradly Deepwater, since you are team captain and Wyman Large is cocaptain, why don't you guys look inside the box that was delivered today."

Wyman's self-confidence had grown since he had a secure home life with Shram Bear. Wyman bounded over the bleacher stairs and ripped open the box sitting in the middle of the gym floor. He lifted out the jazzy nylon shorts and tank tops with number ten written in black bold letters on the white background with red, splashy Indian designs. The track ensemble was stunning! Wren recognized the design from the red, black, and white quilt that Owl's grandmother had made. Wyman's name was printed on the front and back of the sports tank top. A collective aaah sound rose from the bleachers. Wyman lifted out the black shorts trimmed with red Indian design down the side of the right leg. The team could hold back their happiness no longer. They jumped over the first two rows of the bleachers and dug into the box like prairie dogs until each found his own tracksuit. Someone handed Wren the smallest black shorts, and another teammate found her tank top with "Wren" printed on both the front and the back with the number 01. She was delighted

"I'm going to my cell to put these on," she shouted to the coach.

"Be back here in fifteen minutes."

It was a good thing that Wren left, because the boys stripped out of their poverty-home-gathered-track clothes on the spot and donned the new threads. They strutted around the gym mocking the Pavilion team.

"Look what I have, Sister Samantha," Wren called as she held up her new tracksuit.

"*Wow*, they are made from Luise's quilt design. I would recognize that design anywhere. How attractive they look as the team track uniforms. Luise will be so happy to see this! Go put them on and let me see you." Wren shot off, changed in her cell, and quickly returned to Sister Samantha.

"Wren, the suit is beautifully designed and looks snappy, but we will need to make some modifications. The tank top was designed for a boy, and your body is beginning to change like the budding cottonwood leaves." Sister Samantha noticed Wren's despair. "Wren, this will be an easy fix." Sister Samantha ran to the Charity Thrift Shop and returned with a white T-shirt, which they placed under the loose-fitting tank.

"There now! You look great. Run back to practice now."

"I love you so much, Sister Samantha! Thank you! Thank you!"

Coach Gamble noticed the wardrobe adjustment when Wren returned. He could detect the design error and was grateful for the outside help. Wren's maturing body was once again hidden under the loose-fitting fabric.

"Okay, team, line up. Let's have a look at you! You look splendid. Now go take everything off, fold them neatly, and put them back into the box. Fox Goodman, you will be in charge of travel equipment. You will make sure that we have all our belongings to and from our bus trips." Coach Gamble knew that he couldn't allow the suits to be taken home. Some parents would sell them, pawn them, or wear them.

Wren returned to the gym after exchanging her new glitzy track clothes for her ugly blue bloomers. "Team, please come down and sit in the first row. It is time for your second surprise. Let me introduce you to Mr. Steve Roberts, who is the chairman of the board of trustees for the Indian Mission. He has with him two assistants from Hartman's Sporting Goods who will take shoe measurements. Please stand on the papers with both feet so they can order your correct shoe size."

Coach Gamble resumed the regular practice sessions when the shoe measurements were completed. "You guys have experienced the difference when you run on the tarmac of the track and when you run on our gravel roads. Your times are much faster on the track. The board of trustees and the fundraising committee from the Big Brothers Club are donating your shoes. I am predicting that these shoes will make you even faster, but you will need to get used to the shoes. They will feel different, so when the shoes arrive, we are going to bus to the Riverton Middle School track to practice. You will be getting home later, so inform those who need to know. The shoes will remain at school just like the tracksuits for safekeeping. Fox, you will be responsible for all the shoes too."

"The Eagles track team has one month to prepare for the state tournament. Our team will be prepared to compete in our best form, so work hard this month, and then we will taper off before the tournament. Remember that you must individually qualify five days before the tournament. Our relay teams will be formed before the five-day deadline. Right now we don't know the makeup of the relays. Do you have any questions? Yes, Weasel Whitehorse, what is your question?"

"Where will we stay in Laramie, and how long will we be there?"

"Good question, Weasel! We will stay in a dormitory on the University of Wyoming Campus. We will stay there until we don't qualify for the finals. We will qualify! Plan on a three-day stay, and Laramie is a four-hour bus ride. Your meals and room will be provided. Going to Laramie will provide an opportunity for you to see the campus and attend some of their events. Be thinking about what you would like to study after you graduate. Use your time in Laramie to check out what you might choose for a career. For example, check out the building for the college of engineering, science and mathematics, sociology, or maybe education and the arts. Remember that your tribes give full scholarships to any college that you gain acceptance into after graduation, so take a look around. Have a good weekend, and be ready to work out hard on Monday. See you at three-thirty." Coach Gamble's speech motivated Wren to leave the track workout and dash to Little Shield's pasture to run with the antelope.

Wren intensified her self-discipline and ran another hour after every workout. She qualified for the 100-meter dash, 1,600-meter run, 400-meter dash, 800-meter dash, 200-meter dash, and 3,200-meter run. Coach Gamble delayed announcing the contenders for the relays until the state tournament. He was waiting to see which of his runners would run their best times, and then he would announce the relay teams. He knew his lead runner would be Wren. Coach Gamble began to taper his team's workouts. He lessened the intensity of the workouts one week before state tournament, and the week of the meet they did nothing except team bonding. His coaching method was to give his team complete rest in order for their bodies to surge with energy on the days of the meet.

"Listen up, team! Tomorrow we leave for Laramie, and today I have two more surprises for you. I want you to meet Vickie and Janice from the Riverton Beauty School. They have agreed to give haircuts to everyone. I thought that we all should cut our hair out of respect for the twenty Indian Mission kids that committed suicide and dedicate our team energy to the well-being of all athletes. This gift is optional and you are not required to cut your hair, but these ladies know how to make us look like movie stars. Are you interested?" Every hand shot up, and the hair stylists performed their art. The team was transformed into attractively coiffed models, and Wren had her hair cut into a trendy poodle-cut.

After the haircuts, the coach spoke again. "The second surprise today is from Hartman Sporting Goods. In addition to the new track shoes they have donated a pair of new KEDS everyday shoes." Mr. Gamble slowly held up a pair of the trendy white KEDS, and the team gave a collective aah. KEDS was the brand name for the coveted shoes of the Eagles team in the early '60s. With new shoes, new running clothes, and new hairstyles, the team was Laramie bound by 5:00 a.m. Mrs. Gamble had invited Judy to accompany Wren in her car, and they followed the bus only a short way before they deviated onto their own route. Mrs. Gamble wanted to show the girls the beauty of Beaver Rim and took a shortcut across Sand Draw Road. The short cut would put them an hour ahead of the bus, and they agreed to meet in Jeffery City for snacks. The bus packed with 29 kids was too slow and powerless to climb Beaver Rim. It would never make the steep climb and would surely overheat. Besides, Mrs. Gamble wanted to do something special for Wren and her friend. Throughout the track season Mrs. Gamble had become very fond of Wren and wanted her to share this special trip with a friend her own age. Neither Wren nor Judy had ever been off the rez, and they were fascinated by the different landscape.

The view was a series of cliffs that rose in elevation to reach over a mile high. The gravel road twisted, turned, and climbed to level off at a tabletop plateau. Mrs. Gamble pulled the car to the side of the road, stopped, and opened the doors and windows so the girls could experience the ambiance. The sunrise over Beaver Rim would be a lifetime memory. It was eerily magnificent. Beaver Rim was exquisite, and the girls gasped at the sight. Judy reached for Wren's hand, and they hugged each other as they absorbed the landscape into their young systems. The rising sun behind the eastward bluffs cast purple fingers that splayed across the desolate steep rock wall and the lower flat land beneath. The wind whipped the girls' hair as they stood on the edge of the rim looking into the endless beige land that was now tinted lavender. It was a land where nothing but prairie grass and sagebrush would grow, but now momentarily it served as a canvas for the soft painter's pallet from the artisan's dawn. Mrs. Gamble grasped the wisps of hair from her eyes and pointed off into the distance as the girls' eyes followed her direction.

"Buffalo," Judy wailed.

"Keep looking," Mrs. Gamble urged.

"They look like they are running in place. Why would they do that?" Judy puzzled.

"They are lifelike metal cutouts that look like a herd of buffalo. Some creative artist made this incredible sight to look as it did when our ancestors were the only people who lived on this land."

Wren's green eyes opened wide and her perfectly arched eyebrows lifted in their comical questioning manner. "Who made them?"

"We don't know, Wren. Some generous artist gifted this for all of us to see and gave it without needing recognition."

"I love this place. I want to keep this place forever."

"Yes, Wren, it is a wonderful place, but this gravel road we are driving on cuts into the natural scene because workers need to get to the uranium mines, and it is those mineral royalties that give you the monthly per capita check. This is where the aesthetics of a beautiful world collide with modern human needs. If you had to choose between receiving your payday check and preserving the elegance of this moment, what would you choose?" Mrs. Gamble's question made for a lively conversation for fifty miles as they traveled to Jeffery City.

Theirs was the only car. They were the only humans for hundreds of miles in any direction. The road existed because of the uranium mines that sprouted up like weeds across this desolate land, but they remained obscured. Handfuls of new mining investors and developments raged in Fremont County in the 1960s, alleviating poverty for the Indian nations.

"When we reach Jeffery City, what would you like for your snack"? Mrs. Gamble asked.

Wren's eyebrows lifted in her comical characteristic way. "We want peanut butter malts!"

"Hmm, that sounds yummy."

Jeffery City consisted of one restaurant, one bar, and one gas station.

"Why is everyone staring at us?" Judy whispered.

"We are the only females in this restaurant. Look around—the restaurant is full of men who work in the area while the women probably stay at home in Riverton."

"Is this what you feel like being the only girl with all the boys on the track team?" Judy asked her friend.

"Yeah, pretty much."

"Well, male domination just got worse! Here comes the bus." Mrs. Gamble chuckled.

The long road to Laramie was entertaining. Mrs. Gamble followed the bus, and a pizza delivery truck followed her car. The pizza truck passed her and the bus and then slowed going up the hills, and then the bus and Mrs. Gamble's car passed the pizza truck. This leapfrog game went on for miles. Judy and Wren laughed when one of the boys on the bus held up a sign—"Four pepperoni pizzas to go, please"—as the bus passed the pizza truck again. The pizza driver laughed and put on his turn signal as he passed the caravan for the seventh time. The pizza truck pulled over and stopped, and so did the bus and Mrs. Gamble's car. The boys in the bus jumped up and down and cheered when the pizza man produced a stack of pizzas and gave them to the Indian Mission bus driver. Coach Gamble brought Mrs. Gamble and the girls six slices. Each time the bus passed the pizza truck they honked and waved their thanks.

When the Indian Mission parade pulled into Laramie and

the girls saw the Laramie University campus they fell silent. "What's wrong, girls?"

"Judy and I saw this big school building in the cloud game."

Mrs. Gamble remained silent. She didn't know the meaning of the cloud game.

Wren changed into her track clothes in the car before they reached the Laramie High School track. The boys had also changed into their track shoes and clothes on the bus. The car parked, and the dressed Eagles team surrounded the passenger's side of the car while Wren slid out into the center of the pack and was hidden from view. This was a well-rehearsed routine. The team walked together and sat as a group in the giant stadium while Judy and Mrs. Gamble sat several rows higher behind them. She and Judy became the self-appointed educational committee. Mrs. Gamble organized tours of the campus buildings that she thought would be of interest to individual team members. Judy was a major facilitator, as she surprisingly knew the interest of many of the boys. Mrs. Gamble distributed campus maps, provided a list of campus museums, and helped the boys to find buildings that taught their fields of interests.

She saved the performing arts building for Judy and Wren for the night when Mr. Gamble would take the boys to the U of W basketball game. Mrs. Gamble bought tickets to the ballet for herself, Judy, and Wren. Coach Gamble said nothing when Fox Goodman, Wyman Large, and Weasel Whitehorse expressed interest in going to the ballet too. All six of them attended the ballet.

The first day of the track events was a five-hour day. Coach Gamble hovered over his team like a mother hen. "Wyman, I saw Wren talking to you the entire 400-meter dash. I have explained to her that talking while she runs zaps her energy and keeps her from running her potential. What was she saying to you?"

"She said, 'Come on, Wyman, if you don't speed up I am going to pass you,' and she did. She runs and talks at the same time, and still she came in first place."

"Yeah, it's hard to correct her when she does so well. I don't think track seems to be that important to her," Coach Gamble lamented.

Through the rest of the track events, Wren kept talking about the ballet that she would see that night.

Attending the ballet was the highlight of the track meet for Wren. Mrs. Gamble had given ballet programs to the Eagles team during dinner. She explained how the show "Water for Life" promoted environmental protection. The original music and dance portrayed how water pollution killed birds that existed near wetland habitat. The ballet production was an original script and choreographed by the University of Wyoming Dance Department.

Mrs. Gamble, Judy, Wren, and the three boys slid into their ultramarine-blue cushioned seats as the heavy velvet curtains slowly opened in rhythm with the sweet melodic music from the orchestra. Wren was glad that she finally weighed enough to be able to keep her seat from folding up with her sitting inside as it had done at the movies.

The show portrayed flocks of birds, and the climax revealed the prima ballerina in a stunning purple chiffon calf-length dress who danced on point. She represented the purple loon. Her dance was slow graceful arabesque poses. She supported herself on one leg on point (Wren had always called it toe-dancing) while the other leg extended behind her in perfect balance. Wren noticed that she lifted her legs in direct line behind her spine while her shoulders remained straight and squared. Her perfect execution of the jeté gave the illusion of flight. The death of the loon was magnificent. When she died, her purple dress turned white. Judy was so emotionally caught up in the story she released muffled sobs. Wren was so focused on the movements of the ballerina she sat riveted in her chair not wanting it to end. All three boys, and especially Fox Goodman, were mesmerized by the theatrics.

After the ballet, in the motel, under the crisp, cool sheets that were pulled up over their heads, Wren and Judy whispered in excited voices and tried not to disturb Mrs. Gamble.

"I loved, loved, loved the ballet! I watched all the steps and poses that the loon dancer did, and I will go home to practice," Wren whispered to Judy. Wren was so full of love and inspiration she thought she would explode. Wren had never had anyone to sleep beside her before, and she felt the sisterly love for Judy in a way that she had never known. She realized how much that she loved her eleven-year-old friend. Wren loved the beauty of the dance performance, she loved her track team, and she loved the Gambles for giving her this enrichment.

"Let me tell you what happened today at the meet!" Judy whispered. "Mrs. Gamble and I sat beside some senior high school girls from Callie who came to see their boyfriends run in your 800-meter dash. You all were at the starting line, and you shot out like an arrow in a tight bow. One of the prettiest blonde girls said, 'Look at that little boy run.' The other girl shouted, 'I have never seen a boy so small have such long legs.' The blonde girl said, 'That's why he can run so fast!'

"Wren, I couldn't keep quite another minute! I said, 'That's not a boy! That is a girl, and she is only a sixth grader, and she is my friend!' I thought that big senior girl was going to punch me. She doubled up her fist and said, 'You liar! No girl can do that!' Mrs. Gamble stood up and said, 'Girls, girls, settle down! It is true. She is a sixth-grade girl who joined the team so our school would have enough entrants. She will run again tomorrow if you would care to cheer her on.' Wren, I was so proud of you! I feel so special to know someone like you. My mom is special in that way too, since she is the first woman Arapaho council member, but you are only an eleven-year-old kid, and you are my best friend. Anyway, you beat all their boyfriends in the 800-meter dash. Those girls became quiet and watched our Indian Mission team give you cheers."

"Girls! You have to go to sleep now. It is so late, and Wren has her big 3,200-meter run tomorrow and needs to get some rest. Good night!"

The next day was sunny bright, and the day had blessed the Eagles team and kept them from struggling against usual the energy-stealing Laramie wind. The lack of wind was definitely granted in their favor.

Judy and Mrs. Gamble resumed their usual stadium seats to watch their team perform, but it was no longer empty. The lower portion of the stadium was full of girls who had not been there yesterday. At the highest point of the stadium behind them, Mrs. Gamble saw an elegant woman with a stylish black straw hat and sunglasses who sat alone and didn't fit the Wyoming sports scene. The stylish lady piqued Mrs. Gamble's curiosity. Why was she watching the Eagles track team?

Judy spotted the two girls that she had met yesterday and gave a shy smile and a tiny wave. The effervescent blonde girl stood up tall and gave Judy a sweeping giant greeting. Judy was flustered. She had never had any type of recognition in her eleven years and didn't know how to accept it. The blonde girl sat back down, and the entire group of girls turned their heads up to Judy and gave her a closed-fisted power victory greeting. The animated blonde girl sprang to her feet and ascended the bleacher steps to reach Judy and Mrs. Gamble. Judy felt a surge of fear.

"Please come and sit with us so we can cheer for your friend!"

Judy hung her head, lowered her eyes, covered her mouth, and shook her head.

"Oh, come on! We can't cheer without you—we don't even know her name."

"Her name is Wren," Judy replied, barely audible, with downcast eyes.

"Judy, please accept her invitation." Mrs. Gamble nudged her. "I will be right up here, if you don't want to sit with the girls, and you can always come back to sit with me if you don't like it." Judy stood up as the blonde cheerleader took her hand and led her to the seats of her friends.

The 3,200-meter run began with the six members on the starting line. Wren was positioned most unfavorably on the outside lane. When the runners were crouched in starting formation and before the gun went off, the crowd of girls stood up and shouted, "Run, Wren, run!" Wren was surprised and stood up to look at the crowd of cheering girls. Coach Gamble too turned to see the mob that cheered. The starting judge repeated, "Runners, take your mark!" Wren went back down into her crouched starting position. The gunshot was heard, and the runners began their race. Wren bolted out like a chased antelope.

"Wren can never hold that pace. The cheering crowd propelled her to take it out faster than she should," Coach Gamble said to his watching team. "Remember, guys, to pace your energy. Wren is not pacing herself." Wren was already six horse lengths ahead.

The cheerleaders in the stadium went wild. Judy stood in the middle of the girls, shouted, waved her arms, and imitated these older girls. She was overwhelmed with the feeling of crowd energy and never-before-felt experience of belonging. The fervor swelled in her awareness, and she loved this new sensation. The senior girl gave Judy an enormous hug in her excitement for Wren's lead over the other runners. Judy's hug was contagious, and she began hugging the other girls around her. Mrs. Gamble laughed out loud at Judy's exuberance. Judy was becoming self-confident through Wren's efforts.

The 3,200-meter run was four times around the football field. Each time Wren circled the track her length of lead grew—not because she increased her speed, but the runners had paced themselves to her jet takeoff, and she had worn them down. Their start was too fast, and they had no reserve to keep pace with her. Coach Gamble had just observed a new race strategy. Each time Wren passed the cheering crowd, she heard "Run, Wren, run!" Wren had distanced her lead by one length of the football field on her fourth and last lap. Her team jumped the track barrier and lifted her high on their shoulders.

"We want to meet your friend," the girls yelled to Judy.

"Okay, let's go down there!"

Judy and her new friends joined the Indian Mission team on the field. Judy hollered up to Wren, who was riding high on team shoulders. "Meet my new friends."

Mrs. Gamble turned to look for the beautiful woman with the picture hat, but she had vanished.

The team was exhausted and slept most of the way back to Ft. Washakie. The Gambles were tired too, but they felt a surge of contentment as they knew that the team had used their full potential to earn the first-place trophy and that they had a role in broadening these students horizons.

Chapter 17

SHOSHONI CULTURE

It was the last day of school. Wren and Judy felt a pinch of sadness, and knew that the summer months gave little opportunity to be with the nuns or school chums. The quietness of Incaranata Hall was interrupted by the ring of the drumbeat. Sister Samantha picked up the phone.

"I wish to speak to Sister Samantha," the male tribal voice announced as ten clicks of the rubbering community listened on.

"This is she."

"Sister Samantha, I am calling on behalf of the Shoshoni council members who want you and Wren to attend the next Shoshoni council meeting on Tuesday at two p.m. Will you be there?" Samantha had lived with the Shoshoni culture long enough to know that it was impolite to ask questions when explanations were not freely given.

"Well, yes, I guess we can be there. Is this a summons or an invitation?"

"It is both a summons and an invitation."

"Okay, since school is out, we don't have many obligations. We will be there."

On Tuesday morning, Sister Samantha suggested that Wren wear her one dress and her Thrift Charity Shop black patent-leather tap shoes before she outgrew them.

"Why are we supposed to go to the Shoshoni council meeting?"

"I don't know, Wren, but I told them that we would attend."

Wren, Sister Samantha, and Judy moseyed into the familiar Ft. Washakie redbrick government building where Waffle Stomper and Big Boots's trial had taken place nearly a year ago. All the chairs were full of familiar Shoshoni people, and some of her Arapaho track team were there too. Wren felt a stranger's eyes piercing through her as he sat at the back of the tribal hall. The man who stared at her was handsome, nicely dressed, and wore a maroon-colored sports jacket, gray pants, and Italian shoes that she recognized from magazine ads. It was his shoes the captivated her interest. *Who is this man with the shining, tasseled loafer, Salvatore Ferragamo shoes? I know his shoes cost seven hundred and fifty dollars. He does not look like the BIA government men.* Wren remembered that she had seen him at her godfathers' trial too. She searched the other audience members and knew everyone else. Wren was flooded with emotion when she saw her godfathers and bolted to hug them as they sat near the front. They had saved three chairs. One chair was for her, another for Sister Samantha, and a third was for Judy. Waffle Stomper was no longer in a wheelchair and walked with a cane. Tears of happiness ran down her thin nose, fine small features, and dripped into the corners of her rosebud mouth. *Why do I have such a lump in my throat that makes me want to cry?* Wren thought. She sat down beside Big Boots and motioned for Judy to sit beside her. It wasn't until after she settled into her chair that she noticed the traditional formality of the occasion. She saw that the entire Shoshoni council wore traditional dress. They looked like they were ready for a powwow. Their beaded buckskins were colorful, and some of their war bonnets reached to the ground. Wren's godfathers had told her that these council members had served in many wars before WWII. The room smelled pleasantly of buckskin and sage.

Sister Samantha studied Wren who experienced the hormonal change into adulthood, and felt a tearful lump in her own throat. She saw that her foster child was now a beautiful petite eleven-year-old. Wren looked like the diminutive popular comic book character Betty Boop with her fashionable beauty-school-styled haircut and her emerging shapely tiny body.

"Do you know why we are here, Judy?"

"Yes, and so do you. We saw the tribal chief and the child in the cumulus cloud game. Don't you remember?"

"Yes, I remember, but I didn't know what it meant. Shhh—I want to hear what Chief Washakie says."

The chief stood to lead the Pledge of Allegiance, and the crowd rose to their feet and joined in. As the audience sat down, the council members began to beat out a rhythm with their hands on the tabletop in front of where they were seated and chanted songs that Wren had heard many times.

Chief John Washakie, a descendant of the original chief Washakie, was a strikingly handsome man in his seventies. He stood in the middle of the tribal hall and beckoned toward Wren. Wren looked around to see who he could be motioning toward, and then she felt Sister Samantha's nudge.

"Wren, he wants you. Go stand in the center of the room."

Sister Samantha shuddered when she remembered the paper that katybear had given her to read that contained the notes she had jotted down from eavesdropping on the girls' cloud game. The big school building cloud formation was Judy's prediction about University of Wyoming, where Wren won the tournament trophy. The chief pointing his finger toward a child was another image Judy had interpreted that had come true. Sister Samantha noted that she and katybear needed to talk more about Judy's shaman abilities.

"Ladies and gentlemen of the Indian Nation, today we have come together for our Shoshoni Naming Ceremony to bestow a second name to this young lady. Wren generously gave her efforts and her skills unselfishly to the Eagles track team for them to qualify for the State Track Tournament in Laramie, Wyoming. She helped her team to win the 1964 first place trophy for the Indian Mission and gave that honor to her Shoshoni Indian Nation at Ft. Washakie.

"Wren established who she is without any knowledge of an identity or a family. Her only possession from her past is a 1950 Dodge hubcap. She has built her own family of love: Sister Samantha is her surrogate mother, Father Patty fills the roll of her father, Sister Sara is her big sister, Mother Superior and Sister Margaret are her godmothers, and Katy Bear was her wet nurse and now serves as her aunt while Katy's twelve children are Wren's cousins. Judy Bear is her best friend and sister, while Big Boots and Waffle Stomper remain her constant godfathers.

"This little Shoshoni girl has enemies even while her village family love her. Her foe is the unknown and her nemesis is lack of opportunity. Wren is an example of what we all must overcome: we must identify what it is that we want as a nation—what is our collective dream? Wren's dream is to become a toe dancer. Wren works hard each day to reach her goals. She self-teaches, practices her dance, and runs with the antelope to gain endurance. Her tenacity is something that we all should learn.

"This little bird has brought her family great light. She has brought recognition to her school and to her tribe. She is the 'bringer of light' and will forever be named Sun." Chief John Washakie picked up the tribal pipe, inhaled a deep breath of smoke, exhaled, and chanted into the direction of the east. He lifted the pipe to the west and repeated the chant to the direction of the west. He did the same for the directions of the north and to the south. Every councilman and audience member chanted the prayer to Mother Earth and Father Sun.

"Sun, now you must become accustomed to your new name. Sun, please perform these tasks ..." The chief handed her a bundle of flowers. "Sun, give a flower to each of your family members and thank them for your well-being." Sun Wren performed her task with tears streaming down her cheeks. "Sun, take a glass of water to Coach Gamble and his wife."

She performed her task and felt gratitude toward the Gambles. Sun Wren whispered to Mrs. Gamble, "I loved Beaver Rim. Thank you for taking me there." Sun Wren walked back to the center of the room, and Chief John Washakie gave her the last task.

"Now, Sun, say something to the audience and use your new name."

Sun Wren stood silent in the center of the tribal hall for several minutes that seemed an eternity to Sister Samantha, who felt Sun's discomfort and wished that she would hurry up and say something, anything to break the long silence. The nun felt anxiety for Wren, and knew that her little bird was on display to prove her mettle that was being tested.

How can I say anything? I remember Waffle Stomper's story about what the original Chief Washakie felt when he was given a saddle as a gift from President Grant. He said, "When a kindness is shown to a white man, he feels it in his head and his tongue speaks. When a kindness is shown to an Indian, he feels it in his heart, but his heart has no tongue."

Wren's heart was in a state of expansion, but her tongue would not move. At last Wren raised her large green eyes; tilted her head toward her chief; directed her small, fine-featured face forward; arched her eyebrows into a comical position; opened her small, heart-shaped mouth; and allowed her strong, confident voice to ring out in the silent council hall.

"I am Sun Wren, and I thank you for this gift. For a very long time I have wanted to have two names like everyone else. Sister Samantha has two names. Katybear and Judy Bear have two names. Weasel Whitehorse, Fox Goodman, Big Boots, Waffle Stomper, and Mrs. Gamble all have two names, but I only had one name until today, and now I have two names. I am Sun Wren."

Sister Samantha released her breath that she had held waiting for Sun Wren to finish her last task. The audience stood and gave her a standing ovation. Katybear, Shram, and his weight-lifting team scurried around to serve rocky road ice cream and peanut butter cookies. Sun Wren searched the room for the nice-looking stranger that she didn't know, but he had vanished. She ran and threw her arms around Sister Samantha and nearly knocked her out of her chair.

"I have two names, and I love you so much."

"You have earned your two names, Sun, by bringing happiness to others."

"Would you girls like to go to the movies?" Katybear asked, interrupting.

"The movies!" shouted Sun.

Later, while finishing her ice cream and cookies in the almost empty tribal hall, Sun Wren said to Waffle Stomper, "Katybear said that Judy and I can go to the nighttime movie to see *The Gospel According to St. Matthew*. Do you want to go with us?"

"Do you know, Sun, that that movie was directed by Pier Paolo Pasolini?"

Sun Wren shrugged her indifference and asked, "Will you come with us, godfathers?"

"We would love to go, Sun, but I need to ready for the Sun Dance I promised to dance for Waffle Stomper's recovery. It is important I keep my promise."

"I am so glad that Waffle Stomper is walking again, and I want to do the Sun Dance too."

"Sun, the Sun Dance is only for men."

"It is named the Sun Dance, and now my name is Sun, so it must mean that I can dance too."

Big Boots laughed. "You were the only girl on the boys' track team, and you changed the school rules, but you cannot change tribal rules. You can be one of my helpers during the ceremony. I have asked Fox Goodman, Weasel White Horse, and Wyman Large to help with the Sun Dance preparations, and you can help too if you want."

"Thank you, Godfather. I do want to be your helper, and I will learn how to help you with the Sun Dance!"

The Sun Dance took place in August in a remote, secret location, and it was the Shoshonis' most sacred affair. Big Boots began to prepare himself for its rigorous demands two weeks before the scheduled event. Fox, Weasel, Wyman, and Sun Wren walked the country roads for five miles every day with Big Boots to help him gain physical endurance. His support group was already in great physical condition from participating with Shram Bear's weight-lifting team and the completed track season, but they wanted to encourage Big Boots. They all changed their diet to match the nutritious supplements Big Boots ingested. They quadrupled their intake of water, sage tea, and lemonade. They ate, drank, exercised, and attended sweat lodge together in the evenings. At sunrise each morning the helpers combed the prairie and gathered the wild grown herb called kinnickinnick, which was used for smudging and smoking. The gang of court-paroled youth had cared for Waffle Stomper for the past year, and those young men had also bonded with Big Boots to become family. The boys' anger and insecurities transformed into respect and idolatry. Fox Goodman and Wyman Large announced their intention to join Big Boots in the Sun Dance to pay their gratitude for Waffle Stomper's recovery. Sun Wren and Weasel vowed their allegiance to be loyal helpers.

In ancient decades, the Sun Dance was performed when God granted a prayer, and the debtor thanked God with his participation in the Sun Dance. The ancient early native Indian participants cut their pectoral muscles on both side of their chest and run a rawhide string through each laceration. They attached the other end of the rawhide string through the nose of the mounted buffalo head on a pole high in the center of the arbor. The debtors who owed God danced up and back to the pole while the two attached rawhide twine tugged on the pectoral muscle until it wore through. The government forbade this practice before Sun Wren was born.

The forty-foot round red-willow Sun Dance lodge was constructed away from public view on the isolated flat prairie, and only Sun Dancers with their helpers were allowed in the arbor. The opening of the arbor was a five-foot-wide entrance where family or friends could view the participants, but they were not allowed to go inside. A circle of blankets that belonged to the helpers surrounded the arbor interior walls and designated the area where Sun Wren and Weasel White Horse sat. Big Boots, Fox Goodman, and Wyman Large joined their helpers on the blankets for short rest periods and received small comforts.

Sun Wren had three towels to dry perspiration for each dancer, or she used an eagle-wing fan to dry or cool their bodies in the ninety-eight-degree summer heat. When the dancers looked fatigued, she administered sage or kinnickinnick as a smelling salt to help them revive while Weasel administered a beeswax lubricant to their dry lips to keep them from bleeding.

Big Boots, Fox Goodman, and Wyman Large all danced in their separate parallel tracks inside the arbor dirt floor. The dancers always faced the east-mounted buffalo head with their backs to the arbor entrance. The head of the buffalo was thirty feet from the entrance and dancers used this area for their individual paths of dance. They took tiny steps forward to the east until they reached the buffalo headed pole and then walked backward toward the west, but their movement was more like a shuffle than a step. This same pattern and movement was repeated over and over for hours that turned into three days.

Sun Wren's devoted dancers were shirtless, wore shorts, moccasins, and Big Boots donned the traditional head roach, but the boys heads remained unadorned. Small puffs of dust surrounded their feet as they shuffled up and back to the arbors' central pole that displayed the buffalo head. The three dancers tweeted on hollowed reed pipes to a one note monotones whistle as their bodies moved with the rhythm. Some of the other twenty devotees also used pipe whistles. Sun Dance participants continued this routine for three days and three nights without food, water, or sleep. Some of the dancers dropped from exertion, and were carried to the blankets of the caregivers, but if they dropped they were not allowed to continue. Sun Wren and Weasel Whitehorse were pleased that Big Boots and their friends had conditioned themselves well and exhibited their stamina.

In the afternoon of the second day, Big Boots sat on the blankets. Fox and Wyman came to rest while Sun Wren washed their faces with a cool wet face cloth as Big Boots spoke.

"You may begin to lose the sense of your limbs, or you may feel that you have no body at all. This is the time to give full focus to the reason that you dance. Keep your thoughts devoted to your ancestors, to God, and give all your gratitude. If your mind drifts to thoughts of unkindness, resentments, anger, or ill will toward anyone enters your mind, you will drop like a tail feather from the eagle. Keep your thoughts pure and full of thanks." He stood up strongly and resumed his position in his tracks while the boys shuffled determinedly beside him to the tweet of their whistles.

The red-willow arbor held an unmistakable, Sun Dance unique smell. The constructed arbor emitted the fragrance of red willow, and the dancers' bodies produced the aroma of kinnickinnick as they perspired. The smell of leather and earth mixed with the pungent sage produced the smell of Sun Dance. Sun Wren and Weasel remained loyally focused helpers on their blankets, and each of them took turns being on duty. Sun took time off to have lunch with katybear and Judy's family in their traditional tipi that Bears had erected near the other fifteen families that supported their Sun Dancers. The Bear family was Arapaho, but this was the year of peace between the tribes, and they were there to support Sun Wren and the paroled boys that her two lawyers sons attempted to rehabilitate. Katybear made sure that Sun Wren and Weasel stayed hydrated and well fed while they cared for their dancers. Judy took a turn of dancer care while Sun Wren and Weasel walked about the campgrounds for respite.

Sun Wren loved the picturesque sight of this sacred event with the fifteen traditional tipis scattered around the red-willow arbor. The view was bathed in lavender and pink light from the setting sun. The white elk skin tipis glowed electric pink and the human forms were black silhouettes against the lavender sky, and they reminded her of the artful buffalo cutouts on Beaver Rim that Mrs. Gamble had shown to her and Judy.

Sun Wren knew that she belonged to this life. This was her place, and these were her people. The view of the Indian camp was reminiscent of a past way of life before the white man changed their way of living. Evenings on the prairie cooled significantly, and Sun Wren felt the breeze dry her body-dew from the day's heat as she walked back to the arbor to resume her duties.

Big Boots and the boys had put on shirts to block the chill of the night air as they continued the tortures of the grueling task. Judy slid over to allow Sun Wren room onto the blue Pendleton blanket that marked their territory. They tucked the light quilt over themselves as they huddled together beneath, and raised their faces upward to gaze through the open roof of the arbor to see the black velvet night sky with millions of twinkling stars.

Sun Wren whispered to Judy, "Can you predict what will happen by looking at the stars like you do with the cumulus clouds?"

"No, not even a little bit. The stars belong to the light of our ancestors, their ancestors, their ancestors until the beginning of time. Each star is an ancestor to someone. We do not know their thoughts, but we know their protection. Can't you just feel how we are shielded? Look up and see how many ancestors guard us."

The girls wrapped their arms around each other, and felt the love from the beautiful, soft black overhead blanket of twinkling ancestors that cared for them. The small cute curly haired Shoshoni girl and the beautiful Arapaho prophet fell asleep under their cozy world embraced together as the Sun Dancers continued throughout the night.

Big Boots in his hazy mental fog came to rest on the blanket with the sleeping young girls. For the first time in two days, he faced west toward the arbor entrance. What did he see? Had he experienced a vision? In the opening at 3:00 a.m. he saw the man in the shadows that he had seen at the powwow three years in a row, and now he saw him again as he stared at the sleeping girls. Fox Goodman plopped down beside Big Boots on the blankets.

"Fox, who is that man standing in the entrance that keeps staring at Sun Wren?"

"There is no one there, Big Boots! Everyone has gone to the tipis for the night. Are you okay?"

"Yes, I am fine, and it is time for me to get moving." Big Boots struggled to get up onto his knees. Fox helped him to stand, but he was weak and wobbled off to resume his monotonous shuffle forward and backward to the buffalo head as his whistle faltered and faintly sounded into the night air.

The girls woke up to see the prairie cast in a glorious pumpkin golden sunrise. The metallic light absorbed into their young frames and supplied electrical energy that they circuited to their dancers. The two friends determined that they had chores that needed urgent attention. Big Boots and the boys collapsed onto the blankets. Wren and Weasel quickly administered the sage, washed their faces, and applied the bees wax, but the harsh requirements of the Sun Dance had slapped hardships on their beloved, dedicated participants. Wren saw how her tribesmen struggled to endure the agony and fatigue. She suffered with them and understood their depleted energy, but she tapped into the golden sunrise and become a conduit. She transmitted the surge of energy that she felt from the sun and conducted it into her kinsmen. Sun became the needed extension cord that lead from the pulsating dawn, and plugged it into her tribal family. She encouraged them to keep going in the remaining hours that concluded in the early afternoon.   Judy stretched up toward the radiance of morning, shook out her long, black hair, stood tall, and ran to the Bear's tipi to help katybear and the family prepare the food for the feast. The participants' families bestowed honors to those who danced the Sun Dance, and they enjoyed delicious fry bread with honey, hamburgers, hot dogs and Indian stew. Sun Wren and Judy's team finished strong in the brilliant midday sun, but they only drank water, sage tea or lemonade, and ate watermelon, Jell-O, and chicken broth. The sponsor for the Sun Dance feast was Gene Lee Used Cars from Riverton, and he gave the food as a gift.

Chapter 18

CHANGES

Wren's maturity changed to align with the integrity of her newly given name, Sun. Her stalwart character strengthened to wrestle with the suffocating grip of her nemesis LOO (lack of opportunity). LOO pestered Sun Wren at every given chance. It was always there to block Sun's most sought after desires, but inadvertently it presented new avenues to teach her, and today was an example that illustrated Loo's minacious plots.

Sun sprawled in the newly cut alfalfa field for an hour and waited for the antelope arrival. The fragrant alfalfa aroma perfumed the entire valley and sedated her into a listless pleasure. She felt the cool moist clover penetrate through the thinly worn denim of her summer vacation jeans. She was in love with everything within her world. This remarkable pasture filled with wildlife, her family, friends, school, and future were all ingredients that blended into mellifluous prospects for her future. Sun sprang up with the energy from pure joy. She chased the antelope to the west end of the pasture, held her chest, and sobbed with pain. She walked back to the convent with measured slow steps as her gait changed into a nonimpact, cautious glide as she drew nearer to the front door. Painful sobs spilled from her pursed mouth and tears wetted her almond cheeks. Several of the nuns glanced in her direction as Sun searched the galley for Sister Samantha.

"She's at chapel."

"I'll wait for her in her cell," sobbed Sun as she flopped onto Sister Samantha's cot.

Sister Samantha opened the cell door with a jerk. "Whatever is the matter, Sun?"

Without answering, Sun pulled up her oversized tee shirt and exposed a mass of purple-veined stretch-marked breasts.

"I can't run anymore! I think that I have ripped the pectoral muscle just like ancient Indians of the Sun Dance."

"Oh my darling girl! I had no idea! You must be suffering terribly." Sister Samantha retrieved butter from the galley and helped Sun to ease the pain. Sun's small back and rib cage supported large breasts that were a DDD in size, and the stretched skin was bruised and stretched so tight that it made black and purple marks from her collarbone to her abdomen. Sun's chest looked as if it had been clawed by a grizzly bear.

"There are no stores in Wyoming that carry your unusual dimensions. The common size is 34 A, or B at most. I think that you are most likely a 28 DDD bra size. You need a special tailored fit. We will shop locally the best we can to get by until we can get you a decent fit. My parents in Chicago are clothing designers, and they can make you proper undergarments. I haven't seen them for thirteen years, and it is time for them to meet you. I am excited for you to see Chicago, and I have a twitter-pated heart about seeing my parents again. Do you want to go to Chicago?"

"Yes, yes, and more yes!"

Five days later, Sun had the window seat as the Frontier Airlines plane passed over Denver Colorado where they would change planes to American Airlines into Chicago. Sun's eyes stared at the Denver sprawl as the plane circled four times in a holding pattern before it landed.

"How can so many buildings be there?"

"It is just the way the city grew. We have a two-hour layover at the airport, and we can have lunch."

"Will they give us Coke and glazed donuts or maybe a hot dog?"

"I am thinking that we might want to experience Asian food."

Sister Samantha led the way down the corridor to an Asian restaurant, and Sun trailed behind. Sister Samantha turned around and panicked to see that Sun was not behind her. Sister Samantha's heart did the drumbeat dance in her chest as her eyes searched the area. She became frantic in her search before she spotted Sun standing stiffly beside a corridor wall. Sister Samantha dashed to her.

"Sun, you scared me senseless. I thought that I had lost you. Why didn't you follow me?"

"Why are all these people standing so close to me? I feel trapped in a cage." Sun's tawny tiny, fine-featured face asked the question in contorted disdain. Her eyebrows were furrowed into a deep frown, and her big green eyes expressed fright. Sister Samantha understood her discomfort immediately.

"Sun, this is your first experience of being in a crowd. This is just the way that city life is. At home there are not enough people for you to ever be in a crowd, and when the people cluster together at home, you know them all, and it isn't terrifying. Keep a tight hold on my hand, and see if you can relax and learn to enjoy the crowd experience."

Samantha saw Sun relax as she was amazed at the colorful Asian cuisine when it was delivered to their red-cushioned booth by waiters who wore beautiful red-and-black silk kimonos. Sun cautiously attempted the chopsticks after Sister Samantha demonstrated the task with dexterity. Sun Wren's eyes danced with a surprised sparkle as she ventured her first bite.

"This is sooooo good!"

"I thought that you might like it. Do you remember studying about China in Sister Margaret's class?"

"Yes, but it wasn't like this. This is the way I want to learn—through my senses and not through my intellect. Look at those beautiful red paper lanterns, and listen to that unusual tinkle music. It makes me want to get up and dance." Sun sniffed the air. "China even smells yummy. I remember things that Sister Margaret told us about the Great Wall and the Silk Road. I want to go to China someday."

"Me too! Can we go together?" Sister Samantha laughed. The nun and foundling enjoyed each other with a new perspective, and Sister Samantha realized how this travel exposure had already taken hold to develop Sun's education.

"Come on, Sun Wren. We have a plane to catch to Chicago!"

Sun's first view of Chicago from the American Airlines window was unbelievable to her young senses. "Is all this Chicago?"

"Yes, Sun, it is all just one city. Chicago covers 227 square miles"

"How many miles does the rez cover?"

"Hmmm ... it's about 3,500 square miles."

"Are you telling me that this one city of Chicago is 204 times bigger than the whole Wind River Reservation?"

"Yes. You did that math rather quickly. Just look at it! It is the second-biggest city in the United States. New York is even bigger. There are roughly twelve thousand people living in one square mile. That means that all the people that you know on the reservation would easily live in one block of Chicago."

"Well, what about Laramie, Wyoming? That is a big city. What about the whole state of Wyoming?"

"Sun, it would take four times the entire population of Wyoming to fill Chicago. The population of Chicago is almost 2.7 million, and the population of Wyoming is just under five hundred thousand."

"Wow! That is a lot of people down there."

"Yes, Sun, it is, and it is no wonder that you felt trapped in a cage. It will take you time to get used to the crowd and city life. My parents will meet us at baggage claim. Do you have all your stuff?"

"Yup."

"Keep close behind me, Sun. Let's go see my mom and dad!"

Sister Samantha strode out of the plane and down the gangway to baggage claim. She turned to see Sun twirling in circles in the middle of the crowded terminal. Sister Samantha stood and watched this cute, dark four-foot-eleven attractive preteen. Sun wore her new Samantha-designed emerald-green dress that fit the body of an adorable young lady. The dress was the latest '60s design with a fitted bodice and a princess drop-waist skirt that ended just below Sun's knees. Sister Samantha had found ballerina-style flat fabric shoes from the Charity Thrift Shop that she had dyed with green indelible ink to match Sun's dress. She was pleased with Sun's appearance and gazed at her creative handiwork. Sister Samantha watched the dark poodle-haircut girl in the center of the airport terminal.

"Sun Wren, keep up with me, please."

"I love, love, love, it. I can feel the collective energy that all these people are releasing, and I am absorbing it into myself. I feel its power, and it makes me feel strong!"

Sister Samantha smiled as she took Sun's hand.

Sister Samantha's parents didn't have any difficulty finding her at baggage claim since she was the only nun in the vicinity. Sun found her battered gray Charity Store bag and looked up to see a distinguished couple, who hollered, "Sam, Sam," as they rushed to engulf Sister Samantha with hugs and kisses all over her face.

"Mom and Dad, I want you to meet Sun."

"Sun?" repeated a beautiful blonde woman with her hair in a French twist. "I thought you said that your child's name was Wren."

"Yes, Mom, my baby Wren has grown to become Sun. Sun, this is my mother, Bogetta Favre, and my father, Lars Favre."

"I am glad to meet you. You called her Sam, but we all call her Sister Samantha."

"Yes, Sam is the childhood name that Lars and I called her when she was little."

"Your name was Wren, but now you are Sun. Our Sam grew to become Sister Samantha. Come on, everyone, let's go home."

The tall blond man, Lars, had a mustache and a gray sports jacket, and he herded the group to the curb of the terminal.

"Jake will pick us up."

Sun's system was overwhelmed into silence as she watched a white stretch limousine pull to the curb, and a uniformed driver took their luggage and placed it into the luggage compartment. The driver held the door while all four passengers climbed into the back.

"Is this a car or a bus?" Her question remained drowned by the family chatter.

Sun sat beside the window and was spellbound by the

sights and sounds of the city. She heard nothing of the family conversation between Sister Samantha and her parents. Sun wondered if what she saw was real. The contrast between her life and the life that Sister Samantha knew was jolting. What she saw left her to feel small and empty. She watched as skyscrapers, busses, trains, many types of cars, taxies, and fascinating storefronts passed in her view. For the first time in her life, she didn't know who she was. She felt so lost that she wanted to cry, but she didn't. The car passed lovely parks, lakes, and trees until it turned into a narrow paved driveway to a house. Then she vaguely heard Sister Samantha say, "This is my home."

The house was as big as the school building on the University of Wyoming campus and was surrounded by green grass, purple flowers, and trees, trees, trees. Sun had never seen so many trees in one place. The car pulled into a circular driveway and stopped. The driver opened the car door. Another man wearing a blue uniform came out from the house and took the luggage inside.

"Zetta has planned dinner for us at seven thirty, and Janette will show Sun to her room."

"Thanks, Mom, but I can show Sun Wren to her room, and we will see you at seven thirty for dinner."

"Okay, darling. I have laid out a new outfit for you that your father and I thought you might like to wear now that you're home."

Sister Samantha nudged Sun out of the opened car door.

"Sister Samantha, is this place really where you grew up, and how many people live in this house with you?"

"Yes, Sun, it is my childhood home, and only the Favre family live here, my parents and I. Come on, I will show you the house."

Sun Wren had no sense of direction inside the Favre mansion. She couldn't tell the directions because she couldn't see the sun or mountains, and she thought she was a mouse inside a maze. Sister Samantha showed her the exercise room, the indoor Olympic-size swimming pool, and the galley Sister Samantha called the kitchen. She saw the Avonelle design room where Bogetta and Lars each had their design drafting tables for working at home. The place Sister Samantha called the galley was not a kitchen like Incaranata Hall, but it was a long hallway that had pictures from their home country of Switzerland of the Favre aunts, uncles, and cousins. Wren's eyes opened wide and her arched eyebrows lifted when she realized she'd seen more than twelve telephones throughout the house.

"Do you have a lot of rubbering with so many telephones?"

Sister Samantha answered with a laugh, "Nope, we don't even have one person like Hilda who listens in to our conversations. All these phones are a private line. Our family has a number, and it is published in this phone directory."

Sister Samantha held up two big books each the size of a volume of the Encyclopedia Britannica from Sun Wren's school. Sun gazed over the thousands of names listed in the directory.

"All the names are alphabetical. See if you can find our phone number."

Sister Samantha handed Sun the books. Sun Wren quickly understood that she would only need to look near the middle of the first book. She traced her finger down the list and found the name Favre. She found a listing for Bogetta and another listing for Lars.

"Do you have a listing too?"

"I did once, but now I have been gone for too many years, and my parents use my phone as an extension."

The waif and the Chicago princess sat alone on the edge of

Sister Samantha's giant bed and inspected the elegant trendy '60s lavender jumpsuit that was designed by her Favre parents.

"Sister Samantha, will you wear this jumpsuit?"

"Yes." Samantha rolled her eyes and said, "The fifth commandment is honor thy father and thy mother."

"Put it on now, and let's see how you look!"

"I will wear it tonight for dinner. Come on, let's go see your room."

They sauntered down the hall as Sun's eyes drank in the opulence of this grand home.

"Sister Samantha, your house is bigger than Incaranata Hall."

"Yes. When I first went to the Wind River Reservation, I felt like you are feeling now, only in reverse. I had to adjust to the smallness of everything, the lack of my large bedroom, fancy food, silly friends, a car for every occasion, expensive clothing, telephones, domestic workers, and parents. I don't think that I was a very nice person when I first got to the Indian Mission. I was obstreperous. I wanted attention, and I tried to get it by doing stupid things."

"Like what?"

"Like putting a frog into Sister Margaret's denture cup."

"*You didn't!*"

"Yeah, I did."

"Sister Samantha, why did you want to leave all this good stuff?"

"I could see what a waste all this splendor is. There are so many people who are hungry, lonely, and sick. I wanted to help people to have happiness in their lives. All this beautiful stuff doesn't make for real happiness."

"Your parents seem to be happy."

"You will have two weeks to determine if you think that is

true." Sister Samantha gave Sun Wren a little pat on her curly poodle head. "Having you and the Indian Mission in my life has been my greatest joy. Sun Wren, I have loved being your surrogate mom, and no amount of stuff can make me as happy as I am to be with you and doing my job at the school. One of the most valuable things that I can do is to help provide the funds so the Indian Mission can survive, and to help the reservation kids." Sister Samantha stood up.

"I want to take a shower before seven. Did you see your bathroom?" Sister Samantha pointed to show Sun Wren that she had her own bathroom in her bedroom too.

"That is cool."

At 6:45, Sun was startled to hear the phone ring in her bedroom. *Am I expected to answer it?*

"Good evening. This is Miss Sun Wren. May I help you?"

Peals of laughter wafted through the phone.

"Yes, you may, Miss Sun Wren. Are you ready to go downstairs for dinner?"

"I am starving, Sister Samantha, but I don't know where to go. I found a cute pink dress laid out for me in the bathroom, and I am wearing it."

"Great, I will come to your room and get you."

The dress fit perfectly except Sun could not get the chest area of the dress to button, so she wore a white tee shirt under it. She heard the soft rap on her door.

"Princess Samantha may enter. If it is the witch who will erase everything that I am seeing, then she can erase herself!"

Sister Samantha entered, and Sun Wren was in awe. "Sister Samantha! Is that really you? You look like a movie star."

"No, it is not really me, but it is the Samantha Favre that my parents want me to be. You look so cute yourself, Miss Sun Wren! Let's go to dinner."

Samantha Favre was drop-dead-gorgeous fully made up in make-up. Her beautifully dimpled smile accentuate her long-thick black mascara eyelashes, eyeliner, and lavender eyeshadow that matched her jumpsuit and shoes. Samantha's blonde hair was worn down fluffy-long like the actress Farrah Fawcett that Wren had seen in Waffle Stomper's magazines. The two reformed convent refugees glided to the dining room.

The dining room was prepared with linen napkins, tablecloth, china dishes, many silver utensils, and fresh flowers. Samantha gave Sun her first lesson in fine dining.

"You girls look stunning! That little pink dress is one that Sam wore in a fashion show when she was just seven years old. I wanted to compliment you on your green dress that you were wearing at the airport. It suited you nicely."

"Thank you. It was designed by an exclusive fashion designer, Sister Samantha from Wyoming."

Bogetta Favre eyes lit up, and her face broke into a beautiful smile with peels of low laughter. She beamed her acceptance and fondness for Sun Wren at that moment. Bogetta's thick blonde hair was piled into a soft French twist and her dimpled face framed her bright blue laughing eyes. She was tall like Sister Samantha and her slender body was clad in a lavender-gray long evening dress that shimmered.

"I thought that I recognized the creative style, but the choice of fabric was perfect for your body shape and complexion."

"Thank you. What would you like me to call you, Mrs. Favre? Sister Samantha calls you mom. Should I do that too?"

"No, Mrs. Favre will do nicely. Sam, will you please say grace?"

"Yes." Sister Samantha recited her usual mealtime prayer.

"Sam I can't believe that you are with us today after so many years away. Of course we telephone and write, but it's not the same as having you back at our table again. You have become a stunning twenty-seven-year-old model that would turn heads on the runway." Mr. Favre winked at Sister Samantha like a proud father.

"Before I forget, here is an envelope of tickets for you to use to show Sun Wren around Chicago. Tomorrow escort Sun Wren to the Avonelle Building by nine a.m. and we can get started designing the needed undergarments. We have three new designers that will love to compete for the privilege of designing a day dress, sports attire, and a business dress for her too."

"Dad, Sun Wren has no place to wear those clothes."

"Nonsense, all girls have places to wear nice clothes. I think that Sun has grown into her adulthood size and shape even if she is only eleven, and probably won't grow much more. She can use the clothes for many years."

"Thank you, Mr. Favre. What is the Avonelle Building?" Sun Wren tried to learn about the Favre family.

"Avonelle is the name of the clothing line that my parents design and market worldwide."

Janette entered caring a telephone to the table and stood beside Mr. Favre.

"Sir, forgive the interruption, but Felix is on the line with an urgent call."

Mrs. Favre, Sister Samantha, and Sun enjoyed the bountiful gourmet dinner while Mr. Favre accepted the call.

"Yes, Felix, what is it? Did she die? Felix, this is not a problem. My daughter just arrived in town. She is the exact size as Felicity, and she will do the show on Tuesday in her place. My daughter Sam and another young lady are coming to Avonelle tomorrow. They will be there in the morning by nine if any alternations need to be made. She will also be available for hair and makeup instructions before the Tuesday show. Take care of this tomorrow, Felix. This will not be any trouble since my daughter knows the runway business. Let me know Felicity's condition and oh, send her some flowers or something." Lars Favre hung up, and Janette removed the telephone and left the dining room.

"These hungry, emotional, high-strung women are always causing glitches into our perfected shows. The Avonelle show on Tuesday is our most important 1964 fall fashion line, and the success of it finances the business until the Christmas holiday Avonelle line debuts. We are so fortunate to have Samantha here to step in and help out." He winked and smiled at Sister Samantha.

"There is a high turnover of models in this business, but Felicity has been with us for as long as Samantha has been gone. You have met her haven't you Sam?" Mrs. Favre asked as she refilled her wine glass.

"Yes, I was sixteen. It was my last Avonelle show, and it was Felicity's first. Why can't she do the show on Tuesday?"

"I don't know. It seems that she tried to commit suicide or perhaps just overdosed by accident. These women take so many diet pills, appetite control, or nonfluid-absorbing pills to stay thin, and Felicity suffers from bouts of depression. She makes good money as an Avonelle star model, lives in an expensive apartment, has a sports car, but she is just an unhappy person. We are lucky to have Samantha to help us out of this jam. Bogetta and I have work to do tonight. Sam, skip the dessert, but Sun Wren, please have dessert and spend the evening as you wish. Don't forget to use the envelope of tickets. Please excuse us." Mr. and Mrs. Favre pushed back from the table and retreated into the designing workshop office.

"Sister Samantha, I can't believe how beautiful you are. It's like you are a different person."

"Yes, I am a different person, all superficial, glitzy, and ornamental without any substance. My parents don't see the human inner quality in me or in anyone. I was so excited to see my parents, but now I realize that nothing has changed since I was sixteen. Do you want to take a swim and then say compline together before bedtime?"

"Yeah, a swimming pool inside of your house is cool."

Sister Samantha swam many laps with the vigor Sun understood. Wren was in awe of the Olympic home swimming pool. She had only been to a swimming pool once when katybear had taken Wren into Riverton to pick up her kids. Compline was said, and Sun delighted in the bedtime tuck that Sister Samantha gave, but she couldn't fall sleep. The house was too big, too quiet, too lonely, and lacked the emanated love from twenty-four nuns. Wren left her bed, padded down the hall to Sister Samantha's bed, and slipped under the lavender silk sheets that covered Sister Samantha, who slept undisturbed.

"Well, good morning little Miss Sun Wren! I am surprised to see you snuggled into my bed. Couldn't you sleep?"

Sun shook her head and stretched.

"Jake, our Favre driver will pick us up by eight a.m. We will be at Avonelle most of the day. I will be getting groomed for the Tuesday fashion show, and you will be busy being measured, fitted, and altered, but the employees will bring us our meals, including breakfast. Jake will bring us home at five p.m., and we will have dinner with my parents at seven. We have been sucked up by the Avonelle vacuum until after the show, but then we can use the rest of our time to explore Chicago."

The Avonelle building was a cream-colored granite fronted skyscraper with fifty-two floors. Samantha explained that her parents owned the building, used twenty of the floors, and leased the other thirty-two floors out to other businesses. Many of the tall Chicago building had glass that reflected the sunlight, and the Avonelle building was definitively shiny.

The Favre Avonelle schedule of events unfurled as Sister Samantha had related. Sun Wren understood the inhuman experience that she had described the night before. She felt like a piece of machinery, and each of the workers changed her parts, adjusted, transformed, created, and maintained her physical form.

"Dear, you are quite cute, but you are too small to ever be a runway model, but our order told us to give you the works. So, let's get started!"

Sun received a facial, and hairstyle that included a piled high curly hairpiece that sat on the top of her head, which made her two inches taller. She received a manicure/pedicure, massage, skin care, teeth whitening, eye lash extensions, and a total foundation makeover. At the end of the day, Sun looked into the mirror, and she was astounded to see the result. She appeared to be over eighteen years old instead of eleven. She liked the outcome, but she understood exactly how Sister Samantha felt about herself. She understood how the models were pressured and required to maintain this appearance as their persona. No wonder they took pills and tried to end their lives. Sun took one more glance into the mirror. No, truth was she stared at herself for over fifteen minutes. It was magical how she had changed, and who had she become? The Chicago experience answered that question for her. She and Sister Samantha were on schedule for the Favre dinner at 7:00 p.m.

"Sun, you have metamorphosed into a little beauty, and, Sam, your straight auburn hair will accentuate the fall colored outfits that you will wear in tomorrow's show. Lars, do you think that Sam's hair should be redder?"

"No, Avonelle did a great job with her. She will be wearing

gold and rust colored outfits too, and the auburn hair will do nicely for all the clothing. This mint-glazed duck is wonderful tonight. Sun, would you like some more? You don't need to worry about keeping your stomach flat for tomorrows show."

He jived Sun, but his statement was directed toward Sister Samantha. At the end of dinner, Mrs. Favre handed Sun a powder blue silk bag.

"Here is the sleeping face cover to use tonight. Sam already has hers." Sun's expression showed bewilderment.

"You will put the bag over your head and face to preserve your hairstyle and make-up." Sun accepted the silk bag in awe.

"It helps you to stay fresh for tomorrow's event. Mr. Favre and I have loads to do tonight, and you girls need to get lots of sleep to meet tomorrow's demands." Sister Samantha and Sun reluctantly moseyed to their separate bedrooms clutching the powder blue silk bags.

In the morning, Sun and Sister Samantha entered the Avonelle building on schedule. Sun Wren was aware of the heightened tension from employees, models, designers, and owners. The fashion show began at 10:00 a.m., and Samantha left to do her required performance. Sun sat in her reserved seat. She was overwhelmed by the stress of the fashion world. She saw Mr. Favre display anger with an employee, models who cried, employees who clutched pieces of fabric, a young man hollered for people to move as he pushed a cart full of shoes. The atmosphere was unpleasant energy and caused Wren to have inner disquiet. The show was an all-day event that represented many brands from over seven countries. Mrs. Favre had a reserved chair next to Sun, but she only sat down for thirty seconds to invite her to meet in the Avonelle tea room at one-thirty for lunch.

Sun was highly entertained by runway glamour, and the

morning passed quickly. She left her powder-blue cushioned chair at 1:15 in search of Mrs. Favre who waited in the tearoom. The walls of the tearoom were an elegant cream linen color, and the powder-blue carpet gave a sedate, quiet atmosphere. Sun noted that everything the Favres touched had elegance. The smell of pastries permeated the tearoom, and reminded Sun of her hunger.

"Hi, Mrs. Favre," Sun gave a big friendly wave. "I saw Sister Samantha, and she looked beautiful." The other fashion industry diners gave Mrs. Favre and Sun Wren sideward glances of respect as they raised their eyebrows toward their direction.

"I thought so too dear. Sit close so that we can talk without others overhearing." Sun settled into the designated chair.

"What was your favorite outfit that you saw this morning?"

"I thought that the Louis Vuitton emerald-green dress was the coolest, but I thought that Sister Samantha knew how to do her turns much better than the Louis Vuitton model. Avonelle and Sister Samantha when she wore the rust colored skirt and boots was my second most favorite."

"You have a keen eye," Mrs. Favre said. "Louis Vuitton is the most expensive brand in the world, so if you chose Avonelle as second place, I can live with that!" The giddy laughter of the nearby models seeped into their conversation, and disquieted the tearoom.

"Sam is a natural at modeling. You know that she is our only child, and it is our hope that she should come back to Chicago, and take an interest in this business."

"I don't think that Sister Samantha likes the fashion world very much. Do you know that she is a beloved teacher and nun? I love her so much, and so do the kids at the Indian Mission."

Mrs. Favre's smile turned to plastic, the attractive dimples disappeared into the hardened lines around her pursed lips that slammed together into a silence that lasted throughout lunch. Sun Wren said grace out loud, and ate the chicken cordon bleu with great gusto. Mrs. Favre walked Sun back to her seat, but she didn't sit with her.

"Enjoy the rest of the show, dear."

"Thank you and Mr. Favre for the Chicago event tickets. I want to see Chicago."

Sister Samantha and Sun spent the last week of their visit exploring the wonders of Chicago, and on Friday they returned to Wyoming. Sun stuffed her new clothing into her Charity Thrift Shop dilapidated bag, but Sister Samantha left hers in the closet.

"Thank you, Mr. and Mrs. Favre, for everything that you have done for me. I will remember this Chicago visit for the rest of my life. I have learned so much, and the best gift that you have given me has been Sister Samantha. I know what a sacrifice that has been for you, and my thanks is not big enough." Sun gave a heartfelt hug to Mrs. Favre and shook Mr. Favre's hand.

"Mom and Dad, I am proud of you both for your successful show. I love you both very much."

Sister Samantha sat down into the white Favre limousine, and swung her legs in last as she had been taught to do, even though her legs were hidden beneath her long familiar habit.

Sun Wren was glad to be nestled beside Sister Samantha on the return flight. Sun felt a magnified attachment to her nun. She understood and admired the relinquished life that Sister Samantha had released to enable a greater good for humanity by living with less. Sun saw that Sister Samantha had achieved her vows of Poverty and Chasity, but she knew that Sister Samantha justifiably struggled with Obedience toward her parents.

"I am so relieved and unburdened to be leaving Chicago, and that synthetic life."

"Avonelle gave me the hair piece, false eye lashes and makeup. Would you help me to put it all back on when we get to Incaranata Hall? I want to show Judy how I looked. She won't believe this stuff unless I show her," Sister Samantha laughed.

"It all is quite ineffable. I guess that I am bringing some of that synthetic life back to the rez," She chuckled. "Yes, we can get you all gussied up to show katybear too! We will get home this afternoon in time for you to see Judy."

"Can I spend the night? I have so many things to tell her."

Chapter 19

FAREWELL

Sun walked, not ran the three miles to katybear's house, and she moved slowly so she wouldn't sweat under the hairpiece and Avonelle fashion runway makeup. She clutched the powder-blue silk nighttime bag that she had stuffed with Chicago brochures.

"Yoo-hoo! Judy, I am at the back door!" Judy came to the kitchen screen door and saw Sun.

"Sun Wren? What in the world have you done? I wouldn't have known it was you if you hadn't told me you were coming! Look at you! *Mom, come and see Sun!*"

Katybear and Judy stood in the messy kitchen where katybear had fixed food to take to a friend, but turned to gaze in amazement at the transformed Sun.

Sun laughed. "Look at this."

She pulled up her shirt, and showed Judy and katybear her new bra. They were dazzled. Sun brought the blue silk bag from behind her back. "Guess what this is for."

"It's a fancy book bag, right?"

"No, Judy, the models actually put this over their heads,

like this. You put the bag over your head and face to preserve your hairstyle and makeup!" She talked with her head inside the bag. "This is my new Chicago, Avonelle *Sun Wren* look." Sun removed the bag from her head.

"I want to see your eyes. How did you grow the long eyelashes?" Katybear peered into Sun's eyes.

"They come in a box, and are glued onto the eyelashes."

Katybear touched Sun's eyes. "They feel like real lashes, only Indians don't have lashes, and, Sun, you naturally have more lashes than Arapahos or Shoshoni, but now with those lashes, you look as if your eyes are butterflies. You also grew taller." Katybear stood next to Sun and measured up.

"No, I'm not, but I look taller. Look at this." She pulled back some of the curls on the top of her head to show the fake hairpiece. "It just makes me look like I am two inches taller."

Judy continued to stare at her, "When you came to the door, I thought that you were some college girl selling magazines."

"You won't believe the things that the models do to themselves to get the special look that they want. One model put electrical tape under her butt to make it fluff up! Another one put the big boulder marbles into her mouth so her cheeks would look fatter."

"You girls have lots to talk about, but I have to deliver this food. Judy can tell me everything later." Katybear gathered the food trays, put them into the van, and hurried away. Judy and Sun began to clean up the kitchen as they talked.

"Judy, I am glad to be back with real people who are as they seem to be. You should have seen Sister Samantha and what they did to her. She was gorgeous, but I didn't even know her. They painted her hair auburn. Auburn is dark red, and she was so made up with green eye makeup that her blue eyes looked green. Judy, you are as pretty as any of those models without doing any of that fake stuff. You don't even know what a beautiful girl you are. You are a real person in all the world, and your beauty is forever the same. You don't need to do anything to be pretty. You just are! I am glad that you are my friend, not because you are pretty, but because you are beautiful in your mind and heart too."

Judy was surprised when Sun gave her a huge hug. "Sun, I love you too, like you are my blood sister. You have always been the bold one. You are fearless. Even when we were little, it was you that led the way. That's why we have been good friends for each other. You know no fear, and I have no boldness."

"I missed you so much, and I wished you could have been there to see everything. Look at these pictures of skyscrapers!" The two friends sat at the kitchen table talking about Chicago until Homer and the Arapaho Racer Taxi arrived, and seven of Judy's siblings tumbled out. They all clamored to see the pictures and brochures that Sun displayed on the kitchen table. The Bear's house changed from a quiet kitchen into a din of chatter. Sun captured their attention with her stories about the Chicago Shed Aquarium and Zoo. She told about Wrigley Field, and the many baseball teams that played there. She told Judy's captivated brothers about the Chicago Cubs, White Sox, and the Blackhawks. Sun's favorite places were the beautiful Chicago parks with millions of people and trees. She described the strange people who frequented them. Sun lost her captured male audience when she droned on for half an hour about attending the ballet.

Judy and Sun prepared hot dogs and Coke for everyone's supper while she talked about the ballerinas, and while katybear was away. As the dark of night covered the flat plains, the Bear children drifted off to their own amusements, and Judy took her Coke into the living room to gaze out the window at the newly appeared stars, while Sun finished cleaning up the kitchen.

Sun folded up the dishtowel after she wiped the counter surface clean, and swept up the hot dog bun crumbs from the floor. Sun was startled when she heard the sound of firecrackers, and shattered glass from the living room. She set the broom aside and dashed to find Judy. She screamed when she saw the shattered window shards scattered on the floor, the walls splattered with Judy's blood, and Judy's crumpled body in a heap on the floor. She ran, slid to the floor, and cradled her in her lap. Sun looked at her friend, but she had no face. Judy's face had been blown away. Her face, and part of her head were gone, and a mangled red mess of meat remained. She sat hugging the limp body while Homer Bear and the children crowded around hysterically screaming and shouting. Sun felt Judy's blood flow onto her arms and thighs, and she reveled in its warmth. Her clothes were saturated with her friend's blood, and she relished the sensation of Judy's melting spirit. She wanted to absorb this precious life into her own.

Susan Bear had arrived home from work, picked up the phone, and urgently spoke. "Judy's been shot, we need help here!"

The party line was a clamor of voices. She hung up, ran to her sister, Sun Wren, and dropped to the floor beside her dad.

Homer searched for a pulse, but Sun knew that she was gone. Sun sobbed, and shouted,

"She knew! She knew from the cloud game," but Sun's words were wasted on ears that didn't understand, and minds that were in emotional turmoil.

The ambulance lights flashed, and the high-pitched siren screamed, but Sun Wren held on to her friend until the ambulance responders pried Judy's body from her arms.

"She's gone, Sun. She's gone. You have to let her go now," coaxed Homer Bear.

Three reservation police cars arrived with blaring lights and sirens. Katybear's van pulled up in the mix of vehicles, her driver's door flew open, and a horrified katybear sprang out.

"What's wrong? What is going on?"

One of the officers answered. "It looks like a drive-by shooting."

Katybear sprinted up the steps and into the house to see Judy's body being pried from Sun Wren's hug. Katybear wrapped her arms around Sun and wailed. "Oh dear God, no! No! No!"

Sun untangled herself from katybear's arms and bolted out of the door with a track team start.

"Sun," hollered an officer, "where are you going?"

"I am going home," screamed Sun.

"Get into the police car. I will drive you."

During the three-mile drive, Sun was numb. She was cold and hot at the same time. She couldn't think straight, and she wanted to run. The police officer talked to her, but she didn't hear his words, nor did she answer. She ran into Incaranata Hall, and started packing up her things. Sister Samantha had been sewing, but entered Sun's Generosity cell, and saw her frantic behavior.

"Sun, I heard the news, and I am ———."

Sister Samantha was careful to observe the Shoshoni way about not speaking the name of the deceased.

"Take off your blood soaked clothes, and put these on. Please come to Chapel with me." Sun did not respond. She grabbed the scissors from Sister Samantha's sewing basket, and ran to the chapel while Sister Samantha trailed. Throughout the mass that was said for Judy, Sun proceeded to cut off her short-cropped hair to the scalp. Her grief was ineffable. At the end of mass, Sun sprinted back to her cell while Sister Samantha stayed behind to sweep up the fallen curls. Sister Samantha softly entered Sun's cell, and hugged her while she wept.

"I want to run away."

"Okay! I will help you to do that very thing, if you promise to return to me when you are ready." Sun looked at her in surprise.

"Sun, I will never stand in your way. I will not become the obstacle to inhibit your intuition, the way that my parents interfered with mine."

"But I don't know where to go."

"Yes, you do! You have your own secret place." Sister Samantha opened the box that was hidden under her cot.

"Here is the map that I have kept for you for almost four years now." Again, Sister Samantha was careful not to speak Owl's name.

"He gave it to you and told you to go there whenever you wanted. I know that Sister Sara has been giving you driving lessons. Can you drive there by yourself?"

Sun nodded.

"I will pack food and water for you in small bags that will fit easily through the portal. You can leave an extra supply of water in the Chariot and use it as you travel. Sun will you allow me to call Big Boots and Waffle Stomper to tell them of your plans?"

Sun, nodded affirmatively again.

"You may pack up tonight and leave at first light. I love you with all my being, and I share your grief, but you are free to express suffering in your own way without interference from anyone, including me."

Sun threw her arms around Sister Samantha neck and sobbed. "I want to call Big Boots and Waffle Stomper myself right now."

"Absolutely, that is the responsible thing to do. This time of night, Hilda won't be rubbering." Sister Samantha gave Sun a sly little wink and smile.

Big Boots phone rang five times before he picked it up.

"Yup, this is Big Boots."

"I am so glad that you picked up the phone. Godfather, I wanted to tell you that I am gong to run away."

"Hi, Sun. No, you are not running away. You are going on your first vision quest."

"I don't know how to do a vision quest."

"Do you want my help?"

"Yes, I do, Godfather."

"When a Shoshoni boy turns between twelve or fourteen it is time for him to become his own person. He no longer is dependent upon his mother. This is the time when he leaves childhood to become an adult. The vision quest is not a part of the ancient Shoshoni tradition, it is actually a Mandan tribal practice, but it was borrowed from them, and used by our Shoshoni tribe for many years. It is a useful tool to build self-awareness, so it has been followed as our tradition. A Shoshoni must become a responsible member of his tribe. You became your own master when you were seven, but it is important for you to prove to yourself that you have become a responsible adult. Sun, I admire your spunk. I have not known any women who wanted to do a vision quest. It is only for men. The vision quest is similar to the Sun Dance in the sense that the devotee has helpers. This is another reason that you are remarkable. You are doing this alone. Would you like me to check on you?"

"Yes, please, Godfather, but I do not want anyone to know where I am. I am in a secret place, but you can get the map from Sister Sara."

"The vision quest is to be completed in three days, but you can start it whenever you choose. Usually the helpers do a sweat lodge cleansing ceremony, but you will not have helpers or a sweat lodge. Please listen to the list of things that you must take with you. Do you want to write them down?"

"Yes, I have a pen and paper, and I am ready to follow your instructions." Sun compiled her list from Godfather's words.

"Thank you for helping me, Godfather. Running away is much easier now that I know that I have a purpose and that grief is not chasing me off. I will spend the night getting the list together, and I will follow your instructions. I will leave tomorrow at first light, but I will not begin the quest until I am ready. It may be a few days before I begin. I have a long drive tomorrow."

"Sun, one more caution to follow: If you are in the monthly cycle don't go on the quest until you have finished. If you start the monthly period, come home! Don't stay out there by yourself. It is too dangerous with the grizzly and brown bears. They are not mean animals by nature, but they have acute sense of smell, and poor eye sight, and they may think that you are lunch."

"Yes, I understand, and I am leaving in the morning."

"Sun, are you driving alone?"

"Yes."

"Are you a good driver?"

"Good enough to make the car move. I love you, Godfather, and Waffle too. Good night!"

Eleven-year-old Sun Wren's strong intuition to leave Incaranata Hall was on overdrive. Something propelled her to hasten. The sun's morning orange glow broke through the horizon with the strong smell of sage. Sun Wren packed the old gray Chariot with the list of quest survival gear, and returned to Incaranata Hall to load the food and water that Sister Samantha prepared. Sister Samantha padded into the galley as Sun was toting the last load.

"I am so glad that I caught you in time to say goodbye. Please return to me, Sun. I love you beyond words. This is the end of August and school will start on your birthday, but don't come back until it is right for you." Sun gave Sister Samantha a heartfelt hug and kissed her cheek.

"I will return when I have healed my wounds."

Sun laid the map that Owl had given her onto the passenger's seat so she could follow the written directions at a glance. Sun's eyes flooded with tears as she looked at Owl's handwriting, now gone, and it gave testimony that two admirable lives had evaporated. She cleared her vision, and pressed on the execrator. The old Chariot jerked and jolted in the same manner as when Sara began to drive, but Sun knew how to dance, and she used the clutch much smoother than Sara's first attempts. Sun was able to merge with the car's rhythm. The Chariot was Sun's dance partner, and it responded to her agility and dexterous moves as she put Incaranata Hall and the many miles behind her. Godfather said, "Keep the vehicle between the fence posts, sister." Sister Sara taught her to sight the Chariot's hood ornament with the middle of the road to give her driving consistency, and to keep if from wobbling from one side of the road to the other. Sara's hood-ornament lesson gave Sun more control over the Chariot.

Sun focused on her destination, and kept the last images of Judy's face at bay. She matched the map with the visual landmarks along the way. Suddenly she slammed her foot on the brake, and pulled over in the middle of nowhere. She spotted a patch of mature kinnickinnick growing on the prairie. She turned off the car, and sprinted to the plant. This was the only thing on her godfathers' list that she didn't have, and there it grew. She broke off a big piece, and toted it to the trunk of the car. She felt victorious to have completed the needed list. She was set to continue to her sixty-mile destination.

Sun arrived at the same monochromatic sand colored cow path she had walked as a seven-year-old, and parked the Chariot. She carried what she could, and planned to come back to the car for the other things later. She trudged the same trail for an hour, and it was as she had remembered. She arrived at the boulder area. Sun Wren studied the map, and selected the boulder that she thought concealed the portal. She remembered how Owl moved several boulders before finding the correct one. She tried to move the boulder she determined was the entrance, but her tiny size did not have strength enough. *What if this boulder is incorrect and I give all my effort only to find out that it is not the right one?* She sat down beside the boulder and looked at the map again. She knew that her legs were stronger than her upper body. She took a deep breath, closed her eyes to the brightness of the day, and connected with the earth energy. Sun soaked up energy from the universe, searched for her self-determination, and knew that Owl and Judy would assist. She pushed the boulder with all her might, and it moved enough where she could peek underneath to determine that it concealed the portal. She drew her knees up again, pushed with all her strength, and the boulder moved. She scooted her bottom closer to the rock rapidly, used its momentum and her legs to push repeatedly until the entire portal was exposed. *Thank you, thank you, my friends. We have done it.* Sun Wren pushed her bedroll and the food bags down through the entrance, and listened to the thud as they landed. She slithered headfirst like a greased gofer down the hole, and landed on top of the bedroll.

The darkness cast a comfort over her, and she wept with its protectiveness. She was grateful that she had driven the distance without trouble. She sat straight-legged with her long slim limbs splayed out in front of her, and allowed the cool cavern to fill her senses to erase the frantic anxiety she had held within since she had held Judy. She felt safe, free, and the aloneness that she found was pure pleasure. Her intuition had pushed her to ferret out this memorable place, and the same joy that she had felt four years ago erupted again. This cavern bolstered her sense of well-being.

Sun's instincts told her to flee. Psychologists during the '60s believed that a human in crisis would either fight or take flight. Sun's intuitions was to take flight. Sun Wren unfurled her bedroll and arranged it on the level flat ledge landing beneath the portal before it descended and sloped to follow the river downward. Godfather's words proved helpful as she remembered: "Take a comfortable pillow, blanket, and bedroll. Your body must be well rested before you begin the vision quest." Sun Wren quickly fell asleep. This was her first separation from her supportive village family, and from beloved Sister Samantha.

During the two weeks they had spent in Chicago, Sun and Sister Samantha didn't know about the reignited ancient feud between the Arapaho and the Shoshoni. The rez was ablaze with the atrocities of tribal distain and hatred between the two tribes during their Chicago visit. Prior to their trip, the Wind River Reservation enjoyed twenty years of tribal harmony. These were years of childhood happiness that Wren had known. The rez had developed a ShoRap fire department, school system, health clinic, and police department. The joint organizations proved to be more efficient and economical as they worked together. During these peaceful years there were many ShoRap weddings, and an entire generation of ShoRap children were born, but the tribes were not as they had been when they returned. It was a mere blink of an eye, and Indian life was coated in bloodshed and property destruction. It was unclear why the peace ended, or what started the raw conflict again, but there it was.

The last week of August was a true endian-summer with mild tempters and the cottonwood trees showing off their new fall splendor. The day had been a perfectly rewarding day for Sister Samantha, but the prairie night's cool breeze, and the newly emerged stars clustered in the overhead black sky brought melancholy to Samantha. She felt empty, and lonely not knowing the where a-bouts of her Sun-child. Sister Samantha sat on the Indian Mission front steps stargazing when a late model red Ford pickup tore onto the mission grounds, threw gravel, and disturbed the quiet. The red truck blasted its horn, and three angry men jumped out and lighted carried torches.

"We want the little Shoshoni girl who doesn't know how to respect her place under tribal rule." Shouted one of the three inebriated, large Arapaho men who stood outside Incaranata Hall with a lighted torch. The twenty-four nuns had opened the front door and crowded onto the front steps. The nuns were silent, frightened, and didn't know how to respond.

"Call the police and the fire department." Mother Superior directed Sister Margaret, without knowing if any of the first responders would actually arrive. She pushed her way to the front of the crowded nuns to question the three threatening men.

"What do you want here?"

"We want the little girl named Wren," hollered one of the three intruders. Father Patty popped out of the chapel behind the Arapaho men.

The three men turned sharply to place him in their sight of vision as Father Patty stood his ground and answered, "We don't harbor anyone by that name."

"Oh come on now, Father, you know exactly who we mean."

Jason Laughing Dog became enraged, pawed the ground like a rutting Elk, and began to twirl his torch in a threatening manner.

"Yes, maybe I do know who you mean, but Jason, I married you and Thelma, baptized your children, and you are standing beside God's sacred chapel meant for both tribes."

Sister Samantha stood up in front of the nuns, and stepped bravely forward.

"Sun Wren is not here."

Her loud clear words only seemed to further infuriate the three inebriated confrontational bucks. Sister Sara strode closer to the aggressors.

"What Sister Samantha says is true. I have not seen Sun Wren since two weeks ago before she left for her Chicago visit. Maybe she stayed in Chicago. Do you gentlemen wish to search her cell in Incaranata Hall?" Sister Sara spoke her truth since she was unable to attend Judy's funeral mass, and had not seen Sun. Mother Superior grimaced at the thought of these men inside the convent.

"Yeah, we want-a look. Which is hers?"

"I will show you. Follow me." Sister Samantha's confidence further unbalanced the drunk and disorderly unwelcome visitors. They were taken aback by her bravado and by the fact that she didn't cower in their presence.

"I will come with you," said Sister Sara.

The sisters led the way to Sun's cell Generosity, and opened the door so the men could see the half-unpacked suitcase, and jumble of items that suggested a hurried departure. Sister Samantha had disposed Sun's bloodstained clothes into the convent incinerator, and the room revealed that it was vacant. The men grumbled and staggered from the convent, but Laughing Dog threw his lighted torch at the huddled nuns who shrieked and scattered onto the playground to throw sand on their burned garments The three drunks jumped into their pickup, and one of the men fired a shotgun randomly into the chapel area. The shots kicked up the dirt in a series of pings that struck and wounded Father Patty. The firetruck arrived half staffed with only the Shoshoni firefighters, who quickly quenched the remaining flames from the torch, and two Shoshoni policemen applied a tourniquet to Father Patty's injured foot. They took him into Riverton to the Memorial Hospital emergency room. Sister Sara darted to the first aid closet, and attended, six nuns' minor burns that were under their torched habits.

Sister Samantha was unnerved by the anger that spewed from those men, and her thoughts were in a jumble. What would have happened to Sun if she had been here? Were these men responsible for Judy's death? Were they responsible for the random drive-by shootings? Was the attack on Bear's house another random drive-by shooting? Was Judy's death targeted because of Katy Bear's role on the tribal council? Was Judy's death meant to be Sun's? Sun was a Shoshoni who befriended an Arapaho family. Was that the reason these men were looking for her? *Thank God I didn't discourage Sun from using her intuition to run away. I am so glad that she left in the nick of time. It seems years ago that Sun left Incaranata Hall instead of only just this morning. I miss her so much, and it has only been one day that she hasn't been beside me.* Sister Samantha called the hospital to inquire about Father Patty's condition. She was told that he would be released in three days.

The night of Judy's death, Helga told Sister Samantha on the drumbeat about the atrocities that had occurred while she was in Chicago. She was amazed how the rez could be turned upside down in such a short time. The moccasin telegraph related that every night for over two weeks, the drive-by-shootings had become routine. Fourteen injuries had occurred, and two other adult lives had been taken by the random shootings. Jason Laughing Dog's eldest Arapaho daughter had married a Shoshoni, and they had two ShoRap children. She was one of the adults killed in the drive-by-shootings. Sister Samantha felt compassion for the Laughing Dog family, but their expression of grief was poorly illustrated. While she and Sun were in Chicago, the moccasin telegraph told about an Arapaho woman named Feather Music who walked home alone from the Big Chief Casino, and was raped by three alleged Shoshoni hunters who celebrated the kill of a seven-point elk. Feather Music's husband found the drunken men, castrated all three of them, and left them to die on Seventeen Mile Road where a motorist rescued them. Friends bore witness to the Shoshoni hunters' innocence, and retaliated. They burned down Arapaho homes, and three children in a home were burned alive.

For the last few weeks, it was a continual series of violence and retaliation, violence and retaliation over and over again without end. How many winsome people like Jason's daughter, Judy, and Sun Wren would be pulled into the deadly inferno? Sister Samantha felt powerless to stop the reservation rampage, and tonight during compline in the chapel she thanked God for the mission's safety, and prayed for Sun's protection and well-being.

Sun had a long sleep and pleasant night. She woke to a shaft of light that shone in through the portal opening. It perfectly lighted the pictographs on the opposite cavern wall. Sun turned onto her side and studied the magnificent works of art. Now that she was no longer a child, the renderings were far more meaningful. She noticed the menacing figures hidden behind trees that aimed spears ready to target the women who peacefully cooked around the campfire. This was a curious discovery. It was a dominant theme, but she didn't notice it when she viewed it as a child.

Sun knew this was an UP day. She sat up, stretched up, stood up, and felt a surge of hunger. She unwrapped the food bag. The Indian Mission received its share of Indian commodities, and Sister Samantha had packed them for her. Sun ate the most perishable foods first. She drank the milk, ate the banana, berries, and cut off a big slice from the brick of cheese. The tribe's nickname for the US commodities food was commie food, or jokingly slang words for communist food. Many tribal members resented, or disliked the given provisions, which were easy items to subsidize drinking addictions. The commie contraband was taken into town and sold to non-Indian people who were eager to buy the items, and especially the high quality cheese, which was unavailable in local groceries. While the commie food was resented, it was a needed provision that sustained many, including Incaranata Hall.

The Foundling's Chapel and Incaranata Hall training was part of her strong self-discipline. Her first day alone began with matins morning prayers, lauds lunch prayers, vespers were said at four in the afternoon, and at bedtime she completed compline. The rituals gave her a fragment of relief from her overpowering grief.

Sun felt contentment and well-being this morning! She began the preparations for her vision quest as Big Boots had instructed. The track star hotfooted the mile trail back to the car, retrieved the kinnickinnick plant from the trunk, and hauled it up to the boulder area near her clandestine cavern. She dove headfirst back into the portal and scavenged through the food supply to utilize the empty berry bag. She emerged into the outside world again, and began to strip the leaves from the stick like plant. Sun Wren placed the leaves on top of the boulder to dry in the sun before she had crunched and pulverized them. When the leaves were dried into a flakey greenish-brown color she scraped them from the rock, and put them into her salvaged berry bag for safekeeping. She repeated the process until all the leaves were crunched, dried, and stored.

Sun as an eleven-year-old was a pioneer environmentalist. She was very careful not to pollute the water stream, the cavern, or the boulder area surrounding the portal. She skipped down the inclined trail toward the car, dug a hole, relieved herself, and covered the debris with dirt. This procedure discouraged the frequent roaming bears from smelling human scent. The downhill buried waste also prevented water pollution in the cavern where she needed to drink. When Sun took her bath she removed the sparkling pure water from the river in a pail, bathed, and poured the dirty bath water onto the ground outside the entrance where she planted a few of the gleaned kinnickinnick seeds. This ritual left the estuary uncontaminated, and if the kinnickinnick plant grew it would provide a place for her to come for future retreats.

Sun roamed the above ground area several miles in each direction and searched for a suitable rock hollowed like a bowl to place the kinnickinnick when it was time to smudge herself. After several hours she found what she was looking for. In between her projects, her emotional loss consumed her. Her grief was ineffable, but her lack of words were expressed as she wailed loudly into the open landscape. The projects gave her purpose and occupied her thoughts, but she couldn't maintain productivity without tearful bouts of grief. The vision quest required three days without food or water. Godfather told her not to start her quest if she was shedding many tears. It may acerbate dehydration and force her to prematurely terminate the quest. Sun remembered the men's dehydrated condition when she was a helper with the Sun Dance, and she knew the dangers. She was alone without helpers and needed to take care of herself. She cried throughout the day, but she drank quarts of the pure water from the cavern to replenish her water loss.

The waif said lauds lunch prayers, ate the perishable meat sandwiches, the box of Hostess Twinkies, and drank more water. Sun Wren was connected to the sun as well as to the earth. She could tell by the position of the sun the time of day even though she had no watch. In the afternoon she sat directly onto the ground, and allowed the earth energy to strengthen her resolve, and to heal her bereavement. She drank more water, but still the tears erupted, and cascaded down her face like hot lava spewing from a volcano. Sun said her 4:00 p.m. vespers and knew that Sister Samantha would also be saying them at the same time. When she finished her prayers, Sun leaped from vespers and ran the hills with a sweat produced vengeance.

Sun remembered Godfather's quest instructions, and understood the importance of the sweat lodge prior to beginning the quest, but she substituted this strenuous hillside run as her sweat lodge requirement. Her exertion was intense to produce the required sweat in this arid, moisture-sucking prairie. The ragamuffin surprised herself after the hard run. She felt relief from the caged anger, anxiety, and resentment toward Judy's cavalier killers. Now, she felt in control of her despair, but the riddance of anger left a vacant spot replaced by hunger that jumped with a craving for salty stuff. The ravenous orphan dove into the food bag like a starving coyote. She ripped open and crunched down two bags of Lays potato chips, a bag of Fritos, and drank two quarts of cavern spring water. Sun embarrassed herself, and said the dinner blessing after she finished rather than before she gobbled down the salt replacement food. She laid down on the bedroll, but the grief surged again and resulted in a sobbing jag. It was dark outside when Sun Wren pushed up through the cavern opening to feel the cool night wind on her face. The wind blew the sprigs of shorn hair left from the hasty chapel sewing-basket scissor cut straight into a prairie wind-swept salute.

The darkness and quietness were welcomed partners as the castaway listened to the night sounds. She opened her mouth and her lungs inflated into the eerie sad human-animal wail. Her mournful bay disturbed the night for miles. Sun expressed her insurmountable sadness. She shouted into the wind until the clouds parted and the full moon brought wolf cries from the distance to join hers. She enjoyed their company. She and the wolves sang their lament together for hours before her thirst drove her back into the cavern to quench her dry throat. Sleep swept over her as soon as she finished her compline evening prayers

Sun Wren's second day was a repeat of the first with the exception that the tears had stopped. Instead of preparing kinnickinnick Sun returned to the car, and carried the heavy can good commodities up to her hidden campsite. She reasoned that when she completed her quest she would be weak, and the canned goods with the can opener should be near the quest site. She followed Big Boots list, and placed the vegetable soup can, and the empty milk bottle filled with spring water to be within her grasp. She drank quarts of water throughout the day, and sweat after her hard run. She felt renewed when she finished her night howl at the moon, and she had banished tears for an entire day. She ate the remaining peanut-butter-and-jelly sandwiches and homemade pumpkin cookies, and drank two quarts of water to be fully hydrated. She felt ready to begin the quest at sunup.

Chapter 20

THE VISION QUEST

un's internal clock worked like an alarm. She was well rested and pushed herself up through her portal to the outside wide-open spaces. She clutched the bag of kinnickinnick and the box of matches in one hand, and pulled her pillow and blanket with her into the open ground above in case her weakness wouldn't allow her to retrieve them later. Sun Wren took out a box that contained three sturdy twigs she had previously prepared, and pounded one into the ground beside the big boulder for its protection. She carefully replaced the two other thick twigs into the empty matchbox in the manner Big Boots had suggested. This task was to help her keep track of the days during her quest when she might not be thinking straight. She sat on the bare ground to feel the earth's vibrations with the blanket and pillow nearby. She placed the bag of kinnickinnick inside the rock bowl that she had found, and placed the box of matches beside it. She faced the east to begin the quest. She lighted the kinnickinnick just as a tiny shaft of sun appeared above the horizon, and she smudged herself as the day announced itself.

The parentless girl squinted her eyes into the east and could see the Chariot, but she detected movement. Her heart raced at the thought of strangers. She sighted two figures on the cow trail, and they were moving toward her clandestine escape. She watched them as they grew larger in her view. Their movements were familiar. Her fear subsided when she identified them. She jumped up, and ran to greet them on the trail. She threw her arms around her godfathers, and nearly knocked Waffle Stomper over with her zealous happiness.

"I am so glad that you have come. I have been lonely for you. Did Sister Sara give you the map?"

"Yup, Sun, and we came to see how you were getting on. You look well. Are you ready to begin?"

"Yes. Look, Godfather—I am set up to begin at sunrise." She pointed to the smudge pot.

"We wanted to chant the beginning ceremony blessing. It will help you to be strong in your quest. I see that you have pounded your first day stake. You listened well."

Big Boots and Waffle Stomper squatted down near Sun Wren's supplies and began to chant. Waffle used his voice, and his beautiful tenor was restored. Sun was overjoyed by their comfortable and compassionate presence. Big Boots lighted the bowl of kinnickinnick and smudged his small godchild. The three Shoshoni smudged and chanted as the sun sneaked slowly into its full bloom on the eastern horizon. Waffle reached for Sun's hand, and placed it between his own. He looked deep into her emerald green eyes, nodded his head, and smiled at her. Big Boots stood, and patted her on her twiggy shorn head.

"Remember what I told you about your thoughts. Be safe godchild."

Her two beloved protectors walked back down the cow trail. Sun watched them disappear like two black silhouettes against the heavenly glow of sunrise. She was embolden with confidence that she would be victorious in her quest, but already Sun struggled with hunger pangs from the lack of breakfast so, she prayed the matins morning breakfast prayers, without breakfast.

Sun believed that the godfathers' chants had activated the support of nature. The sun rose into its overhead noon position, but it remained soft light throughout the day without its usual fierce late August intensity. She knew that she had been blessed.

Her thoughts were full of love as she thought about her childhood friend Judy. She remembered trying to roller skate on Core's beer cans tied to the soles of their shoes. They were too poor to afford real skates. Sun laughed out loud at the thought about the time when plump Judy fell down the slope of the hill with the beer cans hitting the top of her head as she flipped end over end. Sun remembered the time when they were four years old, made mud pies, and created their own bakery. They decorated their creations with yellow blooming alfalfa, sage, and wild white Lilly of the Valley. They sold their baked-by-the-sun-goods to Shram, Darrel, Susan, and Speedbump for a penny each. They spent their pennies on penny candy at Moss's Grocery Store while they played in the Riverton City Park. She remembered Judy when they were five. They coaxed pregnant katybear to go down the slide with them at the park. Katybear was so wide that she got stuck. She and Judy pushed and pulled her, but she didn't slide. Katybear bellowed so hard with laughter that tears rolled down her face. Memories of Judy filled her mind for hours, and brought indescribable comfort and healing. Her love for Judy was monumental, and she knew that Judy would be the heavenly ancestor who would protect her.

The child devotee from the Indian Mission grew hungrier, but she said the lauds lunch time prayers instead of thinking about food. She felt the hunger grow as she roamed around the boulders outside, but decided she should go into her hole to retain as much water as she could to stay hydrated. Inside her cave the fresh water stream became an enormous temptation. Outside was the arid wind. Inside was the water temptation. She decided to bear each one equally. She found the book that Sister Samantha had gotten for her at the library about Pavlova the great Russian ballet dancer. She read the book as the hours passed, but the hunger and thirst mounted.

Sun Wren tossed the book aside, jumped up to the hole's edge, and pulled herself out to the bolder area. She sat on the rock, and looked at the expansive landscape below where nothing happened. She watched the purple sunset in the west, and thanked God for her successful first day of the quest. Sun Wren watched the stars begin to fill the night sky, and she thought about Judy's star conversation. Judy said that the stars are our protective ancestors. Sun selected the Evening star to be Judy's star. Sun's comfort soared, but her hunger and thirst mounted too. She smudged herself from the rock bowl, and allowed the smoke to drift over her face and arms as Godfather had directed. She chanted the end of quest day chant that he had taught to her, but it got all twisted up with compline prayers. Sun felt no need to howl at the moon tonight as she had mellowed into a state of perfect peace. She looked at the night sky for a long time before she pushed her bedroll back into the hole, slithered down into her comfortable cavern, and slept peacefully through the night on her bedroll.

The little Wren bird woke before there was light and used a flashlight inside the grotto to make preparations before sunrise. She felt wobbly, but she knew that she needed to bathe, and to wash out her Avonelle underclothes. She dipped the bucket into the stream and washed herself from the bucket water. She washed her body, but she didn't trust her will power enough to allow the water to touch her face or mouth for fear that she would gulp it down, and ruin her quest. She washed herself, and then rinsed out her under garments. She lugged the bucket full of dirty water up to the portal with the intention of watering the newly planted kinnickinnick seed as she had yesterday, but she didn't have the strength that she had yesterday. She couldn't lift the bucket. She was forced to set it down on the rock ledge. She put on the soggy underwear, and wondered if by wearing wet underwear she was cheating on her quest. Would her body absorb some of the water through the pores when she was to deny any water intake?

Sun Wren wanted to leave the cavern quickly to resist the temptation of drinking the sweet, pure, delicious, flowing water. She tossed her Pavlova book up through the portal so she could read it in the daylight later, and turned off the flash light and tossed it outside too. The emaciated child jumped to the ledge edge, and tried to pull herself up, but her arms lacked strength. She had done this maneuver many times yesterday, but was frustrated with herself because she couldn't do it today. Disappointed about her weakness she sat down on her bedroll to rest and to think. She gathered up her determination and tried again. This time Sun concentrated on jumping up higher so her arms wouldn't have to lift so much of her weight. She tried again without success. Everything she needed to follow Godfather's instructions was outside beside the boulder. The orphan's cupidity propelled determination, and she rolled up her bedroll as tight as she could, and stood it on end. The tiny girl stood on the bedroll, and jumped up again to grab the edge of the ledge to hoist herself up, but it still wasn't enough.

Panic drove Sun to take drastic measure to get out of the grotto. The young environmentalist poured the dirty water out slowly, and allowed it to run down the ledge rock pathway. She poured the water so it would dry on the rocks before it reached the water below to prohibit contamination from wastewater. The thoughtful child placed the empty bucket upside down on top of the tightly coiled bedroll, and climbed up on both of them. She jumped as high and as hard as she could. Sun Wren landed chest high on the ledge with her legs and body suspended midair, and dangled there. The castaway kicked her legs frantically to give her arms and upper body some momentum. Long legged Sun made contact with the side of the cave wall with one foot. She pushed her body farther out toward the opening, and gained some distance. The weakened small girl, kicked, and pushed her legs again to gain more leverage. Rubicund Sun Wren laid on the ledge with most of her body through the opening and panted like a tired dog. She gave one big surge of an arm pull and was out. The exhausted Waif laid on the ground to regain her energy, but she felt depleted. Sun crawled to her blanket and pillow, and rested while she waited for the daylight.

Daybreak cracked enough to allow some soft gray glow to precede the dawn. Sun used the faint light and found the box of twigs, and removed one. She pounded it into the ground with a rock beside the first one. She sat by the boulder and waited for the dawn. The awareness of her fading strength shocked her. It was a startling lesson to learn how fast the body deteriorates without needed nourishment. This was a lifetime lesson learned about using the body as God's Given Container to fill only with life enhancing stuff. This was defiantly a lesson concerning the use of alcohol, cigarettes, and the reservation lifestyle where fruits and vegetables were scant. Sun studied her newly learned lesson, analyzed her loss of strength, and knew that she could not return to the cavern. *Well, at least I won't be tempted by the cool, sweet thought of water, because outside there is none.*

Sun found her kinnickinnick stash, poured it into the rock

bowl, lighted it with the matches, and breathed it deeply into her nose. It smelled sweet and soothed. The smoke-like vapor was allowed to travel over her face, arms, and legs. She smudged her entire body and made a wide circle around her head to her feet as she sat with her knees drawn up to her chin. She made the wide arc around herself again before the kinnickinnick burned itself out. Sun touched the leftover warm ashes, and put them on her forehead the way Father Patty had done for Ash Wednesday. She hoped that it would help her to retain clarity of mind.

The foundling tried to remember Godfather's morning chant. She remembered some parts of it, but finished by saying matins from her mission training. The morning wind on her skin calmed the tension from her exerted efforts to escape the cavern into the wide-open space of landscape and freedom. It was the openness of the land that gave freedom to her soul.

The day began when the dawn opened its beauty to the earth. She watched the eastern horizon as a tiny sliver of magenta emerged, and slowly grew into a glorious brilliant 1964 psychedelic orange, magenta, red sphere that announced the second quest day had arrived. Sun unfolded her notepaper that she had scribbled over the phone and had tucked it into the twig box. *Second Quest Day: Determine Intentions.* Sun Wren's first assigned room in the convent had been named Determine, and she had already determined many things, but she was four years older now, and maybe it was like the pictographs on the cave wall where she would become aware of other more important details to determine.

Sun entered into adulthood during her Chicago trip. Her damp newly washed Avonelle underwear gave testimony to her womanhood. She stood up, and roamed the ground away from the cow trail to give deeper thought to Godfather's assignment. Sun wondered aimlessly considering what she wanted in this lifetime. Her answer was as clear as the flowing water in the hidden cavern. She wanted to give the same kind of love that Sister Samantha and katybear had given to Judy and her. Sun Wren determined that she wanted to show universal love to everyone she met in her life, and not to ever intentionally hurt anyone. She would have a lifetime to learn how to simultaneously balance that goal while she protected herself from others who intended ill will.

Satisfied with her resolved first task, Sun plopped down in the openness. The day had progressed into a soft, dusky, overcast sky, and very muted from the fireball sun that entered the dawn. She looked up toward the grayness and was grateful that the sun wasn't blasting her with heat. Once again she had been given the support of nature. Suddenly fear struck her! She didn't know where she was, or which way to find the trail back to the cavern. She had been absorbed in her thoughts, and now she was lost. She sat alone in the landscapes vastness of endless sameness. The orphan couldn't even cry. There wasn't any water left in her body. Sun sat in the emptiness for a long time and tried to remember the way, but there were no landmarks. It all looked like the same flatness. She looked twenty feet in front of her, and saw it.

The sage chicken was in full mating plumage strutting alone. There were no female prairie hens to be seen, and prairie chickens were never known to inhabit at this height of altitude. This prairie rooster was out of context, but she was positive that she saw him. He was performing for her! He jumped, spun, and posed. Her voice was dry, but she called to him.

"Owl, is that you"?

The male sage fluffed up his feathers to twice his size, ducked his head, then stretched up as high as his neck would expand. Sun knew that Owl had danced in this same replica.

"Owl, it is you!"

The bird strutted farther away, but abruptly stopped to pose. Sun stood up, but the bird did not take flight as a typical prairie chicken would have done. The bird was beautiful in the same black and white plumage as Owl had been. She crept toward him stealthily so she wouldn't frighten him away. He moved farther away and stopped. She went closer again, and he strutted off again. She followed him again, and realized that this bird wanted her to follow.

The prancing bird with Sun following traveled together several miles. Sun lifted her eyes away from the proud prairie chicken, and saw the cow trail that would lead her safely back to the cavern.

"Thank you, Owl, thank you Owl, thank you!"

Sun would have cried from gratefulness if she had any tears to shed, but she did not. Sun searched for Owl, but he was gone.

Sun sank down onto her pillow and blanket and slept. When she woke she looked at the sky and determined it to be late afternoon, but she was lethargic. She picked up her book and read about the great dancer Pavlova, but it was difficult to comprehend the words. She read until the light had turned to black with thousands of beautiful stars shining in the clear sky. The bright moon gave her campsite visibility like a city street light, but she was listless. Sun Wren said her evening compline and drifted to sleep.

The new day began with the birth of the sun wrapped in hazy gray clouds, like a newborn child. Sun turned over, fluffed her pillow, felt the hard ground against her Levis, but fell back to sleep again. She woke up disoriented and determined the brightest spot in the above overcast sky to be the sun. She guessed the time of day to be 10:00 a.m. The small orphan looked around her camp area and saw the scat from at least three bears that must have roamed the area around her during the night, and she was surprised that she had slept so soundly. The bears had prowled so close to her that she could have touched them. They had overturned her can good box, and the cans were strewn in all directions. She retrieved the can opener, and put it into the box with the gathered cans. The bears had left her undisturbed because she didn't smell like food, or they believed that she was dead. They had moved her book at least ten feet from where she had left it.

Sun Wren was still disoriented but remembered her twig box. She found it scattered toward the west, and gathered it up. The twig box helped her to keep count of the days, and she saw that she had one twig left inside. *Am I still in the second day?* Sun remembered that Owl showed her the path, and that she had forgotten to pound her third twig into the ground because there was no dawn. The foundling fumbled inside the box for the twig and pounded it beside the other two twigs. Her body crumpled back onto the pillow and experienced exhaustion.

The somber stratus cloud cover of morning had graced her with coolness, but now the clouds had changed to plumbeous cumulus, and her thoughts turned to memories of Judy. She lay looking toward the drab, lead-colored billows overhead and wondered what Judy would tell her about the clouds that looked like a basket of soiled laundry and others that looked like discarded moccasins. She watched the clouds change into many shapes, and she wondered what they all meant. Judy's death created a void in her life that lasted forever. Sun Wren had known Judy's kindness for eleven years, and she had demonstrated love to everyone. That was what Sun aspired to do too. Judy had been her spiritual teacher, her confidant, her friend, and her sister. Sun wondered what it would have been like to live with the knowledge that she would die from a speeding car as Judy had. Judy had known for years about her own death but failed to translate the reality to her best friend. Judy had tried to explain, but Sun hadn't understood. Sun had understood the words, but she didn't grasp the scope of the meaning. Judy had tried to tell her many times until Sun eventually refused to play the cloud game. How remorseful Sun felt now as she realized that she had not given Judy the compassion that she deserved.

Sun was overtaken by the image of Judy's mangled face. The anger soared inside her toward the speeding car that took Judy's life. She felt rage, hate, and revenge. Sun screamed into the prairie wind riddled with pain. The stray child doubled over with abdominal pain. What was this belly anguish that she suffered? Sun remembered her godfathers' caution: "Keep your thoughts upon your intentions, and upon the reason that you chose to do the vision quest. If you have bad thoughts, you will suffer pain and sickness. Vision quest participants who had bad or impure thoughts dropped like an eagle feather, unable to finish the quest."

Sun sat up straight on her blanket and persisted to finish the quest. She immediately changed the tone of her thoughts, the pain disappeared, and she felt better.

"I am determined to grow into the best person that I can be."

She looked toward the sky in search of the sun, but saw only more plumbeous clouds. Sun waited for a glimpse of the sun to judge how much time that she had left before sunset— that ended her third day, and the quest. She found the hotspot in the sky, squinted her eyes, raised her hand, and measured the distance of her fingers from the sun to the horizon. The measurement was two fingers!

Sun only needed to endure two more hours before she could drink the cavern's sweet pure liquid that she had placed into the empty milk bottle that Sister Samantha had packed for her. The ragamuffin had planned ahead for her weakened state at the end of the quest. She had placed the precious water bottle into the canned good box of commodities with the soup and can opener. She anticipated the cool water to restore clarity of thought, moisten her parched throat, restore her loss of equilibrium, and regain her lost strength. She remembered retrieving the can goods that were scattered around by the prowling bears, but the bottle of water was not among the goods. Sun scanned the area with her burning dry eyes and spotted the broken bottle with the glass shards next to the bolder where she had planted the kinnickinnick. The bears had flung the bottle, smashed the container, and the water had all leaked to the ground.

The water will nurture and help the seeds to sprout. At least I have done one of the last requirements from Godfather's directions. I gave Mother Earth a drink of water before I drank. Sun sat motionless on her blanket, and considered her options for survival. She had two hours to resolve her water problem, and she assured herself that there was an answer. There was water in the cavern, and there were two water bottles full of water in the parked Chariot. Which of the two options would she be able to achieve? Sun ascertained her energy level could support the one-mile walk to the car. She was more likely to be successful walking than hoisting herself out of the portal where she almost failed yesterday.

Sun's tenacity pulled her to stand, she gathered up one soup can, the opener, and began her trek. She reasoned that she had two hours to walk the mile. She dug deep to gather her fortitude, and placed her pigeon-toed feet one in front of the other on the cow trail down the descending path. She thought, *If I could run the three miles to Judy's house in forty-five minutes, I can walk this mile. I can do this.* Her legs were once strong, but now felt like soggy French fries, her lack of equilibrium made her wobble like a bowl of soup carried by a child as it slopped from side to side, and her fatigue weighted her down like a heavy watermelon, but she was intrepid toward her mission and toward the Chariot. Sun's purposefulness set her eyes on her distention, and she kept going, but the exertion was immense. She was like a dog that couldn't sweat, but she knew that she had to find stamina. The thought of Judy's bravery to live her life knowing her own peril pushed Sun undauntedly onward. She could see Owl's Chariot now which she believed was another half a mile away.

Her disorientated state was equal to her many tribesmen who in their drunkenness were unable to find their way home. She vowed that she would give her body the water that it needed, and vowed to never abuse it with non-life-supportive substances. Her heart rate danced the fast drumbeat, and she couldn't think anymore, but she was able to pull the car handle down, and saw the two bottles of life giving liquid sitting on the seat. The walk to the car had taken her two full hours, but she was elated that she had conquered the distance in her weakness. She sank down and sprawled onto the back seat of the convent's car and looked out the side window toward the west. The glorious purple, orange, and pink sunset was radiant. The Mardi Gras colors were splashed over the landscape by the sunset's reflection. It was sundown, and she had successfully finished the vision quest.

Sun's hands shakily grasped the water bottle, awkwardly twisted off the cap, opened the back seat car door, and spilled some water on the ground to nourish Mother Earth. She lifted the bottle to her swollen, dry, cracked lips, and drank. She slowly sipped the water from the first bottle as she watched the sunset colors fade into twilight. She steadied the soup can between her knees, and struggled unsuccessfully to use the opener. Her hands had no strength, and the soup can remained unopened. She was overtaken by a blackness, from sleep, the night sky, the inside of the grotto, or unconsciousness.

Chapter 21

THE VILLAGE FAMILY

Sun woke with the taste of vegetable soup in her mouth, and the smell of katybear's fry bread with honey. She smelled the damp rock cavern, and heard soft chanted harmonized male tenor voices that sounded like the echo chamber from the '60s disk jockey Wolf Man Jack. Her body was logy, and her mind muddled, but she felt the soft touch of someone's hand, who spoon-fed her cherry-flavored Jell-O. She slowly realized that she laid upon her bedroll inside the cavern, but her eyes remained unfocused in the darkness. She saw three shadowed figures outlined against the cavern walls.

"Hey, little girl, It's about time that you woke up!" Sun recognized Sister Sara's voice.

"I didn't know that I had fallen asleep."

"You are sounding stronger today."

"Who else is here?"

"Katy Bear, Waffle Stomper, and it was Big Boots who carried you back here."

"Is it nighttime?"

"Not anymore—you slept all night, and it is almost noon."

Katybear ambled up on the rock ledge from the stream below and knelt down beside Sun and Sister Sara. Her eyes filled with tears. "You must gain your strength back. Do you want more soup?"

Sun nodded. Katybear opened Campbell chicken noodle soup and put a spoon inside the can. She handed it to her. Sun sat up and eagerly reached for it.

"I thought that I smelled fry bread with honey."

Katybear laughed. "Yes, you did. That was our lunch, and you can have some later tonight, but you should eat more Jell-O and soup for a few more hours before you begin solid food. I am glad that you are feeling better. I need to drive back home soon, but I wanted to be with you. I have twelve kids that I need to keep track of."

"You only have eleven children now, katybear," Wren whispered.

"No, Sun, I have twelve children! You have always been a part of my brood, and I needed to hold you again." Katybear gave Sun a strong, motherly hug. "Please come home soon. Is there anything that you want me to tell Sister Samantha?"

"Yes, Tell her that I will come home when the weather changes."

"By the looks of that overcast sky it may be soon. We all miss you, little Wren, and we want you back in our nest soon."

"I love you, katybear." Tears ran from katybear's eyes as she crawled from the portal into the wide openness.

"I want to go outside. Will you give me a little boost, Sister Sara?"

"Well, okay then!" Sister Sara lifted Sun Wren to the ledge portal and watched her wiggle out.

"Here, take this blanket. It has gotten colder." Sister Sara climbed out behind her. They huddled together under the blanket as they watched katybear saunter to her van.

Sun hollered, "Goodbye, goodbye, goodbye, katybear!" She waved franticly, and katybear turned and waved. Then she and her van disappeared into the vastness.

Sister Sara and Sun plopped down to the ground wrapped together in the gray Pendleton blanket.

"This place has a special meaning for us, doesn't it, Sun?"

"Yes."

Sun never told anyone about her vision quest that included the encounter with Owl, the transmigrated prairie chicken. That spiritual experience of knowing about Owl's continued care for her was hers alone.

"Sun, I will ride back to the convent with the godfathers in the morning. Come home with us."

"No, I will wait for the snow to come. Then I will come home. The snow will erase the tracks of my friend from this earth, and it will heal the hole in my heart."

"Yup, I know. Come back when you are ready. You have learned to be alone, but I want to make sure that you have enough strength to jump to the ledge portal and to close the entrance with the boulder when you leave. This is a special place of our ancestors, and others may not respect the sacredness of the grotto as we do."

"I am stronger already."

"Yes, you are, and we will see how strong you are tomorrow. I won't leave until I know your strength has returned. Sister Samantha sent you another box of food, and katybear made fry bread and honey for you. You are my little sister, and I have great love in the memories that we share."

Sun and her village family ate the vision quest feast that Waffle Stomper had prepared. The godfathers had snare-fished the grotto stream and caught enough fish for two meals. Big Boots and Waffle Stomper had snare-fished all their lives and were experts. The pole was a stick with a metal wire loop attached to the end. The pole with the loop was lowered into the clear, shallow stream, and when the fish had swum into the center of the loop Big Boots's fast reactions would jerk it out of the water to flop on the rock ledge. Sun had snare-fished many times with her godfathers, and she too was a good snare fisherman.

Sister Sara prepared fried potatoes cooked on Waffle Stomper's camp stove, and they shared katybear's fried bread with honey. Waffle Stomper presented the decadent chocolate cake that he had made at home in expectation of Sun's completed vision quest. Big Boots turned on his battery-powered ghetto blaster, and it had great reception at the high altitude. The godfathers, the nun, and the eleven-year-old waif sat under the star splattered sky, and sang their '60s top-ten hits from Wolf Man Jack's Oklahoma radio station. They sang for hours and laughed at the distant coyote howls that had joined in the serenade. The godfathers chanted the closing vision quest blessings before they settled into sleeping bags. Sun and Sister Sara chanted the bedtime Catholic compline, wolves and coyotes chanted their howls, and all these sounds were wrapped together into the colder crisp night air before they squirmed deep down into the cavern's warmth.

Sun realized the comforts that the grotto gave. When it was hot outside the grotto had a pleasant coolness. When it was cold outside the grotto felt snuggly warm. Nature gifted its comforts to humans, and this is what Sun Wren appreciated about Owl's gifted legacy. She possessed the protection from her two friends who had passed to the other side, she absorbed the warmth from her friend who slept next to her on the earthly plane, and she owned the well-being and happiness that she held within her soul. Her contentment was all wrapped together in the vision quest lesson, and it would be permanently within her forever no matter where she lived. Sun melted together with the cavern blackness and slept.

She felt great gratitude to Owl in the morning as she sat next to the boulder that still protected the three standing twigs, and she watched the sunrise crack the twilight. Owl had given her this splendid place to heal from life's injuries. Sun Wren said her morning matins with the light from the dawn.

"Hey little girl, I can't believe you are awake already! I see you were able to jump to the ledge and pull yourself out."

"Well, I think that you also saw the box that I stood on."

"It doesn't matter. I know that you can get out by yourself, and I bet in another day or so you won't even need the box."

"Godfathers are packing up to drive away."

"Yup, Sun all twenty-three nuns miss you, and Mother Superior gave you this—." Sister Sarah held out her outstretched hand and presented a multifaceted crystal rosary that sparkled brightly in the morning sunshine. Sun gasp at its beauty.

"I have never seen such a beautiful rosary."

"It is the most beautiful that I have ever seen!"

"Mother Superior must think that you are pretty rare, and I do too. Big boots checked the Chariot to make sure that it was running okay, and we will leave soon. You have tons of food both perishable and nonperishable to last you until it snows, whenever that may be."

Waffle Stomper came up the cow trail, heard the last few words about snow, and told the girls his true story.

"I was standing outside of the Riverton State Bank last week when a New York tourist come up to me and asked, 'How do you Indians know when winter is coming?' I said, 'I know winter be here soon when I see white man come down from mountain with firewood in pickup truck.'" The girls laughed uproariously as the godfathers gave Sun a hug.

"It is time for us to leave now, Sun."

"Godfathers, thank you for helping me with the vision quest."

"You are a woman now, and you know how to take care of yourself."

Sun Wren watched as her protectors and her big sister blended into the morning light, and she was alone again. She loved being soaked by the morning sun, and filled with the new day sounds. She was jolted by the bellow of an elk giving the mating call, she heard the blades of prairie grass whisper about it with the wind, and the meadowlarks laughed at his unrequited love. Sun Wren loved all this, but her humanness was hungry for breakfast. *What will your breakfast be? Leftover chocolate cake, of course!*

Cake crumbs, empty commie food cans, filled, emptied, refilled water bottles, miles of walked cow trails, the twice read Pavlova book, and Sun Wren's regained agility to jump up to the aperture without the use of the box were all testimonials to the passage of time. Sun sat wrapped in the Pendleton blanket like the ancient people had done on this same land before her. She had waited ten days for fall to change to winter. She noticed that the sand-beige colored landscape had changed to plumbeous. The isolated weather-watcher looked up at the drab lead-colored sky, and felt tiny flakes of snow lite on her face. She stuck out her tongue and caught bigger flakes that tasted of pine. She looked at the snowflakes that stuck to her blanket. It was snowing!

Sun plunged headfirst into the portal, gathered all remnants of her existence, and toted everything on the mile cow trail to the waiting Chariot. The Eagles track-star ran the cow trail back to the grotto in the cold blowing wind to check on the cavern's pristine condition. Sun Wren had finished her mission. She dropped the Pendleton to the ground as she sat down on the snow sifted ground, and pushed the bolder with her feet to close the aperture. She picked up the blanket, shook it free from snow, wrapped it around herself, and ran the mile to the Chariot as the snow and wind blurred her vision. She dived into the warmth of the Chariot the same way that she dove into the portal. Sun knew about windshield wipers and car heaters from riding with her godfathers during snowstorms. Both of these two mechanical amenities worked, thanks to Big Boots years of car service. The car started with a friendly purr, and she used the clutch without even a jolt or a buck. The map still laid on the passenger side of the front seat, but the snow obscured road markings. Sun heard the echo of Big Boots words: "Just keep it between the fence posts, sister." She couldn't see the road anymore, but she looked for the fences, and followed them sixty miles east before she was within the bounds of her own recognizable territory.

The car careened down the driveway to the Indian Mission, and Sun blew the Chariot horn in the manner of the wild teenager that she had become. Black and White magpies swooped from the front door to great her. Sun rushed to Sister Samantha who grabbed her from the underarms, and they twirled together in the white fluffy stuff surrounded by twenty-four flapping nuns. Sister Sara grabbed Sun's feet, and they tossed her into the outstretched arms of the flock of nuns. When Sun's feet landed on the ground again, Sister Samantha and Sister Sara walked her into Incaranata Hall

"I have so much to tell you. Let's go to the galley, and have your favorite glazed donuts and Coke. Sun look what the nuns made to celebrate your birthday. A happy birthday cake!"

Sister Samantha and the nuns all sang to her as she licked the sugary frosting from the side of the plate.

"Sun, I might as well tell you the big news first. It is all over the moccasin telegraph anyway, thanks to Helga. I am sure that Helga was rubbering when they called to talk to you, and that's how the news spread so fast. I wanted to tell you the news before you heard it from anyone else. I received a call from Western Union in Riverton, and they gave you a job offer. It seems that the moccasin telegraph made a connection with the real telegraph in Riverton. Isn't that a good joke? Western Union heard that you were a fast runner, and offered you a job delivering telegrams after school. They want you to work weekends, and during the summer too. They will pay for your car expenses to drive into town, plus pay you twenty-five cents an hour more than minimum wage! That is more than most of our adults make. Isn't that exciting news?"

"That is so cool! I want to do it."

Chapter 22

WESTERN UNION

The vision quest had validated Sun's passage into adulthood, and the job offer soared Sun's grownup self-image. Sun was hired by her new Western Union boss Isabelle Jacobson, and started her job as a twelve-year-old. She drove herself into Riverton during an era when driver's licenses weren't a strict requirement and loosely enforced. Western Union payed Sun for gas money to and from the workplace, which was twenty-five cents a gallon.

Isabelle Jacobson was a slender sixty-year-old stylish woman with big brown doe eyes behind wire-rimmed glasses. She didn't have children of her own, and that may have been the reason why she was fond of the young telegram delivery personnel. Isabelle had a quirky use of humor and enjoyed laughter, especially her own. Her kindness, compassion, and encouragement created Sun's self-confidence to participate in the business world. Isabelle held high moral standards about how business was conducted, and she mandated strict ethical principles for her trainees, customers, and community. Personal, political, economic, and religious data flowed in and out of the small town office, but Isabelle protected everyone's privacy. Western Union employees adhered to ethics that respected the rights of privacy. They never moccasin telegraphed about the telegrams that were sent or received.

Isabelle was the daughter of Pop Logan who owned the popcorn wagon on the corner of Gene Lee Used Cars lot. When Wren was an eight-year-old, she bought popcorn from Pop, and now at twelve she was employed by Pop Logan's daughter, Isabelle. The Western Union office was located across the street from the First National Bank where Sun opened her own bank account and deposited her paychecks. She saved her money, and eventually bought a car from Gene Lee Used Cars who was the only car dealer in 1965 that would deal with the Native American population. The orphan learned, worked happily, and tirelessly as the year passed.

Thirteen-year-old Sun had a good grasp of the telegraph business, and learned to read Morse code. She learned to receive and send messages, plus deliver them. Sun was a pioneer sixty years into her future with "texting and chatting." The Lander Wyoming Western Union office had a young boy named Philip Richards that learned to do what Sun had learned to do in the Riverton office, and when they weren't busy they 'chatted' over the wires in Morse code to each other. This was an exciting time for Sun Wren, and she used the technology socially. She soaked up the attention that she received from other males in addition to Philip while she delivered telegrams.

Sun grew acquainted with the Riverton boys that worked at the First National Bank across the street. They watched her when she left the WU office, and walked with her as she delivered the telegrams. An older high school boy named Gary studied for his Realtor license in a real estate office half a block away, and he escorted her to the post office every day. Sun was a novice to this special male attention, but she learned quickly, and developed an interest in boys.

Western Union was the only company that wired money, and it did a high volume of cash transactions. On one occasion a very elderly woman came into the office, and explained, "I know that you can send money by Western Union, so I think that you can also send my great-granddaughter this cake. It's her birthday."

The old woman placed a huge white cake on the counter where Sun worked. Sun was stunned into silence, but Isabelle jumped up from her swivel chair, and said, "I think that our lines might get a little gummed up, but yes we can do that. You will need to give us an address."

The great-grandmother was delighted with the wonderful custom service, and left the office. Isabelle sent a telegram to a bakery in Laramie Wyoming, and described the white cake in detail. She took ten dollars out of her purse, and placed it into the cash drawer. Sun and Isabelle ate cake all afternoon while Sun rubbed her stuffed belly.

"Isabelle, I think this cake has gummed up my lines, and now I need rotor-rooter so I can unclog. You need to take the leftovers home quickly before I eat it all!"

Western Union was amusing, entertaining, and educational with information that flowed over the wires. Isabelle and Sun bonded as they read telegrams to each other that made them laugh, and sometimes they cried about the news. They knew who was having an affair, who received a promotion, who received a scholarship, what company went bankrupt, what corporation sold out or bought in, what new priest arrived, who died, and the wires were hot with information about uranium. Many uranium companies formed the hub of Wyoming industry, and were located in Riverton. During the early '60s Riverton's population of seven thousand granted itself the title of Uranium Capital. Sun loved working for her boss Isabelle, and she ran the office by herself on weekends when business was slower, or when Isabelle wanted free time.   Sun Wren had changed cells four time at Incaranata Hall since she started her job at Western Union. Her cells were named Humility, Creativity, Intellect, and last September 5, she was changed into the cell Servitude. Sun was now fifteen, and today at work, she was challenged with a new test to determine right from wrong.

It was an unusually busy Saturday at the Western Union office, and Sun worked alone. A telegram came in for a uranium company:

> Susquehanna Western: The United States Federal Government authorized Susquehanna Western license #00994538 uranium mining rights for land parcel 3489; sixty miles northwest of Ft. Washakie: Eastern Shoshoni / Northern Arapaho Wind River Indian Reservation; Begin strip mining operations April, 15 1968. Signed: Thomas Farr Bureau of Land Management. Sent time: March 2, 1968; 4:45 p.m.: Washington, DC. Received Riverton, Wyoming: March 2, 1968; 5:06 p.m.

Sun pushed her office swivel chair away from the telegraph ticker tape, covered her face, and sobbed. She closed the office door so others in the office building wouldn't hear her. The WU operator wiped her face on her skirt and cleared her blurred green eyes. She pushed her chair back in place, took the ticker tape from the machine, glued it into place on the telegram form, sealed it for delivery, and stuffed it into her skirt pocket.

The distraught telegraphy operator moseyed to the back of the office and stared at the trash can that overflowed with erred telegram remnants. She hesitated beside it for several minutes. Sun walked across the room to the customer side of the counter, and sat down beside the window that looked out onto Broadway toward the First National Bank. She knew that she should quickly deliver the telegram. The Susquehanna office stayed open until 6:00 p.m., and the telegram was time stamped, but she couldn't deliver it.

The government had just granted permission to destroy Owl's secret cavern, his legacy. The cavern was her vision quest retreat, and it was Sister Sara's ancestral connection to Sacajawea. The cavern held the Shoshoni tribes recorded history with ancient art etched on the interior rock walls. Sun had found answers inside of its sacred space for her self-development during the ten days that shaped her into womanhood, and if she delivered this telegram she would be the Shoshoni who destroyed it.

Sun moved back to the telegraph and considered her options. She could alter the received time on the telegram, type in the time as received after closing hours, and deliver it on Monday to delay the immense ruin. She looked at the clock on the wall and it read 5:24 p.m. Even if she altered the time, the Western Union headquarters would have a record of the correct time, if it was investigated. Sun's first instinct was to moccasin telegraph this news to the Shoshoni tribal council. Tears erupted with strong, uncontrollable frustration.

She sat staring out the office window when a memory came vividly to mind. After she had completed the vision quest and needed to regain her strength, she had walked five miles from the cavern. Each day she walked in a different direction, and each direction revealed a curious phenomenon. She saw a strange two-inch-diameter hole in solid rock that was about seven inches deep without an exit. Sun had studied these holes to determine what animal made such a hole like that into solid rock. Today, three years later, she knew the answer. Susquehanna Western was the animal that collected core samples to establish the mine area. Core samples were drilled in a thirty-five-mile radius to determine if the land held sufficient uranium to be profitable for a strip mine. Obviously the area was rich in uranium, and the telegram today gave testimony about its profitability.

Sun's loyalty as a Western Union employee kept her from telling anyone about Susquehanna Western's private business. If she should moccasin telegraph this news, Isabelle could lose her job as the Riverton manager. Sun mulled the message over in her mind. She gave the telegram a deadly chokehold as she squeezed her fingers tightly around it inside her skirt pocket. She continued to stare out the window, and she despised the glued words that threatened the land's existence. The big mining company would destroy the Shoshoni sacred place. Sun's tears felt hot and salty on her face, and her jumbled thoughts jabbered away in her head. *I know that it is right to deliver the telegram. It is the right thing to do. It was paid for, and it is Western Union's responsibility to deliver, but if I deliver it, I will destroy the most important place of my life.* Sun placated herself with the notion that it would also grant a larger per capita check to her tribe. She lived in the cell Servitude to learn how to be of service, but should she be of service to her Indian Nation, or should she be of service to Isabelle and Western Union? Should she be of service to perform the spontaneous right action? She stood up to her full five foot two inch height, grasped the loathed thing lodged in her skirt pocket, hung the "Back in 10 minutes" sign on the door, locked it, and ran to the Susquehanna Western office.

The dark-haired, attractive Susquehanna Western receptionist looked up and signed the delivery form that Sun's outstretched hand presented. She looked at the time stamped on the envelope. "My goodness, you ran to our office very fast."

"Not as fast as I should have." Sun stated her truth.

The saltwater tears from Sun's eyes streaked her face, and the wind chapped her cheeks on her run back to the Western Union office. There was a crowd of people who waited for service when she arrived. It was past closing time when she finished sending telegrams and closed out the cash drawer. She locked the office door, turned the sign to "Closed," and sat staring out at the dusk-tinted Riverton streets. She remembered when she was in the third grade and Sister Margaret took her class to the uranium-tailing mill where the kids put their hands into the yellowcake. She remembered Jeffery City as the uranium boom-and-bust town that she visited with Mrs. Gamble and Judy. She thought about their conversation concerning the environment versus the needed per capita checks. That debate rolled around in her head like marbles colliding together. Her choice was money, or the love of nature. Which one was more important? Sun drew her conclusion. She thought about her tribe and evaluated their progress and happiness. The increased per capita checks had brought increased suicides, alcoholism, domestic violence, and child neglect. The increased per capita checks brought fierce resentments between the Shoshoni and the Arapaho tribes, less harmony, and no satisfaction within either. Sun concluded money brought deterioration to the quality of the Wind River Indian Reservation.

Sun knew that the environment encompassed all plant, animal, and human life. Love for the environment lifted the human spirit, but materialism stroked egotism, laziness, and promoted decay. Money itself was not injurious, but how the reservation people used it was detrimental to the human spirit. Sun thought about her happiness, and realized her true teachers had been nature, nuns, and the godfathers who extracted their joy from earthly simplicity.

Sun turned off the lights at the Western Union office, and knew that she had to do the right thing without causing hurt to anyone. It would be difficult to accomplish both goals at the same time, but she had to try. Sun dejectedly sloshed through the new snow to her car. She placed the ignition keys into the Dodge Rambler with the Gene Lee Motors sticker on the trunk and drove south toward the Indian Mission convent while she remained deep in thought. Sun reasoned that time was on her side, and she prepared her strategy. She could talk to Isabelle about her dilemma, but she needed to wait until the Riverton Daily newspaper broke the news publicly before she approached the Shoshoni tribal council. The delay gave her time to prepare a well-crafted plan to protect Isabelle and Western Union.

After school on Monday afternoon, Sun rushed into the Western Union office, and startled Isabelle.

"Goodness, child! You nearly gave me a heart attack! What could be so urgent?"

Sun quickly explained everything.

"I am truly sorry for your dilemma, Sun, but I am so glad that you did the right thing. Tell me more about the pictographs on the cavern walls. I think they may be the treasure to save your land from the rape of the strip mine." Isabelle the listened as Sun described the ancient drawings in detail.

"Sun, my brother Theodore is a professor of archaeology at the University of Wyoming, and he is very influential in his field nationally. He would be the person to help you protect this environmental art. He has preserved many places of cultural interest in New Mexico, Utah, Idaho, South Dakota, and Montana. We have time for him to come to the reservation and document this discovery. Would you show him where it is located?"

"Yes! We can do this before the news breaks about the Susquehanna Western strip mine, and we can be ready to prove the importance of saving this land. I am so glad that you mentioned your brother. When can he come?"

"I don't know, but let's call him now, shall we?"

"Oh yeah, I won't be so troubled in my head if I knew that there was promise we might save this place."

Isabelle dialed the number, and the call was picked up on the third ring.

"Theodore Logan. Hello."

"Theo, this is Isabelle."

"What in the world did I do to deserve a call in the middle of the day from my sister? If someone in the family had died, you would have sent a telegram. So, what's up?"

"Theo, I have some news about an archeological find that may further your career."

"Oh yeah? How's that?"

"I have a Shoshoni girl who works in my office, and she knows where pictographs are in a cavern, wait, I will put her on. Sun, talk to my brother yourself."

"Hello, this is Sun Wren."

"My sister tells me that you have seen some pictographs. Is that correct?"

"Yes."

"Please describe them to me."

"The drawings are very clear of women around a campfire. Menacing men with poised spears and arrows are hiding behind trees. Some of the drawings show victorious pronghorn antelope hunters."

"Hum, that sounds very interesting. Can you show them to me if I come to Riverton this weekend?"

"Yes!"

"Good! Let me talk to my sister again."

"Isabelle, he wants to talk to you."

"Theo, please call me tonight. We are starting to get busy in my office. We will talk later." Isabelle hung up abruptly, because the Western Union business grew briskly. Sun felt a huge sense of relief and optimism. She waited eagerly for the weekend to come.

Sun made a list of needed supplies for Isabelle to give to Theodore to prepare and equip him for the cavern exploration. At the top of her list was a four-wheel-drive, all-terrain vehicle; snow tires with chains; warm clothes; a shovel; water; and food. Theodore lived in Laramie and was sure to know about the frigid March winters, but Sun wasn't sure that he would understand about travel over two feet deep snow-covered areas without roads or visibility.

Sun delivered her last telegram in the painful ten below cold when Gary popped out of the real estate office to escort her to the post office. His mission was to invite her to the movies on Friday like the many times before.

"Thanks for inviting me, but I can't go this weekend."

"Why not?"

"I have something that I need to do, and it will take the entire time. Sorry"

"Like what?"

"Gary, I promise to tell you all about it when the time is right."

"Well, all right then." He strutted off exasperated, and she ran to her car, and felt protection from the biting weather as she slid onto the stiff cold seat under the steering wheel. Sun drove to the convent in deep thought. It was Monday night, and she was eager to talk to Sister Sara before going to compline. Sun parked in her usual spot beside the chapel, waited, and hailed to Sister Sara when she saw her. They sat together in Sun's parked Dodge as the windows fogged over from the steam of their conversation.

"Sister Sara, I want to invite you to go to our special cavern this weekend."

"What? Sun, are you crazy? It is ten below, the snow will be up to our wimples or deeper, and we will freeze off our rosaries." Sun couldn't help but crack a faint smile.

"Yep, I know that's right!" Sun told Sara about the archaeologist from Laramie who was coming to see the pictographs, but she didn't tell her about the Susquehanna Western telegram.

"I don't think that we should expose our sacred place to the public, even if he is an archaeologist. Sun, that is our Shoshoni secret place given to us by our dancing friend."

"You are so right about that Sara, and we promised our prairie chicken that we would protect it." Sara fell silent. She sensed that Sun withheld information, but she didn't press her.

"I am inviting you today so you can plan to have proper warm clothing and boots. You won't be able to wear your habit like you did in August."

"I am twenty-one years old, and I haven't been out of it since …"

"Yes, Sara, I know."

"What if Mother Superior sees me?"

"We will ask Sister Samantha to help us. Okay then, you will come with me?"

"Yeah, you little trickster! I will come with you. Come on, Sun. Hurry up, or we will be late for compline." Sun knew that if Sister Sara learned about Susquehanna Western she would want to help in the cavern preservation, and Sun was obliged to include her now. Sister Sara loved the cavern too, and Sun knew that she would need Sara's help in April before the strip mining began.

Sister Samantha noticed that Sun had developed a surprising new routine of reading the Riverton newspaper every night before she went to bed. She noted that this was a curious departure in Sun Wren's nature. She was always on the move, and never had been much of a reader except for the Pavlova Russian Dance book that she read twice when she was on the vision quest four years ago. Something of vital interest made her so diligent to read the daily newspapers.

Sun skimmed through the newspaper Monday and Tuesday, but read nothing about Susquehanna Western. She traipsed into Sister Samantha's cell after Tuesday compline, and told her about the weekend plans with the archaeologist and Sister Sara, but she held her tongue concerning the telegram.

"Will you help us pack for the trip? Sister Sara will need different clothes, and she must remain clandestine from Mother Superior?"

"Yes, of course, that's no problem, and I will pack a plentiful food basket for you."

"I am waiting to hear from Isabelle about the details, and I will let you know when we will leave. Thanks Sister Samantha for helping us."

Monday through Friday Sun scrutinized the Riverton Daily for news concerning the strip mine, but read nothing.

On Saturday morning, her eyes popped wide at the sight of Theodore Logan's vehicle and equipment trailer as it pulled into the Indian Mission to collect Sister Sara and Sun. The 4x4 Dodge Power Wagon with University of Wyoming colors of dark chocolate-brown with bold yellow letters displayed on the doors with the U. W. Archeological Dept. insignia. The hefty bear of a vehicle also pulled a matching chocolate brown enclosed U-Haul type trailer with the same bold yellow letters; The University of Wyoming splashed on both sides. The two convent residents plus twenty-three window peered penguins were impressed by the spectacle, but Sun was humiliated by the foolish homespun supply list that she had made for Theodore Logan.

Theodore Logan stepped from his Power Wagon with a friendly out stretched hand. Sun and Sister Sara were intimidated by the expensive vehicle and equipment but responded with a confident sturdy handshake.

"I am so glad to meet both of you. You can put your things into the trailer." He opened the double doors on the back of the trailer to reveal two snowmobiles, snowsuits, snowshoes, hydrated food packages, cases of water, and boxes of granola bars, and tools of every kind, including shovels, a hydraulic jack, and spare tires.

Sister Samantha struggled down the Incaranata Hall steps with a heavily laden laundry basket full of fresh food. Theodore Logan rushed to heft the basket into the trailer. He introduced himself to Sister Samantha, and his gaze locked onto the blueness of her eyes as she spoke.

"I hope that this trip will be everything that you are looking for." She gave Sun and Sara a hug, "Have fun and be safe."

The two Shoshoni friends climbed into the Wagon as Theodore Logan remarked, "Sister Samantha is a beautiful nun!"

"Yup, we know that is true, and she is full of love too," Sun emphatically agreed.

The three travelers settled into the cab of the Power Wagon, and Sun fit comfortably in the middle. The doors of the vehicle closed, and Sun's worries opened. The snow depth at the cavern would be a minimum of two to four feet, and it would cover the boulder area that marked the entrance to the cavern portal. With all the preparations that this man had made, it would be humiliating if she failed to find it.

"Mr. Logan, there aren't any roads once we pass Ft. Washakie, and there aren't any snow plows out here either."

"Please call me Theo. I don't think that we'll get stuck, but if we do we can use the snowmobiles."

"There aren't any snow plows because there aren't any roads to plow," Sister Sara corrected.

"We are out in the middle of nowhere! Everything looks the same without any landmarks to give clues about our destination. How do you ladies know where we are?"

"Do you see those little brown spots?" Sun pointed them out. "Those are the tops of fence posts beside range land, and we are to go straight beside them for about sixty miles."

"Oh yeah, I do see them." The Power Wagon pushed through the bumper deep, white powder that fanned the snow out into a spray like a snowplow as the vehicle moved forward. The wild game was forced down from the mountain range by the below zero temperature, and gave the travelers interesting entertainment as they sighted, moose, elk, deer, pronghorn, fox, and a band of wild horses through the defrosted windshield. The fifty miles of white sameness heightened Sun's apprehension to a crescendo about finding the portal. The snow got deeper the closer they traveled to the foothills. Theo slowed the vehicle and stopped.

"Excuse me ladies, but I had better check the hubs to make sure the four wheel drive is clicked into place. The snow is getting deep." He stepped out, and closed the driver's door to retain the cabin heat.

"Sun, how in the world will be ever find the cavern opening?"

"I am counting on you to help me."

"My casino-frequenting grandmother would say, 'If I'm your ace in the hole, we are in trouble!'"

"Well, that certainly threw gasoline on the flame in my stomach."

"Sun, I am sorry, but I don't think you understand that we may be headed for disaster here."

"I think we have about ten miles more to go. Is that what you think too?"

"Yup."

Theodore Logan climbed back into the driver's seat. "The Wagon can push forward for a few more miles, but I think we may have to take the snowmobiles to the higher elevation. How much farther?"

"About ten more miles, Sun assertively stated."

"I have never felt so dependent. This country knocks a hole in my inner navigation system."

"I am an ancestor of Sacajawea, and we both are guides in our country." Sister Sara's comment startled Sun into a five-mile silence.

"Well, this is as far as she goes. Do you ladies know how to drive a snowmobile?"

"No, but I want to learn." Sun reached across Sister Sara, and opened the Wagon door to the cruel, painful cold.

Theo opened up the back of the trailer and handed each of the Shoshoni ladies a snowsuit, gloves, and helmet. They dressed themselves as Theo pushed the snowmobiles from the back of the trailer.

"Wow, I can't believe how warm all this stuff makes me feel. Sun you are a better driver, so you should drive."

"Sister Sara, you are a true archeologist explorer now. Sacajawea would call you a sissy to see you dressed like that compared to what she endured."

Theo gave Sun a quick lesson about the navigation of the snowmobile.

"Sun, have you ever driven a motorcycle?"

"No."

"It doesn't matter. You will get the hang of it soon enough." Theo showed her how to twist the throttle and operate the brake on the handlebars. "Have you ever ridden a ten-speed bicycle?"

"Nope."

"That's good, because most people's tendency to stop a snowmobile is to drag their foot, oops, not a good idea because it could tear it off. At least you won't do that! Sara, I think that you should ride behind me until Sun gets the hang of her machine."

Sara jumped from the snowmobile as Theo was dressing in his snowsuit, dashed to the back of the opened trailer, and prepared a snack pack from Sister Samantha's laundry basket, and placed the food bag into the snowmobiles cargo space. Theo stuffed his pockets with Granola bars and handed a fist full to both of the women.

"The cold air makes you hungry, stuff your pockets full, and put water into the thermos because it will freeze if you don't. I think we are ready to start off. Just take it slow at first, Sun."

Sun felt the snow machine's rhythm the same way that she rode a horse with her godfathers. It moved under her with controlled proficiency. She understood its movements quickly, and was ready to pick up the pace.

"Hit it!" She called out to Theo who laughed into his helmet. Theo was much younger than his sister Isabelle, but he had the same kindness and calm essence that she exuded. He was good-looking with the look of intellect and professionalism, but without prudishness. He was a slender six foot two inches, and lanky like Isabelle, but he had strong defined muscles in his back, arms and thighs that announced he had climbed around many mountains of rocks. He had a pleasant calm featured face, abundant rust colored hair, and beautiful white teeth inside a quirky smile. Sun was glad that he didn't have extra pounds to push through the portal. When she thought about the portal, and the doubt about finding it, her emotions stuck into her throat. Her heart did the war dance again, but the thrill of driving the snowmobile, and being out in this beautiful winter wonderland released her worries. Sara turned around, waved, and shouted to trailing Sun.

"Dr. Zhivago"

They were in the middle of an iced snow covered mountain that looked like the white covered land in the movie of Dr. Zhivago that she and Sara had seen together. Sun lifted her hand in acknowledgement.

These two friends had never seen their reservation look so pristine and beautiful. It was ineffable, and had an indescribable silence. There was no sound because the fifteen below zero mountain air had frozen it into overawe. Sun felt subservient and obedient to its power, and she felt the love that this hushed quiet wrapped around her. She could not articulate her sense of well-being that consumed her into such a deep reverie.

Sun wished that they weren't riding the loud-motored vehicles that disrupted its purity, but they needed to reach their destination, and this was a thrilling way to travel. She revved up the throttle and zipped passed her friends to be in the lead.

She quickly cut the motor to its most silent capability for in the direct path ahead of her was a skinny, trembling elk that was near death from starvation. He had once been a strong animal with a big span of antlers, but now the winter without food had made it difficult for his scrawny neck to support the large rack on his head. Sun followed behind him, as quietly and slowly as she could. She didn't want to frighten him or to cause him any more stress than he already endured. He was so thin that he looked like a moving carcass, and she watched his rib cage heave in and out as the white stream of his breath escaped from his nostrils. She could see the stringy tendons of his legs pump the long bones up and down as he struggled forward. He tried to get hoof traction in the deep snow, and Sun could see that he was exhausted from his effort. She tried to stay far enough away from him so that he wouldn't be inclined to run. The wondrous winter-land had gifted perfect beauty to her senses, but it gave hardships to foodless animals. The snow was so deep that any edible grass had long been hidden from their ability to reach it.

Sun made a large wide arc that passed around the elk, and she stopped sixty feet in front of him. The only loud noise was from Theo's snowmobile, which he quickly turned off when he saw what was needed. Sun stood up on her vehicle, dug deep into her pockets, found the granola bars, and unwrapped two of them. She crumbled them up with her fingers, stepped from the snowmobile, and quickly sunk waist deep into the snow as she tried to walk back to the shaking emaciated animal. She knew that she couldn't walk the sixty feet to feed the elk. She tossed the broken Granola bar into his direction as hard as she could. It landed forty feet in front of the starving beast. His curiosity propelled him forward, and he sniffed at it, but did not eat it. Sara reached into the snack pack that she gathered from the laundry basket, and retrieved two sandwiches. Theo started up his machine, and made an arc shorter than the one that Sun had made around the desperate creature. When Theo and Sara were less than ten feet from the elk Sister Sara tossed a sandwich to him. He pawed at it, sniffed at it, but left it lie in the snow as he struggled forward with every effort from his scrawny legs.

Tears streamed from Sara and Sun's eyes unseen beneath their helmets. Sun was once again supported by nature. The elk traveled on the same summer time cow trail area that she recognized as the mile between the Chariot and the aperture. The elk had guided her to the cow trail. Theo and Sara slid their snowmobile up beside hers, they all removed their helmet, and shut off their motor so they could hear conversation.

"This is the boulder area."

"Sun I think you might be right, by the way the snow moguls over the boulders, but how on earth do you know which hump is the portal." Sun squinted her eyes over the landscape as Sara intently watched her face. Sun broke into a big smile, and their eyes connected.

"I know exactly which boulder!"

"You do?"

"Come on now, ladies, is this the old Wyoming snipe hunt trick?" (A snipe hunt was a Wyoming gag played on greenhorn visitors. They were taken into the prairie, given a gunnysack and told to catch the snipe. They were coached on how to call the snipe. There was no such animal, and the visitor was abandoned to search alone until he realized the trick.) "I don't see any cavern nor mountain where pictographs could possibly be."

Sun spotted a two-inch sprigs of kinnickinnick that protruded in the four-foot-deep snow. She had planted the seeds four years ago when the bears had shattered her water bottle against the boulder, the water leaked out, the kinnickinnick seeds germinated, and the plant had grown. Sun drove the snowmobile directly to the revealed sprigs, jumped from the snowmobile, and removed snow to uncover the plant. Theo and

Sister Sara watched Sun in amazement. After a few seconds, they rushed to help her liberate the plant. The three explorers dug like gofers to free the plant from the blanketed snow. They found the kinnickinnick plant was a full four foot height. Sun began snow removal to uncovered the boulder beside the plant.

"Okay, Theo, this is where your male muscles can help. We need to push this boulder forward."

Theo had no idea what he was doing, but without much effort, he moved the boulder forward to reveal the aperture. Sara grabbed Sun, and jumped up and down. She hugged her and they laughed until they both tumbled over into the deep snow. Theo stood silence, and gave them both a worried look.

"We did it! We found the portal."

"Okay who wants to be first?"

"You should go first Sun. Theo should be second. You can guide him in, and I will push him from the back," Sara laughed. The three amateur spelunkers laid flat on their bellies and disappeared head first into the aperture. Theo Logan uprighted himself,

"In all my years as an archaeologist I have never seen anything as remarkable as this cavern. You have shown me a rare archeological find, and I thank you." The warmth inside the cavern prompted Sun and Sara to unzip and remove their snowmobile suits, but Theo kept his on. He returned to the snowmobile to retrieve equipment. He brought two cameras into the grotto, an instant photo Polaroid, a Hasselblad, and three battery operated lanterns to light the pictographs. He asked Sara to hold the lanterns as he did the photo shoot.

"Theo please tell us about this art." Sara held the light steady as he explained.

"Wyoming has Petroglyphs and Pictographs. We are looking at the rarest of the two archaeological types. These are pictographs as Sun correctly described to me over the phone. Petroglyphs are usually outside in the open, and carved into the side of cliffs, ledges, or mountainsides. They are more abundant than pictographs. Pictographs are painted onto the rock, and in this case protected by the grotto or hidden cave. Pictographs are much older than petroglyphs, and they survived because they were protected from the harsh weather. Without taking samples to be tested my experience tells me that these pictographs are three thousand to five thousand years old, and I believe them to be created by the Sheep-Eaters who were ancestors of the modern day Shoshoni."

"See the variety of pigments the artists used? I think this color was made from blood and iron oxide, which is found in limonite or hematite. Look at these colors. They seem have used charcoal and copper. This is a rare find because of the variety of colors. These pictographs have survived because they have been protected and sheltered from the elements and left undisturbed. The ancient Indians who drew these used pictures and symbols to tell their story instead of words."

"Sun, you explained over the phone about menacing men hidden behind trees, but look how big their drawn bows are, and see this picture of the arrow head?" Sun nodded affirmatively. "These pictures tell the story: The drawn bow is the symbol for hunting. The men had a great hunt of pronghorn, and the women cooked to fill their empty bellies. This picture of the arrowhead is a sign that they protected their tribe from their natural enemies, which were the waring Black Foot and Arapaho tribes. See how big the arrowhead is? That symbolized alertness. Do you see this symbol of the circle cut up into four pieces? That is the symbol of the four seasons. Do you see how much bigger this piece of the circle is than the rest? That tells us that it is in winter, and they have pronghorn antelope for food. They most likely spent their coldest days of winter protected in this cave, and had time enough to paint this picture. It is remarkable that we can know their four-thousand-year-old story about their hunt, and a little bit of the Sheep-Eaters' history. We have been given a rare lesson to learn from their artwork."

Theo took many photos with both cameras, and the Shoshoni women were astounded when the Polaroid camera spit out the pictures. They were amazed by modern 1969 technology. Theo gave Sara and Sun several Polaroid prints of the pictographs. Sun's task of saving this cavern from becoming a strip mine was now more achievable. Theo gathered up his equipment.

"Let's go home, ladies. We have many slow snow miles to cover before dark."

The three victorious explorers slithered out from the hole into the painful sting of the fifteen below zero weather. Sun and Sara helped Theo replace the boulder over the aperture, and the cavern was securely sealed again. The three preservationists stood in silence and realized their accomplishments. They grasped each other in a genuine three-person hug of gratitude. Sun pointed to the single elk tracks, and to the kinnickinnick eaten plant that had lost its four-foot stature, and was reduced to one foot in height.

Six eyes met in silent communication and acknowledged the extraordinary satisfied task that they had played in documenting this rare find, and hopefully saved an elk's life. Everyone climbed back into their snowmobile suits, gloves, and helmets as they climbed onto the snowmobiles. Sun had an enormous surge of energy, and gunned her throttled to race her snowmobile to its sixty-five-mile-per-hour maximum. She became a wild-child, and pounded her machine over the mogul terrain as fast as she could race. Sara and Theo laughed out loud because they too understood her zeal.

By the time they had reached the Power Wagon Sun had already ransacked the laundry basket, and prepared three plates of partly frozen sandwiches, fry bread, and icy Cokes. She turned on the ignition with the keys that Theo had left behind, and turned the heater nob to give comfort to the late arrivals. The heat mostly defrosted the food by the time Theo and Sara loaded the snowmobiles, removed helmets, gloves, unzipped, hung, and stored snowmobile suits. They quickly plunged into the truck's cab, and escaped the biting fangs of the deadly cold.

"Welcome to the Chat-and-Chew Café. We have gourmet lunch on the menu. These are lamb and pickle sandwiches prepared by our head chef, Sister Samantha." Sun presented the plates to appreciative eaters.

"We are honoring the Sheep-Eaters that we have descended from." Theo and Sara laughed at Sun's joke.

"That's a good one, Sun! Anyone hanker for some Lays potato chips?" Sara opened the bag.

"Oh yeah, I can eat the entire bag." Theo grabbed a handful.

"How on earth did you two find this place?" The orphan lowered her eyes and the nun sat in silence.

"Okay, why do I get the old Shoshoni silent treatment?" More silence ensued until Sun finally answered.

"A Shoshoni friend gave it to Sara and me as his legacy."

Theo knew that there would be no further explanation.

The snow had crusted over during the day, and the vehicle pulled harder. It slipped and skidded sideways many times, but it only produced laughter. There was nothing out here in the wide-open frozen spaces to cause a collision. It was dark, and compline had already been held in the chapel when the Power Wagon made its way into the Indian Mission. It pulled into the parking space at Incaranata Hall, and Sister Samantha met her guests in the galley.

"I am glad that you are safely home. I have made hot chocolate and cinnamon rolls if you are hungry."

"We are all starving like a saggy-skinned, scrawny elk." Sun announced.

"Thank you, Sister Samantha, for the food basket. There is only one unopened Coke left." Theo showed her the empty laundry basket as he carried it, and set it on the floor.

"The sandwiches were the best!"

"You are welcome Mr. Logan, and I am glad that you enjoyed them. Was the trip a success?"

"It was the most productive exploration that I have had in years." He removed the pictures from his jacket pocket and showed them to her. She peered at them with intense interest.

"Oh my, these Polaroid pictures turned out very clearly," Sister Samantha jumped up and dashed to her cell. She reappeared as fast as she had disappeared.

"Sun, I have something to show you that might interest you," Sister Samantha held up the Friday's edition of the Riverton newspaper with the splattered headlines: SUSQUEHANNA WESTERN TO BEGIN URANIUM STRIP MINE ON THE WIND RIVER RESERVATION.

Sun's eyes opened wide and her brows lifted as she snatched the paper. Theo and Sara listened to Sun read the article aloud.

"So this is why it was urgent for the archeologist?"

"Sara, I am so sorry that I withheld information from you, but I had to honor my employer, and suppress the moccasin telegraph."

"Sun, I didn't know either. Isabelle didn't tell me anything, but I can help you with this now. What are your plans?"

"I will present the information that you have given about the pictographs to the Shoshoni tribal council, and hopefully they will stop the uranium strip mine."

"Sun I will prepare a document on University of Wyoming letterhead about the importance of this cavern, and I will solicit the University Archeological Department's help. The university will request a restraining order be placed against the Susquehanna Western strip mine project. I will send this information to you at the Western Union office, and you shall have it by next week. You may use the letter as proof that the University of Wyoming does not approve of the location for Susquehanna's Western's strip mine, and we support your cause. Sun these documents are my gift of thanks to you and Sara for sharing this archeological site with me."

Chapter 23

LAND PROTECTION PLEA

"**B**eware the ides of March" stung the nerves of Sun's memory as her woolen forest-green Sister Samantha designed winter coat battered her legs, and the attached wrap around belt at her tiny waist whipped to be free behind her. The cruel fierce wind pulled at the belt straps with the force of a violent rapist. Sun hunched her shoulders, and protected her face with her mitten-clad hands, to fight the savage perpetrator that ripped at her clothing. Sister Sara trailed Sun into the Shoshoni tribal meeting, and wore her habit underneath a man's sheepskin leather coat salvaged from the Charity Thrift Shop.

Sun pulled open the heavy glass doors of the familiar, ugly intrusive, redbrick government buildings at Ft. Washakie where the Shoshoni tribal council met. The Indian council sat at a long table at the front of the room, and the scant audience embodied older men and women from the Shoshoni tribe, but there was a small, dark-haired man that stood alone in the shadows at the rear exit door that Sun didn't know. She feared him to be

Susquehanna Western shareholder. Sun had requested to be placed on the agenda to speak today when the daily agenda was light, and onlookers wanted entertainment. Sun waved to the godfathers and to katybear, who sat with them as she and Sister Sara settled into vacant, straight-backed chairs near the middle of the hall. Sun clutched a manila envelope with Western Union insignia splashed on the exterior. The crowd stood for the Pledge of Allegiance, and the meeting began when seventy-eight-year-old Chief John Washakie presided.

"We will begin today's meeting with announcements of special events"

Sister Sara closed her eyes as if in prayer, while Sun rolled hers and practiced the convent lesson of patience. They listened to announcements about the various sweat lodges, giveaways, school fundraisers, Big Brother and Big Sister benefits, weight-lifting tournaments, and bake sales. These events were held around Fremont County, covered the Wind River Reservation, and part of Hot Springs County. Chief John Washakie called for the secretary and treasurer's reports. He asked for items of old business. The council discussed the progress of needed repairs for the community center and for the library. Big Boots and Waffle stomper contributed to the discussion. At long last Chief Washakie called for new business.

"Sun Wren, it is nice to see you again. Would you like to explain this order of business?"

Fifteen-year-old Sun stepped to the front of the seated council. "Thank you, gentlemen, for giving me this opportunity to speak. Last week in the *Riverton Daily News*, some of you may have read that Susquehanna Western Uranium mine had been given permission from the BIA to construct a strip mine on the Wind River Reservation."

Cheers rose from the crowd like spectators at an Eagles

basketball game. Sun realized that her Land Protection Plea
would be harder to promote than she'd expected, and she
immediately changed the tactics of her oration.

"Wyoming has the largest uranium reserve in the United
States. Twenty counties out of twenty-three Wyoming counties
have been verified with rich deposits. Wyoming produced
uranium has provided the energy equivalent to 5.9 billion
barrels of fuel or 1.9 billion tons of coal. More then one-half
of that production comes from Fremont County which you all
know means that it came from the Wind River Reservation.
Today I ask you as my respected guiding generation, What
benefits have our tribes realized from the uranium profits? The
per capita checks barely feed your families. Reservation alcohol
consumption is higher in 1968 by two hundred percent than
in 1958. Alcohol related illness have skyrocketed, and deaths
on the rez have jumped to three times higher than deaths in
1958. Domestic violence, murder, and crime have risen by four
hundred percent to say nothing about the suicide rate. I don't
see evidence that our Indian Nation is happier even though our
per capita checks are three times higher than in 1958. If the
Susquehanna Western mine is successful, and we accept the
word IF. It is possible that our checks would double in value, but
would our happiness double? Would the reservation children be
among the gifted and talented?"

"It is a known fact that sparsely populated Wyoming has
reported one of the highest rates of cancer. This report includes
the white residents living in Wyoming cities where cancer has
almost doubled the reported number of cases since 1958. A
theory is that radio-active uranium is the reason for the increased
cancer deaths."

"The Susquehanna Western mine would destroy the Wind
River Reservation as we know it visually. It would alter if not

destroy fish and wild game. Many of our tribal clans rely on the fish and game to feed ourselves. The epicenter of the mine would destroy a sacred spiritual place for the Shoshoni tribe." Sun read the legal description from the Western Union telegram that was quoted in the newspaper: "Susquehanna Western: The United States Federal Government authorized Susquehanna Western license #00994538 uranium mining rights for land parcel 3489; sixty miles northwest of Ft. Washakie: Eastern Shoshoni / Northern Arapaho Wind River Indian Reservation; Begin strip mining operations April 15, 1968. Signed: Thomas Farr, Bureau of Land Management."

A younger member in the audience, Justin Iron Eagle, stood up, and drew everyone's attention with his strong words. "I live in the northernmost part of the county, and there is no such sacred place like Sun has described."

> Sun's face flushed red not from anger, but from embarrassment that she had been publicly contradicted, but she continued undaunted.

"The Susquehanna Western Uranium mine would disturb a minimum of a thirty-five-mile radius to begin the strip mine extraction process." Sun opened her envelope, distributed the University of Wyoming letter from Theodore Logan to the council members, and she gave a few extra copies to audience members, to Justin Iron Eagle, and to the godfathers. Justin Iron Eagle read the letter from the university, scrunched it into a wad, and tossed in on the floor.

"I don't care what the university says. I live ten miles from there, and I know that nothing sacred exists. It is flat wasteland. Susquehanna Western can gladly expropriate my land for five times its worth."

Sister Sara, tossed off her oversized man's sheepskin coat, and raced to the front to stand beside Sun.

"Sir, with all due respect, the reason that you have not seen the sacred place that Theodore Logan from the university speaks about is because it is inside an underground cavern, and few Shoshoni or anyone knows about it."

"Yeah well," he responded with doubt in his voice. "Have you seen it, Sister?"

"Yes, sir, I have seen it on two separate occasions. The first time was four years ago, and the second time was last week."

Justin Iron Eagle appeared taken aback, and he sat down into his chair to a murmuring audience.

Chief John Washakie raised his hand with the eagle feather to signal for silence.

"Is there anyone else who has seen this place?" Big Boots, Waffle Stomper, Katy Bear, Sun, and Sister Sara all raised their hands. "Thank you. Five Shoshoni people have seen this place, and validate that it exists plus Theodore Logan makes six, and Katy Bear, one Arapaho, totals seven. These are people that I have known who speak the truth. Sun, is there something more that you wish the council to know about?"

"Yes, Chief Washakie, there is. I would like the council to understand why it is sacred, and why it is important for the university to preserve it as an important archeological site."

"Go ahead, Sun. I would like to hear this."

"The only thing that our people have as our Shoshoni History is our oral history, but these pictographs are our recorded history, and the University of Wyoming is determined to help us preserve it. Very little is known about our predecessor ancestors the Sheep-Eaters. Mr. Logan believes that the pictographs were painted by them over four thousand years ago. He has said that this cave is a rare cultural find. It is the roots of our Shoshoni culture and predates Sacajawea by over three thousand five hundred years. It is our legacy to learn from."

"Sun you said you learned from the pictographs? What did you learn?" Sun was silent for a few drumbeats, and then she cautiously answered.

"Chief Washakie, I have learned that our Native American culture is very slow toward change. It has changed very little since the pictographs were painted four thousand years ago. Perhaps the lack of change happened because our culture is rooted in truth, or it is slow to change because it is rooted in the basic needs for survival. I believe it is rooted equally in both the need to survive and the truth, which are basic laws of nature. It is the laws of nature that have guided Shoshoni's spirituality. To expound upon the need to survive, our tribe is still struggling for food. Many of our tribesmen lack nutrition. One, some clansmen have a shortage of food, or do not have healthy food. Nutritious produce must be trucked into the Riverton or Lander grocery stores, and the expense of buying fruits and vegetables is prohibitive. Two, our tribe has never developed a taste for a more nutritious diet. They also have never developed a desire for farming. The most successful Shoshoni are ranchers, and are outcasts because they have assimilated into the white culture, and are labeled Apples, red on the outside, but white on the inside. An example of that fact is the Arapaho Ranch. Three, our people cannot farm fruits or vegetables because of the short Wyoming growing season. We can grow summer gardens, and we do, but it is not enough to sustain a family or the tribe throughout the winter months. Our tribe's diet is carnivorous, and in 1968 we still eat like the Sheep-Eaters from four thousand years ago.

"Our Shoshoni tribe's truth comes from our education from nature. We live close to the earth, and we feel the earth's heartbeat. We learn about freedom from observing the sky, and from the endless unrestricted land. We can soar like a bird whenever we want too, and we like to roam. We are a nomadic nation by nature like the Sheep-Eaters. Our lessons to live a contented life are derived from observations from trees, plants, animals, weather from the rain, snow, frost, heat, drought, the soil, all from the four seasons. We learn about developing strength, both inner strength, and physical strength. Nature teaches us about patience, compassion, respect, kindness, and survival. Shoshoni's still used the same education from nature like the Sheep-Eaters. We have progressed in very small increments because the rez is insulated by mountains, and we remain isolated from the rest of the world. Our Shoshoni tribesmen who look at the pictographs may learn vital personal information to guide their lives. We must protect these rare and precious lessons for generations because this is who we are! Those pictographs are our Shoshoni photo-album. Council members and Chief Washakie, please help Sister Sara and me to save the cavern."

"Thanks you Sun. The council will take a recess to discuss this issue. We will discuss this among ourselves while you wait in the audience and the council makes their decision. After we find our recommendation we will welcome audience comments."

The audience murmured among themselves as the Shoshoni tribal council discussed the topic of the Susquehanna Western strip mine. Sun and Sister Sara sat demurely silent in their chairs as they waited forty-five minutes for the council to announce their decision.

"Sister Sara and Sun please stand. The members are ready to take a vote. We will have a show of hand from the Shoshoni tribal council. All those in favor of supporting the protection of the pictographs please raise your hand." Four members supported the preservation while two of the six-member council voted against it. The two Shoshoni women nodded their heads in thanks, and returned to their seats. Sun glanced toward the rear exit door and saw that the man she thought to be from the strip mine was gone.

Chief Washakie continued to preside. "The letter from Theodore Logan states that the university will provide funds toward the legal injunction halting the Susquehanna Western strip mine. The council will hear comments from the community. If you wish to speak please stand so everyone can hear your words."

Katy Bear stood and spoke. "I recommend that my two sons serve as needed lawyers to halt the strip mine."

Justin Iron Eagle eyes shot daggers at Katy Bear as she spoke. He stood up and shouted, "What right you have'a be this meet'n? You Arapaho! Get out! Look at 'em two Shoshoni women! They no learnt to keep their place in Shoshoni culture! How dare'm speak as men! Look at Sister Sara wears man's coat. This what Arapaho women teach? Has younger generation women learnt to be show-offs?" Justin Iron Eagle threw his chair at Katy Bear.

Sister Sara grabbed their coats. "Come on, Sun, it is time for us to get out of here." The two Shoshoni friends hustled katybear out, and the three raced to the parking lot stung by the violet cold, and singed by the inflamed words. The storm that blustered outside was less painful than the furious violent storm that brewed within the Shoshoni tribal council. The blustering wind with the blinding blizzard and the ten-below-zero temperature outside of the Ft. Washakie council room couldn't simmer the boil that the strip mine topic had caused.

Tempers ran hot in favor and against the Shoshoni tribal

council who voted in support of the pictographs environment. Indian words seethed inside the council room like a furious storm. Brown faces wore fury and bodies bristled with violent anger as they sat in their chairs. The windows steamed over from stewed thoughts that percolated in the emotionally heated room. The anger surged on for hours until the six council members dispersed into the frigid snowstorm to escape the surge of fiery tempers. Sister Sara and Sun welcomed the calmness of Incaranata Hall.

"Sun I am glad that you are home early. The moccasin telegraph said that the council voted in favor to halt the strip mine. Congratulations! You were courageous, and thank God, victorious! Will you please drive me to the airport? I must depart on the ten-thirty p.m. flight to Denver, then to Chicago. My dad has had a heart attack. I am packed to leave now."

"Of course, let me help you with your bag. Is that all you are taking?"

"Yeah, you know that I have everything in Chicago."

The drive to the Riverton airport took an hour, and the asphalt covered in black ice caused Sun's Dodge Rambler to slide and skid, but she had experienced over four years of driving in blizzards and knew how to control the vehicle appropriately. The Riverton High School hill and the hill on the airport ridge were the most troublesome without chains. The roads were vacant at this time of night, and she had the area to herself. She gunned the vehicle hard at the bottom of the hill, and drove in the center of the two-way traffic to crest the pinnacle. Sister Samantha had trust in Sun's driving ability, and remained relaxed with her young driver in command. They reached the airport and waited for the snow delayed Denver flight.

"I am nervous about my father's condition. It doesn't sound good, and my mother will work herself to death to keep the

Favre clothing line on top. She will be running the Avonelle business alone."

"Please tell your Mom how sorry I am about Mr. Favre. Sister Samantha, I am sorry for you too. You are not about that glitzy pretend world, and you grasp to remain at your nunnery life while your family tugs at you."

"I am always surprised about how much you understand. I can only hope to return soon, but, Sun, it is you that I am most worried about."

"Why me? Why are you worried about me?"

"Alcohol and Native American blood produce unpredictable violence. Please be careful. I love you so very much." Sister Samantha stood on the freezing open gangway that led up to Frontier Airlines while the brutal wind banged her habit against her svelte frame as she blew kisses down to Sun, who was waving from the window inside the terminal. Sun watched the plane disappear into the blinding black blizzard of March.

Chapter 24

SUPPORT OF NATURE

March powered on with killing temperatures that dropped to thirty degree below zero. It killed a large number of prized stock at the Arapaho ranch. Horses and cows froze to death as they stood at the water and feed troughs. The icy fingers of winter split the sparse cottonwood trees in half with the heavy iced snow on their branches, and later they died from winterkill. Seven Arapahos and five Shoshoni were lost during the blizzard, and froze to death before they reached shelter less than seventy feet away. Human internal organs could not function with such cold temperatures. People died from frozen lungs and heart attacks, or suffered from frozen limbs that required amputation and frostbitten faces and skin that caused lifelong problems.

Sun was forbidden to run while she delivered Western Union telegrams, and she could only endure the outside pain for short twenty-minute spurts at a time. She had to resort to telegram delivery by car, but the cold weather nor the hot tribal anger obstructed her endgame. To halt the strip mine operation by April 15, she could not be deterred. Isabelle gave her and

Theo free telephone and telegraph privileges. She relayed to Theo about the Shoshoni tribal council positive vote for the injunction, and she reported about the hotly angered state of the reservation. Sun connected the Bear Lawyers Shram and Darrel with Theo, and he plugged them into the University of Wyoming legal department that had expertise in saving tribal archeological sites.

Theo volunteered his university communications system to relay the news about the strip mine that encroached upon reservation sovereignty to the scattered Wyoming media. The Riverton local newspaper interviewed Sun, wrote about mining news, and activated local interest, but the biggest newspaper with state readership was the Casper News, which was nearly two hundred miles away. She had only three weeks to slay the Goliath creature, and Sara helped to plot its demise. Sun and Sara worked to halt the gladiator corporation with its giant yellow caterpillar equipment that had the power to erase and sweep away the beloved benign beauty. The ugly Cyclops was not the only concern. Sun and Sara had insults and anger rained upon them as they worked and studied at the Indian Mission.

The Shoshoni and Arapaho tribes were on individual rampages, and each tribe had their own warpath. The Susquehanna Western strip mine topic added gunpowder to the existing feud. Any logical mind would think that the torturous cold weather would lower hot tempers, but it didn't work that way. The pain of the cold weather seemed to unhinge and rile normally calm kinsmen. A nun and a waif barred their path to obtain a larger per capita check. Money burned in their Levis pockets, and money burned in their moccasin souls. The thought of money burned in their brains, and ignited their addictions. Katy Bear served as a councilwoman on the board for rehabilitation, and concluded that she had unfinished business to attend.

She gathered up the freshly baked platter of cookies, muffins, brownies and carted them to her van after all the kids had gotten off to school. Her grief for her lost daughter, Judy was a permanent mountain in her chest, but she purged grief by doing extra efforts for any community event. Her bereavement was saturated with thoughts about the Shoshoni tribal council meeting and Sun's presentation. Justin Iron Eagle's comment weighed heavy on her mind, but she knew that he was correct when he said that "she had no right to be at the meeting since she was an Arapaho." She lamented the fact that her presence wasn't understood. Her intentions were to give motherly support to Sun, who had no mother, and they both shared the loss of the precious gifted soothsayer, and their bond would be for a lifetime. Her presence was misunderstood as an Arapaho at the Shoshoni meeting. The meeting augmented the melancholy she already carried.

Katy Bear drove the miles to Justin Iron Eagle's ticky-tacky shack and parked near the front door. The cold ate through her Levis and the down quilted jacket couldn't block the biting thirty-below weather, but she balanced the platter of baked goods through the three-foot-deep snow that had drifted in front of Iron Eagle's door. She rapped loudly on the door and was answered with, "Yeah, who's it?"

"It is Katy Bear, and I have come to apologize." With that response, the door flew open. Justin Iron Eagle was a specimen of strength, and his eyes were fixed into a hard, angry glare. Before he could say anything, Katy Bear thrust the platter into his midsection.

"We don't take charity from no Arapahos."

"This isn't charity. It is baked goods apologies to say that you were right. I shouldn't have been at the Shoshoni members council meeting." Distant child voices surged from the dim interior asking if they could have the cookies and brownies. Justin handed the platter to the four children, and it disappeared.

"Sun doesn't have a mother, and my daughter and Sun Wren had been friends since birth. I was at the meeting to give her moral support, but I shouldn't have spoken. I am sorry."

"You the Arapaho who nursed her?"

"Yes. I brought the map to the cavern if you would like to come with me. I can show it to you."

"I'm gonna grab a couple of those cookies and get my boots. I'll be right back. Linda," he shouted, "get my coat. I'm goin' with this here woman."

Justin Iron Eagle slammed the van door shut against the refrigerator weather. He attempted to make small talk as these two enemies traveled ten miles north.

"The Arapaho ranch laid off four us Shoshoni foreman. This brutal cold winter the ranch lost twenty percent of livestock. The ground's frozen six feet deep, and no way to keep 'em from freezin'. Kept the breeders in the barn, but couldn't save the rest."

"This winter has taken many lives." Katy turned on the defroster to clear the obscured frosted windshield.

"Do you aim to find this place with all this snow?"

"Yeah, I have the map, and Sun told me how to find the portal. We will need to walk a mile, but I brought some boards that we can strap to our boots." Katy was able to drive the van closer to the portal, but the mile walk was strenuous. She panted, sweated, her face was rubiginous, but she spotted the University of Wyoming pendant stuck into a deep mogul.

"I saw that banner last week when I was huntin', but I thought some smart-ass college kid planted it there."

"Yeah well you would have been right! The smart-ass college kid was a professor Theodore Logan from the university. I will need your help to move the boulder." Katy Bear and Justin Iron Eagle dug the snow away to ground level, and Justin moved the stone to reveal the portal. Katy went inside head first, and Justin followed.

"Well, I'll be damned! Ain't this sumthin'!" Katy pulled out her flashlight and shined it on the pictographs. Justin stared at the art, and surveyed the cave as his eyes adjusted to the darkness.

"I can't believe that Arapaho showed me this," his laughter echoed a beautiful sound.

"It's unbelievable that this place exists, and to think that a little Shoshoni girl showed it to me." Katy's laugh echoed in unison with his.

"Here, take the flash light and take a walk down the ledge to the water's edge." Justin took the flashlight and sauntered away. The unlikely pair of Native Americans crawled out of the hole, covered the portal, and replanted the University of Wyoming pennant. Justin Iron Eagle and Katy Bear put the van into four-wheel drive and began the return trip back to his house.

"Justin, I am sorry about your job, but you seem to be a resourceful kind of a guy. You know the old Indian saying, 'That cream rises.' You are cream, and I predict that you will be back on top soon."

"I never'ed believed that cavern story unless I seen it with my own eyes."

"It is unbelievable. I am rewarded, Justin, by your appreciation. We will need to protect it from people who have no value for archaeology. Young vandals from both our tribes could destroy it in a drumbeat. To know that it has survived for four thousand years is really a miracle!"

Justin opened the van door in front of his home. "Thanks for the cookies. Damn good muffins!" He disappeared inside his house.

Katy drove to her house on Deaf Smith Road, and felt majestic. She knew that she had been forgiven. This was a trip that started with two enemies being together, and it ended in a friendship. Katy had accomplished a monumental advancement to promote peace—with at least one Shoshoni. She would live a lifetime without knowing who had killed Judy. It might have been Shoshoni or Arapaho, but it doesn't matter, gone was gone. The two tribes' resentment for government men was stronger than the fury between the tribes, and digging for the truth was futile because a Native American would never reveal anything even a gifted girl's life to a government man, which was another older wound. Katy Bear's focus remained steadfast to help Sun with the protection of the cavern.

Sun Wren planned and plotted to save the environment and the archeological treasures within the cavern from the Susquehanna Western Corporation, but she wished that Sister Samantha was at Incaranata Hall to discuss her thoughts. She decided to call her in Chicago.

"Hi, Sister Samantha. When will you come home? I miss you so much."

"Oh Sun, my sweet girl! Things are going very badly here. My Mom is working herself into a frenzy. I am helping her to organize the business into something she can manage by herself, but she can't accept that my dad is gone and that he won't be here to help her. It may be a long while before I can come back to Incaranata Hall."

"Theodore Logan and I talk often through the Western Union, and he asked me for your telephone number in Chicago. Do you want me to give it to him?"

"Sure, he seems to be a man with a good heart and a higher purpose in life. I am lonely without the sisterhood, and I would welcome some conversation. It is my goal to give this pretend, synthetic life a base for a more life-enhancing purpose, but I can't find one. My mother doesn't understand my unhappiness. Are you doing okay with your job and school?"

"Work is great and I have fun with Isabelle, but school is a bummer. I don't have any close friends, my grades are mostly Cs in everything, but As in creative writing, PE, and art class. Some of the girls at school ask me to draw their assignments, and I do, because I want to make new friends. There are so many people on the line rubbering that I can't hear you anymore. I'm hanging up, Sister Samantha, I love you."

Nature gifted Sun support and showed her its love. The intolerable frigid cold remained, and forced Susquehanna Western to delay the mine construction site for another month. June 15 was the newly scheduled date for the mine to begin opening a thirty-five-mile wound on the earth to extract the coveted prize of uranium. The delay was a heaven-send for Sun. The injunction had time to be properly prepared and recorded. The portal would be more accessible for university archeologists, and she could spend time informing the public about environmental preservation.

The threatening day of June 15, 1968 presented itself like an arrogant mating prairie chicken. The forty-five-degree temperature wrapped the day in sun-filled warmth, and the streets had turned to slush and mud where Sun worked at Western Union.

Sun answered the phone on the first ring.

"Sun this is Shram Bear. Darrell and I would like for you to ride out to the mine site with us after you close the office today at noon. We will come into Riverton to pick you up."

"Thanks, I would love that. We can talk about the injunction on the way. See you at noon."

Sun locked the WU office as Darrell's new gold colored Bronco parked. She sprinted to the vehicle, and slid into the passenger seat while the other Bear brother leaned over the front seat and gave her a bear hug.

"Shram and I have the injunction papers in this folder. We wanted you to be the person who presented them, if Susquehanna workers were out there."

"The truth is, we wanted you to show us the way." Darrell gave her his coy wink and flirtatious smile. Sun grasped the folder and began looking through it.

"It looks very—legal." Sun directed the Bear lawyers the sixty miles through the slushy mud covered prairie. A pasture length before the one-mile cow trail, her eyes were as wide as the Wind River Canyon with awe. She gasped, and her breathing stopped. Darrell slowed the Bronco and parked to view the entire panorama. Sun made a sound of air intake as she had forgotten to breath. Her heart pounded in her chest, and she needed air. Her eyes could not examine the sight quick enough for her brain to compute the image that was in front of her. She reminded herself to breath.

"Sun did you know that all this was going on?"

"No."

Sun couldn't speak. Her eyes were too busy digesting the spectacle. Hugh yellow Susquehanna crawler loaders, earth moving track excavators, long reach excavators, bob cats, dozers, caterpillar loaders, and six dump trucks were parked in reediness. Sun didn't know the names of all the implements that she saw, but the Bear brothers pointed them out to her. All these contraptions were halted before the one-mile cow trail. She saw the same dark-haired man that she had seen at the Shoshoni tribal meeting leaning against a huge front-end loader dressed in nice clothing, and looked out of place. Sun wondered if he was the owner of Susquehanna Western.

The cow trail was strewn with standing humans. The trail had become a human wall that protected the cavern and stretched around the mine area. From the portal she could see nuns with their arms outstretched and grasped the hand of another nun. She recognized the twenty-four nuns with Mother Superior and Sister Margaret in the middle of the penguin-colored human chain. Father Patty had recruited the Jesuits from surrounding towns of Kenner, Pavilion, Morten, Lander, and Riverton. They added a black-colored link to the end of the nuns' black-and-white string. Sun knew that this human wall was Sister Sara's contribution. School buses from the Jesuit participated towns were parked end to end and forbid access to the cow trail. Twenty riders on horseback from the Arapaho Ranch had spread themselves in a protective line around the perimeter, and their horse trailers were parked end to end and blocked egress to the open rangeland.

"Look there is your mom standing with the Arapaho ranch hands," Sun snickered.

Big Brothers and Big Sisters organizations with twenty youth members held their arms outstretched and chanted the Eagles' school song. The weight lifters team, dressed in team suits and held dumbbells stood next to the Shoshoni tribal council who sat to beat on a tribal powwow drum. Big Boots and Waffle Stomper stood next to the drum. The University of Wyoming archeological department with three professors and Theodore Logan stood at the end of the chain. Sun saw reporters from local newspapers interviewing some of the people in the barricade.

"Okay, Sun, it is your turn to do your part. Take that folder, and give it to the grumpy looking man sitting in that red pickup."

Sun opened the Bronco car door, and the smell of the thawed earth bolstered her confidence to slosh across the muddy ground to protect the pictographs. The air tasted like the popularly sold tiny black squares of sin-sin. The mud sucked at her boots with each step. She could feel the suction tug on her shoes inside the green rubber calf high waders, and she hoped that her feet wouldn't slip out of her shoes while the boots remained stuck in the mud. The walk through the mud required the strength of her thighs.

The westward wind blew her long curly hair straight behind her, and the ties of her belted coat were flung backward like stiff cardboard. Her forest-green wraparound woolen coat made her look like a small sprig of sage as she trudged across the open range to meet Goliath. The only prairie sound that Sun heard was the wind that whistled in her ears. All sounds were replaced by ultra quietness and stillness. The air was as tense as a pulled bowstring with a poised arrow ready to fly. She wondered if she would be the target. Everyone's eyes who had been a part of her life were upon her. Her mission was to save the Shoshoni land from the tortures that the machinery would inflict. She was a predecessor for modern environmentalists, and the cave dweller's drawings were predecessors for her. The cavern was Owl's legacy, and she wanted to gift it to the Shoshoni tribe. Sun remained steadfast to her purpose.

Sun paused a few yards from the Susquehanna 1968 red Ford pickup. Darrell tooted his Bronco horn that jarred the soundless air, but gained the driver's attention. She resumed her march with an out stretched arm that prominently displayed the folder. Sun looked like the tiny wren in the foreground of the horizontal line of village and tribal supporters. The Susquehanna Western burly foreman got out of his truck, and slopped toward her. Sun looked directly into his squinted eyes as she handed him the documents.

"Here is the legal and binding injunction to stop the strip mine construction. I am standing here until you and this equipment leave the area." The man snatched the file, and a loud cheer and applause erupted from the border wall. Sun stood with crossed arms defiantly over her chest. The foreman lumbered back to his truck while Sun stood like a stone pillar. Her thoughts questioned whether the grumpy foreman would mow her over in his anger with his huge new truck.

It seemed like hours that Sun waited in defiance. She was aware that the nicely dressed stranger stared at her, but he emitted no anger nor did he threaten her. Ten minutes passed before the Susquehanna Western foreman emerged from his truck with the folder in his hands, and oozed through the mud to each of the equipment drivers. He talked to each of them with hostile animated gestures. Sun stood her ground, waited, and watched. Slowly each piece of earth scraping machinery was put into reverse, and each contraption rumbled across the prairie flinging mud in all directions as it headed east.

Chapter 25

REOPENED RAW WOUNDS

The mission chapel stood in stillness under the clear star spangled night with the windows aglow from the interior lighted votive candles offered in thankfulness for a peaceful resolution, and for the Jesuits contributions to help end the strip mine. The nuns' compline was a glorious chanted melody that reflected order. The nuns sang the last cantata, and each carried a votive from the chapel as they reverently filed into Incaranata Hall for the night. Contentment washed over the mission as the clergy sank into the reverie of deserved deep dreams.

Sun startled upright in her cot from the intense heat that woke her. She wiped the river of sweat that poured into her sleepy eyes as her feet touched the floor that felt like hot beds of coals. She stopped at her cell doorframe and peered down the hall. She saw lashing tongues of orange flames that licked the seared cell doors. She ran in panic outside to the Incaranata Hall entrance steps in her thin white cotton nightgown in the freezing temperature. She fiercely tugged on the rope that rang the mission bell. She rang it as long as her ears could withstand the painful sound, and she returned to the smoke filled sweltering hall. On her return down the blazing hall, she picked up the telephone to call the fire department, but the phone line had been cremated. She dashed to Sister Sara's cell, but saw that she had been awakened by the mission bell. Sun shouted, "Help me save the nuns!"

The sonorous mission bell had alerted the sleeping nuns and Father Patty in the chapel rectory. Screams and shouts mixed with the crackling sound of burned timber told that the residents of Incaranata Hall were alive with blistered fear. Sister Sara jumped into her boots, and ran to as many cells as she could. She grabbed many of the singed doors and ripped them from their hinges to free trapped sisters, and she shoved nuns toward the only exit with her burned hands. Sun flung open the heavy front door, and propped it with a long brass candlesnuffer that served as an exit for escape, but the opened door gave more oxygen for the flames to ignite into a larger and faster blaze, and the convent enkindled into a roaring bonfire. Sun shouted as she ran.

"Get out. Run to the gymnasium now! Look for other sisters as you go!"

Sun ran barefooted to Mother Superior's charred quarters stepping on pieces of glowing burned embers, but found the cell empty. She dashed to Sister Margaret's cell but couldn't enter through the savage flames that blocked her entrance and consumed the cell. Sun shouted for Margaret as she stood on burning plank flooring and hot embers, but her voice was muted by the fiery din. Sun ran to as many of the cells as she could, but every cell was engulfed in a smoke-filled inferno. She could no longer see through the smoke and flames, so she crawled on her hands and knees. She reached the front door just as the roof collapsed behind her. The front door had burned from its hinges and glass shards were thrown onto the steps. Sun ran to the gymnasium with cold, burned, injured feet, and she was met by Sister Sara, who flung open the door.

"Thank God you escaped."

"How many survived?"

"There are eleven of us, but more may come." Sister Sara and Sun waited by the front door to receive other sisters, but there were no more. After Sun's watery, singed eyes adjusted to the dark, she scanned the room of huddled nuns, and shouted,

"Has anyone seen Mother Superior or Sister Margaret?"

A small, whimpering voice came from a dark corner of the large empty gymnasium.

"I saw Mother Superior enter Sister Margaret's cell."

Sister Sara and Sun, with their backs supported against the hard surface of the gymnasium wall, slid down to the floor as they held each other and wailed in grief. They listened in a fuzzy mental haze to the blaring firetruck siren and watched the red-and-blue lights flash into the gymnasium windows and onto the walls like a '60s ballroom dance party. Sun floated from reality into a dreamlike surreal state as she opened the heavy door to watch the firemen as they sprayed the school building and the gymnasium roof. She watched as the firehose spray of water doused the flames that ate the steeple and half of the mission chapel. She watched the firemen enter the chapel, and she waited to see Father Patty emerge, but her view was interrupted by a pathetic, remote voice: "Please close the door. We are freezing."

Sun slipped out the opened door.

"Sun, you can't go out there. Your feet are bleeding and you have no coat."

Sun allowed the door to close behind her. She stood on

the iced cement before she ran across the schoolyard in her thin white nightgown. A Lander fireman ran to meet her, and wrapped her in a Pendleton blanket.

"I have a nun in shock here." A different Riverton firemen carried her to the waiting ambulance.

"Please Sir, would you take more blankets to the nuns huddled in the gymnasium? There are eleven who have survived." Sun stood up to return to the gymnasium.

"Just sit right back down there little lady. We are going to treat your mangled feet."

"There may be others with injuries in the gymnasium."

"Someone is already on the way."

"Did you find Mother Superior or Sister Margaret?"

"The convent roof collapsed. We don't know about survivors. Just rest now, and let me tend to your feet."

"Did you find Father Patty?"

"Fifty percent of the chapel has been saved, and the firemen are searching now." Sun jumped down from the gurney.

"I'm going to find him. I know the rectory part of the chapel, and he may be in there."

The medic grabbed Sun forcefully around her waist, and sat her back up on the gurney.

"Let the firemen do their job, bossy woman! If you don't let me finish closing these wounds, I am going to give you a sedative."

He injected Sun into sedation, closed the wounds, and treated her third-degree burned, lacerated, and glass-embedded feet. She had big white wrapped clumps at the end of her thin sinewy legs. She sat on the edge of the gurney in displaced suspension as she looked out of the ambulance door at the carnage of Incaranata Hall. She watched the smoldered roasted roof timbers that looked like beef from the Sunday mass barbecue. She watched the glow of the bright orange embers as they cooled into white-hot gray charcoal, and later turned black. The cinderblock walls still stood upright exposed to the beautiful star filled sky. The smell of bonfire-roasted Incaranata Hall smelled tastier than roasted marshmallows. The many years of ensconced rose water and incense had saturated and penetrated into the wood that burned, and released the smell of pleasant potpourri. Sun watched as the firemen carried a gurney from the rectory and place Father Patty next to her. She looked at his Irish, round, jowled kind face, and tears slid down her charcoaled dirty face.

"Father Patty, can you hear me? This is Sun Wren. Thank you for your recruitment of the other Jesuits that saved the Shoshoni ancient art today. You have been my father figure, my spiritual inspiration, and my teacher. You have made me into the Sun that I am. I came to you as a ragamuffin inside a hubcap, but please don't leave me to be an orphan again. You are not finished growing me. I need you more now than I ever have. Our world has just been burned into a black pile of ashes, and I need fatherly guidance. Sun took Father Patty's hand, and she saw his eyes flutter. Please stay with me."

"We need to move Sun into the gymnasium so we can have room to treat two other badly burned nuns, and a third with severely burned hand." Sun was whisked off the table as Sister Sara walked in her black rubber waders beside two of the new postulants who were carried in on stretchers. Sister Sara said the Rosary to the two postulants as they entered the ambulance.

"Father Patty, if you can hear me please say a blessing for these sisters who will be traveling companions as you ride into the Riverton Memorial. I love you, Father Patty."

Sun still talked to Father Patty as the medics carried her back into the gymnasium and placed her on the cold floor where a pallet had been made. Sun's pallet was among eight other traumatized nuns. Through her sedated foggy mind, Sun was aware that katybear had handed her a glass of water. Sun broke into a soft crying binge as she hugged her surrogate mom, and wouldn't turn her loose.

"Please, Sun, drink the water you must be dehydrated, and don't cry anymore. It will only deplete your body fluid. I need to bring in a barrel of water, pitcher and Dixie cups for everyone. Darrell, Shram, Speedbump, and Susan are helping to sift through the debris looking for anything that hasn't been incinerated to determine the cause. I promise that I will return, and we can chat after I help with the others. Sister Sara will be back into the gym when they finish bandaging her hands. The heat will be turned on in here soon, you have the locker rooms to shower, and you can use the restrooms. Please try to sleep now." Katybear rose from her knees as her family carried in barrels of water, large pots of soup, and fry bread with honey. Sun flopped down exhausted under the ambulance blanket and fell asleep. It was dawn before the firetrucks finished, the ambulances delivered patients into Riverton and Lander Hospitals, and the light of day assured that life went on.

Sun woke and discovered Sister Sara slept beside her with big white bandages on her hands similar to the bandages on Sun's feet. Sister Sara's hands were badly burned as she removed the doors from the cell hinges. Sister Sara managed to save seven nuns who would have been trapped in their cells. Sun gazed at beloved Sister Sara, and smiled a coy smile to herself as she thought, *I will need to be Sister Sara's hands, and she needs to be my feet. We need to be together to make a whole person.*

The Bear family with charcoaled smeared faces and soot covered clothing paraded into the gymnasium. Darrell and Speedbump grasped the corners of Sun's pallet with her riding on it, and pulled it away from the other sleeping nuns. Shram approached Sun and stood before her with outstretched arms.

"Look what we found!"

"Oh, for heaven's sake! Sister Samantha had saved this, and decorated it into a wall hanging for my room, of all the things to survive, who would have ever guessed that it would be the hubcap! Thanks!" she laughed. Shram laid the hubcap on Sun's pallet.

"Look what else that we found." Speedbump held up the crystal rosary that Mother Superior had given to her for the vision quest. Sun's eyes filled with tears and her sobs reverberated off the gym walls.

"We gotta go, but Mom is coming to visit you!"

Ten minutes after the Bear family left the gym, katybear slid across the gym floor in her socks and sat down on Sun's pallet. "How are you doing?"

"Thanks for the great fry bread. You know that's my favorite. Do they know who set the fire?"

"Yes, it is the same men that would have tortured you if you hadn't been on the vision quest, but nothing will come of it. Tribal police won't press charges, state police have no jurisdiction, and no Native American Arapaho or Shoshoni will involve a federal agent. Nobody will even speak to a government man. They were drunk, and who knows the reason. It could have been revenge for loss of per capita. It could have been resentment against bold women taking charge. It could have been yours and my ShoRap friendship. It could have been that they were mad at the church for marriage to their wives that are giving them trouble. It could have been me, a woman member on the Arapaho tribal council. The men themselves can't even answer why they did it. They took thirteen lives without consequences."

"Should I be afraid they will be after me?"

"Sun, you have no more reason to be afraid than the rest of us. They may think that you were one of the thirteen that were cremated. Alcoholics are unpredictable. Sun, I am so sorry to tell you, but Father Patty died at the Riverton Hospital. I called Sister Samantha in Chicago. She knows about Susquehanna Western, and now this disaster. The convent won't be replaced, and there aren't enough nuns to staff the school, so the board of trustees will bus the kids into Riverton and Lander. Sun, Sister Samantha's mom died too. She died of a stroke two months after her dad's death. Sister Samantha runs the Favre operation and the Avonelle Design Line. She isn't living the life of a nun anymore since the fire, and she might not—"

"It's okay, katybear. We are each born with our own blueprint, and nature directs the show. Everyone must live the life that is given to them. How well you and I know that!"

"Sun you are welcome to live with us. You can finish out your high school years at Riverton High School. I need to take the kids into Riverton to school, and you can ride along, or take your own car since you have a job."

"Your house would be the right place for me, katybear. Susan, Speedbump, Shram, and Darrell are on their own. I want to be with you."

"The kids took the van, and Homer is waiting for me out on the Arapaho Racer. Do you need anything before I go"?

"Can you pull my pallet back over next to Sister Sara?"

"Yes. Come to our house whenever you are ready. You belong with us."

Sun fell asleep again while she waited for Sister Sara to wake up, but she awakened a few minutes later to a soft touch on her face. She opened her eyes to see Isabelle's soft smile.

"How are you doing today?"

"I am fine, but I don't think that I will be very fast delivering telegrams."

"You will always have a job at Western Union. You can work in the office, and we can hire a boy to deliver the messages until you get well. What is this hubcap here? Do you use it for a bed pan?"

Sun laughed. "That's a great idea! I just might need to do that if I can't make it into the john."

"Theo told me that he and Sister Samantha have hit it off, and he has been seeing her in Chicago".

"Yeah, I thought that might happen. I will live with katybear until I graduate. I love my job at Western Union. Please call me at katybear's if you need to talk to me. I will come back to work as soon as I can."

"Sun, you are a good worker, and you don't need to worry about job security. I don't want anyone else."

"Thank you, Isabelle. You are the best boss that I ever had." Isabelle laughed.

"I am the only boss that you have ever had. You were only twelve!"

Sun flashed a coy smile.

"See you at the office whenever you can. Happy trails!"

The nine surviving nuns camped out in the gymnasium for three weeks until the group dwindled. Five nuns went to nearby Catholic schools to teach, two others transferred to schools out of state, and both postulants were transferred to the Denver Burn Center in critical condition. Sun and Sister Sara were the last two that camped in the gymnasium.

Their injuries improved, but Sun didn't have crutches. She couldn't put weight onto her feet, and Sara's hands remained bandaged. Sun and Sara lay on their pallets the night of July 15, 1968, one month after the fire. The gymnasium grew larger with only the two remaining survivors. The room echoed with their words.

"Sara, we have been together in the most unusual predicaments, haven't we?" The two friends memories reverberated from the steel-beam ceiling and bounced across the boundary-lined floor of the gymnasium, but most of all, their memories hung on the basketball hoop. The silence communicated their bond.

"I have had thinking time, and I am riddled with guilt from the deaths and destruction that my actions have caused. I grieve for Mother Superior, Sister Margaret, Father Patty, and the nuns, but I suffer from thinking that I am to blame for these ashes and the lost lives."

"Sun Wren! Don't you dare think that way or say another word about accepting blame. You are not at fault! You did the right thing to save the reservation treasure and our tribal history. You did a universal good for many people. You cannot accept responsibility for the addictions of our people. If you even dare to utter another blame thought I will be angry. You are responsible only for spontaneous right action!"

"My vision quest was to always show love and never to intentionally hurt anyone."

"Yes, and you have done that. Never blame yourself for the weakness of others. Forget those thoughts. Yep, tomorrow the Doctor will bring your crutches, and then you can go to Katy's."

"I would never leave you alone here. Sister Sara what will you do?"

"I will live with Luise, and help her with our friend's half brothers and sisters. It would be the right thing for me to help his family. I can use my education for the benefit of those kids, and hopefully they will never choose suicide."

"Sister Sara, take the Chariot even though you gave it to Incaranata Hall for the giveaway. Incaranata Hall is gone, and the car runs great! Big Boots and Waffle Stomper gave it an overhaul. Luise could certainly use it, and she would appreciate that you had it again. It belongs with you and Luise. What goes around comes around. I think that some of his brothers and sisters should be able to drive by now, and they could help out."

"I had forgotten about the Chariot. Yes, I will take it! I will be happy helping Luise and the kids."

"I have been thinking about what I want to do, and realized that I haven't finished my very first assignment that Mother Superior gave to me. She assigned me to the first cell Determine, and told me to determine who I was. The vision quest determined the inner me, and who I am, but I still don't know about the hubcap baby that I was. I have never thought about my parents, or tried to find them, but now I want to." Silence overtook the survivors that had been together since Sun's childhood and they were contented. Their friendship had evolved into a younger version of the friendship that the godfathers had for each other. Conversation was unnecessary.

The two Shoshoni friends fell asleep contented with their reinvented lives. They quickly released the past and accepted what had been given to them as their future. They didn't wallow in the muck or sink into the black ashes.

The next morning the Indian Health Service arrived to examine Sun and Sara's injuries. The doctor removed the bandages from Sun's feet, and gave her pink socks and a pair of crutches. Sun's nemesis LOO had been lounging in the stadium bleachers, jumped the railing, and tromped on her toes.

"When will I be able to practice toe dancing again, Doctor?"

"I don't understand toe dancing."

"For the last five years I have practiced standing and dancing on the end of my toes. My toes are very strong. See? They are as long as my fingers, and I want to be in the ballet."

"Sun, the shard pieces of glass were embedded very deeply and shredded tendons in your toes. I don't think that you will ever be able to stand or dance on the end of your toes again. I think you will be able to dance, but ballerinas have special shoes to dance on point."

"Are you telling me that I won't be able to stand on my toes anymore?" LOO gave a wicked little smile and slunk off to a dark corner under the stadium seats.

"Probably Not, The injuries have healed nicely, but I don't think you can stand as you have described. Keep the feet covered with the socks, and use the crutches to assist walking. In another week you should be able to wear shoes and maybe walk without the crutches."

The Doctor examined Sister Sara's hands, rubbed in new salves, and rewrapped them, but exposed the finger that allowed her to have limited use.

"Your hands need to heal a little more before we remove the bandage. Sun, I won't need to see you again, but Sara I will need to see you in another week."

The sound of the doctor's footsteps faded from the gymnasium as he walked away, and the girls were alone. Sun rolled up their pallets, folded their blankets, and the two friends left the gymnasium empty to harbor past stories and accept future ones. Together they packed up their stuff while Sister Sara steadied Sun on the crutches. Sister Sara guided Sun to her black Rambler and then she marched to the Chariot that still had the keys in the ignition.

Chapter 26

SIFTING THROUGH THE ASHES

It was a brand new day in August 1969. Seventeen-year-old Sun had been back to work for two weeks without needing crutches, walked with no limp, and felt like a nun in a full-grown woman's body. Her dark brown hair was a mass of long curls that had grown to the middle of her back. Her small fine features magnified huge round 7UP-bottle-colored green eyes. She lifted the old charred hubcap from under the Western Union counter, picked up the pile of telegrams to be delivered, locked the office door, sashayed her pigeon-toed, shapely five foot two inches, small boned frame, swung the hubcap like a call girl, and headed west down Main Street. Her erect posture commanded attention like an on-stage actress as she walked three blocks past the Acme Theatre, the Teton Hotel, across the street to Pop Logan's wagon, and to Gene Lee Used Cars. She saw Gene Lee leaning on the counter with his elbows. He was a good-looking, friendly, older man with wavy dark hair, bright blue eyes, an Indian nose, and a crooked, womanizing smile.

"Hi, Gene Lee."

"Hi, I remember you. You are the little Western Union girl that bought the black 1955 Dodge Rambler about three years ago. I may have forgotten your name, but I never forget a car. Whatcha got there? A hubcap? Okay I'll give you $1.25 for it."

"Nope."

"Okay, a buck forty that's my last offer."

"I don't want to sell it."

"Oh! You don't?"

"Nope, I want you to tell me about it."

"Oh, okay you are holding a hubcap that's probably as old as you are. It's from a 1950 Dodge four-door sedan."

"Did you sell the car?" Gene Lee stroked his throat as he thought about it.

"You know I might have! I sold a dark blue 1950 Dodge four door sedan to a couple of tourists, but it wasn't in 1950 it would have been later probably in 1953 because I don't sell new cars, only used, and back then the cars that I sold were no newer than three years."

"Do you remember the people that bought it?"

"Naw," Gene Lee shook his head, "not really. I just remember cars."

"Okay, thanks for your help," Sun headed out for the opened door of the small office.

"Wait a minute, little lady. I do remember something. I remembered that the woman was very pretty. Women I also remember." He gave Sun a flirtatious wink. "I don't remember their names, but I do remember that the lady was a good looker."

Sun walked back to the counter where Gene Lee rested, and she leaned on the counter next to him. He had renewed her interest in conversation. "What did she look like?"

"I remember that she had tons of long thick very curly dark

hair. They came by taxi, and I remember that her husband was a small man, don't remember him much."

"When you said they came by taxi, do you mean Arapaho Racer Taxi Service?"

"Exactly! They are the only taxi in Fremont County, been here for years. I sold twelve cars to Homer Bear over the years, come to think of it, he's behind on his payments."

"Thank you, Gene Lee, for your help."

"Remember, to come back if you want to sell that hubcap."

Sun waved to him as she bounced down the street to deliver the last telegrams. She was excited to continue her search for her identity. When her telegrams were delivered, she jumped on her Rambler and drove a little too fast to get back to the Bear's house to talk to Homer.

Sun waited until after Homer had finished dinner, and was relaxed before she asked questions.

"Homer, Can I talk to you?"

"Shoot the air is full of pigeons!"

"Homer I talked to Gene Lee today, and he thinks that he sold a car to a couple that you brought to his car lot in 1953, and you might remember them. Do you remember taking a couple to his car lot?"

"Sun, don't even remember what I ate for dinner yesterday. How can I remember something like that when it was long ago?"

"Gene Lee said that you brought a couple in your taxi, and that the lady was pretty. Do you recall anything about that?"

"Yeah, I remember that! The lady was so beautiful that I stared at her. I picked them up at the airport charged thirty dollars, normally it is a ten-dollar cab ride. Didn't look like the run-of-the-mill tourist; looked like they had plenty of money. They said they wanted to buy a car, so I took them to Gene Lee Used Cars."

"Why did you think they had a lot of money?"

"It was their clothes. Maybe from another country or something, but clothes looked different."

"Tell me about their clothes."

"Just different, like people in magazines."

"Like the pictures in Sears or Penny's catalogues."

"Naw, expensive, foreign, I remember the man's shoes." Sun's thoughts circled like a dog chasing his tail, and her excitement soared.

"What do you remember about his shoes? What did he look like?"

"He was a small, dark-haired man, maybe five foot six, wore a suit, not like a government man—pants, jacket, and vest that were all the same gray color—and shoes were sissy-looking."

Was this the same man that she had seen at the Shoshoni tribal council when she spoke about saving the pictographs? She also saw him at her naming ceremony, and she too had noticed his shoes. Sun jumped up, ran to the magazine heap, and pulled out the magazine that showed Italian shoes. She showed the picture to Homer.

"Yep, this is the kind of shoes that he had. See how sissy they look." Homer selected the picture of the Salvatore Ferragamo loafers made in Italy. Reservation men wore moccasins, field boots or cowboy boots. Sun understood the shoes could be described as sissy-looking.

"Homer, what were the lady's clothes like? What did she wear?"

"Don't remember nothing about her clothes; only remember how beautiful she was."

"What did she look like?"

"Little, lots of black curly hair, not black Indian hair, just dark."

"If you think of anything else that you remember, would you please tell me?"

⟵━━⟪

In 1953 on September 4, at five-thirty in the late afternoon, one day before Wren was born, the Arapaho Racer Taxi Service, owned by Judy's father Homer Bear, pulled up to the car lot, and two people got off. The expectant pair was tired from the long Delta plane ride from Los Angeles to Denver, and then from Denver to Riverton on Frontier Airlines where Katy Bear's husband charged them thirty-dollar cab fare at the airport and delivered them to Gene Lee's Used Car Lot in his taxi to buy a car.

The couple was an elegantly dressed man and a beautiful young woman who hid her nine-month pregnancy under a fashionable London Fog coat. The couple purchased a 1950 dark blue Dodge sedan with bad tires, but Gene Lee threw in two spares to cement the cash transaction, and the pair was assured that the car would reach their destination in Lander, but it didn't.

High above the mountainous switchbacks, the car jerked and jolted, and the sound of rubber slapped on payment and alerted the fatigued couple. The tires had given out and couldn't continue. Tracy Grant Richards managed to steer the crippled car onto a dirt road leading to Silas Lake and parked the car in a hidden gully. The evergreen forest sent a fresh fragrance of pine tar into the air, and the sun behind the hills filtered through the changing golden leaves of the cottonwood trees to cast a soft, romantic haze over the ravine.

"Dominique, I am so tired I can't change the tire. Let's car camp for the night and head to Lander first thing in morning."

Dominique felt extreme fatigue herself and quickly agreed.

She opened the car door to the strong smell of spruce pine and breathed deeply.

"This is a beautiful, serene place. I haven't felt such peace since I left Italy. I certainly haven't felt this relaxed in Los Angeles."

"No one feels relaxed in LA." Tracy opened his car door and heard the squish of the thick pine forest mulch underfoot. The pine-scented forest was pungent and acted as menthol upon his lungs as he sucked in the late afternoon air. He walked around to the passenger side of the car, reached for Dominique's hands, and pulled her to her feet. He kissed her with tender affection as they stood by the impaired Dodge.

"Look at the canopy of autumn color. Let's sleep beneath it."

"Great idea, Dom. Let's do."

Tracy spread his charcoal-gray cashmere topcoat onto the ground away from the injured car, and she removed her London Fog and placed it beside his on the soft, comfortable ground. They snuggled together under the darkening twilight. He placed his arm to cushion her thick, voluminous curly black head and kissed her beautiful almond face.

"Miss Pasolini, I think that we did well to find such a remote place as Lander Wyoming to place the baby up for adoption. No one will ever know about this. There are no TV stations, no movie cameras, no movie directors, and no producers to withdraw your contract because you got pregnant. Hell, there aren't even any people here!"

"Tracy, I love you so much, and I am grateful you stuck with me."

"Dom, I have loved you from the first moment that I saw you. I'm with you because I love you, and not because you need my help."

The two exhausted travelers watched the twilight transform

into the black as ink night sky sprinkled with glittery bright specks. They listened to the sounds of nighthawks, hoot owls, and unidentified nocturnal animals rooting for food, and each of the sounds was wrapped in the cool, crisp breeze. They slept soundly until the morning sunlight filtered through the trees.

Tracy sprang to his feet, and began the repair task. He handed Dominique the hubcap to hold while he proceeded to restore the dismembered auto back into service.

"I need to take an urgent walk into the woods." Dominique moved into the forest, and she absentmindedly carried the hubcap with her.

Tracy chuckled as he watched his aqua-blue sweater–clad pregnant little duck waddle away.

Sun Wren thought about the conversation with Homer and Gene Lee. Her distracted thoughts almost made her late for work. She scurried into her place behind the telegraph where the telegrams were rapidly coming in. Isabelle was at her desk doing the office accounting.

"Good morning, Sun! Looks like a busy day. After you compile the incoming telegrams and deliver them, could you please sift through that stack of 'nonurgent' stuff, toss out the junk mail, and act on the required ones? I have neglected that pile for over a month."

"Sure enough! I would be glad to." Sun took in more than twenty telegrams that morning, and it took her from midmorning until after 2:00 p.m. to get them all delivered.

For the first time in her life, Sun's mind was consumed with thoughts about her mother as she walked the miles and delivered the telegrams. Perhaps Sister Samantha's absence, Sun's maturation, and her identification with womanhood prompted the desire to learn about her biological mother. She had never before questioned her abandonment. Sister Samantha and katybear continued to be her moms, and now that Sister Samantha was in Chicago Sun was closer to katybear than she had ever been. Even though Katy had eleven other children, Sun had absorbed Katy's love that would have been bestowed on Judy. Their bond was a grief soother, and this triangular love was a comfort for both mother and friend toward their absent Judy.

Sun returned to the Western Union office with lunch that Isabelle suggested she should pick up on her return. They ate the garlic-seasoned hamburgers from the A&W drive-in known for curly fries. Sun ate lunch as she sorted through the heap of mail. Her hands crumpled fliers, advertisements, and old community notices and tossed them into the trash. Her fingers wrapped around a thick, cream-colored envelope addressed to Sun Wren Richards.

"What's this?" Isabelle glanced up, wiped the ketchup from her chin, and smiled.

"Sun, I forgot to give that to you. I am sorry. Phillip Richards from the Lander Western Union office attempted to either court you or that was his inept, hen-house way of a marriage proposal." She laughed. "Do you want to read your love letter in private?"

"This letter is almost two months old. He might have forgotten me by now."

"I'm sorry that I forgot to give it to you. Susquehanna Western and the Indian Mission fire distracted me."

Sun ripped open the envelope, and her eyes scanned the words. Her eyes and face expressed bewilderment.

LAST WILL AND TESTAMENT
of
TRACY GRANT RICHARDS and DOMINIQUE PAOLO PASOLINI

STATE OF CALIFORNIA X KNOW ALL MEN BY THESE PRESENTS
COUNTY OF LOS ANGELES X

We, TRACY G. RICHARDS and DOMINIQUE P. PASOLINI RICHARDS, husband and wife of Los Angeles County, California, being of full age, sound mind, disposing memory, under no restraint, and over the age of eighteen (18) years, do make public and declare this instrument to be our Last Will and Testament and hereby revoke all Wills and Codicils ever before made by us.

This Will is not the result of any contract between ourselves and any beneficiary, fiduciary, or third party. Any Will made by us may be revoked at any time at our sole discretion.

ITEM #I

If, subsequent to the execution of this, our Last Will and Testament, there shall be no additional children born to or legally adopted by us, TRACY G. RICHARDS and DOMINIQUE P. PASOLINI RICHARDS, and no relatives or acquaintance shall share in the benefits of our estate.

ITEM #II

TRACY G. RICHARDS and DOMINIQUE P. PASOLINI recognize and attest that SUN WREN RICHARDS is our biological and legally adopted daughter and is the sole beneficiary of: ARISTOCRAT TYPEWRITER MANUFACTORY INC. and ARISTOCRAT FILM PRODUCTIONS estate.

We hereby direct that no action be had in the probate court in relation to the settlement of our estate other than the probate and recording of this, our Last Will and Testament, and the return of an inventory appraisement and list of claims of our estate.

ITEM #III

We hereby authorize our Executor to utilize the services of an attorney, accountant, and any other professionals as may be necessary in the administration of this, our Last Will and Testament. The expenses incurred by the Executor using such professional services shall be an expense to our estate and shall be paid by our estate.

"Isabelle, please look at this! This is no love letter."

"Uh-oh, I think it may be called a Dear John letter?"

"I don't know what it is called. See what you think."

Isabelle reached for the letter and read it. "Oh my God!"

"What, Isabelle! What is it?"

"Sun, this is a will that explains that you have inherited a fortune." Isabelle swiped the envelope from Sun's hands and examined it.

"It was sent from Larson and Haze Attorneys from Los Angeles." Isabelle opened the envelope and discovered a newspaper clipping stuck inside. "Sun, read this news article," she said.

Sun read the newspaper clipping out loud.

June 18, 1969
Los Angeles Daily News
Hollywood, California

Dominique Paolo Pasolini and husband Tracy Grant Richards were killed 3:33 p.m., June 17, 1969. Their private aircraft Cessna 182 crashed at the Denver International Airport. Aviation examiners determined the crash was caused by engine failure. It was reported by Pasolini relatives that the Richards were vacationing in the mountains of Wyoming and Colorado when their aircraft crashed. They were on their return trip to their 1577 Bel Air Beverly Hills, California, home. Funeral ceremonies are pending and notification for burial details are forthcoming.

"Sun, let the rest of this stuff go. Take this letter upstairs to the Bear Brothers Law Firm and see what they have to say about this. If it is true, you are one rich little girl."

Sun carefully replaced the newspaper article into the envelope, and dashed up the steps to the third floor of the Masonic Temple Building above the Western Union office. The receptionist in the law office looked up. "Hi Sun, how have you been?"

"I'm good. Is Darrell or Shram in the office?"

"Yes, Darrell is here, but Shram is out with his weight-lifting team. What can I do for you?"

"Please tell him that I have an emergency and need to talk to him."

"Oh no, Susquehanna Western giving you trouble?"

"No, it is another matter. I need him to examine some papers that I have."

Shiela, the svelte receptionist, crossed the anteroom and tapped on Darrell's office door. "Sun is here to see you."

"Send her in." Sun slipped into Darrell's office and closed the door. "Hi Sun,—-What's up?" Sun didn't respond, but handed Darrell the envelope. He casually received it, opened it slowly, and began to read the will. "Holly shit!" He sat straight up in his chair, and fervently unfolded the newspaper article. His eyes ate hungrily at the words, and he digested the article as well. "Sit down, Sun, let's research this." He picked up the letter and dialed the numbers slowly on the rotary as he read the phone numbers out loud from the letterhead.

"Good afternoon. This is attorney Darrell Bear from Riverton, Wyoming. I would like to speak to Counselor Larson or Haze. It is in regard to Sun Wren." The Larson and Haze legal secretary left Darrell hanging. Darrell raised his hands into the air and shrugged in puzzlement to Sun. Thirty seconds later Darrell and Larson had a discussion as Sun waited eagerly to learn the facts. Darrell hung up the phone after the twenty-minute conversation, gave a low whistle, ran his hands through his hair, and leaned back in his swivel chair.

"Sun, the law office of Larson and Haze has been waiting to hear from you. Tracy Grant Richards was the richest man in the United States in 1953. He was sole heir to the Aristocrat Typewriter Manufacturing Inc. They proclaimed that you were their daughter, legally adopted you in 1958 when you were five years old, and in 1964 when you were eleven they created the will with you being the only beneficiary. You must be stunned and need time to absorb all this. I know that I do. I want to talk to Shram about how to financially protect you. I think that you need to appoint Shram and me as your new godfathers because you have outgrown Big Boots and Waffle Stomper. Who all knows about this envelope?"

"Isabelle, my boss at Western Union. No one else knows, not even me really!"

"Oh, Sun, I totally get it! Don't tell anyone about this for now. I am so excited for you that I can't even think straight. Do everything in your usual way, go to school, go to work, do everything as normal, and don't tell my mom. I know that you and she are close, but this news would reach the moccasin telegraph like wild fire, and staying with Arapaho's is not the safest thing for you under normal circumstances. Come upstairs and talk to Shram and me whenever you want. I think that we have ourselves a new VIP client." Darrell laughed, expressing total disbelief. "Sun, I'll get copies made of this will at the bank in private for you, and I'll put this envelope into my office safe. The will is properly recorded in LA, but you need us as your bodyguards." Darrell roared with nervous laughter. "Shram has been lifting weights, and he looks like a bodyguard. Who would have guessed to what end he would use his bodybuilding workouts!" Darrell was still laughing as Sun left his office and closed his door. Shiela looked up at her.

"What in the world is Darrell so happy about?"

"A new dirty joke. See you later."

Sun went back into the Western Union office to finish her aborted task. Isabelle looked up.   "Well, is it true?"

Sun nodded her head in the affirmative.

"My God! Do you want to leave work early?"

"Nope, I'm to carry on in my normal way until Darell and Shram can sort it out. I am not to tell anyone about it except for you, but I can't quit thinking about it."

"Well, I'm not even you, and I can't quit thinking about it either! You know our office policy what news comes through this office stays in this office. We have many years of observing that rule, and now it seems like a good idea to keep it."

"Yup, but I am glad that I have you to talk with. In 1953, Tracy Grant Richards was the wealthiest man in the United States. He was into typewriter manufacturing. I am their natural biological daughter, and they legally adopted me when I was five. My new name is Sun Wren Richards."

———◄———

"I put the baby into the hubcap, and now it's gone," Dominique shouted. Tracy ran up the path to meet Dominique, swept her into his arms, and raced to the repaired car. He gently sat her down in the passenger's seat and closed her door as she sank into exhaustion.

"Dom, it's okay. An old rattletrap of a green truck just passed the ravine without seeing us. They must have found the baby. I can't believe that you had the child so quickly. We will follow the truck to see where it goes. Are you okay?" Tracy was in pursuit of the truck but kept distance so the truck passengers wouldn't see them.

"I am okay."

"Was it a boy or girl?"

"I don't know. I quickly wrapped the baby in my sweater and crawled to sit in the lake while I washed off." Tracy kept the truck in view and watched it turn into the Indian Mission. He parked the car behind an old barn, walked down Deaf Smith

Road, crouched in the sagebrush, and watched the fisherman hand the hubcap to the nun. He waited until the old green truck left the area, and he returned to Dominique who had fallen asleep in the car. Tracy drove the back roads into the Lander Hospital.

"Dom, wake up," he said softly as he touched her face. "We need for you to get checked out by a doctor to make sure that you are okay. The baby was placed into Incaranata Hall, a nunnery, and a nun took the baby. This was an even better plan than the one that we had made. The child will be cared for, and we didn't have to go through an adoption agency. We know the baby's location and who is taking care of it. The child will have a Catholic education which is what we wanted, the environment will teach resourcefulness, and natural law will teach the child to be a sturdy, secure person. This is better than adoption where we would have no knowledge of anything. Come on. Let's go inside."

Sun waited a few minutes before she went inside. She had finished her work at the office, and came directly to Waffle Stomper's house. The dogs barked her arrival, and she stepped out of the Rambler to greet them. "Good boy, Fast Forward. Don't jump, Rewind. Stay down, boys."

"Well, looky, looky who came to visit me."

"Hi, Waffle Stomper. How have you been?"

"Come in, let's drink kinnickinnick tea"

"Oh, that sounds good. I can't stay long. I promised katybear that I would deliver some baskets for her after work. I know that she is waiting for me, but I wanted to ask you some movie questions."

"Movie-goin' days slowin' down."

"That may be true, but you know your movie-stars better than anybody that I know."

"Gave old movie magazines to the Bear kids. They loved 'em."

"I know, I read those magazines with them for years. Still do."

"What's your question, Sun?"

"Do you know a movie star by the name of Dominique Paola Pasolini?"

"Sure do! I'll give you magazine tells 'bout her." Waffle Stomper limped into the back room and retrieved the tattered periodical. "I think as you get older you look like her."

Sun's heart skipped and fluttered in her chest when Waffle Stomper said those words. Could his words be true? He handed her the magazine.

"Keep it. Dominique is my favorite actress. Read about her when you have time. See if you like her." Waffle Stomper walked Sun out and held the dogs as she got into her Rambler. "Thanks for visiting. You bring me happiness."

————◄———

Sun Wren brought no happiness on September 5, 1953, when she was born and placed into a 1950 Dodge hubcap by a seventeen-year-old Sicilian film actress named Dominique Paolo Pasolini. Miss Pasolini represented the 1 percent privileged social Sicilian aristocracy. Sicily's economy was in parlous poverty when the war ended in 1946, and envy was the aristocrats' most treacherous enemy. Aristocracy was all about family roots, nobility, and inheritance. It was said that J. Paul Getty was denied membership into aristocratic clubs because he did not have old family monied roots sunk into his pockets even though he was well-to-do. Unlike J. Paul Getty, Dominique

Paolo Pasolini was an undeniable Sicilian aristocratic with her acres of land that supported ancestral estates of grandeur, while the average citizen was hungry, desperate, and despised the wealthy. Their envy sought revenge.

The creamy almond complexion was hallmarked upon the selected, curly dark-haired, blue eyed, 1 percent aristocrat, Dominique. Her slender, petite five-foot-one-inch frame was supported by long, thin, shapely legs that wore Hanes nylon stockings when rags were the acceptable fashion. She would have been described as stunningly beautiful, but she gained no compliments, compassion, or concern from the war-torn citizens of Sicily who held malevolence and distain for the privileged. Dominique Paolo Pasolini was privileged, and narrowly escaped her death as she was forced to the Atlantic port to set sail for the United States. Her cousin, a film director, Pier Paolo Pasolini, introduced her to Orson Wells where good fortune struck, and she was cast in a movie and earned instant stardom.

Chapter 27

NEW BEGINNINGS

Black mosquitoes and silver powdered millers flew under the bedside lampshade, singed their wings, and some fell to their death attracted by the blaze from the bulb, but Sun could not turn off the light. She was as entranced by Dominique Pasolini's story as millers were attracted to the flame. Sun Wren Richards read the magazine that Waffle Stomper had given her until late in the night. Her thoughts drifted to past events when she questioned who was the man shrouded in shadow. Big Boots had told her about the man hidden between the cars at her first powwow when she was eight, and he had cautioned her about feminine safety. Mrs. Gamble had told her about the elegant woman who had watched the Eagles' track team victory race when she was eleven, and Sun Wren remembered the man at the back of her naming ceremony with the Italian shoes. Big Boots remembered his hazy sight of a man standing at the entrance of the Sun Dance, and he had told her that he had a vision of a foreign man who watched her and Judy as they slept. Sun wondered about the unknown man in the Shoshoni tribal hall when she had delivered her environment speech to the council when she was sixteen, and he had quickly vanished after Justin Iron Eagle threw the chair at katybear. Her parents had been present at every important phase of her life.

Sun Wren Richards was calm as she began to fit the pieces of her puzzled life into a new family frame. This was the most satisfied adventure she had encountered, and she had no idea where it would lead. Katybear noticed her heightened energy the next morning.

"What's with you, girl? That Gary kid still following you to the post office every day? Is that what's makin' you so full of light?"

"Yeah maybe. We are going to the movies Friday night."

"He's a good-looking young man, and he's studying to take his Realtor exam—not a bad catch, if you ask me!"

"I only want a friend—not a husband!" Sun darted out the kitchen door, letting it slam behind her. Sun rushed off to the Western Union office in Riverton. She efficiently received the morning's coded ticker tape and pasted them onto telegram forms. A telegram came in that startled her: "To Miss Sun Wren Richards (stop). From Larson and Haze Los Angeles (stop). Please receive ownership of Aristocrat Film Industry and Aristocrat Typewriter Manufacturing as soon as possible (stop). Give possible travel dates to Los Angeles (stop). Larson and Haze will make arrangements (stop)." Sun halted the stream of telegrams and showed this one to Isabelle.

"Wow! Sun, this is happening very fast. Let's look at our work calendar for possible available dates. I think that you should go for a visit to see if that lifestyle is really what you want." Sun and Isabelle chose three possible dates to give Larson and Haze. They chose August, 15, August 25, and September 5, which would be Sun Wren Richard's seventeenth birthday.

During Sun's afternoon work break, she climbed the stairs to the third-floor Bear Brothers law office.

"Hi, Shiela. Are Shram and Darrell here?"

"They are both here."

"Thanks, may I see them?"

"They gave me clear instructions to allow you to see them anytime. I will tell them that you are here." Shiela motioned for Sun to enter. The Bear Brothers' interior was separated into two separate small offices with nameplates upon their office doors. The small offices were joined by a commons area. The brothers were seated in the comfortable commons space where she entered.

"Hi, guys." She gave a small Wyoming howdy wave.

"Hi, Sun. What have you got?" Sun ambled to the sectional where Darrell was seated and handed him the newly arrived telegram.

Darrell read it through. "This is a good sign that the law firm is efficient. They want closure on the will. Are these the dates that you have decided upon?" Darrell passed the telegram to Shram. Shram glanced at it. "I think you should choose your birthday as the day to travel to Los Angeles, but it was courteous to give them the three dates for consideration. You should go, and check out your new life. You are not yet eighteen, and you can't legally sign anything until you are, but you could certainly live there, and begin to learn the business for a year. You could live in your LA house, or you may have more than one home. You have some great options! You should go to see what you own." Sun inched a little closer to Shram and retrieved the telegram from his hands.

"Shram, your brother told me that you know about business law. Do you know anything about Tracy Grant Richards?"

"I know a little bit. In law school we studied his wealth as a case study for a required business law class. I can tell you what I remember about him. He was about fifty-four or fifty- five years old when he died in the recent plane crash. That's not very old! His parents were immigrants from Sicily who founded the typewriter manufacturing industry in New York in 1904. Tracy and his twin brother, Trenton, were Nicoles Racinellie's only heirs. Their mother died in childbirth, and Trenton died of polio as a child. Tracy Grant Racinellie changed his last name to Richards to sound more American. He grew up in New York City, attended Harvard, became a genius at business, and is … was one of America's wealthiest men. His father Nicoles Racinellie may still be alive, but he retired from the business world when it was handed over to Tracy."

Sun's eyes were huge green saucers as she registered her truth. Her thoughts tumbled out into hasty words.

"The Susquehanna Western strip mine injunction was June 15. The plane crash was June 17, and the newspaper article said that Tracy Richards and his wife were vacationing in Wyoming. I know that I saw him leaning on one of the front-end loaders as I carried the folder to the foreman who sat in the red pickup that day of June 15. I felt his presence, and I knew that he watched me. I thought that he might have been the Susquehanna Western owner or a major corporate stockholder. Richard's plane crashed on the way back to LA. They had come to check on me. My parents abandoned me as a baby, but the fact that he was at the injunction shows that my parents cared about me, and they crashed to their death two days later. The will assigned me everything, and that also proved their love."

Shram lowered his eyes and looked at the telegram in Sun's hand. "Sun, we saw the stranger beside the equipment too. We wondered why he was so intent on watching you, and now we know." The sound of the wall clock echoed in the office silence. The silence offered compassion and acknowledged Sun's emptiness.

"It is strange to feel no sadness for the death of my parents, but they were people that I didn't know. A Shoshoni never says the name of the deceased out loud, and I feel that I am Shoshoni, but I know that my blood is Sicilian. I feel at home with my Indian culture, but natural law tells me that my blood is a different truth. The will has given me an opportunity to determine my identity, and it has defeated LOO." Sun sat without tears and was jolted by the new reality.

Shram and Darrell sat in silence. Sun walked across the aqua colored carpet to the Bear Brother Law office door as the old grandfather wall-clock ticked its loud time. No one spoke. Sun moseyed toward the door, and ambled down the stairs in a blue blur of bewilderment. She sat behind the telegraph machine of the Western Union office and sent an acceptance reply to the Larson and Haze Law office in Los Angeles.

"Isabelle, I have a favor to ask."

"Okay, Sun. My telegraph is waiting to receive. What's your favor?"

"I need to call Sister Samantha in Chicago, and katybear has a ten-party line that is full of rubber ears. I will pay Western Union out of my paycheck for the call."

"That's fair and reasonable. Just ask the operator for time and charges when you finish the call."

"I have finished with the day's incoming telegrams, and I am feeling desperate to talk to her. She is living the life that will be my future."

"Yes, I understand and I know that you miss her." Isabelle respectfully walked across the street to Burlesons Drug Store to buy herself a chocolate Coke. Sun made the call, and Sister Samantha picked up on the third ring.

"Hello, Sister Samantha, I am so glad that you answered. I have so much to tell you!"

"It has been too long since we have talked, Sun. I have missed you terribly. Katy Bear told me about the Incaranata Hall incineration and that you and Sister Sara were safe. I grieved and prayed for the souls of Father Patty, Mother Superior, and Sister Margaret. I am saddened to know that I will never be able to return to the Indian Mission." She paused. "I have made you another green dress similar to the one that you lost in the fire. You haven't gotten fat or anything, have you? I got your measurements from the Avonelle Designers. I sent a package with the dress, new bras, and matching shoes to Katy Bear's house, and you should have it soon."

"Thank you, Sister Samantha. I need them desperately because I am going to Los Angeles."

"Really? Why to Los Angeles?" Sun took twenty-five minutes and forty-two seconds to tell Sister Samantha about the will and the research that she had done on her parents.

"Sun, always stay grounded in your Shoshoni culture. Natural law is the strong steel core of who you are. All else that Los Angeles presents is pleasing, exterior shiny glam and glitz that can suck you into pretentious untruths."

"I will call you lots of times when I learn about my new LA life. I can take possession, but I can't legally own anything until I am eighteen. I will spend my seventeenth year learning about the business and discovering who I am."

"Sun, I encourage you to embrace your new LA business path. Our lives remain parallel. I was a novice nun, and you were a newborn. Now you are an heiress, and our worlds will be similar again. We can put our good fortunes to the betterment of humankind. I work to benefit the poor in Midwest America, and you can do the same for the West Coast. We will be sister warriors."

"Yes, we will be fearless! I am on telegraph time and need to hang—"

"Sun, wait! There is another important thing that I want to tell you. Theodore Logan and I are engaged."

"I could see it coming! I want you to know happiness in Chicago, and I believe that Theo can be the person to fix that! I love you, Sister Samantha, but you will always be my mother." Sun replaced the receiver with contentment.

Sun Wren Richards knew that it was time to say goodbye to her former life when the Larson and Haze Law firm accepted her birthday, September 5, 1969, for her arrival date to Los Angeles. Isabelle returned to the office with a cherry Coke and handed it to Sun.

"Thanks for the Coke. Sister Samantha and your brother Theo are engaged to be married."

Isabelle smiled a knowing smile. Sun showed Isabelle the newly arrived telegram that accepted her birthday as the arrival date. Sun Wren gave Isabelle her two-week notice that terminated her pleasant job, and the notice accompanied a strong, heartfelt hug. Two weeks quickly passed, and Sun brought Isabelle's favorite A&W drive-in meal into the Western Union office, where they shared a last meal together.

"Isabelle, thanks for teaching me about useful business skills. I will apply the learned office integrity into my own Aristocrat Film and Typewriter Manufacturing business practice once I became old enough to own it."

"You are always welcome to work for Western Union anywhere in the United States, and I would gladly give you a favorable recommendation. You are a good kid, and I will miss you."

Sun walked away from a valuable experience with Isabelle. The job had helped her to gently transition away from reservation life. Sun Wren knew that it was time to cut other leather thongs that bound her to the stationary Sun Dance pole. Sun struggled free from the rustic native culture that strangled education, self-development, and was a friend to LOO.

Sun accepted her boyfriend Gary's invitation to have a cherry Coke at Burlesons Drug Store. The Riverton High School couple known as an "item" settled into the high-back wooden booth, and Sun told Gary about her upcoming move to Los Angeles. He was angry and reluctant to receive the news. He said, "You have dumped me to be with Philip." With pouting, whining words he added, "I just don't trust you."

Sun presented the copy of the telegram from Larson and Haze Law Firm.

"You constructed this telegram yourself!"

Sun's eye's blazed with fury, and she pulled a copy of the will from her folder. He read it carefully. She showed him the Dominique Paola Pasolini magazine, and Gary resented her new Los Angeles opportunities. Sun realized that he would never trust her, and she would always need to prove herself to calm his doubts.

"I don't understand why you can't be content in Riverton with me. We could invest your inheritance into real estate and I could build us a good life." Sun raised her brows, and her big green eyes met his jealous attitude and selfishness with alarm. He knew her answer. He displayed his arrogance and left her sitting in the booth alone with her full cherry Coke.

Sun enjoyed the Coke until the straw made empty sucking sounds, and then she finished his Coke too. She could not be tethered to this man like the torturous thong was tied to a Sun Dance pole. Gary's farewell granted great relief, freedom, and a pathway for possible adventure. It would be much harder for her to loosen the grip of attachments that bound her heart to her other village family.

Sun met katybear an hour before school got out at the Riverton Jefferson Elementary School where katybear's youngest kids were bussed while the Indian Mission School remained closed. Katybear waited and watched Sun park curbside in front of the school. She grabbed the package that Sister Samantha had sent, darted across the street to Sun's 1955 Black Rambler, and slid into the passenger seat next to her.

"I am glad that we could meet for a chat so I could give you this box from Sister Samantha."

"Thanks, katybear! Sister Samantha made a new dress for me to wear to Los Angeles."

"Los Angeles! What's in Los Angeles?"

"My life has expanded in the most unusual way. I am moving to Los Angeles."

Katybear's eyes opened wide in surprise. Sun pulled the will from the folder and showed it to her. Katybear slowly read through the document.

"Sun, this document needs legal eyes. You should show this to the boys."

"Yes, I have. I showed them this will a few weeks ago. They know what has happened, but I couldn't tell you until they did the research for authenticity."

"Sun, you have become Cinderella and a wealthy girl without having to try on shoes."

Sun laughed. "I am leaving for Los Angeles on my seventeenth birthday, but I wanted to talk to you before I left. Katybear, the will completes Judy's last prediction. In one of our childhood cloud games, she said that I would wear a very expensive dress like the one we saw in the magazines. The will points to my future and shows that she was once again correct about my life. Look at this!" Sun pulled out the movie magazine featuring Dominique Paolo Pasolini and pointed to the name on the will. "She was my mother, but it was you that sustained my life. You raised me to become who I am, and you accepted me—a Shoshoni—into your Arapaho family. You gave me the best childhood and the best childhood friend that anyone could have ever had. You and Sister Samantha will always be my mothers, and I love you for giving me such a wonderful start in life. Judy pointed out my future, and I want to accept the opportunity that this will has given to me."

Katybear grabbed Sun and hugged her through loud sobs and tears. They cried together in a tearful, soggy hug until the school bell rang, and the Bear kids filled her parked van.

"Sun, you will always have a home with Homer and me anytime that you need us."

"Katybear, I don't know what is in Los Angeles, but I must go to discover my roots. You are always in my heart."

Sun's Arapaho mom rushed to her carload of kids, and Sun heard one of the children ask, "Why are you crying, Mom?"

"My tears are about good things."

Sun Wren Richards watched the Bear car pull from the curb before she turned her ignition key and drove in the opposite direction.

Sun drove across the roadless prairie, crept across the narrow cow trail between the bluff ridge and the irrigation canal, and parked in front of Waffle Stomper's house. She was glad to see Big Boots's truck, which indicated he was inside too. The dogs barked and told her that she was welcome. Waffle Stomper opened the front door.

"Well, looky, looky who's here ta see me. Come on out of the wind."

"I am here to see both of my godfathers. Hello, Godfather Big Boots."

"You get prettier every time I see you," Big Boots said. Sun gave him a hug.

"I told her last month, she looks like Dominique Paola Pasolini." Sun stood frozen as she remembered that he had said those exact words before, but they had meant nothing to her.

"Godfather Waffle Stomper, look into my eyes. Really look at my face. Do you honestly believe what you say?"

Godfather Waffle Stomper was silenced by her directness.

Big Boots answered for him. "Sun, you have features that resemble hers, but I have never known you to care about your appearance before. Why are you concerned about your appearance now?"

Sun rummaged through her folder and pulled out the will. She handed it to her godfathers, and Big Boots read the will over Waffle Stomper's shoulder. They took their time reading it and spoke to each other in the Shoshoni language.

"Great Spirit above!" Big Boots shouted. Waffle Stomper sat down, covered his face with his hands, and sobbed. Sun Wren Richards pulled the movie magazine from her folder and held it up.

"Do you understand that she was my mother?" She showed the godfathers the telegrams. They looked astonished.

"I am going to Los Angeles on my birthday, September 5. You have been my godfathers and my protectors, and I have loved you for many years. The Bear brothers said that the will has changed my life. They said that I have outgrown my reservation godfathers' protection, and now I will need their legal protection, maybe even a bodyguard. But I will always use your godfather Shoshoni protection. It is with me always, and I thank you for that." Sun Wren Richards threw her arms around her godfathers as rivers of tears ran down their weathered faces like rain runs down the eroded face of the mountain. "Thank you for teaching me about the Shoshoni way. It lives inside me. I will do what I can do for my Indian Nation. Money is not the root of all evil. It can be the instrument to create goodness."

"No! That is what is wrong with our people! They have yet to learn to develop themselves to have strength of character. They have forgotten the old strong ways and who we are deep inside our redskins. Any money bestowed on individual tribal members is wasted. They need new experiences, education, and opportunities. They cannot see that imitating the white culture without strength of character leads to Lucky Strike cigarette, new Chevy pickups, Jim Beam bottles, tight-rolled marijuana, *Playboy* magazines, and random sex. The old Shoshoni way is to always do the right thing. You have learned that lesson. You are Shoshoni!"

Sun could not control the flood of tears. She sniffled as she made her way to her car and then sobbed over the steering wheel.

"I will always love you, Godfathers!" Sun shouted as she drove away. The bark from Rewind and Fast Forward grew fainter.

Big Boots's words lodged into her soul, and she would remember their protective warmth in future times. Sun Wren felt that her old identity was dissolving across the Wind River Reservation, but she continued her farewell trek as she drove to Owl's Grandmother Luise's house. Sun Wren parked her car beside the Chariot and marveled that it was still usable. She saw many teenagers coming in and out of Luise's house. She watched Sister Sara give two boys instructions for something and saw that she was joyously in her element. Sister Sara looked up and waved her in like a happy flagman at a car race.

"Hi, Sun! Come and sit with me on the steps awhile." Sister Sara's tight-fitting jeans and sweatshirt had replaced her Catholic habit.

"You look great, Sister Sara. Your hands have healed."

Sister Sara looked embarrassed with downcast eyes. "I think they will have the school back together by next fall, and I have been asked to teach the fourth grade!"

"I am so glad for you! You have wanted that position for the last few years! Sara, I came to give you and Luise my Rambler. It looks like the Chariot wants to be turned out to pasture."

"You just got it paid for! Why would you want to give it to us?"

"On my birthday, September 5, I am leaving to go to Los Angeles, and I want you to take me to the airport. You and Luise can keep my car."

"Why are you going to Los Angeles?"

"Because my name is now Sun Wren Richards." Sun told her the long story. She showed Sister Sara the will so that she could understand more clearly. They talked about the will and the wealth that had been heaped upon her, and Sun showed Sister Sara the movie magazine.

"This movie star Dominique Paola Pasolini was my mother." Sister Sara sat in stunned silence. "Sister Sara, you helped to fulfill the promise we made to protect the legacy and to save the pictographs. I have truly loved you as my sister through our shared grief and the loss of Incaranata Hall."

Sun Wren and Sister Sara had learned the Shoshoni art of communication through silence. They had unfurled into the same space that Big Boots and Waffle Stomper occupied. Sun Wren Richards and Sister Sara nudged the older generation to make space for them in their Shoshoni growth. They sat together in the present sound vacuum and watched the wind spank the sagebrush, and Sun's words stirred up dust devils when she spoke.

"I have no idea what is in Los Angeles, but it is an opportunity that I can't be hesitant to accept. Some force is pushing me forward. I want to expand and develop with the opportunity that was given to me, and I want others to have opportunity too. I want to diminish or slay LOO, which looms and dominates reservation life. LOO will not triumph over strength of character, determination, and perseverance if it is squelched."

Sister Sara threw her arms around Sun Wren Richard's shoulders and hugged her. "I hope the roll of your dice brings good luck, my little Wren. *No*, you are not a tiny Wren anymore! You are a brave Shoshoni eagle, and I will take you to your airport bird in the morning."

Sun Wren Richards boarded the plane for Los Angeles on September 5, 1969. She was excited to meet her true-blood Pasolini cousins and her grandfather Nicoles Racinellie. She vowed that she would strive to become a worthy Sicilian family member, but she knew that her inner core was Shoshoni. Sun was determined to follow in Sister Samantha's footsteps to be a West Coast warrior for the betterment of her tribe.

EPILOGUE

The multicolored shafts of neon Hollywood lights reached skyward and elbowed and shoved the starlight from the night sky into oblivion. Electrical currents and the pulse from technology replaced the drum and human heartbeat. City glitter had the potential to tarnish or bolster individual creativity, and Sun Wren Richard's choice remained to be determined.

ACKNOWLEDGMENTS

Special thanks to family members for contributing memories:
Shawn Bonsell
Tiffany Egnor
Sharon Starks

Special thanks to friends for contributing memories:
Barbara Fregger
Jim Bonsell
Scott Ratliff

Special Note: The book cover is a painting by Wyoming artist
Georgine Lee